Eternal Magic

Books by Alexandra Ivy

Guardians of Eternity
WHEN DARKNESS COMES
EMBRACE THE DARKNESS
DARKNESS EVERLASTING
DARKNESS REVEALED
DARKNESS UNLEASHED
BEYOND THE DARKNESS
DEVOURED BY DARKNESS
BOUND BY DARKNESS
FEAR THE DARKNESS
DARKNESS AVENGED
HUNT THE DARKNESS
WHEN DARKNESS ENDS
DARKNESS RETURNS
BEWARE THE DARKNESS
CONQUER THE DARKNESS
SHADES OF DARKNESS
DARKNESS BETRAYED
BEWITCH THE DARKNESS
STALK THE DARKNESS
SATE THE DARKNESS

The Immortal Rogues
MY LORD VAMPIRE
MY LORD ETERNITY
MY LORD IMMORTALITY

The Sentinels
BORN IN BLOOD
BLOOD ASSASSIN
BLOOD LUST

Magic for Hire
WILD MAGIC
ANCIENT MAGIC

ETERNAL MAGIC

Ares Security
KILL WITHOUT MERCY
KILL WITHOUT SHAME

Romantic Suspense
PRETEND YOU'RE SAFE
WHAT ARE YOU AFRAID OF?
YOU WILL SUFFER
THE INTENDED VICTIM
DON'T LOOK
FACELESS
UNSTABLE
DESPERATE ACTS
THE MURDER CLUB

Historical Romance
SOME LIKE IT WICKED
SOME LIKE IT SINFUL
SOME LIKE IT BRAZEN

And don't miss these Guardians of Eternity novellas
TAKEN BY DARKNESS in YOURS FOR ETERNITY
DARKNESS ETERNAL in SUPERNATURAL
WHERE DARKNESS LIVES in THE REAL WEREWIVES
OF VAMPIRE COUNTY
LEVET (ebook only)
A VERY LEVET CHRISTMAS (ebook only)

And don't miss these Sentinel novellas
OUT OF CONTROL
ON THE HUNT

Published by Kensington Publishing Corp.

Eternal Magic

By Alexandra Ivy

LYRICAL PRESS
Kensington Publishing Corp.
www.kensingtonbooks.com

LYRICAL PRESS BOOKS are published by
Kensington Publishing Corp.
119 West 40th Street
New York, NY 10018

Special book excerpts or customized printings can also be created to fit specific needs. For details, write or phone the office of the Kensington Sales Manager: Kensington Publishing Corp., 119 West 40th Street, New York, NY 10018. Attn. Sales Department. Phone: 1-800-221-2647.

Lyrical Press Books and Lyrical Press eBooks logo Reg. U.S. Pat. & TM Off.

First Electronic Edition: March 2025
ISBN: 978-1-5161-1140-4 (ebook)

First Print Edition: March 2025
ISBN: 978-1-5161-1143-5

150150871

Chapter 1

Spring was springing. Or at least there was a faint promise of spring in the air, luring the winter-weary citizens of Linden, New Jersey, out of their homes. Who cared if the wind whipping through the narrow streets was more frigid than refreshing? Or that darkness was already gathering as they headed out of their offices after a long day of work? Or even that it was a random Tuesday in mid-April. Tonight they eagerly celebrated happy hour at the local bars and jammed the sidewalks as they wandered in and out of the various shops.

Including the Witch's Brew.

The brightly lit coffee shop with a white tiled floor and lavender walls wasn't the largest in town, and it wasn't part of a chain, but it was always packed with customers who crowded into the narrow space and battled to claim one of the small tables set near the large front window. Most were eager to munch on the variety of muffins and scones and brownies, not to mention enjoy the freshly brewed coffee. But there were a few who wandered into the attached bookstore in search of a good novel to enjoy during a quiet evening alone.

The private office at the back of the shop, however, was strictly off limits. The only customers allowed through the door were by appointment. And only for those select few clients who could afford Maya Rosen's outrageous fees. As one of the most powerful mages in the world, Maya could name her price.

And she did.

Plus, she only offered her considerable skills to demons. They were split into two categories. The goblins who had long ago been giants, ogres, and trolls. And the fey creatures who had been fairies, sprites, and imps.

She never worked for vampires. Ever. And, of course, the local humans didn't have a clue that she was anything other than a successful businesswoman who was always generous with the neighborhood charities. Just as they didn't know that they were living on the outskirts of a pool of ancient magic called a Gyre that fueled the demons who infested New York City. Or that the territory was ruled by Valen, a powerful member of the Vampire Cabal.

Ignorance could definitely be bliss, Maya wryly acknowledged as she calmly watched a male demon storm around the barren office like a caged lion, waving his arms as he vented his seething fury. At first glance, the intruder appeared to be a regular guy in a tailored gray suit with his dark hair smoothed from his square face. Maya, however, could see the dark crimson aura that throbbed around his large body. It revealed that he was a goblin, but also that his blood hadn't been diluted over the centuries.

She could also smell the sour stench of his fear that he was trying to hide beneath his loud bluster.

Understandable. She had, after all, created a truth potion that had caused him to blurt out the fact that he'd been routinely overbilling vendors and pocketing the money during a meeting with his manager. Plus he'd shared his nasty habit of forcing himself on his young female employees.

Now he was out of his job as an accountant at the glitzy nightclub in New York City, and soon he'd be facing Valen's wrath for his sexual harassment. Something no demon wanted.

"Who was it?" he ground out as he stomped past her desk, his face an interesting shade of purple.

Maya pretended to be confused by his question. "Excuse me?"

"Who paid the contract to have my coffee spiked with a truth potion?"

Maya shrugged, not surprised he'd managed to figure out she was responsible for the potion in his coffee. But that's all he'd ever know. There was no way in hell she would reveal that the contract had been negotiated by his last victim. The pretty fairy had sold everything she owned, plus taken a loan from the bank, to ensure that the goblin was exposed and punished for his crimes.

The payment would be returned to the fairy through some covert means. Maya had too much respect for the female to refuse the stack of cash she'd proudly handed over. Just as she hadn't told the younger woman that she intended to add a secret layer to the potion. A layer that hadn't kicked in yet.

A week from now the demon was going to develop a mysterious rash with oozing pus and a disgusting odor. It wouldn't kill him, but it was going to make him miserable for several days.

"My clients are guaranteed confidentiality," she informed the seething demon. "Unless they specifically request I share their name."

"I don't give a flying fuck about your—"

"Enough," Maya snapped. She'd allowed the idiot to indulge his rabid temper—which was more than he deserved—but she was done. Beyond done. Opening the top drawer of her desk, she pulled out a small glass vial. "This meeting is over."

"What do you mean, over?" His face darkened from purple to puce as the male moved to slam his palms on her desk, spittle hanging at the corner of his mouth. "I'll tell you when it's over, bitch." The threat was unmistakable, but Maya didn't flinch. Instead she calmly pulled the stopper out of the top of the vial. The demon stiffened, the fury fogging his brain penetrated by the acrid odor that abruptly stained the air. "What's that?"

"A very powerful potion."

The male scowled. "Are you threatening me?"

"I'm giving you an opportunity," Maya corrected in a soft voice.

"An opportunity for what?"

"You can walk out of here, and never return. Or I can toss the contents of this vial on you and various parts of your body are going to start shriveling." She paused, studying the liquid that was beginning to bubble inside the glass container. "Perhaps even fall off," she conceded with a small shrug. "I haven't used this recipe before so it's hard to say how bad things might get for you."

The male stumbled backward, his jaw bulging as he clenched his teeth in frustration. He was a cliché bully who used bluster and intimidation to manipulate others. The fact that he couldn't terrorize her was pissing him off as much as the knowledge that he'd lost everything.

"You wouldn't do it," he snarled. "Those potions are illegal."

They were. And the foaming liquid in the vial was nothing more than a harmless cleansing potion, but he didn't know that. Maya slowly rose to her feet, stretching out her arm as if preparing to launch a spell.

"So is stealing. And lying. And being a pervert," she reminded him in overly sweet tones. "Should I go on?"

The male smacked into the wall with a heavy thud. "I hope you rot in hell, you...you witch," he rasped, his insult ruined as he hastily turned to wrench open the door and flee like a coward.

With a roll of her eyes, Maya tossed the contents of the vial onto the floor, allowing the potion to spread through the office and purify the air. The demons couldn't touch their ancient powers when they were outside the magic of the Gyre, but that didn't mean they couldn't buy hexes and leave them behind.

Better safe than sorry. That was her motto.

Then, moving toward the open door, Maya paused to wipe her hands down her yellow cashmere sweater that she'd matched with a pair of ivory slacks. The meeting had gone pretty much as expected, but this was her least favorite part of her mage-for-hire business. Next, she combed her fingers through her shoulder-length black hair that framed her face. There was no gray to be seen in the silken strands, just as there were no lines on her oval face. As a mage, she stopped aging around thirty, but there was no mistaking the hard-earned wisdom in her bright green eyes.

The only visible mar to her polished beauty was the silvery spiderweb of scars that ran from her ear along the line of her jaw. The remnants of the magic that had nearly destroyed her.

Once she was confident that her composure was firmly in place, she walked through the empty bookstore and into the coffee shop that was serving the last of the customers. It was after six o'clock and the shop was officially closed, but even on a Tuesday it was closer to seven before the staff could shut off the lights and call it a day.

Well, most of the staff, Maya grimly acknowledged, her gaze locked on the young woman who was tossing aside her apron as she grabbed the purse she'd stowed beneath the front counter. With long strides, Maya was across the white tiled floor to stand directly in front of her newest employee.

Courtney Tate had appeared at the coffee shop a week ago, pleading for an opportunity to work with Maya. She wasn't the first mage to apply for a job at the Witch's Brew. Not only because Maya had mentored Peri Sanguis, a mage who'd recently ignited the wild magic that had been out of reach for as long as they could remember, along with Skye, a seer whose visions had recently saved the world. But because Maya's own magic was off the charts.

Maya had been wary. The young woman's magic was mediocre at best, which meant that Maya's assistance would be limited. She couldn't perform miracles. And worse, there'd been a hard arrogance beneath the mage's pretense of eager longing that had rubbed against Maya's nerves.

She'd lost Peri and Skye, who were her two best friends over the past year. Okay, she conceded, that was overly dramatic. She hadn't *lost* them. But they'd both recently fallen in love with members of the Cabal and they'd moved out of the Witch's Brew to be with their chosen mates.

Leeches... A shudder raced through her body. The worst sort of creature as far as she was concerned. Unfortunately, they hadn't asked her opinion.

But despite the very large hole that had been blasted into her life with their absence, Maya wasn't desperate enough to take in the first mage who wandered off the streets. Especially one she didn't even like.

Still, there'd been something suspicious about her. Maya couldn't put her finger on what was off, but she knew without a doubt Courtney had no interest in being mentored. Not by anyone, including Maya. She also knew the only way to discover the reason the young mage had gone to such an effort to get access to the Witch's Brew was to hire her. Eventually she would reveal the truth.

Now she studied the younger mage with a suspicious gaze. Courtney was several inches shorter than Maya with blond hair that was cut pixie short to frame her round face. Her eyes were blue and so wide they gave her the appearance of being perpetually surprised while her lips were plumped with some sort of artificial filler. She wore figure-hugging dresses and designer heels nearly as high as Maya's.

"You're leaving?" Maya demanded, glancing toward the last of the customers who were shuffling out of the shop. "You haven't finished cleaning."

Courtney shrugged. "Yeah well, I gotta bounce."

"Is something wrong?"

"Hard to say. My mom called and said she's not feeling good. It's probably nothing, but I gotta check on her." Courtney widened her too-wide eyes. "You don't mind, do you?"

Maya felt a surge of annoyance. Did the stupid girl think her innocent act could sway a battle-hardened mage?

"I assume you'll be back tomorrow?" Maya asked in dry tones.

"Maybe. Maybe not. We'll see." With a finger wave, Courtney swayed her way to the door.

There was a snort of disgust from behind Maya and she turned to discover Joyce Shelton removing the unsold pastries from the front case even as she glared at Courtney, who was out the door and headed down the street.

"Sketchy," the older woman muttered.

Maya arched a brow. Joyce had been working part-time at the Witch's Brew for over a decade, and while she was a human with no idea that she was employed by a magic user, she'd been one of Maya's most loyal staff members.

"Why do you say that?" Maya demanded.

The older woman wrinkled her nose. She was in her mid-sixties with a square face and frizzy hair she kept dyed a bright red. She wasn't fat, but she was solid beneath the baggy sweater and yoga pants.

"She comes in late and leaves early," Joyce said, loading the pastries into one of the glass coolers that lined the far wall.

"She's young," Maya pointed out.

"Young doesn't mean stupid. She can tell time, can't she?" Joyce pointed out. "And it's not like she doesn't have a clock. Her eyes are glued to that phone of hers like she's expecting a message from the Almighty."

Maya studied the woman's stiff back with blatant curiosity. Joyce was gruff, but she never complained about the girls Maya took under her wing. In fact, she'd doted on Peri and Skye as if they were her own daughters.

"Anything else?"

Joyce shut the cooler with a snap and turned back to face Maya. "While you were in your meeting I caught her coming out of the basement."

Maya stilled, her gaze moving toward the steel door behind the counter. "You're sure?"

Joyce clicked her tongue. "Of course I'm sure. I'm old but I'm not blind. I saw her sneaking up the stairs with my own eyes."

"How did she get past the lock?"

"Don't know." Joyce grabbed a mop from the utility closet. Maya would cast a cleansing spell later, but she requested her human staff to follow a typical closing routine. Otherwise they would wonder how the place was always spotless. "I told her it was off limits to everyone, including the staff, on the first day she came to work."

So had Maya, but she wasn't surprised that Courtney had sneaked down to the cellar. As a mage, the younger woman would know that the steel door was installed as a secondary layer of protection in case the vault where Maya kept the most dangerous potions and spell books was breached.

It could have been natural curiosity that led her down there, or something more sinister. Maya had several rare and valuable items stored in the vault. But what did surprise her was the fact that the girl had managed to break through the warding spell she'd placed on the door. Maybe she had more power than Maya had originally suspected.

"Did she say anything when you caught her?" Maya abruptly asked.

Joyce shrugged. "She claimed she'd gone down there to look for extra napkins, as if there weren't plenty under the counter."

"Hmm. Maybe I should have a word with her."

"Good luck with that. Doubt she bothers to show up again."

"You're right." Maya felt a stab of urgency slice through her. "I need to speak to her. Can you lock up?"

"Yes, but—"

"Thanks."

With brisk steps, Maya returned to her office to grab a leather satchel filled with several vials of potions along with cash and a variety of ID cards. She paused to scoop her phone off her desk before she was heading back into the coffee shop. She was halfway to the front door when she felt Joyce reach out to touch her arm.

"Be careful."

Maya blinked at the edge in the older woman's voice, as if she was genuinely concerned for Maya's safety. Strange.

"Always," she murmured.

Continuing her path out the door, Maya touched the emerald pendant she wore on a gold chain. It was more habit than a necessity. She didn't need the extra magic she'd stored in the priceless gem to track her young employee. Or even to blend in with the pedestrians who clogged the sidewalks.

She did slow her pace once she'd left the brightly lit business area of town and followed the trail that led her across a large parking lot and up the steps to the commuter train. Once on the platform, she paused to scan the waiting crowd. Courtney was easy to spot. She was standing near the edge, impatiently glaring toward the approaching train as if it was running late.

Maya edged her way around the gathered passengers, prepared as the train stopped and the doors slid open. There was the usual push of people trying to exit while others were wiggling their way into the carriages, but Maya waited to make sure Courtney was settled in a seat before scurrying onto the train just seconds before the doors slid shut.

The younger woman appeared impervious to the fact that she was being followed as she pulled out her phone and scrolled with a bored expression. Or maybe she was trying to blend in with the horde of passengers who were equally engrossed as they stared mindlessly at their screens.

Maya remained standing in a shadowed corner, shuddering as they moved from the outskirts into the full power of the Gyre. As a mage she didn't need the ancient magic to create spells or potions, but it intensified her power until it pounded through her with an addictive force.

This was the reason most mages were willing to bend the knee to the Vampire Cabal. They considered it a fair trade-off to pledge loyalty to the leeches so they could create magic inside the Gyre.

Not Maya.

Avoiding the mass exodus as they came to a halt at Penn Station, Maya waited until the carriage was empty. She wasn't going to risk exposing her presence. Mages weren't as rare as vampires, but there wasn't an abundance of them either. It was simple enough to follow the trail of magic Courtney left in her wake.

Heading up the escalators and onto the streets of Manhattan, Maya turned south, away from the bustle of Times Square. Within a couple of blocks she once again had the younger woman in sight.

Courtney was walking at a rapid pace, not slowing until she entered the Meatpacking District. Even then she hurried past the redbrick buildings that had been refurbished into trendy apartments and rooftop taverns as if she was on a mission. It wasn't until she reached a shabby building near the river that she paused, glancing side to side before she pushed open a wooden door to disappear inside what appeared to be an abandoned slaughterhouse.

Maya waited a full five minutes before she hesitantly moved to stand in front of the squat building with boarded windows and a rusted tin roof. Holding out her hand, she felt a familiar warmth tingle against her palm. Maya arched her brows. There was a protective barrier wrapped around the building, but it wasn't an active spell or incantation created by a mage. A demon had woven this strand by strand, using the power of the Gyre. Just like a spider weaving a web.

Interesting.

Valen was more tolerant than most members of the Cabal when it came to demons running their own businesses in his territory, so why would they go to such an effort?

The obvious answer was that the owner was hiding something worth the bother and expense of such an elaborate barrier.

Debating the wisdom of entering the building without backup, Maya muttered the words of a defensive spell. She no longer had Peri and Skye to call on when she needed assistance. Time to adjust to the fact that she was on her own.

The ancient words seared her tongue, the bitter taste a deliberate warning to be careful. As if the scars on her face weren't enough to remind her of the dangers of using magic as a weapon, she wryly acknowledged. At the same time, the sweet, intoxicating power swirled through her veins, enhanced by the hum of the Gyre beneath her feet. The turbulent magic added a seductive edge to the anticipation that sizzled through her, threatening to demolish her usual caution.

Grimly squaring her shoulders, Maya forced herself to step through the magic. The spell was locked and loaded. There was no reason to wait.

A prickle of heat crawled over her as she moved forward. It wasn't the delicate power of a fairy. It was raw and intimidating. Goblin. With a grimace, she pushed open the door and cautiously headed down the steep staircase that led her beneath the empty slaughterhouse. The steps ended at another heavy door, but this one was lit with blinking neon lights that spelled out:

SLAUGHTERHOUSE CLUB
Enter at your own risk

Maya rolled her eyes. Goblins were powerful, cunning, and ruthless, but they had the creativity of a turnip.

Pushing open the basement door, Maya winced at the avalanche of noise that assaulted her. Not only the heavy thump of music that spilled from the overhead speakers, but also the harsh cries of bloodlust from the crowd gathered at the far side of the long room.

Maya paused, allowing her vision to adjust to the thick gloom that surrounded her. She wanted to follow Courtney, not stumble over her because she couldn't see. Or worse, stumble over one of the numerous demons who would love to rip out her heart and eat it.

At the same time, she studied the brightly lit corner where the crowd was gathered. They circled something that looked like an elevated square. A stage? No, it was a boxing ring surrounded by a tall, chain-link fence.

The flashing lights caught the outline of a large male goblin with a deep red aura who was holding a slender fairy over his head. She watched as he turned in a slow circle, obviously prodding the crowd into a frenzy of excitement before he launched his opponent through the air to hit the fence with enough force to bend the metal post.

An underground fight club.

The crowd roared and Maya turned away with a disgusted shake of her head.

At least she understood the need for the layers of protection. Valen had strict rules about this type of club. And the first rule was that no one could run one that wasn't personally under his supervision.

It wasn't that he worried about the fighters being injured. He was a leech, not a saint. But these types of places tended to attract a violent crowd who lost all common sense when they were in the throes of their bloodlust. It was all too common for brawls to erupt in the club and then spill onto the streets where innocent humans could be injured or killed.

That was never good for business.

Using the distraction of the crowd, Maya edged through the thick shadows, absently absorbing the waves of demon energy that pulsed through the room. She could store it in her emerald pendant to amp up her magic. Another benefit of being in the Gyre.

But again, not worth having to bend the knee to a vampire.

Reaching an opening at the side of the room, Maya glanced around before she peered into the narrow hallway lined with closed doors. Ah. So that was it. Now she understood why Courtney had deliberately gone into the off-limits basement at the Witch's Brew when she was bound to be spotted. And why she'd waited for Maya to conclude her business with the demon before she'd taken off from work.

This was a trap.

Honestly, Maya couldn't help but be offended. Did Courtney think she was that stupid? Or was she just lazy?

She was going with the lazy theory. Her ego couldn't accept that she'd reached an age when the younger generation assumed she was so old and feeble she could be this easily fooled.

Following the tingle of magic to the end of the corridor, Maya pushed open the wooden door and stepped into the small, square room. She didn't have to search for hidden dangers. The floor was cement. The walls were cement. There was a single bare light bulb hanging from the ceiling and zero furniture. The only thing to see was the young mage watching her with a smug expression.

"Hello, Maya."

Magic lashed out, wrapping around Maya as if she was a mummy being entombed. She didn't fight the spell. Her own magic was primed and ready to shred through the invisible bonds. For now she wanted Courtney to believe she was in control of the situation. It was the only way she was going to discover why the younger mage had lured her to this location.

"Courtney." Her voice was calm as she inspected her captor with more curiosity than fear.

Courtney's pleasure dimmed, her eyes narrowing. "Surprised?"

"Not really. Why have you attacked me?"

"Hardly an attack." The mage clicked her tongue. "It's no more than a binding spell."

"Answer me."

"Answer you?" Courtney stepped forward, her heels clicking on the cement floor. "Are you seriously giving me orders?"

"I asked a simple question."

The younger woman snorted. "After enduring a week of being treated like I'm your slave, I can happily tell you to fuck off," she hissed. "You're not the boss of me." She snapped her fingers in Maya's face. "I quit."

Maya arched a brow. The girl didn't qualify as an employee, let alone a slave. "If you didn't want to work at the Witch's Brew, why did you apply for the job?"

"Because I need the money."

"There are lots of jobs available. Most of them pay more than I can offer."

Courtney released a sharp laugh. "Do you really think I'm the sort of woman who works for minimum wage?" She deliberately glanced down at her designer outfit and manicured nails. "When I say I need the money, I'm not looking for a lousy paycheck. I want the sort of payout that can keep me in luxury for the next year."

Maya wasn't offended by the snarky words. In fact, it was reassuring to know her instincts about this mage hadn't been wrong.

"And how do you intend to get your generous payout?"

The woman lifted her hand and gestured toward the door. A second later it slammed shut, muting the music and roar from the distant crowd. Maya breathed a sigh of relief. Maybe she *was* getting old. Her ears were ringing from the noise.

"Obviously by capturing the infamous Maya Rosen," Courtney informed her.

"Infamous?" Maya kept her expression mildly curious, even as she inwardly dismissed the various fears that had run through her mind when she'd been following Courtney. In the past year Peri had battled an ancient evil magic. And then Skye had been swept into a plot that would have bathed the world in fire. It was almost boring to discover this was nothing more than a mundane desire for revenge. "Should I be flattered or insulted?"

"Be whatever you want. I don't give a shit," the younger woman snapped. Clearly, Maya wasn't as terrified as she'd hoped. "I just want my money."

"Who's paying you?"

Courtney rolled her eyes. "What a stupid question. In my business we don't exchange personal information. I do my job and I get paid."

"Your business?"

"Assassin."

"Ah." Maya rolled her eyes. There might be a handful of demons and mage assassins who had the skills to kidnap or kill her, but they weren't stupid enough to try. On the other hand, there were a whole plethora of assassins who plied their trade without an ounce of talent. Most of them bumbled from one job to another, hoping to get paid before they could be exposed as incompetent amateurs. "I hope you offer coupons."

Courtney blinked. "Excuse me?"

"Just a little warning, my dear, from one mage to another," Maya said with a smile. "If you're as bad at being an assassin as you are at being a barista, then your client is going to want a discount."

Courtney flushed, the bonds around Maya tightening as the woman struggled to maintain her temper. Clumsy. Emotions were the enemy of any mage. Especially when they were actively using magic.

"You're here, aren't you?" Courtney taunted. "Exactly where I wanted you to be."

"If you say so." Maya deliberately paused. "Now what?"

"I send word to my contact and he comes to pick you up."

Good. There was no point in going through this charade if she wasn't going to discover the person responsible for hiring Courtney.

"How?" she demanded.

Courtney flashed an impatient frown. "I don't know. And I don't care."

"How do you contact him?" Maya clarified.

"Oh." The mage reached into her purse to pull out her phone. "Through the app."

For the first time since entering the trap, Maya was genuinely surprised. "There's an app for assassins?"

"There's an app for everything, you stupid hag. Not everyone is stuck in the past." Courtney dropped the phone back into her purse. "Some of us are smart enough to change with the times."

Maya grimaced. The words didn't hurt. Not exactly. But there was enough truth in the insult to rub across a raw nerve. There were times when she did wonder if she was becoming obsolete. Not because it was increasingly difficult to keep up with technology, but she couldn't deny there were occasions when she considered selling the Witch's Brew and moving to a tiny cottage in the middle of nowhere with a dog and stacks of books to keep her company. A little peace and quiet sounded like heaven.

A worry for later, she sharply reminded herself. There wouldn't be any cottages in her future if she didn't get out of this basement alive.

"So you have no idea who hired you?"

"I get a job, I do it, I get paid. Simple." Courtney pursed her lips, her gaze flicking over Maya with blatant dislike. "Of course, on this job I have the added bonus of never having to hear the name Maya Rosen again."

Maya was baffled by the angry sincerity in the younger woman's voice. Okay, she could be cold and demanding and sometimes impatient, but she wasn't a monster. Was she?

"Is there a particular reason you dislike me?"

"I don't dislike you." Courtney leaned forward, only to flinch as she encountered Maya's protective spell. Unlike other mages, Maya's magic didn't spark and flicker around her. It blasted out with the force of an industrial furnace. Even humans who had no idea mages existed avoided standing too close to Maya. The younger woman sniffed, pretending she wasn't unnerved by the thunderous power. "I loathe you."

Loathe? Well, that seemed unnecessarily dramatic.

"Why?" Maya asked. "You know nothing about me."

"Seriously?"

"I'm always serious."

Courtney made a gagging sound. "Every young mage in the world is sick of listening to stories of how you battled against a vampire and forced the Cabal to bend to your will. The older generation whisper your name in tones of awe, and your enemies tremble in fear. It's even worse now that your precious protégée, Peri Sanguis, has tapped into the wild magic. A magic that's out of reach for the rest of us." Her voice was thick with envy as her gaze moved to the scar on the side of Maya's face. "There are some of us who realize that you're not some sort of hero just because you survived. And that it doesn't give you the right to be a bully."

Maya kept her features smooth even as the accusations pierced her heart. She never revealed the torment she'd endured from her former master or how she managed to escape. Which no doubt explained the endless rumors that had swirled around her for decades. If the gossips couldn't get the real story, they would just make one up.

More importantly, she never ever discussed why she refused to bend the knee to the Cabal. That was a secret she would take to her grave. And beyond.

"I've never claimed to be a hero," she informed the younger woman. "And I'm certainly no bully."

"No, you just suck up all the jobs that offer a hefty payout and leave the rest of us to squabble over the crumbs."

Maya silently released the breath stuck in her lungs. Okay. She could deal with petty jealousy. The past? Not so much.

"You forget, I've seen your work," she reminded Courtney with a mocking smile. "Maybe if you were actually willing to put in an effort and learn some skills, you wouldn't be squabbling for crumbs."

"You—" Courtney raised her hand, as if she was going to strike. Then, watching Maya's smile widen in anticipation, she wisely backed away. "No. You're not worth the effort," she muttered, angling until she was close enough to pull open the door. She paused to blow Maya a kiss. "I hope whoever paid to have you captured intends to kill you. Very, very slowly."

Courtney exited the room, slamming shut the door with a dramatic flick of her wrist. Maya shook her head as she listened to the heels clicking against the cement slowly fade into the distance.

"Drama queen," she muttered, easily busting through the magical bonds that held her.

Once free, she did a mental sweep of her body, making sure Courtney hadn't left behind a nasty curse or a hex that would trigger as soon as Maya lowered her defensive shields. It was something Maya did on a regular basis. If her head-on attack failed, she had a backup in place.

Not surprisingly, Courtney hadn't bothered with the additional layer.

A hack, Maya thought as she moved to press her back against the wall next to the open door. Whoever had trained the younger woman was an embarrassment to mages around the world.

Keeping her shields in place, Maya began to weave a delicate web of magic over the door. It was designed to allow anyone into the room, including her mystery enemy, but they wouldn't be able to escape. She intended to get her questions answered one way or another.

She was still in the process of weaving her spell when a frigid gust of air swirled through the room.

A shiver raced through her as she instantly recognized her danger.

Vampire.

With the skill that came from decades of practice, Maya grimly re-formed the spell she'd been weaving, thickening the strands of magic to slam against the blur of darkness that darted into the room. It wouldn't hurt a leech, but it would hopefully catch him off guard. She needed time to dig through the potions she kept stocked in her satchel.

Unfortunately, she only had one laced with enough silver to cause actual pain. It hadn't occurred to her that she might stumble across a leech when she'd followed Courtney into the city. Valen had a low tolerance for allowing his brothers into his territory. Especially after the Cabal had descended on New York City a few months back to determine if Valen's mate—and Maya's best friend—was a danger to the vampires.

Watching the waves of magic smack against the shadowed form, Maya's eyes widened as the powerful spell fizzled and sputtered, as if being absorbed by the darkness.

Genuine fear pierced her heart as Maya shoved her hand into her purse to grab a vial. Right now it didn't matter what was in the potion. She needed a distraction to get the hell out of here.

Her fingers wrapped around the glass tube, but before she could pull it out, the shadow had moved with blinding speed to stand directly in front of her.

"Easy, Maya," a male voice murmured.

A voice that she easily recognized despite the years since she'd last heard it.

Shock slammed into her, the ground feeling as if it was buckling beneath her feet. Or maybe it was her knees that were buckling. Whatever the case, Maya would have collapsed if strong hands hadn't reached out to grasp her arms, keeping her upright.

At the same time, the shadows dissipated, revealing a tall, heavily muscled male with silver-blond hair shaven close to his scalp and chiseled features. His skin was smooth with a hint of gold and his eyes were the precise shade of turquoise rimmed with silver.

He wasn't handsome. That was too small a word. He was...brutally, ruthlessly gorgeous with the sort of raw animal magnetism that made her entire body sizzle with awareness. This male didn't seek attention, he demanded it.

Ravyr.

Emotions erupted through her, so intense they were impossible to contain. Astonishment, bewilderment, and a strange sense of giddy relief. As if the sight of him healed a wound she didn't even know she carried deep inside.

The last emotion to bubble out was fury.

The sort of high-octane fury that shattered her hard-earned composure and demanded a physical release. Lifting her hands, she pounded them against his chest.

"No. It can't be," she hissed. "You're dead."

Chapter 2

A low growl rumbled in Ravyr's throat. A growl of hunger. Need. Want. Endless, desperate want.

It'd been over forty years since he'd seen Maya Rosen, but that hadn't lessened the impact of being in her presence. In fact, gazing down at the impossibly beautiful face, he experienced the same thrill of anticipation as the time he'd been tossed off a cliff during a battle. Plummeting through the air with no idea if he was going to survive the landing.

Planting his open hand on the wall, Ravyr leaned forward, effectively caging Maya in place. Not as a threat. But this woman was a powerful mage who possessed the sort of magic and cunning to escape before he could talk to her. Plus, if he was being entirely honest, his reaction to seeing her again had knocked his equilibrium off a bit. He needed the extra balance.

At last regaining control of his composure, Ravyr met his companion's horrified gaze, trying to recall what she'd said. Something about him being dead, right? Not surprising. He'd gone to a great deal of effort to convince the world he'd perished in Cambodia four decades ago.

"I suppose it's technically true that all vampires are dead, but it's not entirely accurate," he retorted.

She shook her head. "How?"

"A story for later. Right now we have to get out of this building."

"What?" She lifted her hands again to press them against his chest. "Let me go," she commanded, futilely attempting to shove aside his considerable weight. Obviously realizing it was an impossible task, she tilted back her head to send him a glare that would wither a lesser male. "Are you deaf? I said—"

The sharp, acrid smell of nitrate cut through Maya's rich scent of orchids. An urgent reminder of why he'd interrupted his original purpose for being in the building to track her down and get her the hell out of there.

"You can indulge your desire for a hissy fit later." Keeping one hand wrapped around her upper arm, he tugged her toward the door. "Let's go."

Predictably she dug in her high heels, painful pricks of magic stabbing into his hand.

"Stop it. I'm not going anywhere with you."

"Fine." He parted his lips to expose his massive fangs, a gesture of intense irritation. "Enjoy the fiery explosion. You might survive, but I wouldn't put money on your chances."

She blinked. "What?"

"Maya, don't you feel it?"

He could tell she was forcing herself to battle through her hatred and concentrate on the hum in the air. It wasn't magic or the power of the Gyre. It wasn't even the echo of the demons screaming and stomping their feet overhead. It was the buzz of a lethal explosive about to be unleashed.

"Dammit."

Maya darted out the door and down the hallway, moving with remarkable speed considering she was wearing heels that could be used as weapons. Ravyr followed close behind, his gaze scanning the area as he searched for a hidden enemy. He didn't know why Maya was at this particular location, but it had to be shady. No one came here to conduct legitimate business.

Keeping a respectable pace, they were up the stairs and darting out an emergency exit. On the way, Ravyr hit the fire alarm, hoping at least a few of the demons had enough sense to get out. Then, feeling the pressure build at an alarming rate, Ravyr ignored Maya's angry tirade as he scooped her off her feet and held her tight against his chest.

She already hated him, what did it matter if he infuriated her by saving her life?

Running across the street and down the block at a speed no other creature could match, Ravyr vaulted onto the balcony of a towering apartment building. He'd barely landed when he was jumping to the balcony above his head, zigzagging his way upward until they were at last on the top of the roof. A second later the explosion hit.

Ravyr turned his back, keeping Maya wrapped tight in his arms as the searing wave passed over them, busting windows along the block and sending lethal debris flying.

It wasn't until the last of the tremors shaking the neighborhood settled that he reluctantly lowered Maya to her feet and stepped back. He wanted enough space to defend himself if she decided to strike out. A very real possibility.

Instead she whirled around to study the empty space where the Slaughterhouse Club had been standing minutes ago.

It was a full and utter devastation. Not only had the walls and ceiling collapsed, but they'd also tumbled into the basement, leaving behind a hole that resembled a gaping wound. Smoke billowed from a fire that burned beneath the rubble, tainting the night with the charred stench of burned wood and melted plastic.

Nasty.

At least there were a few customers fleeing down the street, he acknowledged. Several dozen had escaped the inferno and were desperate to disappear before the authorities arrived. Or worse, before Valen, the Cabal leader of this Gyre, made an appearance.

"Is that your work?" she demanded, turning back to him with an accusing expression.

He wiped his face to an unreadable mask. The next few minutes were going to be...interesting.

"Why would I blow up a building?" he demanded.

"You're a leech." She lifted her hand to touch the scars on the side of her face. "You don't need a reason to destroy things. Or people."

He leaned forward, refusing to offer sympathy. She had survived her past. More than that, she'd thrived. It was nothing less than a miracle.

"Still bitter after all these years, Maya?" he drawled.

Narrowing her eyes, she refused to back away. In fact, she stepped closer, blatantly proving she wasn't going to be intimidated.

"Not bitter, just reconciled to the fact that vampires are ruthless, untrustworthy bastards who will sacrifice anyone and everyone to gain power."

Her smile widened a millisecond before the spell smashed into him with shocking force. Ravyr used his specialized skill to absorb the magic, oddly pleased to discover it was a defensive spell rather than an attempt to genuinely hurt him.

Wrapping his arms around her slender body, he contained her struggles, careful not to bruise her delicate skin. He needed to talk to her before she managed to escape, but he wasn't going to risk hurting her.

"Glad to learn that some things never change," he murmured, lowering his head until their lips were nearly touching.

"Same." She jerked her knee up, trying to smash his tender bits.

Ravyr lifted her off her feet, chuckling even as he tried to remember that Maya Rosen wasn't the reason he traveled to New York. Even if he wished things could be different.

"I'll release you if you swear not to use your magic to hurt me," he murmured.

Her eyes smoldered with a fury that had been festering for years. But with an inner strength he'd always admired, she battled back the ferocious desire to lash out at him. Grinding her teeth, she released a slow breath through her nose.

"I..." A word appeared to stick in her throat, but stiffening her spine, she at last managed to spit it out. "Swear."

He resisted the urge to close the small space and claim a kiss. He'd spent far too many nights fantasizing about the precise taste and feel of this woman's lips to ruin the moment by taking what she was unwilling to give.

Instead, he slowly lowered her to her feet, reluctantly loosening his arms and taking a step back.

"That wasn't so hard, was it?"

Her jaw clenched, emphasizing the silvery scars. "I will kill you."

It wasn't a threat. It was a promise.

Ravyr's lips twisted. Fate had created them to be enemies. It wouldn't be easy to overcome that destiny.

"Perhaps someday, but for now I need you to explain why you were in that building tonight."

She made a sound of disgust. "You should know. You're the one who paid to have me lured into a trap by that pathetic excuse for a mage."

He studied her in confusion. He had no idea what she was talking about. He'd been at the fights to track down the magic that had lured him to New York. It'd been a genuine shock when he'd caught the familiar scent of orchids when he'd entered the basement.

Of course, he'd known she lived in the area, but he hadn't expected to encounter her. Just the opposite. The plan was to go out of his way to avoid her.

At least until he realized the building was about to explode.

Then nothing would have stopped him from getting her to safety.

"If I wanted you trapped, why would I pay someone to do it?"

Her brows snapped together. "You don't expect me to believe it was just a coincidence that I happened to be led into that particular building at the same time you were there?"

Ravyr stiffened. "You're right. It seems highly unlikely," he slowly admitted. Was it coincidence that the two of them had been in that building together? Or a deliberate ploy? "How were you lured to this area?"

"Why should I answer your questions?"

"The sooner I know the truth, the sooner I'll disappear," he promised. "That's what you want." He lowered his gaze to her lips. "Isn't it?"

She trembled. Desire? Or fury. He allowed her delicate scent to flood his senses. Charred orchids.

A combination of desire and fury.

Interesting.

"The mage you hired—"

He immediately interrupted. "She wasn't hired by me."

"Fine," she snapped, clearly willing to do whatever was necessary to get rid of him. "I discovered a new employee was sneaking into the private vault beneath my shop. Naturally I followed to ask her a few questions. That's when she lured me to the Slaughterhouse and trapped me in the basement."

"You walked into a trap?" He arched a brow. "Sloppy."

"Of course not," she retorted, clearly insulted. "I knew from the minute Courtney took a job at the Witch's Brew she was trouble. I followed her to discover why she was spying on me and who she was working for."

That explained why Maya had been at a fight club, but not how her presence might be connected to his prey.

"Tell me about this Courtney," he abruptly demanded.

Maya shrugged. "Young. Arrogant. Mediocre magic." Her lips curved into a humorless smile. "She claims to be a mage assassin."

"You don't believe her?"

"If she is one, she's not very good."

"Not many can compare to you, Maya," he pointed out in dry tones. She blinked, as if she wasn't fully aware that her magic was off the charts. "Was this Courtney a local mage?"

She cleared her throat. "I'm not sure. I've never seen her before."

"What did she want from you?"

"She claimed she'd been hired to kidnap me, but she didn't know the identity of her client."

Ravyr felt a pang of frustration. Of course it couldn't be easy. Like a name and location of whoever had lured her to this location.

After chasing shadows for the past forty years, he was accustomed to smashing into one dead end after another.

The story of his life.

"Do you have any enemies?" he asked.

"Hundreds."

He arched a brow. "Any who would be willing to blow you up in a building?" He tried to narrow the list of potential suspects.

"Hundreds, but we don't have any proof it exploded because of me," she reminded him.

"True."

It didn't feel like a coincidence that they were both in the same location when someone decided to plant a bomb, but then the explosion could have been intended to destroy him, while killing Maya was just a bonus.

Considering the limited number of suspects who would know they were acquainted, let alone that they had a complicated past, it should be a simple matter to—

"Why were you there?"

The sharp question cut into Ravyr's musings. He glanced across the street, where fire and smoke continued to belch out of the large crater. In the distance he could hear sirens screaming through the air as a crowd of humans gathered along the sidewalk to watch the show.

"Vampire business."

She narrowed her eyes. "You forced me to explain why I was there. I insist you offer me the same in return."

"Insist?"

She folded her arms over her chest, her expression defiant as the emerald necklace hanging around her neck glowed with power.

"I don't remember you being hard of hearing, Ravyr," she taunted. "Of course, that was a long time ago and you were old even then."

His gaze focused on the soft curve of her mouth, the scent of her desire abruptly spicing the air.

"Dangerous games, my Maya."

As expected, she went rigid with outrage. At the same time, Ravyr sensed...something. A strange layer of power that shrouded her. As if she was being protected by some unseen force.

"Never yours," she hissed. "Never."

Without warning, she turned and with one fluid motion dove over the edge of the building and plummeted toward the ground. Muttering a string of ancient expletives, Ravyr rushed forward, glancing down just in time to see Maya land feet first on the cement parking lot before disappearing into the shadows of the night.

Ravyr shuddered in relief. She'd used a spell to ease her landing.

Not that he was entirely happy. She'd used that same spell to escape him, which broke her promise. Then he shrugged. Actually, he'd only demanded that she swear not to use the magic on *him*, he reminded himself, not a ban on magic in general, so...

"As charming as ever, Ravyr," a deep male voice drawled from behind him.

Ravyr slowly turned. He'd already sensed Valen's approach when Maya took her nosedive over the edge. Now he studied the slender male with pale hair that lay smoothly against his head and chiseled features that gave him an austere beauty. His eyes were the precise silver of the moonlight that pooled over the rooftop, and his gray suit, along with his crisp white shirt, was hand tailored.

The Cabal leader of the local territory possessed an elegant sophistication that disguised the power that roared just below the polished exterior.

"I'll agree my charm is dubious, but that's not why the lady jumped," Ravyr said. "We have a history."

Surprise flickered through the silver eyes. "Interesting."

Sensations that Ravyr hadn't felt in years jolted through him. He shuddered, not sure if it was a good or bad thing. It was certainly dangerous.

He'd been chosen to complete a delicate mission because of his unique skills that included a mastery over his emotions.

"You have no idea."

"Actually I do," Valen insisted, his expression wry. "Maya is the best friend to my mate, Peri, and fiercely protective of her. She scares the shit out of me."

Ravyr congratulated his companion. "I always suspected you were smarter than you look." Only a fool would underestimate Maya Rosen and the damage she would do to keep her friends and family safe.

A dead fool.

Valen hesitated; then, obviously sensing that Ravyr wasn't going to share any details of his relationship with Maya, the older male glanced toward the smoldering hole across the street. Several firefighters had arrived and were gathering to assess the flames that continued to shoot upward while cops were climbing out of their vehicles and heading toward the gawkers with their hands raised in a futile effort to push them away from the destruction.

"Are you responsible for the explosion?"

Ravyr folded his arms over his broad chest. "Why do people keep asking me that?"

"Something that deserves some deep introspection, old friend," Valen murmured.

Ravyr shook his head. "I assume Sinjon told you I was entering your territory?"

Sinjon was the current leader of the Cabal and the reason that Ravyr had spent the past four decades on a frustrating search for an enemy that stayed just out of reach.

"Yes, but not the reason why," Valen admitted. "Or why the world thought you'd perished along with Batu in Cambodia."

Ravyr shrugged. The death of Batu, the Cabal leader of Cambodia, had been a perfect opportunity for him to become a ghost so he could continue his position as Sinjon's hidden spy.

Or at least, that was the hope.

Lately he wasn't so sure they'd been successful.

"He likes to keep his business quiet," Ravyr said.

"Too quiet," Valen groused.

Ravyr sensed that the older male wasn't discussing the rumors of Ravyr's death, but rather Sinjon's decision to send several Cabal members to discover the danger that Valen's mate, Peri, posed to the vampires with her wild magic. And the disaster that had been narrowly avoided.

"I'm sure Sinjon would be happy to discuss a change in leadership if you'd like to take over the Cabal," Ravyr assured him. "Last time we spoke, Sinjon was telling me about the lair that he's building on a private island in the Mediterranean. He's anxious to enjoy a long overdue retirement. The sooner the better."

"Rule the Cabal?" Valen shuddered in horror. "Do I look like I've lost my mind? No one would want that constant headache."

Ravyr winced as another wave of emergency vehicles descended on the jam-packed neighborhood, their sirens blaring and their flashing lights threatening to give the crowd a seizure.

"Your headaches aren't going to go away anytime soon."

"Is this involved?" Valen nodded toward the crater.

"That has yet to be determined."

"By you?"

"Yes."

"How hands off do I need to be?"

Ravyr considered the question. He hadn't had the opportunity to discover if the explosion was related to his investigation. Or how Maya might be involved. Or even if the mysterious enemy he'd been tracking was still in the area. All he did know was that something had changed tonight.

After remaining an elusive shadow that managed to stay one step ahead of Ravyr for years, this felt like a direct attack.

"You might consider a vacation for the next week or so," he warned his companion.

Valen shrugged. "I could use some time alone with my new mate far away from the city. We never did have a proper honeymoon."

"Good idea." Ravyr grimly ignored the pang of envy at Valen's besotted smile when he spoke about Peri.

He'd accepted Sinjon's offer to become his secret weapon. The position had taken away the possibility of controlling his own Gyre despite his massive power. As well as denying him the ability to settle down with a mate in a cozy lair.

There was something about making a bed and lying in it, right?

Even if it did feel like a punch to the gut on occasion.

"Feel free to stay at my penthouse," Valen offered.

Ravyr shook his head. "Thanks, but I'd rather keep under the radar. At least for now."

Chapter 3

Maya limped her way from the train station to the Witch's Brew. She should have called an Uber. Her impulsive dive over the edge of the building had left her with a twisted ankle and magic so depleted she might as well have been a human. It made her vulnerable. Never a good thing. And especially not on a night when she'd been lured into a trap, nearly blasted into oblivion, and confronted by a ghost from her past.

Only Ravyr isn't a ghost, a voice whispered in the back of her mind. He was as solid and as gorgeous and epically irritating as ever. And sexy... had she listed the sexy part?

Maya muttered her opinion of leeches who refused to stay dead, forcing herself to concentrate on the reason she was wandering through the dark streets instead of being whisked to her front door in comfort.

Joe.

The strange male who skulked around the neighborhood, pretending to be a vagrant who enjoyed calling out rude insults whenever she passed him on the street and stealing pastries out of her shop with a complete lack of remorse.

Only he wasn't just a vagrant. Or even a man.

Over the past year, Maya had become increasingly convinced that Joe had a deeper purpose for hanging around the Witch's Brew. And she assumed it was connected to her, since both Peri and Skye had recently moved away.

Unfortunately, her efforts to follow him when he left the area had been a waste of time. He either disappeared or deliberately led her into some sleazy joint where she'd stood out like a sore thumb. She'd even tried to place a location charm on him, only to discover her spell had been transferred to a stray dog and that she'd been following it around all day.

She didn't have any idea how he'd done it. She'd never heard of anyone able to transfer a spell. All she was sure of was that Joe was playing with her. And enjoying every second of her frustration.

Grimly hobbling around the corner, Maya headed down the narrow street toward her shop, which was squished between a tanning salon and a falafel restaurant. Although the inside lights had been switched off when Joyce had closed for the day, the neon sign with a witch's hat and coffee cup in the center blinked with a happy glow.

A small smile curved her lips. She'd opened the shop almost twelve years ago, but that sign brought a burst of pleasure every time she caught sight of it. The Witch's Brew was her creation. Her business. Her home.

Most importantly, it was her independence.

A rare gift for any mage.

Nearing the front entrance to the coffee shop, Maya was prepared as a dark form detached itself from the nearby lamppost.

Joe.

As always, the strange male was wearing a velour tracksuit with a battered fishing hat tugged down to hide his hair and shadow his eyes. A bushy beard obscured the lower half of his face, making it impossible to determine the male's age and ethnicity. Maya assumed it was a deliberate disguise to allow him to roam the neighborhood without attracting attention.

Most pedestrians scurried past homeless people without looking at them. They were an uncomfortable prick to their conscience. And as long as Joe didn't cause trouble, no one was willing to try to run him off.

"There you are," Maya muttered, halting in front of the male.

Joe made a sound of disgust. "You smell like a possum that—"

Maya interrupted his insult. "Not now."

"Rude," Joe groused before he jerked in surprise, his gaze sweeping over her disheveled appearance. "Why are you covered in ash?"

"You tell me."

"Oh sweet. Are we playing a guessing game?"

"No. I'm sick of games," Maya snapped. "You've been leading me from one false trail to another. I assume you think it's funny?"

He tilted his head, as if considering his response. "Mildly amusing."

Maya would have stomped her foot if her ankle wasn't throbbing. Instead she glared at the massive pain in her ass.

"But tonight wasn't a joke. You tried to kill me."

Joe's eyes suddenly burned with an emerald fire, and the air thickened with an oppressive sense of warning that pressed heavily against Maya. It wasn't the same as standing next to Ravyr. The vampire's power was a raw, almost feral energy that pulsed around him. Like a lion on the hunt.

This was an ancient, terrifyingly vast sense of dominion. As if she was gazing into a void her brain couldn't comprehend.

"If I desired you dead, you wouldn't be standing here to complain about what almost happened, Maya Rosen."

Maya struggled to breathe as the air was squeezed from her lungs. With a desperate effort, she jerked her head to the side, breaking contact with the emerald fire in his eyes.

"I was lured into a trap that I barely escaped before the building exploded," she rasped.

"Who lured you...ah." He slowly nodded. "Courtney."

Maya glanced back, relieved to discover that Joe was once again the harmless vagrant.

"I knew it," she ground out. "Courtney is one of your minions."

Joe snorted. "I wouldn't mind having a few minions, but they wouldn't be immature mages with anger management issues."

Maya planted her fists on her hips, determinedly dismissing the glimpse of infinite power she'd witnessed just seconds before. She was afraid. Not just because of Courtney's treachery or the building exploding or even the resurrection of Ravyr in her life. She'd been plagued by a strange unease for months.

She'd tried to dismiss it as the upheavals in her life. First Peri discovering her wild magic and mating with Valen. And then Skye leaving Jersey to be with Micha. It was an unsettling time. But now she was certain there was something more than constant changes causing her anxiety.

And she wanted answers.

"If she doesn't work for you, how did you know she's a mage?" she demanded in accusing tones. Although humans were familiar with witches who could use rituals and incantations to perform small spells, they had no idea there were women who possessed magic in their very blood. Just as they had no idea there were demons and vampires walking among them. And dragons sleeping beneath their feet. "Or that she has anger issues?" she added for good measure.

Joe shrugged. "She's been leaking all over the place."

"Leaking magic or anger?"

"Both," he said, confirming Maya's suspicion he wasn't just another human. Not that it got her any closer to figuring out his true identity.

A worry for later, she reluctantly accepted. If Courtney hadn't been working for Joe, then Maya needed to find out who'd hired her. The sooner the better.

"What else did you notice about her?"

"Nothing really." He reached up to scratch at his chin through the bushy beard. "Unless you count the fact that she was sneaking around the neighborhood for a week before you hired her."

It took a full minute for Maya to battle back her burst of anger at his offhand revelation. Thankfully her magic was too depleted for her to do something she might regret.

"She's been sneaking around the neighborhood and you didn't think to mention it to me?" she ground out.

"You didn't ask."

"Anything else that I might have forgotten to ask?"

There was more chin scratching. "She didn't come into town on the train."

Maya's anger was forgotten at the unexpected words. "Did she drive?"

"Nope. She walked."

"In those heels?" Maya blinked. "She can't have gone very far."

"Don't know about that."

"What direction did she come from?"

"That way." Joe waved a hand in a vaguely northern direction.

"Did you see her anywhere else in the neighborhood?"

"Like where?"

Maya heaved a frustrated sigh. "A restaurant. A grocery store. The laundromat."

"Nope," Joe murmured, his tone distracted as he leaned forward to smell her hair. "What's that?"

"Stop sniffing me," Maya protested. "It's vulgar."

Joe ignored her protest. "Who were you with?"

"You know who I was with. Courtney."

He was shaking his head before the name left Maya's lips. "Courtney smells like bitter lemons." He sniffed again, barely avoiding the slap that Maya aimed at his face. "This is power. A ruthless hunter."

Maya hissed, taking a painful step backward. It was Ravyr's scent. It had to be. "You're imagining things."

"It's later than I thought." Joe's eyes glowed with that emerald fire as he regarded her with an unnerving intensity. "The past is here, Maya Rosen. For both of us."

Maya shivered. The words sounded like a warning.

"What past?"

In typical Joe fashion, the male turned to scurry down the sidewalk, quickly disappearing into the shadows. Maya didn't bother to follow him. It would be a waste of time. Instead she limped to the front door of the Witch's Brew.

Once inside, she whispered words of protection, laying a web of magic over the door. She was still unsettled, and she needed the comfort of knowing that nothing could enter her home while she was sleeping.

Making her way upstairs, Maya headed into the bathroom, standing in the shower until the hot water was gone and her skin was wrinkled. Then, pulling on her most comfy nightgown, she crawled into bed.

She expected to spend the night tossing and turning. Her days were rarely boring, but it wasn't often that she was nearly decimated by a bomb and rescued by a vampire she thought was dead. Instead, she fell into a deep sleep the second her eyes closed.

For a few precious moments she simply drifted in a soothing darkness, her tense muscles relaxing as she burrowed into the mattress. This was exactly what she needed.

The peace, however, couldn't last. Not when the tumultuous events of the evening continued to nag at her. Plus, there was a new, bone-deep fear that was burrowing into the center of her heart.

It'd started the moment she'd caught sight of Ravyr and realized he'd survived the collapse of Batu's lair. The knowledge had sparked a disturbing sense of relief along with an equally disturbing sense of dread.

If Ravyr had survived, then who else had?

The question whispered over and over as she moved through the dreamscape, the shadows parting to reveal that she was walking along a pathway. It was paved with smooth stones worn by endless centuries of worshippers and buried in the moist jungle soil. A shiver of horror trickled down Maya's spine as she recognized where she was, but she made no effort to shake herself awake.

She had to make sure.

Continuing past the round, ornately carved temples coated in mold and occasionally fractured by the trees reclaiming the land, Maya kept her gaze locked on the pyramid towering above the thick vegetation. Inside, a voice was screaming for her to flee. She'd sacrificed everything to escape this hellhole. She would rather be burned alive than return.

Step by painful step she forced herself forward, ignoring the distant cries of pain and even the silvery swirl of magic that hung thick in the air. Nothing could touch her. Not when she was safely tucked in her bed.

At last reaching the main temple, Maya angled away from the staircase that led toward the top of the pyramid. She wasn't here to worship the bastard who'd done his best to destroy her life. Her route took her to the side of the temple where a door was set in the stone. Predictably the years of abandonment had covered the opening with a layer of invasive foliage, and with a muttered profanity, she grabbed the largest vine, intending to tug it away. Instead, she gasped as she felt a sharp stab of pain from a thorn.

Jerking back, Maya glanced down at the thin ribbon of blood dripping from her wounded hand. *Damn. That hurt.*

Another shiver raced through her. *A dream. That's all. Nothing more than a dream,* she sternly reminded herself.

Refusing to give into her pounding sense of dread, Maya clenched her hand and muttered words of magic. A minute later the plant was neatly cut in two, dropping from the opening to lie in a tangled mess on the ground. Without hesitation, Maya stepped through the narrow doorway and headed down the tunnel that led to the vast chambers dug deep underground.

An inky blackness shrouded her, but Maya's steps never faltered. She'd walked this passage a thousand times. She could find her way blindfolded. A few minutes later, there was a stir of musty air as she entered the lower cavern that was filled with a soft glow. Maya had never known where the orangish light came from, or why the power that hummed beneath her feet felt different from the other Gyres she'd entered, but there was no questioning the magic in the air. It was so thick it made it hard to breathe.

It was, no doubt, the reason that Batu had chosen this place.

He was an ambitious vampire who believed he was destined to rule the Cabal.

As if the mere thought of her former master had conjured his evil soul, the orange glow flickered. Maya froze, her breath lodged in her lungs as she watched the vision appear in front of her. Swallowing her scream, she stumbled back, her hand outstretched as she prepared a hasty spell.

"Don't you dare," a female voice snapped, the murky vision coming into focus to reveal a starkly beautiful woman with silvery hair pulled into a bun and large dark eyes that regarded Maya with icy arrogance.

"Tia," she rasped.

The powerful mage was older than Maya, although she wasn't sure how much older. It was extremely rude to ask.

Long ago Tia had been Maya's friend and mentor, but that had all changed forty-five years ago in this precise location. Now they were bitter enemies who coexisted by staying far away from each other. Maya in Jersey, and Tia at her isolated estate in Colorado.

"Do you have to be so noisy?" Tia groused, tightening the belt around her satin nightgown.

Maya furrowed her brow. "Are you real?"

Tia smiled. Or at least she curved her lips into what passed as a smile. This woman was as cold as a snake. A second later Maya felt a stinging slap hit her cheek.

"Does that settle the issue?" Tia asked in overly sweet tones.

Maya ground her teeth together. Tia hadn't physically smacked her, but the result had been the same.

"Bitch," Maya ground out. "Why are you in my dream?"

Tia sniffed. "Because you keep disturbing mine."

"You're the dream teller, not me," Maya protested.

Tia wasn't a clairvoyant. Not like Maya's protégée, Skye, who'd recently used her visions to save the world. But Tia's dreams gave her glimpses of the future and how she could manipulate it to feed her insatiable ambition. And long ago, it'd allowed the two of them to speak in this dreamworld. The only place they could be assured complete privacy.

"No, but our past bond obviously keeps us tied together." Tia pointed out the obvious, slowly turning until she was facing the side of the cavern that had collapsed into a pile of rubble. Maya had done her best to avoid looking at the destruction. Now she allowed her gaze to trace the scorch marks that blackened the floor along with the lavish collection of furniture and rare objects that had been melted into globs of rubbish. Slowly, Tia turned back to face her. "Why are you in this place?"

Maya shivered. "You don't have nightmares?"

Tia's smug confidence slid away, revealing the woman who'd been molded in a crucible of ruthless torture. A woman who would destroy the world before she was ever a victim again.

"Often, but this isn't a nightmare," she retorted, dark eyes narrowing as she studied Maya. "You're searching for something. Or someone."

Maya hesitated. She didn't trust Tia as far as she could throw her. The mage had proved that she would sacrifice anything and anyone to achieve her selfish goals. Still, no one else would understand the fear that bubbled inside her like a potion in a hot cauldron.

Plus, there was always the chance that this woman was involved.

Tia bitterly blamed her for destroying the partnership that had allowed them to survive endless decades of hell.

"Ravyr's alive."

Tia sucked in a sharp breath, genuine shock widening her eyes. "You're sure?"

"Painfully sure."

The scent of scorched cloves filled the cavern. "Did he attack you?"

Maya grimaced. "Just the opposite. He saved me from a messy death."

Tia sucked in a deep breath before she grimly replaced her shocked expression with the familiar mocking sneer.

"You allowed yourself to be a damsel in distress?" Tia clicked her tongue. "Did I teach you nothing?"

The older mage was deliberately trying to provoke Maya. Unfortunately, it worked like a charm. No one could piss her off quicker than Tia. *Well, maybe Ravyr,* she silently conceded.

"I will never be a damsel in distress," Maya snapped. "Not again."

Tia sniffed. "Then why would you need to be rescued by a leech?"

"I was lured into a snare by a mage named Courtney Tate."

"Courtney Tate?" Tia shrugged. "Never heard of her."

"Me either, but she claims to be an assassin."

Tia arched a brow. "If she were an assassin I would recognize her name."

Maya believed her. Tia possessed an impressive network of spies spread around the world. Only the Cabal could match her in the sheer amount of information she managed to acquire. If Courtney was a professional assassin, Tia would know.

"She told me that she gets her jobs through an app," Maya said.

"An assassin app? Is that a joke?"

"Not according to Courtney."

Tia rolled her eyes. "This generation. They make me tired. They really do."

Maya pursed her lips. Time to ask the obvious question. "I don't suppose you hired her, did you?"

Tia narrowed her gaze. "I assume you're trying to offend me. If I wanted you dead—"

"Okay, okay." Maya waved her hand. She really didn't suspect Tia. The woman was many things, but she was never sloppy.

"Why are you here?"

Maya flinched at the abrupt question. "I don't know."

Tia stepped toward her, her dark gaze watchful. "Yes you do."

Did she? Maya glanced around the desolate cavern, her head tilting back to study the high balconies that were carved into the stone. Many had crumbled away, but the one that she'd used remained. As if to taunt her with the endless nights she'd been forced to sit in full public view while her master had entertained his guests. She lowered her gaze, swiveling until she was staring at the lump of melted gold in the center of the tiled floor.

Once it'd been a throne encrusted with precious gems and velvet cushions. A throne fit for a king...

"Is he dead?" she rasped.

"Ravyr?" Tia demanded in confusion. "You just said he was alive. The bastard."

"Not Ravyr." Maya ground her teeth until she thought they might shatter. This place was scraping her nerves raw. Or maybe they were already raw and this place was pouring salt on the wounds. Whatever the cause, she desperately wanted to be somewhere else. *Anywhere* else, including the pits of hell.

"Batu," she at last managed to mutter. "Could he be alive?"

Tia's face paled, her eyes revealing a fear that came from the very depths of her being.

"Why would you ask that? Maya?"

Tia reached out, as if she was going to grab Maya's arm, but even as her fingers brushed over Maya's bare skin, she was fading into a gray mist. No, wait. It wasn't Tia.

She was the one who was fading, Maya abruptly realized.

Suddenly she was caught between relief to be out of the cavern with its smothering sense of tragedy and a sharp apprehension as the gloom was replaced with a blindingly bright light. Lifting her hand, Maya shielded her eyes. She was either being sucked into the center of a star, or surrounded by a power so vast it threatened to drown her.

Wild magic, a voice whispered in the back of her mind. The primitive source of power that mages tapped into when they created spells and potions and curses. For most it seared through their veins as they matured, transforming them from human witches into mages, before it retreated. Only Peri Sanguis had managed to tap back into the seemingly infinite power.

Maya trembled, bracing herself as the outrageous power churned and pulsed around her. Was it alive? It felt like it was trying to delve deep inside her, seeking out her secrets.

Struggling to stay upright, Maya didn't notice the silvery form that was moving toward her. Not until the magic slowly settled to flow past her at a steady pace, like a river of power rather than a raging storm. Finally able to catch her breath, Maya belatedly realized that there was a man standing directly in front of her.

No, not a man. A vision from a dream. He was shockingly beautiful, with skin that shimmered like bronze and eyes that burned with an emerald fire. His features were chiseled and too perfect to be real. Wearing a green robe that draped over his large body, he towered above her with an unspoken threat.

Maya grimly refused to kneel. She'd seen this male before. He'd been a glimpse in the distance, but he wasn't the sort of male you forgot.

"Who are you?" she whispered.

He stared down at her with an aloof arrogance. "You know."

Maya licked her dry lips. She had so many suspicions. "The Watcher?" she demanded, referring to the mysterious creature who was responsible for keeping the dragons from wakening from their hibernation. He remained silent. "Are you my Benefactor?" she pressed. "Are you Joe?"

"I have many names," he murmured, refusing to answer. "I'm here to offer a warning."

Maya didn't press him. She wasn't sure she truly wanted to know. "What warning?"

"The past will never be forgotten, but don't become so lost in your memories that you allow it to blind you to the danger that is rising," he informed her.

Maya frowned. "A rising danger? What's that supposed to mean?"

"You've encountered it."

Maya tried to hold the smoldering emerald gaze. It was one of the most difficult things she'd ever done. His mere presence slammed against her with brutal force, but she was determined to stand her ground.

"Ravyr?" she demanded, not surprised when the creature waved an impatient hand of dismissal. If Ravyr was the threat, she would never have seen him coming. He could have destroyed her before she realized he was still alive. "Courtney?" she guessed again.

The male dipped his head in agreement. "A pawn, but one who can lead you to the truth."

Maya made a sound of annoyance. "She's not leading me anywhere if I can't find her."

"You are Maya Rosen," the male reminded her, as if she'd forgotten. And maybe she had. "Do what you do best."

The words whispered through her mind even as the light faded and she was once again snuggled in the soft warmth of her bed.

Do what you do best....

Chapter 4

The sun had barely slipped over the horizon when Ravyr was settling in the back of the black Suburban with tinted windows and bulletproof modifications. The vehicle had been arranged by Valen, who'd promised it would be available during his stay in the city, although Ravyr hadn't planned on accepting the offer.

There was a reason he'd allowed the world to believe he'd died during the collapse of Batu's empire. And why he spent the day resting in one of the dusty tunnels that ran beneath the city instead of Valen's luxurious penthouse. The most dangerous hunter was the one you didn't see coming.

Unfortunately, his arrogant belief that he was capable of lurking in the shadows had been blasted to smithereens at the same time as the Slaughterhouse Club. He'd traveled to America in search of the echo that was once again sending pulse waves through the world. He hadn't been surprised when the vibrations had led him to New York City. This Gyre was the current epicenter of magic. It made sense that it would attract any creature or object seeking power. And once he was here, the pulses had led him directly to the fight club.

But the long daylight hours he'd spent pacing the abandoned subway tunnel had eventually convinced him that it wasn't an accident that the building had exploded less than ten minutes after he'd entered it. Or that Maya had been lured to the same location.

Those sorts of coincidences didn't happen.

Which was why he had given up on his stealth mode and called for the ride to Jersey. Now he leaned back against the plush leather seat, his fingers tapping an impatient tattoo on the armrest as they raced through the city and over the bridge.

Ravyr tried to ignore the anticipation that seared through him at the thought of reacquainting himself with the exquisitely beautiful mage who'd captured his attention the moment he'd caught sight of her. Hadn't he learned his lesson when he'd been forced to play Batu's games while he was watching Maya Rosen sitting on the balcony, gazing down at the obscene revelries with open disdain?

A sharp stab of something that felt like regret sliced through his unbeating heart. He'd dedicated his life to duty and loyalty, but that didn't mean he wasn't painfully aware of what he had been forced to sacrifice.

Finally reaching the town where Valen had assured him he could locate Maya, Ravyr was startled when he caught the unmistakable scent of orchids. He frowned, rolling down the window. They were still several blocks away from the address Valen had given him, but that intoxicating scent wasn't a figment of his imagination.

He leaned forward, tapping on the glass that separated him from the driver. "Stop," he commanded. On cue, the heavy SUV swerved next to the curb and rolled to a halt. "Wait for me here."

Exiting the vehicle, Ravyr jogged up the sidewalk, ignoring the pedestrians who stopped and stared at him with various levels of fear, lust, and envy. It didn't matter that he was wearing jeans and a plain black T-shirt to avoid attracting attention. The humans instinctively sensed that he was a predator.

Ravyr slowed as the scent of orchids intensified. Maya was nearby. He melted into the shadows, his gaze skimming over the faded houses that lined the street. Most were on cramped lots framed by wrought iron fences and patches of grass that passed as front lawns. At one time, it'd no doubt been a decent neighborhood, but now it had gone from genteel shabby to just plain shabby.

His brows arched. Why was Maya here?

His confusion only deepened as he caught sight of her slender form inching through the hedges in front of a nearby house, trying to peek into the front window.

What the hell was she doing?

Moving in silence, Ravyr approached her from behind, leaning forward to whisper in her ear.

"We have to stop meeting like this."

She froze, magic sizzling in the air before she turned to face him.

"Ravyr." She spit out his name like an obscenity. Then, with a frustrated glance toward the nearby window, she shooed him toward the side of the house.

Ravyr arched a brow. He'd been alive for twelve hundred years, and never once in all that time had he ever been shooed. Amusement raced through him. This was the confident, outrageously courageous woman he'd always known lurked beneath her pretense of meek subservience.

His amusement quickly faded, however, as his gaze caught sight of the pallor of her skin and the circles under her eyes. Something had disturbed her sleep.

He'd like to think it was him. After all, he'd spent more time than he wanted to admit fantasizing about her over the years. But logic assured him it was far more likely that she was upset by the suspicion that she'd been deliberately lured into a building that was about to explode. The gods knew it was giving him nightmares.

Backing up until they were around the corner of the house, he folded his arms over his chest and studied her with a curious gaze.

"What are you doing here?"

She pinched her lips in annoyance. "Are you following me?"

"You didn't answer my question...." He caught a sudden scent on the crisp night breeze. It wasn't an intoxicating orchid perfume. This one was sharp and acrid. Like bitter lemons. He'd smelled it at the club. "Ah. The mage you were with last night." He glanced toward the house. "She lives here?"

Maya managed to pinch her lips even tighter. Impressive. "I'm not sharing information unless you're willing to tell me why you're here."

He leaned his shoulder against the aluminum siding that threatened to buckle beneath his considerable weight. "You always were stubborn."

Her eyes narrowed. "Tell me."

"Very well." He shrugged. "I didn't intend to follow you. I was heading to your coffee shop in the hopes we could join forces to track down the demon responsible for setting the bomb when I caught your scent." Another shrug. "Now here we are."

"Why would I join forces with you—"

Her words were cut short as a breeze whipped around the corner of the house, bringing with it the unmistakable scent of blood. Her eyes widened in shock, but before she could move, Ravyr had already spun on his heel to rush toward the back of the house. Leaping onto the cement porch, he shoved open the locked door, his fangs fully extended as he entered a small kitchen littered with takeout boxes and empty bottles of wine.

He wrinkled his nose. The house was a mess, but it wasn't from a battle. Just laziness. Moving through the darkness, he followed the thickening stench wafting from the front room. As a vampire he was a connoisseur of the various forms of blood. Both human and demon. But he never drank from a corpse. And that was what was waiting for him.

No, not a corpse. *Two* corpses, he discovered as he cautiously stepped through the connecting door. A male goblin and the mage. Both were lying in the middle of the floor, as if they'd dropped dead in place without ever realizing they were in danger. As he neared he caught sight of a symbol in the center of each of their foreheads. Matching tattoos? Weird.

Even more weird were the daggers sticking out of their chests. They were matching as well with wooden hilts carved with powerful glyphs. Had they stabbed each other in the heart? Like a suicide pact with cursed daggers?

The sound of Maya's approaching footsteps broke into his musings. He moved to block her view. It wasn't particularly grisly, but she'd fled Cambodia to open a coffee shop in Jersey. Obviously she was hoping to put her violent past behind her.

"Maya. This isn't good," he warned.

She tilted her chin. "I need to know."

Ravyr didn't bother to argue. Maya would do what she wanted. More importantly, she had the skills to discover more than he could from the dead bodies.

"I'll search the house," he murmured, leaving her to reach into her satchel to pull out a potion. Minutes later, he'd returned to the living room. The house was too small for an intruder to hide from a vampire. His senses would have pierced through the thickest shield. "All clear," he announced as he returned, standing next to Maya as she circled her hand over the bodies. "Any indication of what happened?"

She shook her head. "They couldn't have died more than an hour ago. If a killer had entered the house, I should be able to detect their presence." She grimaced. "It looks like they killed themselves or killed each other. Which doesn't make any sense."

Ravyr shared her obvious frustration. During his inspection of the house he hadn't identified anything out of the ordinary. That, however, didn't mean that there hadn't been someone who'd managed to slip in and out before they'd arrived.

"Or a genuine assassin who has the skills to kill without leaving a trail," he warned. "That might explain the marks on their foreheads. Some sort of calling card."

Her jaw tightened; then she nodded toward the dead male. "Do you recognize him?"

"No."

"Wrong place, wrong time?"

"Perhaps." Ravyr shrugged. "He's lived in this house for longer than the mage. His scent is deeply imbedded. The mage is a recent addition. A couple of weeks or so."

"A couple of weeks was just long enough for her to scope out the Witch's Brew before taking a job there so she could lead me into a trap."

Ravyr agreed. "If there was a killer, they must have shadowed Courtney back to this location."

"But why?"

"Either she saw something she wasn't supposed to, or someone didn't want her sharing the information that she led you to that building. That could be a secondary reason for the marks. It could be a warning to anyone else who might have information to keep their lips shut."

Maya appeared to consider his theories before she heaved a harsh sigh. "None of this makes sense. Courtney didn't know anything about who hired her or why. And she was too self-centered to notice what was happening around her." She sent him a worried glance. "So does that mean she was killed as a warning? And was it a warning to me or you?"

"Both." Ravyr didn't have proof of the assassin's intentions, but he was smart enough to assume the worst. "Tell me about the mage."

Her brows snapped together. "I did."

"Tell me again."

There was a tense silence before Maya forced herself to respond. "Courtney arrived at my coffee shop last week asking for a job. I suspected she had another purpose for being there, so I agreed to hire her. It seemed the easiest way to discover what she was up to."

Ravyr skimmed his gaze over her pale face. Maya was a natural nurturer. Even from a distance he'd seen how she protected the weaker magic users whom Batu held captive. But she was also willing to punish those who preyed on the vulnerable. He'd once seen her curse a goblin who'd strangled a female human to death. The male's skin peeled off like a molting snake, leaving him so raw he spent a month screaming in pain. It didn't matter to her that Batu would eventually punish her for using her magic without his permission. Her sense of justice demanded vengeance.

"Why did you follow Courtney last night?"

"She was caught by one of my employees sneaking out of the basement where I keep my private vault." Maya shrugged. "She had to know she would be spotted, which meant it was a blatant attempt to gain my attention. So I gave her what she wanted."

Ravyr nodded, assuming that the scheme to lure Maya to the Slaughterhouse had been left up to Courtney to plan. A trained assassin wouldn't have been so obvious, and more importantly, they wouldn't have left so much to mere chance.

What if Maya hadn't followed? What if she'd sensed the bomb before she ever entered the building? What if Maya had struck out as soon as the mage tried to trap her? Courtney would have been dead before she knew what was happening.

He urged her to continue her story. "You said she was hired by someone to lure you to that location."

Maya nodded. "She told me that she'd been contacted through an app and that she didn't have the name or location of who wanted me trapped."

"We might be able to trace the person who hired her."

Maya blinked, as if startled he might have a suggestion that didn't include blood and violence.

"You're right," she breathed, turning in a slow circle until they both spotted a phone left on the coffee table.

Ravyr struggled not to be offended as she moved to grab it. If he was being honest, he had to admit that he looked like a barbarian. And when he'd been spying on Batu, he'd been forced to blend in with the violent horde who filled the vampire's vast lair. It was no wonder she assumed he was a mindless brute.

A worry for later.

"How did you know she would be here?" he instead demanded, watching as Maya slid the phone into her satchel. "I can't imagine she was stupid enough to give you her home address."

"She was seen walking to work," she informed him. "Since she wears three-inch heels and complained if she had to do any sort of physical labor, I assumed she had to be staying fairly close to the shop." She glanced around the shabby house. "It took a while, but I finally caught her scent. I followed it to this place." Her gaze moved to linger on the dead mage, as if she was debating whether to grieve for the overly ambitious woman. Then, with a faint shake of her head, she smoothed her beautiful features into an unreadable expression and returned her attention to him. "That's all I know. Your turn. Is the demon who blew up the building the reason you're in New York?"

"I'm not sure."

Her gaze narrowed, the green eyes flashing in anger. "That's not an answer."

Ravyr wasn't trying to piss her off. He understood that he couldn't expect her to trust him without sharing his reason for being in the Slaughterhouse last night. And he *needed* her trust if they were going to figure out why they'd both been in the exploding building at the same time.

Unfortunately, he didn't have any simple answers. And even if he did, he was breaking Cabal law to share them. Eons ago—during the reign of the dragons—the vampire population had dwindled to the brink of extinction. And while the demon inside them survived most deaths of their mortal host and were eventually resurrected into a new body, they didn't possess the ability to procreate. They'd been trained from the moment they were reborn to protect any secrets that might make them vulnerable.

"I'm not tracking a specific demon," he finally forced himself to admit. He had to risk the Cabal's anger if he intended to get to the truth.

She paused before she asked, "Is it some sort of gang?"

"No. It's an..." Ravyr held up his hands. She wasn't going to like his explanation. *He* didn't like his explanation. "An echo."

"An echo of what?"

"Magic."

"I don't know what that means. Are you talking about a spell?"

"I—" Ravyr cut off his explanation as Maya released a shocked gasp of horror. At first he didn't know what had captured her attention. Not until she was scrambling away from the two bodies lying at his feet. With a frown he glanced down, revulsion crawling through him as the bodies began to decay before their eyes. One moment they were fresh corpses, and a second later their flesh was rotting away as if they'd been decomposing in this house for days.

"What the hell?" he muttered.

"Magic," she rasped. "It has to be some sort of spell."

Mesmerized by the gruesome spectacle, Ravyr was caught off guard once again as Maya abruptly lunged toward him. Not out of fear. Maya was powerful, but she wasn't a fool. She was no match for a vampire in a physical fight. No, it was pure shock that clenched his muscles as her hand slammed over his mouth. He'd been alive a long, long time. And never had anyone dared to treat him with such casual impudence.

"Hush." She added insult to injury.

Ravyr arched a brow, more curious than offended as she cocked her head to one side, as if listening to a voice he couldn't hear. Then her hand was jerked away from his mouth and she was charging toward the front door. "We need to get out of here. Now!"

Ravyr didn't hesitate, rushing out of the house behind her and vaulting off the porch. The urgency that caused her pulse to race wasn't faked. Something had truly spooked her. A second later he heard the crash of glass as someone threw a heavy object through the kitchen window.

It took less than a second to discover that the object was some sort of bomb, which exploded with enough force to shatter the house. Instinctively, Ravyr lunged forward, wrapping Maya in his arms before driving her to the ground. Splayed on top of her struggling form, he shielded her from the projectiles that aimed toward them with lethal intent.

Ravyr grunted in pain as he felt the bite of glass and metal siding and rusty nails as they embedded themselves in his back. The wounds would soon heal, but that didn't mean it didn't hurt like a bitch as they slammed into his flesh.

The shock wave from the blast seared over them, and Ravyr angled his head down to block the worst of the heat. Maya wasn't as fragile as a human, but the explosion could easily burn her skin. At the same time, he brushed his lips over her ear.

"I told you we have to stop meeting like this."

* * * *

Tia paused to smooth back the silver-gray hair that she'd pulled into a neat bun at her nape. It was the only indication that she was anything but icily composed. Certainly no one would detect any hint of nerves on her smooth, elegant features. Or in the tall, slender body that was currently wrapped in a silky caftan. She'd learned two centuries ago that emotions were the enemy. The same time she'd been sold to Batu by her mother and imprisoned in his hellish lair.

Nothing mattered but power. Who had it. Who didn't. And how she could get more.

Tonight, however, she couldn't get rid of the unease churning in the pit of her stomach. *Damn, Maya Rosen.* Tia had spent the past forty-plus years doing everything in her power to forget the past. She'd survived, and now nothing mattered but her plans for a very bright future.

But the mere possibility that Batu—the leech who'd tormented her for decades—might somehow have survived had shattered her promise that she would never look back.

If he truly was alive...

A shudder raced through Tia, and with an effort, she squared her shoulders and stepped out of her private chambers. She'd been called many things in her life. Bossy. Ballsy. And bitchy. But never a coward.

If the bastard was out there, she had to know.

With her head held high, Tia walked down the shadowed corridor lined with tapestries from a twelfth-century palace. It matched the rest of the medieval castle that she'd chosen to build in a valley near Pike's Peak. The sprawling estate that she'd named Emerald Glade in a rare whimsical moment was intended to be more of a statement than a home. Not only did it have enough fortification to keep out a small army for several weeks, but there were also fifty demons who patrolled every inch of the thousand acres 24/7.

At last reaching her personal study, Tia stepped into the vast space that echoed the Gothic style of the castle. There were large, arched windows currently hidden behind crimson velvet curtains and floor-to-ceiling bookshelves that displayed her impressive collection of leatherbound first editions. A large, handwoven rug was tossed in the center of the wood plank floor, and overhead a purple-tinted chandelier dangled from one of the heavy beams.

Her attention, however, was locked on the tall male with bulging muscles and a shaved head who was standing next to the fourteenth-century writing desk. Lynch was a male goblin, although his crimson aura was barely noticeable. Outside the Gyre his strength was mediocre at best.

Not that Tia cared. He was loyal to the point of obsession and he would die to protect her. Who needed raw power when you could get a faithful hound? Besides, she would never allow anyone in her home that could be a potential threat.

"You've made sure the staff are gone?" she demanded as she closed the door behind her.

Lynch nodded. "I did a sweep of the entire property. The place is empty."

It *was* empty. Tia had become accustomed to the hectic buzz of dozens of servants rushing through the castle. Not only did she run a million-dollar business trading in black-market magical items, but she gathered information from around the world like other women collected designer shoes.

There was nothing more valuable than information. Nothing.

"Wait here for me," she commanded, moving to lay her hand on top of the heavy globe that consumed one corner of the room.

With a tingle of magic the globe glided forward, revealing the hole in the floor where it had been standing. The scent of dirt and moss swirled through the air, and with a last glance at Lynch, Tia forced herself to climb down the steep stairs to the vast cavern that was hidden beneath the castle.

There'd been more than one reason she'd chosen this particular location. Not only did it offer stunning views of the Rocky Mountains, but there was also a deep pool of natural spring water that bubbled in the center of the cavern. She'd sensed the magic in the water the moment she traveled through the area. It'd drawn her like a moth to a flame.

Not the magic of Gyres. That was a lingering power from the dragons who were currently in hibernation. This was pure magic. Wild magic. Not a lot, but enough to enhance her natural talent as a dream teller.

The stone floor was cold and rough beneath her bare feet, but she ignored her discomfort as she moved toward the pool and slid off her caftan. Her physical pain was a small sacrifice if she could reassure herself that Maya's fears were nothing more than a reaction to the discovery that Ravyr was alive. Once she was naked, she waded into the water, which shimmered with a silvery light. The magic was tangible as it rippled against her skin, the icy sting wrenching a gasp from her lips.

There's always a cost to power, she silently reminded herself, continuing to the center of the pool even as her muscles spasmed in protest of the cold.

Once the water was deep enough to go over her head, Tia leaned back and stretched out her arms, allowing herself to float in a slow circle. Then, closing her eyes, she cleared her mind.

For several minutes she drifted in the heavy silence, hovering somewhere between consciousness and the sweet oblivion of sleep. It was there she could enter the minds of others. She could reach out to anyone she'd met, even if it was a casual encounter, but it was easier if she had an intimate connection. Like with Maya.

Thankfully—or rather, sadly—the mind she was seeking was painfully intimate.

Lowering the shields that guarded her mind from being invaded, Tia released a shaky breath and reached out. It wasn't as simple as locating the person she wanted and knocking on their brain to be let in. Instead, she visualized herself walking through a barren landscape, ignoring the endless shadows that pressed against her, begging to be seen. In the distance was a shadowed form, but even as she neared the fuzzy silhouette, she refused to accept that it could be anything more than a memory.

The water lapping against her was suddenly so cold it sent sharp stabs of pain through her, but she barely noticed as the shadow cleared to reveal a large, bulky male with roughly chiseled features and long black hair that hung down his back. His eyes were a weird shade of yellow and glowed with a malicious cruelty, as if something in his soul was jaundiced. He was wearing his usual leather vest that revealed his bulging muscles and matching leather pants.

"Batu," she breathed in horror.

The male's strange eyes widened, as if he'd just caught sight of her. "Tia." His harsh voice didn't echo her horror. Instead, there was a sickening hunger that reached through the distance to wrap around her in an unspoken threat. "My love. This is a surprise."

Tia arched in the water, desperate to break the connection. "No."

He seemed to step toward her, his raw musk tainting the air. "I didn't expect you so soon."

"You're dead." She hissed out the words, hoping to convince herself that this was no more than a bad dream.

It wouldn't be the first time the bastard had appeared in her nightmares.

Batu laughed, obviously aware of her panic. "Did you truly think a mere mage could kill me?"

"I watched you die."

He shrugged. "I've returned."

Tia struggled to breathe. Vampires were resurrected, but they were placed in new hosts with no memories of their past. This was...hell, she didn't know what it was, but it was seriously freaking her out.

"This isn't real," she muttered, fiercely trying to move her clenched muscles.

If only she could wake up.

Batu stretched out his hand, blood dripping from his fingers. "Come to me, sweet Tia, and I'll prove how real I am."

"Never."

"Never say never, my love."

The fingers inched closer, and Tia's fear became a living thing, pulsing through her with savage force. If he touched her...

"No!" Tia screamed, pain bursting through her mind as she ripped free of their mental connection.

It was like someone cutting through her brain with an ax, and she abruptly sank to the bottom of the pool, her body too weak to fight against the current.

For a shocking moment Tia thought she might die. That Batu might finally achieve what he'd wanted forty-five years ago. But the inner core that had kept her surviving through abandonment and violence and betrayal hardened her spine and forced her trembling muscles to battle their way through the water.

She was crawling out of the pool, no doubt looking like a drowned rat, when Lynch vaulted down the stairs with a gun in one hand and a hexed dagger in the other.

"What's happened?" he barked, his gaze scanning the empty cavern in search of an enemy.

Tia managed to drag herself out of the water, although she was too shaky to stand. Instead, she grabbed her caftan, wrapping it around her shivering form.

"Start packing," she commanded through chattering teeth.

"Packing?" Lynch eyed her in confusion. "Where are we going?"

"New York City."

Chapter 5

Maya sucked in a deep breath as Ravyr rolled off her with a low groan. It wasn't that she didn't appreciate his efforts to block the worst of the shrapnel, but he weighed a ton. He was squishing all the air from her lungs.

Then, Ravyr flowed gracefully to his feet, revealing the savage wounds beneath his shredded T-shirt, and she forgot her lack of oxygen. Damn. It looked as if he'd been in a fight with a woodchipper. And the woodchipper had won.

If he hadn't shielded her...

She'd be dead. As simple as that.

Grimacing, Maya pushed herself upright, her gaze landing on the decimated house. The explosion hadn't been as powerful as the one that had destroyed the Slaughterhouse, but it had been big enough to kill her and severely wound Ravyr. Had that been the purpose? Or was the killer covering their tracks and they'd been an added bonus?

"Was the bomb on a timer?"

Maya jerked her attention away from the shattered house to meet Ravyr's hard gaze. It took her a second to grasp why he was asking her anything about the mysterious explosion. She'd been the one to warn him to get out of the house.

She shook her head. It had been the whispered warning of her mysterious Benefactor who'd urged her to run, but she'd sensed the danger had been approaching from the shadows, not already in the house.

"No."

The dark eyes flared with brutal satisfaction. "Then whoever set it off is still in the area."

Maya's smile was equally brutal as she pointed toward the north. "You go that way."

His jaw tightened, almost as if he wanted to protest. "Whoever did this is willing to kill without hesitation," he finally rasped, as if she hadn't noticed the buildings that kept exploding around her.

"So am I," she said in cold tones.

With a sharp nod he turned to melt into the shadows, the chill in the air warning that he intended to do very bad things to whoever had tried to kill him. Maya frowned. She was in the mood to make her tormentor pay. In blood. But first they needed information. Something they couldn't get if the culprit was dead.

Trusting that Ravyr would have enough sense to ask questions before ripping off any heads, Maya moved toward the back of the house. Squatting down, she reached her hand into the heavy satchel she'd filled with potions before going in search of Courtney. She wasn't surprised to discover they were undamaged. She'd placed a protective spell on the glass vials before pouring in the potions. Some of them were too dangerous to risk being accidentally released.

Crouching a few feet from the smoldering embers that had once been the kitchen, Maya slowly poured one of the potions onto the grass. She could cast a spell to trace the various footsteps that had recently crossed the lawn, but she was still recovering from the drain on her powers the previous evening. She wanted to save her magic for the very real possibility she would need it to protect herself.

The thick liquid pooled at her feet, bubbling and hissing as the magic was activated. Maya whispered a word of power, sending the liquid spreading over the grass. Seconds later the outline of various footsteps shimmered with different colors. Red for goblin. Green for fey. Silver for vampires. And gold for mages. She didn't bother to track the humans.

Leaning back on her heels, Maya studied the various footprints as the magic slowly settled to a dull pulse. The darker the outline, the more recent the person had passed through.

"There," she muttered, easily picking out the deep crimson tracks that had approached the house from a nearby alley.

Straightening, Maya followed the prints that had retraced their path back down the alley. She paused next to a line of trash cans, ignoring the stench as she carefully scanned her surroundings.

If the demon was truly trying to kill her, it might be smart enough to realize she would be in pursuit if she managed to survive the initial blast. This would be the perfect place for a trap.

Counting to one hundred, Maya grimaced at the sound of opening doors as the neighbors came out of their houses. They remained on their porches for now, no doubt worried that there might be more explosions, but soon the local authorities would arrive with their flashing lights and loud sirens and the gawkers would be unable to resist the lure of watching them up close and personal as they went about their business.

Maya inched forward, her gaze locked on the footprints that headed down the sidewalk. They continued to the corner, but then they abruptly disappeared.

Frustration speared through her at the same time she felt an icy blast of air. Ravyr.

"Anything?" he whispered next to her ear.

She pointed toward the corner. "He got into a vehicle and disappeared."

"Damn. I don't have the talent to track him." Ravyr pulled out his phone and typed in a quick message.

Was he checking in with Valen? Or did he report directly to Sinjon, the big cheese of the Cabal? Maya abruptly turned on her heel and marched back down the alley. Why would she care who he was contacting? He was nothing to her. Not unless you counted him being a gigantic pain in the ass.

Okay, he'd saved her from a nasty explosion. Twice. But it was possible that the bomber wouldn't have targeted the Slaughterhouse or Courtney's house if Ravyr hadn't been inside.

Her attempt to deflect the blame to Ravyr faltered as she skirted past the house, which was lying in shattered ruins. No. The aggravating leech might be included in whoever or whatever was hunting her, but she sensed she was the primary target.

Ravyr easily kept pace next to her, standing close enough for her to feel the thunderous power that pulsed around him. It was a physical force that pressed against her. Not a threat. More of a promise that he was there to protect her.

Which was more terrifying.

She'd labeled Ravyr as the enemy. She wasn't ready to accept that he could be anything else. Even if he was the sexiest, most deliciously gorgeous...

"Where are you going?"

Thankful to have her treacherous thoughts interrupted, Maya stiffened her back and picked up her pace. The sound of sirens was echoing through the night air. She wanted to be far away from the house before they arrived and started asking questions.

"Home."

"Good."

He continued to walk next to her, seeming oblivious to the lingering stares from the neighbors who were beginning to creep their way toward the noxious smoke that belched from the shattered house.

"Don't you have somewhere else to be?" she snapped.

"The only place I have to be is where you lead me."

His soft words brushed over her like a caress and Maya's heart slammed against her ribs.

"Not even in your dreams," she muttered, power walking with a new purpose.

She was cold and tired and her entire body ached. She needed some alone time to gather her composure.

Of course the aggravating male refused to take the hint. "You were, you know."

"I was what?"

"In my dreams."

Maya stumbled. Was he flirting with her? She tilted back her head, her breath catching in her throat. His savage beauty slammed into her, knocking her off balance. Each perfectly carved feature, the eyes that glowed with a luminous turquoise fire, the silver rims shimmering in the moonlight, and the powerful body that moved with a liquid grace.

For one breathless moment she recalled the first time she'd seen this male. Batu had forced her to attend his nightly entertainment, insisting that he wanted her close to his side as he welcomed an ambassador from the leader of the Cabal. It wasn't that he valued her presence, but he enjoyed exhibiting his collection of rare artifacts, along with his most powerful slaves. The vampire version of show-and-tell.

She'd been late and hurrying to the throne room when she'd slammed into Ravyr as he'd stepped out of a side tunnel. He'd wrapped his arms around her before she could bounce off his hard body, keeping her upright with a gentle hug. Fear had blasted through Maya, her muscles clenching as she prepared for him to punish her. It was a routine event since she'd been captured by Batu. Any leech in the lair was welcome to beat her senseless, as long as she wasn't permanently damaged. But instead of a vicious blow, Ravyr had asked if she was hurt, genuine concern in his voice.

She'd tilted back her head, just as she was doing now, and the world had spun away, leaving her floating on a giddy wave of awareness.

It wasn't just that he was gorgeous. Or that she was shivering with longing as he pressed her close to his hard muscles. It was a gut-deep recognition that this male was special. That her life would never be the same now that she'd been in his arms.

But that breathless fantasy had been shattered the moment Batu had strolled into the tunnel and Ravyr had shoved her away as if she were infected with the plague.

The rejection had left a wound that she abruptly realized had never fully healed.

And the realization pissed her off.

Stopping in the middle of the sidewalk, she turned to face him, her fists planted on her hips.

"When was I in your dreams?" she snapped. "When my magic was being drained from my body? Or when I was being paraded before Batu's gathered guests like a prized heifer?" She narrowed her eyes. "Or maybe when I was locked in a cell without food or water for endless days?"

Ravyr grimaced. "I'm sorry."

A tense silence filled the air between them. A combination of anger and regret and missed opportunity. The turquoise eyes darkened, as if offering a promise for a different future, but Maya was spinning away to march down the street.

"It's in the past." She tried to ignore him as he trailed behind her. A wasted effort, of course. How did you ignore a six-foot-five vampire who made the earth shake with his power? And worse, her ankle was beginning to throb. She'd taken a healing potion that morning, but it was starting to wear off. The dull ache was becoming a sharp jab with each step. At last she sent a glare over her shoulder. "Stop following me."

"You have our only clue." His expression was unreadable as he held out his hand. "Give it over and I'll go away."

"Clue?" Her brows snapped together. "What clue?"

"The mage's phone."

Maya ground her teeth. He'd noticed her slipping it into her satchel? Damn.

"No way." She continued down the street, but at a slower pace. It was taking all her effort not to limp. "Finders keepers."

"Finders keepers?" He sounded genuinely confused.

"It's mine."

"Then we stay together."

"You're not invited."

Moving too fast for her to track, Ravyr was abruptly standing directly in front of her, forcing her to stop.

"I have a car."

She turned to watch the large black SUV as it swerved to a halt next to the curb, the windows tinted and the engine purring with power. *That's why he was texting earlier,* she silently realized. He'd been arranging transportation.

A stubborn part of her wanted to ignore his offer. She wasn't Cinderella to be tempted by a carriage ride to the ball. But a more logical part of her brain reminded her that her ankle was throbbing, the sidewalk would soon be crowded with humans flocking toward the sound of sirens, and the sooner she could get home, the sooner she could figure out what secrets Courtney had on her phone.

"Argh."

With a toss of her head she marched toward the SUV, prepared when the back door opened to allow her to slide onto the buttery leather seats. The vehicle was identical to the one Peri used when she visited Maya.

A pang tugged at Maya's heart.

When her friend first mated with the Cabal leader of New York, she'd been determined to continue her work at the Witch's Brew. She was far too independent to wait around on Valen to keep her entertained. But as the weeks and then months passed, she'd naturally developed her own interests. Plus the rigorous, time-consuming training she endured in an effort to control her wild magic.

Ravyr slid in beside her, claiming more than his fair share of space and splintering her wistful musings. As soon as he closed his door the SUV melted into the thickening traffic before turning a corner and heading straight for her shop. Less than ten minutes later it was parked in front of the brightly painted window with the blinking neon sign.

In silence they climbed out and headed toward the door. Maya instinctively glanced around, making sure they hadn't been followed, before gripping the door handle to break the spell that guarded the lock. The magic would have alerted her if anyone had tried to enter the building.

Once convinced it was safe, Maya pushed open the door and led Ravyr inside before she flicked on the overhead lights. A soft glow spilled over the white tiles and reflected off the stainless steel coolers.

Ravyr wandered toward the middle of the floor, his brows arching as he took in the open shelves loaded with delicate china plates and matching cups along with hand-embroidered napkins. He continued turning to study the festive tulips and daffodils painted on the front window along with a bunny rabbit holding an Easter basket.

"This isn't what I was expecting," he at last murmured.

Maya's mouth was dry. This had always been her safe space. A place that was untainted by her past. Allowing Ravyr to enter changed everything.

With an effort, she forced away the unnerving thought and closed the door, not bothering to lock it. If anyone was ballsy enough to attack a powerful mage and vampire, no lock was going to stop them.

"What did you expect?" she demanded, trying to pretend that his presence in her shop wasn't scraping against her raw nerves.

"More fire and brimstone and less caramel latte with sprinkles."

"Caramel latte with sprinkles pays the bills," she said. "Along with a dollop of magic."

He turned back to face her. "You were always so fierce."

"Not by choice." She crossed into the attached bookstore. "My office is this way."

She led him past the bookshelves and into the room at the back, dropping her satchel on the desk before turning to watch him enter. He took a quick glance around, giving an absent nod as if he wasn't surprised by the barren space. He had to know that no mage would meet with potential clients or enemies in a place that wasn't stripped of potential weapons.

Maya leaned against the desk, asking the question that had been nibbling at the edge of her mind since the demon who tried to kill them had disappeared.

"You said that tracking wasn't your talent," she reminded him. "What is?"

He arched a brow. "Would you like a list?"

"I'd like the truth." She deliberately paused. "For once."

Amusement shimmered in his eyes at her less than subtle prod. "My talent is the ability to absorb magic."

Maya had suspected he could manipulate magic. She'd seen him open treasure boxes that were coated in protective hexes when he thought no one was watching. But absorbing it...that was unexpected.

"Does that mean you're impervious to spells and potions?"

"Not completely, but I can dispel most minor magic."

Maya studied him with genuine curiosity. "What happens to the magic after you absorb it?"

"It disappears." He paused before grimacing. "Usually."

"Not always?"

"Not always." His tone was clipped, as if he didn't want to discuss the times the magic hadn't vanished. "Now it's my turn."

"Quid pro quo?"

"Exactly." He folded his arms over his chest. He looked like a male determined to get answers. "How did you know that the house was about to explode?"

Maya flinched. That wasn't what she'd been expecting. "I could smell—"

"No," he interrupted.

She struggled for a plausible lie. "I sensed the danger."

"How?"

"I'm a mage."

"A very powerful one, but your senses can't compete with mine. How did you know?"

Maya hissed out a sigh. He wasn't going to let this go. Not without some sort of explanation.

"I occasionally have assistance from my Benefactor."

He studied her, as if waiting for her to elaborate. "A partner?" he finally asked.

"Not a traditional partner. More of a fairy godfather." She wrinkled her nose, abruptly recalling the last time the voice had demanded she sneak into a demon's nest where she'd nearly died before jumping out of a second-story window and landing on her head. Not very fairy-godfather-like. "No, not that," she conceded. "Honestly, I'm not sure what he is. I began to feel his presence when I first arrived in Jersey."

"What do you mean by presence?"

"It's hard to explain." She instinctively wrapped her arms around her waist. Just mentioning the Benefactor was enough to heighten the sense of her constant companion. "It started with a suspicion that I wasn't alone in a room. Just a feeling of being watched. Then it began to whisper in my mind. Honestly, I thought I might be hallucinating. Then I convinced myself it was some sort of spirit."

"But it wasn't?"

"No." Maya didn't question that the creature was real. "It's far too powerful."

Ravyr's confusion appeared to transform into suspicion as he glanced around the office, as if seeking the creature.

"What does the Benefactor do?"

"He provides a layer of protection to me, as well as my business." Maya tilted her chin, feeling oddly defensive as his brows furrowed. "It means I can remain independent." She didn't have to explain what she meant by independence. They both knew she was speaking of the Cabal. "Something I deeply value."

He narrowed his gaze, but he didn't chide her for her refusal to bend the knee to the vampires.

"I think I felt it."

She blinked in surprise. "When?"

"Last night on the roof. Just before you did your swan dive over the edge of the building."

On cue Maya's ankle twinged with pain. "Hardly a swan dive," she said dryly. "And I can't believe you sensed him. No one else ever has, even Peri and Skye who lived with me for years."

Ravyr shrugged. "If he's attached to you in some way, perhaps I absorbed a portion of his magic."

"I suppose," Maya murmured.

"There must be a cost to his protection," Ravyr pointed out, obviously more interested in what the Benefactor wanted than his identity. "There always is."

"I'm requested to do random tasks. Some are small and simple, others have been dangerous, and at times he tells me what I can or can't do."

"He tells you what you can do?" Ravyr arched a brow. "And you listen?"

She didn't blame him for his surprise. "It pisses me off, but he's prevented more than one nasty disaster. Like avoiding the explosion in Courtney's house."

"And he's what? Invisible?"

Maya swallowed a sigh. It was remarkably difficult to articulate the precise nature of her Benefactor. Probably because she didn't know what his precise nature *was*.

"He's usually an aura that I feel rather than a physical form, but I'm beginning to suspect he's closer than I ever realized," she admitted, resisting the urge to glance over Ravyr's shoulder.

"The creature sounds dodgy."

"So far he's offered more than he's demanded in return. If that changes..."

"What?"

Maya shivered. It was a question that had been on her mind more than once lately.

"I'm not sure." With an abrupt motion, Maya moved around the desk, taking a seat. Then, opening her satchel, she pulled out the phone she'd grabbed before the house exploded. "Let's see who Courtney was chatting with."

Ravyr crossed toward the desk. "I assume it's locked?"

"Yes."

"Valen no doubt has someone who can break through her passcode."

"No need. I've got a shortcut."

Maya leaned to the side and breathed a spell of protection before she tugged on the handle of the bottom drawer. She kept the more lethal potions, spell books, and magical artifacts in her vault. But there were a few dangerous objects that she kept on hand in case of an emergency. She dealt with pissed-off demons on a regular basis. It would be stupid not to have backup.

But beyond the expected curses, hexes, and loaded Glock, she kept a few items that weren't particularly dangerous, but she didn't want them to fall into the wrong hands.

It was the latter sort of potion that she pulled out, along with a small mirror, and placed on the desk in front of her.

"What's that?" Ravyr demanded.

"Watch."

Maya closed her eyes, visualizing Courtney. The round face framed by the short blond hair. The wide blue eyes and pinched lips. Then, grabbing the potion, she wrenched out the cork and downed the liquid in one gulp. It flowed smoothly down her throat, tasting faintly of peppermint. The only potions that tasted bad were those she used as punishment, or a warning. Like healing potions for Peri and Skye after they'd done something stupid to get hurt. A weird tingle spread over her face and crawled over her scalp. It wasn't painful, but it made her toes curl. A disguise potion was never pleasant. Once the tingles faded, she opened her eyes and grabbed the mirror to glance at her reflection. Courtney stared back at her. It wasn't perfect. The eyes were too far apart, and the lips too thin, but it was close enough.

Maya grabbed the phone and held it up to her face; a beat later the lock screen vanished.

"Astonishing," Ravyr muttered.

Maya concentrated on reversing the temporary illusion. "A simple potion."

"I doubt it was simple." He reached out to run a finger down her cheek. "But I prefer this face."

Maya struggled to keep her expression smooth as awareness scorched through her. How could his touch burn her skin when his hand was so cold?

"Thankfully I do too." Maya grimly focused on plugging the phone into the computer. Once it was connected, she searched through the numerous apps. "Got it."

Chapter 6

Ravyr moved to stand behind Maya's chair, allowing him a clear view of the computer screen. He didn't recognize the danger until the intoxicating scent of orchids swirled through the air, clinging to him with a warm promise. Oh hell. He wanted to bend down and bury his face in the satin strands of her dark hair. He wanted to drown in that sweet perfume. Or better yet, to drag the tips of his fangs along the curve of her throat before sinking them deep to taste her blood.

It would be powerful, he silently acknowledged, rich with her magic. And addictive.

So addictive...

"This is the website where Courtney was registered as a potential assassin."

Maya's words thankfully intruded into the sensual fog that was starting to cloud his mind, forcing him to study the image on the screen.

Just for a second he couldn't focus. The hunger for Maya pulsed through his body with a brutal demand. A gnawing, relentless need that had been waiting to explode for over forty years. Then with an effort that was physically painful, he regained command of his passions.

Concentrate, he sternly reminded himself, skimming his gaze over the screen that was so generic it was impossible to know what business owned it or what it might offer. No doubt it was intentional to avoid unwanted interest, but still...

"Pedestrian," he muttered, thoroughly disgusted.

"The website?"

"Everything." He waved a hand toward the computer. "What self-respecting demon would order an assassin like a burrito with extra cheese?"

He sensed her shock before she turned her head to stare at him with an unreadable expression.

"Did you just say burrito with extra cheese?"

"Why?"

"It was a joke."

"So?"

"It's...unnatural."

He held her wary gaze. "Like a caramel latte with sprinkles?"

"Worse." She turned back to the computer, but not before he caught sight of something that might have been amusement smoldering in her emerald eyes. Tapping on the keyboard, she managed to bring up a new screen. It was equally bland with a photo of the blond-haired mage and a list of her supposed skills. "This is Courtney's profile," Maya murmured, leaning forward. "Wait. She called herself Maleficent. You're right. Pedestrian." She pressed on a link that took her to Courtney's banking account. "It looks like she got paid for two jobs in the past year. Including the one to trap me. Less than five thousand dollars total."

"Not the most popular assassin," he murmured. "Can you tell who hired her?"

"This is the account that contacted her." Maya pressed on a link and a second later her magic blasted through the air. "No," she breathed in shock.

Ravyr leaned forward, planting his hand on the desk as he took in the name at the top of the screen.

"Batu," he read out loud, skimming down the screen that had been left blank. No picture, no address, no phone number. Just an online bank account that had no doubt been closed as soon as the money had been transferred.

"It's impossible," Maya hissed.

"Agreed." Ravyr's fangs lengthened as he felt the shivers racing through Maya's body. He was going to rip out the throat of whoever uploaded the profile. "Someone is deliberately taunting you."

Her hands clenched into fists, her back rigid. "You're certain he's dead?"

Ravyr could have described in exquisite detail the end of Batu's life. He'd been hidden in the shadows near Batu's secret lair, hoping for an opportunity to slip through the thick layers of magic. Then he'd heard the screams. Reacting on instinct, he'd rushed forward, charging through the barrier without concern that he was about to destroy the years of effort he'd put in to earning Batu's trust, or the loyalty he owed to Sinjon to discover the source of the strange magic. He recognized that scream. It belonged to Maya....

"Yes, I'm very certain," he assured her in sharp tones, shoving away the unwelcome memory.

"Then why was he hiring an assassin to lure me into a building that was about to explode?"

Ravyr was forced to step aside as Maya jumped to her feet and backed away from the desk, as if she was desperate to get away from the computer. Or was she trying to put space between them?

No. He refused to contemplate that explanation.

"I have no answer," he reluctantly admitted.

She wrapped her arms around her waist, making a visible effort to calm her shattered nerves.

"This mysterious echo you're following," she at last said. "Does it have anything to do with Batu?"

"Yes. I first felt it in his lair." Ravyr paused, debating how much to reveal. "That's why I kept returning to Cambodia." He held her gaze. "And why I couldn't interfere with his control of the Gyre. Sinjon wanted to know the cause of the strange power and determine if it was a danger."

Her lips pressed into a tight line, clearly unimpressed by his excuse for not stepping in to halt Batu's abuse.

"Was the magic throughout the lair or in a specific spot?"

"There was a faint pulse everywhere, but I traced the center of the magic to a hidden chamber beneath his private rooms."

She flinched, as if she was recalling the last moments she'd spent in that chamber.

"If the echo is in Cambodia, then why are you here?"

Ravyr moved to lean against the edge of the desk. "After Batu's death the echo vanished. At the time I couldn't be sure if it had been connected to Batu or his followers. Or if it had been destroyed along with his lair."

"It hadn't been destroyed?"

He shrugged. "A few months later I sensed it again. It was possible that it was a new echo created by an entirely different source, but I don't think so. It was exactly the same as before."

"Where did you sense it?"

"Moving through Asia." Ravyr had been resting in his lair, attempting to recover from his latest journey with Sinjon to Russia. It hadn't been the traveling that had exhausted him. It'd been listening to Kane, the local Cabal leader, gripe and complain that his Gyre was losing its magic and his whiny demands to be moved to a new location. "As soon as I felt the first echo I went in search of it, but the sensation disappeared before I could pinpoint a precise location."

"How could it disappear?"

His lips twisted. He'd arrived in Hong Kong, anxious to confront the magic and stop it from haunting him. Not only was it distracting, but it was also a painful reminder that he'd failed everyone he'd tried to help on the day that Batu died. Especially the woman standing a few feet away from him.

Instead, he'd found nothing. As if he'd imagined the echo.

"Good question," he growled with a frustration that had gnawed at him for years. "Unfortunately I don't have an answer. All I know is that it appears and disappears without any discernable pattern. Just as it moves through the world without a logical path to follow. I've traveled from New Zealand to Africa to South America." He glanced around the barren office. "And now here."

She thankfully didn't ask the obvious question. *Are you losing your mind?* It had been a real concern when he first started sensing the strange magic. And later, when it continued to stay just out of reach.

Now, he didn't worry about his sanity. He worried that he was going to waste an eternity chasing the elusive magic. Or worse, that it was going to cause irreparable harm before he could figure out what the hell it was.

"It could be running from you," she at last suggested. "I assume you've tried to track it down each time you feel the echo?"

"Yes, but why not stay in the same place?" he countered. "From my experience, the only time I sense it is if it moves. Except when Batu was still alive and I was in Cambodia. And even then, I didn't know it was there until I was physically in the lair. It's as if whoever is using it can't completely contain the power when it's being transported."

Maya frowned, absently rubbing the tips of her fingers over her scar as she considered the various possibilities. Then her eyes widened. "It's searching for something."

"Or someone," he murmured, abruptly realizing that was his greatest fear from the moment he'd sensed the power travel to this Gyre.

If the demons who'd pledged their loyalty to Batu were involved in the magic, then they would do anything to punish the woman who was whispered to have been involved in his destruction. They weren't just slaves like most of the servants. They treated Batu as if he was their god.

A shadow darkened Maya's eyes, revealing that she was thoroughly aware of her danger. Then, with her typical courage, she clenched her jaws and dismissed her fear so she could concentrate on what needed to be done to end the threat.

"I'm not sure how to discover the identity of the mystery account," she said. "I can give the phone to a tech friend. They might be able to get more information, but it's going to take some time. I also have acquaintances who owe me favors in the banking world. They should be able to discover who authorized payment to Courtney."

Ravyr didn't doubt that she had hundreds of contacts spread around the world. A mage without the protection of the Cabal would be under constant threat. She needed more than her magic to survive. But he didn't have the patience for her sensible suggestions.

"I have a faster way," he muttered, heading toward the door.

"How?"

Anticipation tingled through Ravyr. For the past four decades he'd been forced to maintain a low profile, hoping to sneak up on the magic before it could disappear. Now, there was no reason he couldn't go on the offense. He was getting the truth, one way or another.

"I'm going to rattle a few cages," he admitted, stepping through the door into the shadowed bookstore.

"I'm coming with you."

There was a clink of glass as Maya grabbed her satchel filled with potions and hurried to walk at his side. Ravyr didn't bother to argue. He wanted to keep her close, not only because it was the only way he could protect her, but he'd spent far too long yearning to have her near. He didn't want her out of his sight for a moment. And there was the very real benefit of having a powerful mage at his side. Together there wasn't anyone who could defeat them.

In silence they moved into the coffee shop and out the front door. Ravyr stopped in the middle of the sidewalk as he waited for Maya to lock the door and place a warding spell. As always, he was on full alert. Over the centuries he'd collected more than one enemy, which meant he was never allowed to let his guard down. That was the only reason he felt the soft brush of power that moved over and through him, as if it was seeking the secrets buried deep inside his soul.

He braced himself for an attack, his hands clenching. Maya whirled to face him, her hand reaching into her satchel.

"What's wrong?"

"I feel a presence. And..." He scowled. "A warning."

Maya furrowed her brow, glancing down the empty street. Over the past couple of hours the breeze had gained a sharp chill and the businesses had closed. Most of the local humans had scurried home to snuggle in for the night.

He envied them. He wouldn't mind being burrowed in a cozy lair. As long as Maya was burrowed next to him.

"The Benefactor," she abruptly announced, shrugging her shoulders as she moved toward the waiting SUV.

She obviously was accustomed to having her unseen guardian check out her companions.

Ravyr hurried to open the back door, waiting until she was settled before he shut the door and tapped on the window next to the driver. The smoked glass slid down to reveal the uniformed goblin, and Ravyr gave the male directions back to the city. Moving to the opposite side of the SUV, Ravyr had started to slip in next to Maya when he caught sight of a shadowed shape across the street.

At a distance they looked like a street person with baggy clothes and a strange hat stuck on their head, but no human could possibly radiate the sort of power that rumbled beneath his feet like an earthquake. Ravyr paused, trying to determine if the stranger was a threat. When nothing happened, he grudgingly settled in the soft leather seat and closed the door.

He assumed that was the mysterious Benefactor. Which meant he was a worry for later.

"Where are we going?" Maya demanded as they pulled away from the curb and squealed down the street at a speed that could have gotten them arrested if the vehicle didn't belong to Valen.

"To track down the owner of the fight club," Ravyr answered.

"Do you think he was involved?"

"No, but I'm hoping he will have video surveillance that survived the explosion."

Maya pursed her lips, calmly tugging the seat belt across her slender body as they bounced and jolted through the side streets before racing across the bridge.

"You aren't going to find anyone to admit that they were in charge of an illegal fight club," she warned. "Valen has strict laws that include the banishment of any demons involved."

Ravyr wasn't concerned. "I can be very persuasive," he assured her.

With a roll of her eyes, she turned her head to watch the stunning skyline as they dodged through the thickening traffic and into narrow alleyways to make their way to the Meatpacking District. Then, with a dramatic flourish, the vehicle swerved to the curb and jerked to a stop.

Ravyr steadied himself to keep from flying out of his seat. He'd told the driver he needed to get to the exploded building ASAP, and the male had done precisely as he'd requested. Thankfully, they'd made it in one piece, and as a bonus, the screech of the tires had attracted the attention of the gawkers who were gathered around the smoking hole in the ground. There weren't as many as the previous evening, but there were still dozens of humans and demons who turned out to discover what was happening.

Ignoring his disgust for melodrama, Ravyr shoved open his door and stepped out of the vehicle to stand in full view of the gathered crowd. As he hoped, the sight of his massive form and the icy power that radiated through the air created a stir of interest. Even the humans who didn't know he was a vampire were able to detect that there was something different about him.

There was the sound of footsteps before the delicious scent of orchids wrapped around him as Maya appeared at his side. She was clever enough to realize what he was doing and, with a cold smile, she tilted her head to make sure the streetlights revealed the silvery web of scars on her jaw.

Demons around the world would recognize Maya Rosen.

Keeping his gaze locked on the group of male goblins standing closest to the smoldering pit, Ravyr started a mental countdown.

Five, four, three, two, one...

On cue the largest of the goblins turned to sprint around the gaping hole, knocking both humans and demons out of his path.

"There he goes." Ravyr didn't bother to wrestle his way through the mob, choosing a casual pace as he strolled up the block as if he didn't have any interest in the fleeing male.

He'd marked the goblin's scent; now there was nowhere in the world he could hide. And he preferred for the male not to realize he was being followed. He wasn't in the mood to be led around the city as the goblin futilely tried to avoid him.

Keeping a pace that Maya could match without having to jog to keep up, Ravyr followed the scent of fear past a block of elegant restaurants and bakeries until they reached a row of brick apartment buildings.

Ravyr halted near the corner, allowing his senses to sweep through the neighborhood for potential danger. He detected a family of fairies as well as several lesser demons in the building, along with several humans. This obviously wasn't an area where the more elite demons gathered, but that didn't mean there weren't threatening creatures lurking in the dark.

Following the trail to the side of the six-story building, Ravyr easily broke through the flimsy lock and shoved open the steel door. He paused again, determined to avoid an unpleasant surprise. When nothing shot at him or leaped out of the dark, he entered the small foyer, waiting for Maya to join him before closing the door.

Overhead an Exit sign flickered with a weird red glow, revealing another door that led to the main part of the building. Predictably the scent of goblin led down the narrow cement steps to the basement, which smelled like rotting garbage. It would be too much to hope he would have a lovely condo on the first floor.

Sharing a wry glance with his companion, Ravyr cautiously headed down the stairs, grimacing as they passed a large dumpster set beneath an overhead chute. A few feet away was a door that pulsed with an unseen magic. This was where the demon was hiding.

He reached out, but before he could grab the knob, Maya was smacking his hand away. His brows lifted as she whispered soft words, creating a spiderweb of threads that coated the door from top to bottom. The strands of magic shimmered with a silvery light before they abruptly caught fire and burned with a blinding speed. Acrid smoke added to the stench of garbage as the charred threads floated to the floor like bits of ash.

Ravyr shuddered. It'd been a nasty hex. One that would have caused him considerable pain. His confidence that having Maya as a partner was going to be beneficial was already paying off.

In more ways than one, he silently acknowledged, savoring the rich scent of orchids that covered the nasty odors filling the hallway.

With an effort, Ravyr returned his concentration to the demon they were chasing. The creature had no doubt sensed his hex being broken, which meant he knew they were there. The time for subtlety was over.

With one swing of his arm, Ravyr smashed open the door, ripping it off its hinges and sending it crashing into the apartment. Or at least what

Alexandra Ivy

passed as an apartment. One glance around the cramped space was enough to reveal that it'd once been a storage room that had been converted into a living space. The owner of the building was clearly taking advantage of the renaissance of the neighborhood to cram in as many tenants as possible.

A cloud of dust filled the air as the door landed on the filthy floor, and the goblin inside coughed as he lifted his hands in a pleading gesture.

"Please. I didn't do anything wrong," he choked out.

Ravyr stepped forward, acutely aware of Maya who remained behind him, guarding the door to make sure they weren't interrupted. They really did make the perfect pair, he mused, studying the male standing in front of him.

The goblin was nearly as tall and wide as Ravyr with a dull crimson aura that revealed he was on the lower end of the demon hierarchy. His long black hair framed a square face and brushed his broad shoulders. His features were bluntly cut and set in a defiant expression even as fear shimmered in the dark eyes. The Cabal was no longer led by savages, but they maintained an iron control over the demons who chose to live in the Gyres.

"You broke my door," the goblin groused, licking his lips as he tried to act outraged.

"What's your name?"

"You can call me Pike," he grudgingly offered, waving his hand toward the broken door. "Are you going to pay for the damages?"

Ravyr folded his arms over his chest. "You shouldn't have run."

"What did you expect? Leeches are always trouble."

Well, that's true enough, Ravyr silently agreed. Not that he was going to share his opinion with the goblin.

"I'll pass your opinion on to Valen."

"I didn't mean Valen," Pike hastily corrected. "I'm a loyal servant to His Excellency."

"Good. Then you'll be happy to assist in my investigation."

"Sure. What investigation?"

"The explosion at the Slaughterhouse."

Pike slowly lowered his hands, his wary gaze darting toward Maya before returning to Ravyr.

"Sorry, I'm afraid that I don't have any information about that." He did more lip licking. "I heard it was a gas leak."

The temperature in the small space dropped by several degrees. "Show me the security footage from last night."

Pike cleared his throat, sweat beading on his bulging forehead. "Security footage? I don't know what you're—" The male's words were cut short as Ravyr strolled forward, grabbing the idiot around the throat and lifting him off the ground. "Argh."

Ravyr calmly watched Pike's face darken to a peculiar shade of puce. "Let me give you a bit of friendly advice," he said, although there was nothing friendly in his tone. "I have two moods. Pissed off. And homicidal. Right now I'm pissed off. Understand?"

"Right, yeah," Pike managed to wheeze. "I understand."

"The security footage."

The goblin waved a weak hand toward the desk at the back of the room. "TV."

Ravyr tossed the goblin aside and headed to the small flat-screen television that was nearly hidden behind stacks of invoices and empty coffee cups.

"Show me," he commanded.

There was a grunt of pain as the demon picked himself up off the floor and reluctantly moved to stand next to Ravyr.

"Fine, but I've watched the footage a thousand times and there's nothing to prove who set off the explosion," he muttered, grabbing a remote control. He scrolled through the apps until he reached the one he wanted.

Ravyr felt a stir of air as Maya moved to stand on the other side of them, watching the grainy video that flickered into motion. The screen was divided in two, including the inside of the fight club as well as the front entrance.

Grabbing the remote control, Ravyr fast-forwarded through the footage.

There was nothing obvious to point out who might have planted the bomb. Unlike Valen's expensive clubs, there was no bouncer at the front door or security to keep the crowd under control. During the evening there'd been dozens of pushing and shoving episodes that had escalated into full-blown brawls, scattering the crowd and causing complete pandemonium. There could have been a dozen bombs planted during the chaos.

"Is there another camera angle?" Ravyr at last demanded.

"No," Pike admitted.

Reaching the moment of explosion, Ravyr ground his fangs and rewound the tape to start from the moment the first employee had arrived. There had to be something....

"Stop," Maya abruptly breathed.

Ravyr hit pause on the remote control. "Do you recognize someone?"

"Hexx," she muttered, pulling her phone out to take a picture of the customers entering the club.

"A hex?" Ravyr asked in confusion.

"No, his name is Hexx," she clarified. "Fast-forward." Ravyr did as she commanded, prepared when she lifted her hand. "Stop."

Maya leaned forward to take another picture; then, leaning close to Ravyr, she turned her phone so he could see the screen.

"This is Hexx going into the club." She zoomed in to reveal a male goblin with crimson flames tattooed along the line of his jaw. His hair was long and pulled into a ponytail and his face narrow, like a rodent. He was wearing a sleeveless leather vest and jeans despite the chilled night air and he had a pale red aura. "Look at his backpack."

Ravyr studied the bag slung over the male's shoulder. It looked like a regular backpack you could pick up in any department store.

"What about it?"

"It's full there." Maya swiped to the second picture. The one of the male heading out of the building. "And empty there."

"That bastard," Pike snarled from the other side of Ravyr, slamming his fist on the desk. "I should have known he was there to cause trouble. He's been avoiding me for six months."

"Why?" Ravyr demanded.

"He owes me money." Pike turned toward the door. "I'm going to kill him."

Ravyr grabbed him by the neck, pushing him against the wall. "You're going to do nothing. The Cabal is in charge of this investigation."

"Why?" Pike stuck out his chin, his aura swirling with frustration. "It was my building. I should get to beat the shit out of him."

"A building that was being used as an illegal fight club." Ravyr flashed his fangs. "Something I'm sure Valen intends to discuss with you."

"Fight clubs are illegal?" The angry scowl melted away, replaced by a pretense of shock. "Really? I had no idea."

Ravyr rolled his eyes, loosening his grip so he could join Maya as she headed out the door. He would send word to Valen that he'd discovered the owner of the Slaughterhouse.

Thankfully Pike wasn't his concern.

He had enough problems without adding to his list.

Chapter 7

Maya was acutely aware of Ravyr as she scurried back to the waiting SUV to give the driver directions. Ravyr was a vampire, which meant he was used to snapping out orders and being in charge, but he readily followed her lead as she hopped into the vehicle and they pulled away from the curb.

The complete opposite of Batu, who'd casually broken her jaw when she'd suggested the human slaves were going to starve to death without more food.

Maya's stomach clenched, but oddly the feel of Ravyr's massive body settled next to her eased her anxiety, allowing her to shove aside the unwelcome memory.

"Tell me about Hexx," he said, offering her the perfect distraction.

Maya eased back in her seat. It would take a few minutes to reach the Bronx, even with the chauffeur determined to drive as if he was in a Formula One race.

"He's a low-level goblin who used to own a pawnshop."

"Used to?"

"I ran across him when the Cabal was in the city a few months ago trying to bully Peri because she gained powers they didn't understand."

Ravyr arched a brow at her tart accusation. "Bully?"

She ignored his interruption. There was no other word for the collection of vampires who'd descended on New York City and demanded that Peri prove she could control her wild magic. Well, she had several other terms she used on a regular basis. Jerks. Monsters. A-holes. Bullies was as polite as she was prepared to offer.

"When I visited the pawnshop I discovered he was selling black-market items. I had them confiscated and shut down the shop."

"I assume he's not happy with you?"

"You assume correctly. Valen was the one to officially force him out of business, but he blamed me."

Hexx had shown up at the Witch's Brew late one night, pounding on her door and threatening to burn the place down if she didn't let him in. Maya had been more annoyed than frightened. Away from the magic of the Gyre the goblin wasn't any more powerful than a human. He did, however, create an unpleasant scene.

At last she'd been forced to lean out her bedroom window and pour an itching potion over his head. The last she'd seen of Hexx, he'd been fleeing down the street, screaming in frustration.

The rest of the journey was made in silence as Ravyr turned his head to peer through the back window. No doubt he was making sure they weren't being followed. A reasonable precaution, considering someone had tried to kill one or both of them. Twice.

At last they reached a shabby neighborhood with rows of small businesses squashed into narrow brick buildings. The SUV halted next to the curb and Ravyr leaned to the side, studying the nearest shop, hidden behind a security gate and with windows covered with plyboard.

"This is the place?"

Maya shoved open her door and climbed out of the vehicle. "He has an apartment above the shop."

Crossing the sidewalk, Maya entered a narrow alleyway that led to the back of the building and the steel stairs that led to the upper floor.

"No lights," Ravyr murmured as they headed up.

"Hexx has the survival instincts of a cockroach," she said dryly. "He's not very smart, but he'll realize that Valen isn't going to be happy about a huge explosion in the middle of his territory. And that anyone connected to the destruction is going to be in a lot of trouble. He'll try to lay low and hope no one noticed his involvement."

They had reached the top of the staircase when Maya felt an unpleasant heat brush over her skin followed by a pungent scent of sulfur.

"Do you smell that?" she demanded. A stupid question, of course. Ravyr's senses were a hundred times more sensitive than her own.

"Dragon scale," he murmured.

Dragon scale was exactly what it claimed to be. Tiny flecks of scales that had been left behind when the dragons went into hibernation long ago. Once they were ground down to a powder they became a powerful drug that demons paid top dollar to obtain. Not only was it rare, but it was also illegal.

"Valen's not going to be happy," Maya murmured as they got to the door. "Time for a new lesson."

"Good."

A pulse of power warned her that Ravyr was about to smash through the steel door.

"Wait, Ravyr, I can open the lock."

He sent her a smile that revealed his massive fangs. "This is more fun."

With a swing of his arm, he knocked the second door of the evening off its hinges, sending it blasting into the apartment. He was flowing inside before the door hit the floor, and Maya followed with her hand in her satchel. She didn't trust Hexx as far as she could throw him.

On cue, Maya felt Ravyr's arm wrap around her as he knocked her aside. They stumbled into a stack of crates, barely escaping the bullet that whizzed past them and hit the doorframe with a splinter of wood.

The ringing of the gun was still echoing in the air when Maya pulled a vial out of her satchel and tossed it toward the shadowy figure crouched in a back corner. The glass shattered as it hit the mark, and the scent of lemongrass, lavender, and mint wafted through the air. The sweet perfume disguised the powerful magic that was brewed into the potion.

Stepping away from Ravyr's protective arms, Maya fumbled to switch on the overhead light. She blinked as the barren bulb flared to life, revealing the open loft that was stuffed from floor to ceiling with wooden crates on one side, leaving only a narrow space for a cot, a battered recliner, and a table that was stacked with empty pizza boxes. Her jaw clenched as she realized Hexx had smuggled a portion of his illegal merchandise out of his shop to hide up here.

Her freeze spell had caught him between crouching next to the recliner and trying to flee toward the large window near the cot. It left him bent in an awkward position with his head swiveled in their direction and his greasy hair hanging over one shoulder. His face was paler than usual, emphasizing the crimson flames tattooed along the line of his jaw.

Her gaze lowered to his naked chest and the running shorts that left far too much of his pasty body exposed. It looked as if he'd been sleeping when he sensed their approach. Fury exploded through her at the sight of the handgun clenched in his frozen hand.

"Did you seriously try to shoot me?" She pointed a finger toward his face to release the magic that held his lips shut.

With a choked gasp, Hexx sucked in a harsh breath. "I didn't know it was you."

"Who were you expecting?"

"No one. I mean..." His voice trailed away as his attention moved toward the huge vampire standing next to her. His eyes widened, as if he understood he hadn't just pissed off a powerful mage. He'd nearly shot a vampire. That was the sort of thing that got demons dead in a hurry. "It's dangerous times," he weakly concluded.

"It's certainly dangerous for you," Maya warned.

With an effort, Hexx returned his attention to her. "I don't know why you're here, but I haven't done anything. Not since you shut me down."

"I shut you down because you were trading in illegal magic." Maya glanced toward the piles of crates. "And here you are. Still dealing."

Hexx strained against her spell, no doubt hoping he could jump out the window before Ravyr could rip out his throat.

"Is that why you're here?" he clearly forced himself to ask at last. "To take the few crumbs I managed to salvage? My life is in the shitter because of you. The least you could do is leave me something to sell off."

Maya rolled her eyes. "If your life is in the shitter it's not my fault."

Hexx's face was threaded with irritation, no doubt at the thought of losing the rest of his merchandise. "Look, it's all low-value stuff. Just an emergency stash."

She shrugged. She didn't have to look in the crates to know he was telling the truth. The items he was hoarding barely registered as magical, and none of them offered a real danger. It was the sort of stuff that charlatans sold in stores to gullible humans.

"It doesn't matter. Your black-market trade is the least of your worries."

"I told you—"

Maya cut short his whining. "You set off a bomb that destroyed the Slaughterhouse Club, killing several demons and nearly me." She wasn't in the mood. "Not to mention a vampire."

Hexx was clearly caught off guard by the accusation. Not that he was innocent—he just hadn't realized they'd connected him to the explosion.

"Bomb? Seriously? It wasn't me. I swear."

"A lie," Ravyr murmured, folding his arms over his massive chest. It was an unspoken warning that Hexx surely didn't miss.

The stench of goblin sweat combined with the stale pizza as his gaze abruptly darted from side to side. He looked like a cornered rat.

"Okay. I might have gone to the club, but I didn't know what was going to happen." He stared straight at Maya, as if hoping that by ignoring the lethal leech, Ravyr might not carve out his heart and eat it. "This time I swear for real."

Maya didn't need the shake of Ravyr's head to know that Hexx was still lying.

"Tell me exactly how you got involved," she commanded.

Hexx paused. Maya knew that he was debating whether to continue with his pretense of innocence or to hope the truth might keep him breathing another night. At last he settled on the truth.

Or at least, his version.

"A few nights ago I was coming home and a stranger approached me in the alley with a job offer," he admitted.

"A demon?"

"Yeah. Goblin."

"What was the job?"

"Just delivering a package to the Slaughterhouse Club. It seemed harmless enough."

"Harmless? You planted a bomb that destroyed half a city block," Maya bit out.

"I didn't know it was a bomb."

"Lie," Ravyr warned.

Hexx grimaced. "Fine. I didn't know it was a *big* bomb," he insisted. "It was just supposed to..."

Maya clicked her tongue as his words trailed away. Did the idiot think that dragging out his story was going to make it any better?

"Supposed to what?" she snapped.

He lowered his gaze to the floor. "Hurt you."

Before she could fully process the knowledge that the bomb had undeniably been tended to harm her, an icy blast of power exploded through the loft, knocking over crates and busting a lamp next to the bed. Maya risked a quick glance at the male standing next to her. There was nothing to reveal why he'd lost control of his temper. His expression was grim, but there was nothing unusual in that.

With a shrug she glanced back at Hexx. "Me specifically?"

Hexx was staring at the shattered lamp, his face draining from pasty to pallid. "Not to kill you," he finally rasped. "The dude promised it was a small explosion that would cause a few injuries." He warily glanced back at Maya. "Nothing permanent, I swear, but enough to stop you from sticking your nose in demon business. It wasn't supposed to be any big deal."

Maya tried to imagine who she'd pissed off enough that they would destroy an entire building and kill dozens of demons just to get rid of her. It seemed like an obscenely flamboyant way to kill her. She shook her head, refusing to dwell on the nasty thought that she could be so profoundly hated.

"If it wasn't a big deal, then why didn't the person who wanted me hurt plant the bomb? There was no need to include you."

"They were supposed to make sure you got to the club and were in place when the explosion went off."

Maya shook her head in disgust. "So once again a random demon contacts you with a crazy scheme and you just say yes?" she asked, referring to Hexx's involvement in Skye's kidnapping six months ago.

"Not at first," the goblin protested in a petulant tone. "But then he handed over a very large stack of cash. Thanks to you I'm deadass broke. What do you want me to do?"

"Did you wonder why this mysterious demon would want to hurt me?"

"No. Every demon in this city would love to see you suffer."

Okay, he does have a point, Maya silently conceded. But while she might have angered a large part of the demon population, not many of them would be stupid enough to risk Valen's fury by blowing up a building in his city. Why not come to Jersey and do the deed?

"Where is the demon now?"

"I have no idea." Hexx winced as another stack of crates toppled to the side, smashing whatever was inside. He sent a pleading glance in Ravyr's direction. "Honestly, I don't know. He hired me to arrive at the Slaughterhouse Club last night and told me to pick up a package he was going to stash behind the dumpster. I got it and went into the men's bathroom where I tossed it in the trash can. After that I headed home. I got a block away when the damned place exploded. I couldn't believe it. I mean...how crappy can my luck get? It's one disaster after another."

His babbling words had an edge of sincerity, but Maya had zero sympathy. She twisted her features into a mask of disgust.

"You killed innocent bystanders and shut down every business in the area, but you're the victim?"

"It wasn't my fault," Hexx insisted.

Maya shook her head. She was wasting time. This goblin was a selfish prick. He would always do what was best for him, regardless of who might suffer from his lack of morals.

"Tell me about the demon. What was his name?"

"I don't know."

Maya ground her teeth. "Describe him."

"Average."

"Average what."

"Average height. Average age. Average."

Magic sizzled through Maya as she struggled to contain her temper. She wanted to flay the stubborn male, then roll him in salt until he screamed in agony. Or—

"Allow me." Ravyr thankfully halted Maya's impulsive desire to strike out at Hexx, who was still frozen by her potion.

She might be furious with the goblin and unnerved by the thought that someone wanted her dead, but she didn't use her powers when someone was helpless to defend themselves.

"No, I'm trying to help," Hexx squealed as Ravyr slowly approached.

"Shut up." Ravyr reached down to grab Hexx by the hair, placing his free hand against the male's forehead.

All vampires possessed the ability to enter the minds of demons and humans, although it wasn't as simple as reading their thoughts. The brain was a complex organ that stored information in fragments.

Still, he should be able to discover something to help them in their search for the mysterious demon.

For a full five minutes, Ravyr searched through Hexx's mind, ignoring the goblin's pleas for mercy. Finally he appeared to concede defeat as he released his hold on Hexx's hair and turned to face Maya with a troubled expression.

"I see the male who approached Hexx in the alley, but his features are too bland to be real." He frowned. "It's like he's wearing a mask."

"No," Maya abruptly breathed. "It's a potion. A very expensive potion. And I know who bought it."

Chapter 8

They were out of the city and zooming northward toward the Hudson Valley before Ravyr turned in his seat to study the silent woman at his side.

"Talk to me," he murmured, easily able to see her troubled expression despite the thick darkness.

"I should have suspected something when we smelled the dragon scale," she said, annoyance edging her voice. "There's no way Hexx could ever afford the drug."

Ravyr had limited experience with dragon scale. Sinjon had dozens of enforcers who were in charge of tracking down the potent drug and destroying it. All he knew was that it could allow any demon to tap briefly into their ancient magic, giving them a surge of euphoric power that often led to violence.

"What are you suggesting?" he asked.

"That it had to be someone besides Hexx who was in that alley smelling like scale."

Ravyr nodded, recalling the goblin's babbled story about a stranger handing him money in the alley.

"The demon who hired Hexx to sneak the bomb into the Slaughterhouse."

"Exactly."

"And you know who it is?"

"I have a good suspicion." She turned her head to gaze at the passing scenery. Not that there was much to see. They'd left behind the sprawling city and plunged into the rolling hills that framed the nearby river. They'd also left behind the magic of the Gyre, easing the pulse of power that usually beat through Ravyr. He didn't mind. He was still stronger and faster and more lethal than any other creature in the area. "When I first arrived in Jersey the Yalick clan approached me with a job offer," Maya continued.

"Yalick." He sent her a wry glance. "Even I've heard that name. They're some sort of demon royalty, right?"

"They're the oldest, most powerful demon clan in America."

"You refused their offer?"

"More than once." She shrugged. "Eventually they sent their goon squad to convince me I needed their protection."

Ravyr shook his head. Only Maya Rosen would refuse a position that would have paid her a fortune and solidified her place on top of the magical hierarchy. Of course, she didn't need the Yalick clan to give her any of that, he wryly conceded. There wasn't a Cabal leader in the world who wouldn't offer her a king's ransom to have her a part of their Gyre.

"I doubt that turned out as they expected," he said dryly, not doubting for a second that she sent the poor demons fleeing in terror.

"I made certain they understood that no means no."

At some point, Ravyr intended to hear the full story of how she'd gotten rid of her unwelcome visitors. Now, however, he needed to prepare for what new disaster they were about to confront.

"How are the Yalicks connected to Hexx?"

She turned back to meet his curious gaze. "When they approached me, they specifically requested that I provide them with a potion that would allow their servants to go about their business without being noticed."

"Like a disguise amulet?"

"Not exactly. The magic doesn't physically alter their features, but it encourages people to ignore them, if that makes sense."

Ravyr considered what he'd glimpsed in Hexx's mind. Reading the memories of others was never an exact science. It all depended on how closely they were paying attention to something and their personal prejudices that colored what was happening. Even faces were colored by emotions. Were they a friend, a lover, a threat...

But Hexx's memory of the male was like an outline that had never been filled in.

"A blank slate," he murmured.

"Yes, so whoever is looking at them rarely takes notice of anything but the fact that they have the usual eyes and nose and lips. Nothing that stands out."

"Convenient. I assume since I've never heard of that particular potion it's not the sort of thing you can get at the local magic shop?"

She shook her head. "It's very rare. Not only are the ingredients difficult to obtain, but it takes a level of magic most mages don't possess to brew. A small vial can go for thousands of dollars on the black market."

Ravyr tapped his fingers on his knee. Even for a wealthy family it would be a considerable investment if you included the salary for a powerful mage and the cost of the ingredients. There had to be a hell of a payoff.

"Did they say why they wanted the potion?"

"They claimed that their business required their staff to transport large sums of money as well as priceless artifacts, and they preferred that servant remain incognito to avoid being robbed."

"What's their business?"

She pursed her lips, the scent of her disapproval thick in the air. "Officially they have a traditional auction house that caters to humans, as well as several smaller auction houses that deal exclusively with demon artifacts and objects of power."

No doubt a lucrative venture, Ravyr acknowledged. Demons were always eager to buy anything that might connect them to their glorious past, but it didn't explain the clan's massive wealth. "And unofficially?"

"The rumor is that the bulk of their money comes from dealing in dragon scale."

"Ah." Ravyr abruptly understood. "That's why they want their servants to be unrecognizable. No one could describe them or pick them out of a lineup. Sinjon takes a dim view of anyone caught in the drug trade."

"So does Valen," Maya added. "Which is one of the reasons the family chooses to live in such a remote location instead of in the city. They try to keep a low profile."

"If the demon was helping to manufacture the drug, it would explain why we smelled it in the alley," Ravyr added.

"Yes, it would easily linger for days," Maya agreed.

Ravyr considered the various implications as the SUV turned off the highway and followed the narrow path up the slope of a hill. For several miles there was nothing to see but the trees that formed a low tunnel over the road, but as they at last reached the summit, the view cleared to reveal a massive stone wall that towered ten feet into the air and sprawled in both directions as far as the eye could see. On top of the wall were marble statues that peered down at the world with arrogant disdain. They were also perfectly positioned to hide potential snipers.

"Is this the place?" He leaned to the side to peer out the window. "Impressive."

"It's obscene," Maya retorted, the sweet scent of orchids more pungent than usual. "They protect the place like they're expecting an alien invasion. Fences, guards, even attack dogs."

"But no magic."

"No *demon* magic," Maya agreed, her features tense as the SUV bumped over the road, which was scarred with ruts and deep potholes. A visible warning that visitors were unwelcome. As if the formidable walls weren't enough. "Which means they can't be attacked by demons and avoid unwanted attention from Valen's servants. But they can pay for snares and curses created by mages. I don't doubt they have them hidden around the entire estate. It will be hard to sneak up on them."

"No worries."

Ravyr leaned forward to rap on the window dividing them from the driver. On cue, the SUV swung into a narrow opening in the wall that served as the front entrance. As expected, there was a heavy steel gate that blocked the road with razor wire added at the top. There was also a large, thickly muscular goblin who stood guard. His crimson aura was impressive, but he was too far from a Gyre to tap into his demon powers, so he'd compensated by arming himself with automatic rifles, large daggers, and what looked like a hand grenade dangling from his heavy utility belt.

Talk about overkill.

The SUV rolled to a halt and the guard strutted up, banging on the top of the vehicle.

"No visitors."

The chauffeur rolled down his window. "I have—"

"I don't care if you have the Easter Bunny," the guard interrupted. "Turn around."

Ravyr pressed the button on the door, sliding down the passenger window. "Open the gate."

The guard grabbed a handgun holstered at his hip. "Go get fu—" His lips snapped together as an icy blast of power slammed into him, sending him to his knees. "Shit. Master. Forgive me." He pressed his face to the hard ground before rising to his feet and slamming a beefy hand against the steel barrier. "Open the gate!"

Ravyr heard Maya mutter something under her breath, but his focus remained locked on the guard, who was nervously shifting from foot to foot, a cell phone in his hand.

"Forgive me, Master, but I need a name. For Mr. Yalick."

"Ravyr."

The dark eyes widened as he easily recognized the name. The lesser demons didn't bother to pay attention to the various members of the Cabal. Just as they lacked the same wary respect for the vampires. The royal families, however, depended on their ancient bloodlines to maintain their power. Which meant spending at least a portion of their time in the local Gyres. Without the goodwill of the Cabal leader they could be shut out, leaving them near human.

Something none of them could stomach.

"Ambassador Ravyr?" The goblin blinked, then blinked again. "I thought you were..."

"Dead?" Ravyr helpfully added.

"Yeah."

Ravyr parted his lips, allowing the tips of his fangs to shimmer in the moonlight. "A dangerous mistake."

The goblin once again slammed his hand against the steel gate. "Get this damned thing open," he bellowed.

"Chillax, dude," a voice groused as the gate shuddered upward. The guard on the other side bent down to peer beneath the rising barrier, no doubt intending to chastise his companion. Instead, the redheaded fairy abruptly dropped to his knees. "Oh shit."

Maya clicked her tongue, her hands clenching into tight fists as she watched the groveling fairy.

"What?" Ravyr demanded. He knew why she looked like she wanted to throat punch him, but he needed her to admit it. If they didn't acknowledge the elephant in the room it was going to destroy any hope of getting past Maya's prejudices.

And he very much wanted to get past them.

"Nothing," she retorted in tones that indicated it was very much something.

"You're dripping with disapproval."

She jerked, her eyes narrowing. "Dripping?"

"I was going to say oozing."

"I'm not dripping or oozing anything."

"But you do disapprove." It wasn't a question.

She waved a hand toward the fairy. "I don't think anyone should have to grovel. Even if they are a demon."

"Especially if they're groveling to a vampire?"

She shrugged. "You said it, not me."

"Would you believe me if I agreed that our class division is antiquated? And that I have no interest in being involved in Cabal politics?"

"Do you have a choice?"

Ravyr grimaced. It was a direct hit. And she knew it.

For now he didn't have the luxury of indulging his personal desires. Not until the danger had been eliminated.

But someday...

Anticipation sizzled through him, his mind overwhelmed with vivid images of carrying Maya to his bed and stripping off each icy layer until she was warm and naked in his arms. He wanted her trembling with need, the air scented with her desire. He wanted her nails raking down his bare chest and her legs wrapped around his waist as he plunged deep inside her.

Not waiting for the gate to fully open, the SUV gunned forward, skimming up the road that was suddenly as smooth as glass. Ravyr leaned his head out the open window, studying the massive redbrick mansion that loomed at the top of the hill. He wasn't interested in the mullioned windows, fancy cornices, or the ivy that coated the wide verandas and climbed up the turrets at each end. He was locating each guard who was strategically placed around the house. He assumed there were an equal number hidden in the surrounding woods.

Enough to make his visit uncomfortable if the Yalick clan decided he was a threat to their luxurious lifestyle.

The vehicle swerved around the circle drive, parking directly in front of the sweeping staircase. With a fluid motion, Ravyr was out of the SUV and moving to place his body between Maya and the sniper crouched on the gable roof. Then, allowing his icy power to jolt through the air, he escorted her up the steps and across the wide veranda.

As they approached, one of the double doors was pulled open and a servant dressed in a crimson-and-gold uniform bowed before leading them out of the foyer without speaking.

Ravyr sensed Maya's tension as they walked into the paneled corridor, her lips moving in a silent incantation. He shared her unease. There was no overt threat. Just the opposite. The vast mansion was an exact replica of an English country manor with lots of polished wood and open beamed ceilings. The artwork hanging on the walls was worth a fortune and enhanced the dark, stuffy atmosphere.

It seemed that the Yalick clan was just another stodgy, obscenely wealthy family with nothing to hide, but underneath the scent of beeswax was a fetid stench. As if something was rotting beneath their feet.

The uniformed servant led them into a long, formal salon before melting into the shadows, leaving Ravyr and Maya standing alone in the center of the handwoven carpet, directly in the pool of light from the overhead chandelier. As if they were actors on a stage as the demons who were gathered near the massive fireplace elegantly sank to their knees and bowed their heads.

"Master Ravyr." A large male with silver hair brushed from his square face spoke for the clan. "This is an unexpected honor."

Ravyr took his time analyzing the kneeling demons. The older male was obviously the leader. He was wearing an expensive black suit that molded to his thick, corded muscles, but it was the deep crimson of his aura that revealed his true power. Next to him was a slender female with dark brown hair carefully tinted to hide the gray, and wearing a black satin gown. Three more demons were fanned behind them. Twin males who were exact replicas of their father, although their auras were obviously diluted, revealing that a distant ancestor had human blood. No doubt a severe disappointment to their parents. Sometimes it took several generations for the weakening pedigree to appear. Next to them was a female with long brown hair and an aura that was much darker than the males. Her expression was carefully bland, but Ravyr didn't miss the hint of arrogant disdain that smoldered in her eyes. Her designer dress was short and tight and sparkled in the light from the chandelier.

Did the family always wear fancy clothes, or had they rushed to change when the guards had warned there was a vampire at the gate?

"Rise," he at last commanded.

The demons pushed themselves to their feet, the older male stepping forward to take charge.

"I am Lord Yalick, as I'm sure you are aware." His expression was one of smug expectancy, as if he assumed that Ravyr's arrival revealed respect for his clan's power. "How may we serve you?"

Ravyr swept his gaze over the rest of the family. All of them appeared more curious than concerned.

Dammit. They obviously hadn't been involved in the explosion.

His gaze moved toward the guards standing at attention on each side of the long room. They both wore uniforms and both had crimson auras, although the one who was standing in front of the towering bookcase had a much darker aura. He also had a hardened expression that spoke of a male who enjoyed violence.

Ravyr watched as the guard rested a protective hand on the back of a wing chair beside him. Seated on the soft leather was a slender woman with blond curls and a narrow face. She was modestly dressed in a black turtleneck and slacks, as if she was deliberately attempting to blend into the shadows, but even at a distance he could see the stark hunger that burned in her pale eyes as she glared at Maya.

A mage.

She looked young, although he couldn't determine her precise age, or how powerful she might be, but there was no mistaking the malicious envy that simmered inside her.

Those two, he silently acknowledged. They knew something.

The sound of Lord Yalick clearing his throat forced Ravyr to return his attention to the pompous goblin. The guard would eventually make a move, he knew. The male was nearly vibrating with the vicious urge to strike out.

And Ravyr would be ready.

"Valen has requested that I take charge of the investigation into the explosion that occurred last night," he said, the scent of orchids suddenly thick in the air.

Maya had easily sensed the danger from the younger woman and was making her own preparations for an attack.

"Explosion?" Lord Yalick furrowed his brow.

The female next to him reached out to lay her hand on his arm, the large diamonds on her fingers threatening to blind Ravyr.

"It was on the news, dear."

"It was?" The older male took a second before he abruptly nodded. "Oh. That squalid building in the Meatpacking District. I thought it was a gas leak?"

"There was no gas leak. A bomb was intentionally planted in the men's bathroom."

Ravyr kept his gaze on Yalick but didn't miss the sound of the guard shuffling his feet. The male had to realize that they'd spoken to Hexx.

There was no other way they could know that the bomb had been placed in that specific spot.

"Tragic, but I'm not sure what this has to do with us," Yalick retorted, his brow still furrowed as if searching for some way to profit off the news. "The property isn't owned by my clan. And I assure you, we don't go around setting off bombs. We are business owners, not terrorists."

Ravyr allowed his fangs to lengthen, a chill blasting through the air. It was time to get to the truth.

"Then how do you explain the fact that your guard paid a large sum of money to a local goblin to carry the bomb into the Slaughterhouse?"

"My guard?" Yalick blinked in confusion. "That's impossible."

Ravyr curled back his lips, exposing his shiny, lethally sharp fangs. "I have proof."

"No...I mean you've made a mistake.... I swear on my life we had nothing to do with the bomb," Yalick stammered.

With a slow, deliberate motion, Ravyr turned to stare at the goblin across the room. On cue, the male pulled a semiautomatic handgun that had been holstered at his side and sprayed the room with bullets. At the same time, the mage jumped out of her seat and waved her hands in a series of circles. A dormant spell she'd no doubt cast when no one was around burst to life, shattering the overhead chandelier and sending the shards of glass zooming through the air. Most of them were aimed at Maya, who was using her own magic to deflect the jagged missiles while the Yalick clan dropped to the floor with screams of terror.

"What's happening?" the clan leader demanded.

"Get your family out of the way," Ravyr barked.

He wasn't worried about the arrogant goblins. Once he informed Sinjon they were dealing in the scale trade, they were destined to end up in a very deep dungeon for a very long time. But he didn't want one of them knocking him into the flying bullets or accidentally tripping him.

Remaining on their hands and knees, the clan scrambled for the main doorway, along with the second guard who'd obviously decided to bail on his duties and flee from the danger.

Alone with the demon and the mage, Ravyr released a low roar and launched forward. A bullet slammed into his upper thigh and shards of glass burrowed into his chest, but he never slowed. Once he had his hands on the bastard he was going to squeeze the truth out of him.

He was savoring the image when there was a soft whoosh of air and the floor beneath his feet abruptly disappeared. He growled in fury as he tumbled into the ten-foot hole and hit the rocky bottom with a heavy thud.

Chapter 9

Maya watched in horror as Ravyr dropped through the trapdoor in the floor. She had no idea if the fleeing Yalicks were responsible for his disappearance or if the goblin charging toward her had opened the hidden trap. Not that the *who* mattered, she decided as she reached into her satchel and pulled out a vial of potion. Not when she was about to be smooshed by a furious demon.

With a flick of her wrist, she tossed the vial toward the male's head, grinding her teeth when he abruptly ducked to the side and without slowing dodged toward the nearest window and threw himself through the tinted glass. Scowling in frustration, she watched as he ran through the garden and disappeared into the trees.

Once she was certain that he wasn't coming back, she whirled around, prepared for the mage to attack. She hadn't missed the younger woman's spiteful glare when they'd entered the room. She could almost smell the envy that drenched the air.

She assumed this mage had gotten her information about Maya in the same place as Courtney. What else would explain the jealousy burning in her eyes? At some point Maya intended to discover who was fueling such hatred among the younger mages, but until then, she had no choice but to defend herself.

Whirling back, she grasped another vial. Unlike the younger mage, she'd learned through years of experience never to waste her magic. It was used as a last line of defense.

Surprisingly, however, the woman wasn't headed in her direction. Instead, she was standing over the hole in the floor where Ravyr had disappeared.

What was she doing?

It wasn't until she felt the tingle of heat in the air that she recognized the spell she was attempting to conjure.

A firestorm.

Dammit. Ravyr might be immune to most magic, but the searing flames would eventually consume him if he couldn't escape.

Racing forward, Maya intended to knock the woman to the ground before hitting her with a stun potion. That would keep her contained long enough for Ravyr to climb out of the hole so they could track down the goblin. Once they captured him, Maya had the perfect potion to force him to talk.

She was still formulating her plan when it all went to hell. The younger mage's spell snapped into place while Maya was too far away to disrupt the magic, and a wall of flames exploded from her fingers.

Maya should have turned and run away.

The mage was obviously focused on killing Ravyr. A wise decision considering the vampire was going to rip out her throat the second he crawled out of that hole. Her distraction would give Maya ample opportunity to escape.

It wasn't like she owed Ravyr anything, right?

He was a vampire. Her mortal enemy.

And even if they did appear to be hunting the same prey, that didn't make them partners. And certainly not friends.

But she didn't turn. She continued to run toward the mage, who was weaving her hands in a gesture to squeeze the searing flames into a cylinder. Another wave of her hands and the flames were spinning and lengthening. She was creating a tower of fire that would fill the pit from top to bottom.

The mage screeched in frustration as Maya finally reached the edge of the trapdoor, no doubt hoping for the opportunity for a face-to-face battle once the vampire was dead. It'd been obvious in her glares that she ached to prove that she was the superior mage. Maya managed a mocking smile before she plunged directly through the flames and into the open pit.

Excruciating heat swept over her, singeing her hair and charring her flesh. It wasn't just fire, it was magically enhanced flames that clung to her even after she was through the tornado and plunging downward. Only years of training allowed her to ignore the pain and tap into the magic that she'd stored in the emerald around her neck. Instantly the power blasted through her veins. Unless she could block the flames, her attempt to play hero was going to get her killed along with Ravyr.

Maya didn't bother to try to conjure a spell. Right now she needed raw magic, not a complex incantation.

As she hoped, the blast of energy pushed back the flames, temporarily driving them backward. At the same time, it smashed into the walls of the pit, shattering the cement as well as the thick foundation of the house.

An avalanche of cement and rock and thick earth collapsed over the top of the pit, sealing away the flames. It didn't stop there, of course. There was no time to create a protective shield, so the landslide slammed into Maya with a brutal force as she plunged downward.

A particularly sharp shard of cement sliced through her temple, carving a deep wound and thankfully knocking her unconscious. She didn't want to be awake when she hit the bottom.

Lost in the thick darkness, Maya dreamed that she didn't smash into the cement floor. Instead, she was caught in strong arms that held her tight against a broad chest.

With a sigh, she relaxed in the strong grasp, sheltered from the rubble that continued to rain from above. It was nice, she decided. She never allowed herself to depend on another creature to protect her. Not ever. But for once she didn't try to fight against her dreams. Instead, she allowed herself to float in the oblivion.

It was impossible to know how much time passed—maybe a second, maybe an hour—but her sense of peace was shattered as a scream pierced the darkness.

Maya's heart struggled to beat, as if it was being squeezed in a vise. She recognized that scream. And the last time she'd heard it. Desperately she tried to wake herself even as the darkness faded and she was transported to the cavern beneath Batu's lair.

This isn't real, this isn't real, this isn't real...

She repeated the mantra over and over, but it did nothing to lessen the sensation of running through the shadowed tunnel, desperate to reach the source of the screams. She wasn't in control of the dream or vision or whatever the hell was happening. She was reliving the past, whether she wanted to or not.

Reaching the end of the tunnel, Maya slammed into the thick webs that protected the entrance to the chamber beneath Batu's private rooms. The shimmering barrier was created out of a strange combination of demon and human magic, interwoven so tightly that no one could unravel the strands. And Maya had tried. On more than one occasion.

She'd always known that the secret to Batu's power was hidden in that secret room. But it'd been impossible to penetrate the wards.

The sounds of the screams intensified and Maya stepped back, adrenaline thumping through her body. She had to do something. Closing her eyes, she grasped her magic and wrenched it into a ball of fury. Before she could consider the consequences of what she was about to do, she smashed it through the shiny strands. The barrier quivered, visibly attempting to remain intact despite the blast of power. There was a high-pitched squeal that blended with the continuing screams; then with a force that shook the ground, the barrier shattered into a thousand pieces.

Maya didn't wait for the air to clear before she was charging through the opening, discovering Batu standing in the center of the surprisingly small chamber. Kneeling in front of him was Tia, her head tilted back and her lips parted as she shrieked in pain. Horror swept over Maya as she watched the magic being drained from her friend. She could see the shimmering waves being sucked out of the trembling mage, the pull so intense it was draining the color from her long brown hair, leaving it a pale silver.

"Tia," she breathed, her voice barely above a whisper.

It was enough, of course, to attract the attention of Batu. Swiveling his head in her direction, Batu glared at her with eyes that glowed with a jaundiced fire, as if he was feeding off the magic like other leeches fed off blood. Maya didn't know if he actually absorbed the magic, or how he managed to use it to gain power, but he'd been draining Tia and her for over a century.

Never like this.

They were two of the most powerful mages in the world. They were too valuable to destroy. But something had obviously caused the vampire to snap. There was death etched on his pale face.

"Get out," he snarled.

Every instinct told her to flee. The vampire was too strong for her to battle alone, not to mention the fact that it was a death sentence to kill a member of the Cabal. It would be suicide to interfere, but she couldn't force herself to turn around and walk away.

Enough was enough.

Reaching beneath her robe, Maya pulled out the tiny vial she'd kept hidden for decades. Batu allowed them to use spells when he needed their magic to create illusions and barriers to keep out the local humans. Or to punish his demon servants. But he refused to allow them to brew potions. Decades ago, Maya taken the risk of creating one vial, accepting that one day she would be driven to the point of no return.

Either she was going to kill Batu, or she was going to die in the attempt.

The yellow eyes narrowed as the vampire caught sight of the potion in her hand, but it wasn't concern that twisted his thin features. It was a sadistic humor.

"You want a fight?" He parted his mouth, his fangs gleaming in the glow from the stone that was buried in the center of the dirt floor. "Go ahead. I dare you."

Maya... The sound of Tia's voice whispered through her mind.

"No, it's over," Maya muttered, the endless years of torment and fear colliding together and creating a nuclear fission that exploded with a force she couldn't control. "I can't stand this another day."

She raised her arm, and Batu laughed, blatantly taunting her pathetic attempt to destroy him. Aiming at his smug face, Maya was distracted when Tia's voice once again echoed through her brain.

Toward me.

Her arm was already snapping forward, but twisting herself to the side, she managed to launch the vial toward the kneeling mage. Batu watched in confusion as it sailed harmlessly past him, no doubt assuming she'd lost her nerve for a direct confrontation.

It wasn't until the vial had whizzed past his face that Tia jerked her hands up, using the last of her strength to gain command of the magic being steadily drained from her and squeezing it to a thin strand. Then, whipping it upward like a lasso, she used it to place the vial high above the vampire's head before she shattered the glass.

In perfect position, the potion poured down to cover Batu in a sticky green acid that smoked and sizzled as it seared into his flesh. He bellowed in pain, the stench of burning flesh tainting the air.

The lethal potion would have melted any other creature into a puddle of goo, but leeches were capable of healing everything but flames and sunlight. Or wounds that refused to heal. Which was the extra layer of magic that Maya had placed in the potion.

"Now!" Tia screeched as her own magic failed and she collapsed at the vampire's feet.

Tia was right. It was now or never. Maya ground her teeth, concentrating fiercely on the male who was desperately attempting to wipe off the clinging sludge. Flooding the potion with her magic, she tapped into the spell that she'd brewed into the mixture. A glow surrounded Batu and the potion thickened, hardening into an unbreakable shell.

Batu hissed, his nails furiously attempting to dig through the potion that continued to sear deep into his flesh.

"Stop, you bitch," he roared, stumbling forward as he tried to get close enough to physically punish her.

Maya wasn't done. Standing her ground, she lifted her arm and sent a jolt of power toward Batu's unbeating heart. He flinched but continued forward, blinded by the potion that smoked and smoldered as the acid ate through his flesh. Maya made a strangled sound of fury, sending another bolt of power followed by another and another....

Batu at last tumbled to his knees, but he refused to die despite Maya's fierce efforts. She couldn't fail, she told herself. She was going to send Batu to hell, even if it meant she joined him in the fiery depths.

Trembling with exhaustion, Maya continued to pour her magic into the potion, knowing that she was dangerously close to a fatal collapse. She could feel it in the agonizing heat that was spreading over her face, destroying her skin as it consumed her flesh to continue drawing power. She had to stop or she was going to burn herself out. Literally.

With a last blast, she had the satisfaction of watching Batu slump onto the hard ground, his skin turning gray as death claimed him.

It was at this point that the dream always fragmented. She'd passed out just seconds after Batu died, and hadn't awakened for nearly a week. By that point she'd been safely hidden in a hut with Tia, who was tending to the deep scars on her face.

This time her dream didn't fade to dark. Instead, she floated on a wave of excruciating pain, choking on the gagging stench of seared flesh. Not just Batu as he was consumed by her magic, but her own charred skin that had been the cost of success. She thought she heard running footsteps and then a muttered conversation before the sense of Batu disappeared. In her dream state she assumed the demons who'd sworn allegiance to the vampire had rushed in to scoop up his ashes, but she couldn't open her eyes.

Then, icy fingers touched the side of her face and the pain eased, as if she was being healed. Moments later, she was lifted off the ground and cradled in strong arms. It wasn't Tia. Or even a demon who might owe her a favor.

It was a vampire.

She cracked open her eyes.

Ravyr...

The darkness crashed over her with enough force to drag her under, shattering the memories and allowing her the peace she'd craved.

She didn't know how much time had passed when the sensation of strong arms cradling her against a hard body penetrated her exhaustion. It'd been years since she'd spent the night with a man. And never had his cool touch sent shivers of pleasure through her.

Slowly she opened her eyes, already prepared to discover Ravyr holding her tight against his body. But even prepared, she gasped at the impact of being up close and personal to his raw beauty. His stunning turquoise eyes with their shimmering silver rims. The features that were crafted with a hint of savage resolve. Even the lethal fangs visible between his parted lips sent tingles of excitement racing through her blood. Which was insane.

She'd seen Batu rip out countless throats with his teeth. Or drain the poor fey females who were forced to feed his perverted hungers. The sight of the fangs should have made her nauseous. Instead, her breath locked in her lungs and her body instinctively arched to press against the chiseled muscles. As if she was eager to feel the sharp stab of Ravyr's bite.

His hands pressed against her back, his eyes darkening as the scent of her awareness perfumed the air.

"It was you," she breathed, her brain still fuzzy from her lingering dream. Or maybe it was fuzzy because she'd landed on her head and cracked her skull.

That would explain so much.

His brows arched as a slow, sexy smile curved his lips. "Probably. What did I do?"

"You were the one who carried me out of Batu's lair."

His smile faded, his expression suddenly impossible to read.

"Yes," he slowly admitted.

"Why?"

"Because I couldn't bear to live in a world where you didn't exist."

I couldn't bear to live in a world where you didn't exist...

The simple words shook her to the core.

They echoed the darkness that had lurked deep in her soul since she'd discovered that Batu's lair had been destroyed and Ravyr was missing. A part of her had been mourning his loss for over forty years, even if she refused to acknowledge her pain.

"And Tia?" she asked, not sure what was unnerving her the most. The fact that Ravyr had been the one to rescue her from Batu's lair? Or that she'd been grieving for his supposed death at the same time she'd sworn she hated vampires? Or that her body continued to sizzle with a desire that was becoming increasingly difficult to ignore?

He grimaced. "If I'd left her behind there would have been questions of how Batu was killed. It was easier to get rid of both of you while I waited for the staff to flee and I could split open the lair as if there'd been an unfortunate earthquake that had exposed Batu to sunlight."

"Wait." She stared at him in disbelief. When she'd returned to Cambodia twenty years ago she'd discovered the soaring stone temple that had stood for thousands of years had been turned into a pile of rubble and covered in a thick layer of foliage. She'd assumed that human looters had caused the damage. "You destroyed the lair?"

"A few well-placed explosives did the work," he admitted.

A surge of anger washed over her. How often had she dreamed of blasting the hellhole into oblivion? Or sending it up in flames?

"I wish you would have done that the first night you arrived," she muttered.

His hands smoothed up the curve of her spine, his cool touch setting off sparks of pleasure. "Me too," he said, his jaw tightening at the edge of accusation in her voice. "Why didn't you leave? You might have been a prisoner, but he couldn't have kept you hostage if you truly wanted to escape."

Her anger was abruptly replaced with smoldering regret. "You're right. I could have blasted my way past the guards the minute Batu was distracted."

"What stopped you?"

"He told me that he would destroy my family if I tried to leave the lair without his permission." A humorless laugh was wrenched from her throat. "It didn't matter that it was my own mother who'd offered me to Batu in exchange for a large sum of money that she used to move herself and my siblings far away from Cambodia."

"She was a witch."

The words were a statement, not a question. Only a witch could give birth to a daughter who had the potential to become a mage. Most of them were horrified when they discovered that their child possessed wild magic in their blood, convinced that it was mages who'd caused the various witch hunts over the centuries. Other mothers were savvy enough to try to profit off their daughters. No doubt Batu had sensed the moment Maya's magic had manifested and approached her mother with his generous offer. And while her family wouldn't have recognized that he was a vampire, they had to have suspected there was something wrong with a man wanting to buy a sixteen-year-old girl.

"She was the local healer," Maya said, her voice not quite steady. "And I worshipped the ground she walked on. Even after my father died, she managed to keep a roof over our heads and food on the table along with tending to the needs of our village. I couldn't believe she would betray me like that."

His jaw tightened, as if her words troubled him, but his touch was light as he slid his fingers under her hair to massage her tense nape.

"Fear will drive even good people to do desperate things," he murmured. "Especially humans."

Maya forced her clenched muscles to relax. A part of her understood that her mother had been doing what she thought was best for her other children. Maya's wild magic had ignited during the middle of a Water Festival, the power sizzling out of her with enough force to flatten the nearby dam and allow the flooded river to gush through the streets of the village. The locals had called her a demon, and a few had whispered that she should be sacrificed to cleanse the evil.

Still, she'd assumed her family would stand by her.

That was why it'd hurt so much when she'd been handed over by her mother and locked in Batu's lair.

Maya shook away the painful memories. "It was difficult to accept what my mother had done, but my brothers and sisters were innocent. I couldn't let them be hurt because I'd been exposed as a mage. Besides, I'd decided just days after being imprisoned that I wasn't leaving until I could destroy Batu. It became my only reason for surviving."

Ravyr slowly nodded, as if he understood her obsessive hunger for revenge, but thankfully he sensed her reluctance to dwell on the darkness.

He sidetracked the conversation. "Now it's my turn to ask the question. Why?"

"Why what?"

"Why did you risk your life to protect me?"

Maya swallowed a sigh. Talk about going from the frying pan to the fire. This was the last conversation she wanted to have. Or, at least, the second last.

"You're the only one who can sense the magic if it leaves New York," she pointed out.

His fingers traced the line of her jaw, deliberately emphasizing the stubborn angle. "And that's the only reason?"

"What else could there be?" Her tone was dismissive, but the sharp tremor that raced through her body ruined her pretense of indifference.

His eyes smoldered with turquoise fire. "We've both tried to deny the awareness, but it's always been there." He lowered his head, pressing a light kiss on her parted lips. "From the very beginning."

It was nothing more than the sweep of their mouths together. A barely there caress. But there was nothing "barely there" about the shock waves of hunger that swept through her. They clenched her stomach into a tight knot and jolted her heart into overdrive.

Instinctively she lifted her hands to press them against his chest. Her desire for this male was alarming. "Don't flatter yourself."

He chuckled at her ridiculous words. "You know I can smell your desire?"

Of course he could. As if her flushed cheeks and racing pulse weren't enough to reveal her urge to climb into his lap and wrap herself around him.

"I also desire cheesecake and double espresso shots, but I know they're bad for me."

The tips of his fangs pressed against her lower lip. Not hard enough to break the skin, but enough to assure her that his bite would bring nothing but bliss.

"It's good to be bad," he said quietly.

Her fingers splayed over the hard width of his chest, forgetting to shove him away. Maybe because she was preoccupied by the sensation of his muscles rippling beneath her palms. "Good to be bad?" She rolled her eyes. "Seriously?"

"I've never been more serious." His fangs skated over her cheek and down the curve of her neck. They hovered over her thumping pulse as if battling the need to sink deep to taste her blood. Her nails dug into his chest. Protest or invitation?

She wasn't sure. Obviously, neither was Ravyr. With a harsh groan he lifted his head to stare down at her with a passion that he clearly struggled to leash.

Minutes ticked past as the turquoise fire burned in his eyes and his fangs shimmered with lethal promise. Then, a shudder shook his body, signaling him regaining command of his hunger.

Maya felt a distinct pang of regret.

She detested those stories about damsels in distress being ravished by their saviors, and the damsels somehow enjoying the ravishing. She'd been confident that she would shrivel up the dangly bits of any male stupid enough to try to treat her like anything but a competent, independent woman.

Now, she couldn't deny a treacherous wish that Ravyr would have rolled her onto her back and covered her with his hard form. And even ripped off her clothes so she could feel the cool touch of his fingers against her bare skin.

Ravyr's nostrils flared, as if he was drawing in the scent of her desire, but his touch was gentle as he cupped her cheek in his hand. "I wish I could change the past."

Maya's lips parted to agree, but her words dried on her tongue. There was nothing about Batu's imprisonment that hadn't been sheer torture, but a part of her accepted that her time in his lair had forged her into a powerful mage who could overcome any obstacle. And without Batu, she would never have encountered Ravyr.

A thought that was strangely unbearable.

"All we can do is try to change the future," she said.

His gaze lowered to linger on her lips as his thumb stroked over her cheek. "Together?"

"For now," she warily agreed.

"I'll take that."

She trembled as his thumb deliberately skimmed over the scars that most men tried to avoid. Abruptly she remembered her dream, and the cool touch that eased the agonizing pain as she was carried out of Batu's lair.

"You healed my face," she breathed.

"I did what I could," he admitted, continuing to caress the rough skin. "The burn came from inside."

"My magic nearly consumed me when I battled Batu."

A distant echo of the pain pulsed through her cheek as she remembered waking in a hut with her flesh still raw and oozing. Tia had been there with her herbs and potions, implying that she'd been the one to rescue her from the lair and begin the healing of her face. The older woman had also implied that she was now in her debt.

It had been the beginning of the end for their friendship.

"Have you fully recovered?" Ravyr asked, his fingers moving to tuck her hair behind her ear.

"Physically." Her hands stroked over his chest; she felt like she needed the reassurance of his solid body to confront her deepest fear. "Batu haunts me. I've tried to tell myself it's because I was so young and impressionable when he captured me that it was inevitable I would be scarred. But now..."

Her words trailed away. She couldn't force them past her stiff lips.

Ravyr wrapped his arms back around her body, tugging her close as if he sensed her need to be protected. Even if it was from her own nightmares.

"If Batu survived, we're going to track him down and destroy him," he assured her in grim tones.

Maya didn't doubt that Ravyr had every intention of discovering who was causing the strange pulses of magic, even if it meant exposing Batu. But the ultimate decision of what happened after they discovered the truth would be made by the Cabal. And more specifically, by Sinjon.

It was a fact she would be a fool to forget. Even if she did allow him to sate the hunger he'd stirred to a fever pitch.

"*If* we can find him," she reminded him.

"It's only a matter of time." Ravyr didn't seem insulted by her lack of faith in his hunting skills. Like all leeches, he possessed an arrogant, unshakable confidence. "Did you recognize the mage?"

Maya shook her head. She'd used the demons' intense focus on Ravyr when they'd entered the Yalick estate to concentrate on the mage. She'd been young, only a few years older than Courtney, but far more powerful. Magic had pulsed in the air with an open challenge. As if she actually thought she could intimidate Maya. Amateurish theatrics.

A skilled mage never allowed their opponent to sense the level of their magic.

"No, I've never seen her before."

"She looked like she held a personal grudge against you," Ravyr said, stating the obvious.

"It seems to be a trend," Maya retorted, genuinely miffed. She'd accepted that she would always have enemies. Her line of business meant she was constantly pissing off one demon or another. But she didn't expect such animosity from fellow mages. "I don't know why. I'm a very friendly person."

His lips curved into a smile that set off scorching zings of anticipation. "*I* like you, if that counts."

Her pulse raced, but she refused to be distracted. "I don't recognize her, but she thankfully wasn't trained by Tia."

"How do you know?"

"She doesn't mask her magic."

"I'm not sure what that means."

"A mage who has more power than the minimum will leave behind a trail of magic."

He studied her in confusion. "You mean their scent?"

Maya wasn't surprised he'd never heard of that particular weakness. Mages were like leeches and demons and even the slumbering dragons. They hid anything that might make them vulnerable.

"Not a scent, but a visible shimmer of magic that lingers in the air. And depending on the strength of the mage, it can remain for days. Sometimes weeks."

He didn't ask why he couldn't see the trail. Only another mage could detect the magic. *And Joe,* she silently acknowledged. He had abilities he shouldn't possess.

"I assume you can mask yours?"

"Only with an iron control that took years to perfect," she said, battling the urge to grimace.

She would never forget the endless hours Tia forced her to build layer after painful layer to shield her power, only to shatter it with a burst of magic and insist she rebuild it until it could hold against the most vicious attack. At the time, she'd been willing to endure the agonizing training—even if she wanted to pin Tia to the wall and pummel her. It wasn't until later that she realized the older mage had her own agenda. And it had nothing to do with any concern for Maya.

"That iron control is impressive, but it's also intimidating." Ravyr's gaze swept over her face with a slow intensity, as if he was memorizing each feature before lingering on her mouth. "Do you ever let your guard down?"

She allowed her gaze to do an equally intense survey of his face, although she didn't need to memorize anything. Every line and curve had been seared into her brain decades ago.

"Do you?" she challenged.

"Touché." His smile was wry. "I've had to develop a hard shell over the centuries."

"The lone wolf syndrome?"

He parted his lips to reveal his massive fangs, as if insulted by the question. "Never a wolf."

"More like a snake in the grass?"

"Sometimes," he surprisingly agreed. "Being an ambassador to Sinjon has meant making hard choices and ignoring my own desires. I told myself I was serving a higher purpose."

Maya arched her brows. "Higher purpose?"

"Okay. That sounded..."

"Unbearably pompous?" she helpfully supplied.

His fingers glided over her brow, his expression impossible to read. "You're right. It does sound obnoxiously conceited, but I wanted to feel like I was making a difference in the lives of my people."

Something melted inside Maya, destroying yet another layer of hatred she'd built over the years.

"I get that," she breathed.

His fingers skimmed down the side of her face, lingering to caress the spiderweb of scars.

"But I'm discovering that the ends don't always justify the means."

Maya sucked in a sharp breath. The lust scorching through wasn't a surprise. Even when she wanted to stick a stake in this male's heart, she found him sexy as hell. Who wouldn't? The brutally handsome face. The short hair that shimmered like silver even in the darkness. The outrageously exotic turquoise eyes. And the hard, muscular body she'd dreamed of stripping naked to lick from head to toe. But the tenderness tugging at her heart?

That was a whole different danger.

"Where are we?" She determinedly turned the conversation to their current situation.

He paused, as if reluctant to follow her lead. Then, with a last brush of his fingers against her cheek, he settled his back against the dirt wall and tugged her even tighter.

"In a tunnel beneath the Yalick estate," he revealed. "I think it will eventually lead to their hidden drug lab."

Maya wrinkled her nose, belatedly noticing the sulfurous stench that wafted through the air.

"That's what I smell." She tried to determine if there was anyone nearby. Unfortunately, she didn't have the über skills of a vampire. All she could sense was the weight of the house above them and a looming emptiness in the tunnel. "Why are we waiting to leave?"

"It's close to dawn and I have no idea if there are enemies waiting to attack once we find an exit." His head tilted to press his cheek against the top of her head. "We both need some time to recover."

She didn't even consider arguing. Every muscle in her body felt like a wet noodle, and there was a dull ache at the base of her skull that warned that she'd drained her magic to a dangerous level.

"Agreed," she conceded with a deep sigh.

"Rest," he murmured, the cool brush of his power wrapping around her in a protective barrier. "We'll return to our hunt once the sun sets."

Chapter 10

Tia waited until darkness shrouded the busy neighborhood and the streets emptied of traffic before she approached the coffee shop. She'd arrived in New York hours ago, but after settling into the elegant apartment her staff had arranged, she'd taken time to brew a new batch of potions. It wasn't often she spent an extended amount of time in a Gyre—especially one this powerful—and she fully intended to take advantage of the extra magic.

She was a woman who *always* took advantage.

Life had taught her that if she wasn't on top, she was on the bottom. And she was never going to be on the bottom again.

Stepping out of an alley, Tia walked to stand directly in front of the glass door of the small coffee shop. *The Witch's Brew.* Tia rolled her eyes. Everything about the place was chintzy. From the coffee cup in the center of the witch's hat on the neon sign. To the windows that were painted with Easter Bunnies. Breathing a soft incantation, Tia released a burst of magic that sliced through Maya's layers of protection before crushing the lock. It didn't matter that she was destroying property and breaking several laws. She wanted inside, that's all that mattered.

Pushing open the door, she closed it behind her before turning in a slow circle. The inside was just as chintzy as the outside with gleaming white tiles and frilly dollies on the tables. The sort of place for a basic human, not a mage with extraordinary powers.

With a shake of her head, Tia moved into the attached bookstore, pausing to absorb the peaceful atmosphere. There weren't any spell books on the shelves, but there was some sort of magic drifting in the air. It brushed against her with a delicate urge to sit and relax.

Once she accepted that there was nothing of value in the room, she moved toward the office. She'd kept a close watch on the shop for the past two hours, making sure that Maya was gone. She wanted to discover what Maya had unearthed about Batu and his potential return to life without enduring a face-to-face conversation. The stubborn mage would withhold the information just to be a pain in the ass.

Skirting past the long table in the center of the room, Tia was a few feet from the private office when she abruptly spun around, her gaze darting from side to side.

There was nothing to see beyond the shadowed outline of bookshelves and large, cushioned chairs set near the table, but Tia wasn't fooled. There was someone lurking in the darkness.

"Who's there?" she demanded, more annoyed than frightened. She was in a hurry. She didn't have time to be interrupted.

"Jinx," a male voice responded. "I was going to ask you the same question."

Tia slid her hand into the pocket of her Burberry jacket that she'd matched with a pencil skirt and three-inch heels. She'd filled a dozen round vials no bigger than pearls with a variety of potent potions. They weren't designed to kill, but they would make any attacker very sorry they'd chosen her as a potential victim.

"Show yourself."

She sensed rather than heard the approach of the intruder, and, moving until her back was pressed against the wall, she reached out to switch on the overhead lights. Instantly a soft glow spread through the room, revealing the short, oddly dressed male with a hat shoved down to his eyes and his face hidden behind a thick beard.

He looked like a garden gnome wrapped in a velour sweatsuit.

"Go away," she commanded, assuming he was a homeless person who'd followed her into the shop.

"Jinx," he said.

"Jinx?" She scowled. That was the second time he'd used that word. "Is that your name?"

"Name?" He clicked his tongue, continuing toward her until he was standing just a foot away. A tremor shook beneath her feet. An earthquake in Jersey? Odd. "My name is Joe," he chastised.

"So why do you keep saying Jinx?"

"Don't you know anything? You say 'jinx' when you both say the same thing. Although it's usually at the same time or something—"

"Shut up," she interrupted.

"You shut up."

"Seriously, stop talking," she hissed between clenched teeth. "You don't want to piss me off."

"Why not?"

Tia forced herself to count to ten. She didn't want to hurt him. Not when she suspected he struggled with his mental health. She might be the bad guy, but she didn't abuse the defenseless victims of the world.

"Unfortunate things happen when I'm mad," she ground out.

Joe tilted his head to the side. "Like what?"

Tia allowed her magic to tingle through her blood. She didn't have to physically hurt him to drive him away. Lifting her hand, she was preparing to launch her spell when her magic abruptly faltered, her breath tangling in her throat. The male in front of her was no longer an annoying pest. He might look the same, but a fierce emerald fire burned in his eyes and the tremors beneath her feet buckled the floorboards and sent several books flying from the shelves.

It was a blatant warning not to use her magic.

"You're not human?" she breathed, trying to determine what he was.

The creature shrugged. "Neither are you."

She ignored his accusation. "Not vampire. Demon?"

He sniffed, as if offended by her question. "There are no words to describe me."

She narrowed her gaze. "Oh, I can think of a few."

Joe smiled, the air scented with...what? Power. That's the only way she could describe the sharp, painfully crisp odor. Power at its most raw and basic form.

"Feisty," he murmured.

Tia battled against her strange urge to cower from the stranger. She'd faced down murderous humans, feral demons, and the Cabal. She wasn't going to bend her knee now.

"Did you just call me feisty?"

"Hmm. Let me think." The creature had the audacity to stroke his beard, as if in deep thought. "Yes. Yes, I rather think I did."

"You." Tia wrapped her fingers around a potion bead in her pocket. She was going to singe that beard off his face. Then they would see who was laughing.

"Enough playing." Joe abruptly interrupted her angry thoughts, stepping so close she could feel the heat pulsing off his body. "Why are you here?"

Her lips parted to tell him to go to hell when she was captured by his emerald gaze. Suddenly the room disappeared and there was nothing but her companion and the need to offer him the information he wanted.

"I'm looking for Maya."

"Why?"

She licked her lips, struggling against the compulsion to answer his questions. "What do you care?"

"She's under my protection."

Tia released a humorless laugh. Only Maya would have this mysterious, insanely powerful creature as her personal protector.

"Of course she's under your protection."

The male arched his shaggy brows. "You sound jealous."

"I'm not jealous, I'm...annoyed." The words were wrenched from the deepest, darkest part of her soul. Words she would rather cut her tongue out than admit. "Precious Maya was too valuable to be sacrificed by Batu, but he had no hesitation in trying to destroy me. And naturally she had to be rescued by Ravyr, who would have happily left me to rot in that hellish lair if he hadn't been protecting his beloved woman. Then she manages to stumble across two of the most powerful mages to walk the earth in centuries, and instead of using their devotion to challenge the Cabal, she hides herself in a cheap coffee shop."

Joe pursed his lips, glancing around the bookstore. "It's not really cheap. You should see what she spends on those fancy little napkins and hand-painted teacups. Then there are the trips to buy her coffee beans—"

"What have you done to me?" Tia furiously interrupted the ridiculous babbling. As if she cared what Maya spent on teacups.

"Nothing." There was a deliberate pause. "Yet."

Tia didn't believe him. Not for a second. "You forced me to say those things."

"I only did what was needed," he assured her. "My grandmother would tell you that bitterness is better out than in. It eats away your soul. Plus, it gives you heartburn."

"There's no way you have a grandmother," she snapped. "You crawled from beneath a rock."

Joe shrugged. "Busted."

Tia pulled her hand out of her pocket. The urge to toss a few potions at the aggravating creature was overwhelming, but she hadn't survived for centuries by being impulsive. "What do you want from me?" she instead demanded.

"Tell me why you're here."

She answered before he could force her. "I had a dream. Maya's enemy is still alive."

Joe muttered something under his breath. Words that Tia had never heard before. Then, without warning, he stepped forward and placed his palm against her forehead. "Let me see."

"Stop."

She lifted her hands, pressing them against his chest as she tried to shove him away. A mistake. As soon as she touched the velour jacket, she was sucked into a silvery mist that was bright enough to hurt her eyes. It was impossible to determine where she was; the only thing she could see was the towering form in front of her. She blinked, clearing her fuzzy vision to study the angular face that was framed by long, coppery hair that shimmered in the strange glow.

A choked sound of disbelief was wrenched from her throat as she tried to accept the blinding perfection of the male. He was gorgeous. Fairy-tale gorgeous with elegant features and bronzed skin so smooth it couldn't be real.

It wasn't until she concentrated on the stunning beauty of his emerald eyes that she was struck with the mind-numbing realization that she knew this male.

Joe. It was Joe.

Seemingly unaware that he'd wrenched her into this strange, misty bubble out of reality, the male abruptly dropped his hand, his expression grim as a thunderous power smashed into Tia, nearly driving her to her knees.

It wasn't the icy pulse of a vampire. Or the blunt force of a demon. This seemed to well from beneath her feet. Like lava erupting out of a volcano.

"This can't be allowed to happen," he growled, turning away to disappear into the mist.

Tia watched in dumbfounded bewilderment, her hand reaching out as if she could stop him. Then, still struggling to wrap her brain around what was happening, the mist swirled and there was a weird popping sound. A second later she was once again in the bookstore. Tia slammed her back against the wall to keep her balance, gasping for air as if she'd been holding her breath.

"What. The. Hell."

Chapter 11

Ravyr gently cradled Maya in his arms long past the time he should have wakened her. He understood the urgency of their mission. And that each tick of the clock meant that the mage had an opportunity to slip further away. But he'd spent endless centuries alone.

Achingly, profoundly alone.

Mostly by choice, but also circumstance.

Who could blame him for wanting to savor the feel of her warm body pressed against him for a few extra minutes?

He was softly stroking his fingers up and down the curve of her spine when Maya began to stir, her long lashes fluttering open to study him with a fuzzy confusion. A full minute passed before she appeared to recall why she was lying in a dark tunnel wrapped in his arms. And another minute to battle back her surge of annoyance.

Obviously she was trying to accept the fact that she'd fallen willingly asleep in his arms. A week ago she would have walked through the pits of hell to avoid his touch.

Clearing her throat, she pushed herself into a sitting position and shoved her hair from her face. "Has the sun set?"

"Yes." He studied the elegant sweep of her features. She appeared rested but there were shadows beneath her eyes. "Are you fully recovered?"

"I'm ready."

"That's not an answer."

She planted her hands on the ground and shoved herself upright. Then, with brisk movements, she brushed off the clinging dust. "That's the only one I have."

Ravyr rose to join her, not bothering to argue. Neither of them were 100 percent. He needed to feed to regain his full strength, and Maya had drained an enormous amount of magic. It would take her days to be ready for round two with the mage.

Unfortunately they didn't have days.

"Fair enough," he murmured, taking the lead as he headed down the tunnel. It wasn't that he had to be in charge, but he was able to absorb a magical attack, giving Maya time to fight back.

They were nearing the end of the tunnel when the scent of goblins filled the air.

"Ravyr," Maya whispered.

"I smell them," he assured her, halting beneath the opening carved in the stone ceiling.

He paused, absorbing the scents of the demons. Three males and two females. He felt a stab of surprise. The whole gang was gathered in the building above them.

Maya moved close enough to press against his arm, her head tilted back toward the light that filtered through the iron grate. "Is there another way out of here?" she asked.

"No. This is the only exit." He reached up to lace his fingers through the grate. "Besides, I want to have a word with the Yalicks."

"Now?"

"They might not be responsible for the explosion, but they have information about the demon who paid Hexx to plant the bomb."

She slowly nodded. "And the mage."

Careful to avoid scraping the iron against the cement floor, Ravyr cleared the opening and reached out his hand. Maya grabbed his shoulder before lifting her leg toward him. He wrapped his fingers around her foot, and with one smooth shove he had her launched through the opening. Magic tingled through the air as she whispered a hasty spell that would disguise their presence. Ravyr jumped up behind her, his gaze sweeping the room.

It was a long, open space, with a vaulted ceiling that was cut by a dozen ventilation vents, and a smooth cement floor. It was built separate from the main estate, and from outside it no doubt looked like a detached garage with three bay doors that were currently closed and no windows.

But inside it was lined with wooden tables that were carved with hexes and sparkled with dragon dust in the overhead lights.

The dragon scale lab.

His attention turned to the back of the room where the demons were stacking heavy steel boxes onto a wheeled dolly.

"Hurry up, you fools," the eldest male snapped, still wearing his expensive black suit, although it was wrinkled and covered in dirt as if he'd spent the day hiding in the dark tunnels. And he probably had. But like a rat, he'd crept out of his hidey hole to try to salvage what was left of his empire. "We have to get this stuff loaded on the van within the hour."

"An hour?" The daughter whirled to face her father. Her long brown hair was disheveled and her gown had lost its sparkle. "I still have to shower and pack my clothes and—"

"We leave within the hour," her father interrupted. "With or without you."

The boys muttered under their breath but they continued to stack boxes, their muscles bulging as if the things weighed a ton. And it was possible they did. Dragon scale was worth a fortune on the street. They wouldn't willingly leave behind a single ounce of powder.

Ravyr stepped out of the protective bubble of magic, folding his arms over his chest.

"In a rush?"

The five demons turned in perfect unison to glare at him in horror. Then, with a strange choreography, the younger twin males stepped back, their auras a dull glow. The sister, however, remained standing in place, her chin tilting to a defiant angle.

"You," the older male breathed, his face pale and doughy. Like bread that hadn't baked long enough. "I thought..."

"That I was dead?" Ravyr folded his arms over his chest. "That would have been unfortunate for both of us. Valen would most certainly come looking for you with uncomfortable questions. No doubt that's why you're so anxious to disappear."

"Disappear?" The demon forced a stiff smile to his lips. "Why would I do that? I didn't have anything to do with what happened in the city. I'm just a businessman."

Ravyr glanced toward the long table where the illegal dragon scales were crushed and turned into powder before being packaged for sale.

"You're a scale dealer." He curled his lips in disgust, revealing the tips of his fangs. "Which means that not only do you have to answer to Valen, but Sinjon is going to want to interview your entire clan."

"No, no." Yalick moved to stand in front of the dolly, as if he could hide the large boxes. "You have it all wrong."

"Do I?"

"Yes. I had no idea what was happening in here. This garage is for my favorite Lamborghinis that I had transported to my home in Florida last summer. Which is why I haven't been out here for months. I had no idea that Bastian and that mage...what's her name? Allie? No, Alison."

"The demon and mage who attacked us?" Ravyr asked, more interested in the names than the lies Yalick was desperately weaving.

"Exactly." The demon pounced on the opening to scapegoat his servants. "I've been searching for the renegades everywhere. I wanted to personally capture them so I could turn them over to the Cabal for a suitable punishment. It's the least I could do."

Maya snorted at the flimsy story, but Ravyr kept his gaze locked on the elder Yalick.

"And the dragon scale just magically appeared in your Lamborghini garage?"

The demon released a shaky laugh. "No, of course not. Bastian must have been using this place to store his illegal drugs. My family had no idea—"

"Enough," Ravyr snapped. "The Yalick dynasty is at an end. Whether or not any of you"—he swept his gaze over the gathered demons—"survive to pass along the family line is entirely dependent on the next few minutes. Do you understand?"

"This is absurd," the older male tried to bluster, only to cringe when his wife's sharp voice overrode him.

"Shut up, Gaylord."

"But—"

"Not another word." The older woman stepped forward, her aura flaring as if she kept it tightly muted. Not unusual in a demon household. The male's pride would demand that his shine brighter when they were in public. The aura, however, meant the woman was most certainly in charge of the family unit. She studied Ravyr with a resigned gaze. "I am Lady Ramona. What do you want from us?"

Ravyr didn't hesitate to switch his focus to the slender female who stood at rigid attention.

"Tell me what you know about Bastian."

"He's been with the clan for over a century. He's always been loyal and willing to do whatever my husband asks of him. I truly had no idea that he might be plotting to blow up a building. In fact, I can't imagine why he would do such a thing."

"There were no changes in his behavior over the past few months?"

She shrugged. "Not that I noticed."

"There were changes." The daughter abruptly moved to stand next to her mother, her own aura flaring brightly.

The Yalicks' power came from the females.

Which didn't make them any less dangerous.

Just the opposite.

"Once the mage moved into the house, he spent less time taking care of our business and more time running errands for her." The demon's voice was cold and edged with bitterness. Ravyr suspected that she was a spoiled brat who was used to every male in the vicinity worshipping at her feet. To have one of her minions distracted by another woman would be unacceptable. "Sometimes they would disappear together for the entire night."

"Where did they go?"

"I have no idea." She pursed her lips. "But he always had mud on his boots when he came back."

Ravyr tucked away the information, along with the knowledge that the younger demon kept a close eye on the demon. If she'd noticed anything that might get her family out of trouble, she would have shared it with him.

He switched his attention back to the Yalick matron. "Where did you find the mage?"

"She was recommended to me by my sister, who has a home in the Bronx. I should have suspected she would deliberately urge me to hire a treacherous bitch. She was always jealous of my position." Ramona clenched her hands into tight fists.

"Did Alison live at this estate?"

"Of course. All of our staff are expected to live here. They're no use to us if we can't depend on them to be around when we need them."

Maya muttered something about slave labor and arrogant bastards under her breath.

Ravyr didn't allow himself to be distracted. "Did you notice anything strange about her?" he asked.

Easily overhearing Maya's insults, Lord Yalick puffed out his chest, his doughy face reddening with outrage.

"She's a mage." He glared in Maya's direction. "Everything about her was strange. If you ask me, they're all more trouble than they're worth. Our ancestors had it right, burning them at the stake."

Magic trembled in the air, but before Maya could release the nasty curse that was no doubt poised on the tip of her tongue, Ravyr pointed a finger toward Ramona.

"Your mate's inability to control his tongue is going to be the death of your clan. We can start now if you want."

With a nonchalance that came from centuries of practice, Ramona moved toward her husband. He made a futile attempt to back away, but with one powerful swing of her arm she connected her fist with his chin, sending him flying through the air to land in an unconscious heap next to the dolly.

Once he was down for the count, she smoothed her hands down her gown and turned back to Ravyr. "Continue with your questions."

"Anyone notice the mage acting suspicious?" He glanced toward the two male demons, who blinked as if they weren't quite sure what was happening. Ravyr shook his head in disgust and returned his attention to the females. "Maybe meeting with strangers or having conversations on the phone she didn't want you to overhear?"

The daughter was the one to answer his question. "I don't know if it means anything, but I happened to notice her heading into the woods one night so I followed her."

"Why did you follow her?" Ravyr demanded. He didn't want the girl making up stories in the hopes he would offer her mercy.

He had none to give.

"She kept looking around like she was worried about being seen from the house. It seemed sketchy. I wanted to know what she was doing."

Ravyr believed her. The girl obviously was jealous of the mage. Plus, there would be the constant fear of the family business being discovered. All it would take would be one of their staff being bribed to expose their illegal activities and bring the empire crashing down.

"And?" he prompted. "Did you find out why she was in the woods?"

"Not really," the demon grudgingly admitted. "She had some sort of altar set up, but I don't know what she was doing out there. I assumed she was into some weird religion."

Ravyr was confused. He didn't know why a mage would have an altar. "Could she be using the area to brew her potions?"

"No, she insisted on having two hours alone in the kitchen every evening to cook up her disgusting concoctions," the elder female interjected, her expression sour. "My chef threatened to quit more than once. He claimed she left a disgusting mess when she was done."

Maya stepped forward, indicating she wanted to take command of the encounter. "Describe the altar," she insisted.

The girl shrugged. "There's not much to describe. All I could see was a big stump that was carved with a bunch of weird hexes and surrounded by candles. Oh, and there was a mirror leaning against a tree."

"A mirror?" Maya stared at the younger female with a frown. "You're sure?"

"It was impossible to miss," the demon insisted, glancing toward her twin brothers. "It was bigger than Claude's and his is six foot tall so he can gaze at himself with endless adoration."

One of the twins scowled, his face reddening with an embarrassed blush. "Shut your face."

"It's true."

Maya abruptly turned toward him, laying her hand on his arm as the younger demons squabbled over mirrors and who was more vain.

"I need to see the altar," she murmured softly.

"Now?"

"Now."

"Okay." Ravyr was ready to move on. The demons had given them the limited amount of information they possessed. It was time to track down Bastian and Alison. But first, he intended to make sure the Yalicks weren't stupid enough to think this was over for them. He swept his gaze over the five demons. "Try to leave this estate, and you will be branded as traitors and a bounty will be placed on your entire clan," he warned, his gaze locking on the matron. "Got it?"

She bowed her stiff neck, her expression pained. "Yes."

Grasping Maya's hand, he headed for the door at the end of the room. He'd call Valen as soon as they were off the estate. Once out of the garage, Ravyr allowed Maya to take the lead. She would be able to sense any concentration of magic in the area.

"Why are you interested in an altar?" he asked as she angled across the wide lawn toward the back of the estate.

"Mages will brew potions that are infused with their power or store excess magic in gems, but they don't have any need for altars," she explained in distracted tones, picking up the pace as if she was being drawn to a particular location. "Only witches call on mother earth to create spells."

The darkness crowded around them as they reached the edge of the nearby trees. It wasn't just the fact that they were miles from the nearest town, there was a magic shrouding the area as if hiding what was inside the woods.

"So she's a witch, not a mage?" Ravyr swiveled his head from side to side as they weaved their way through the trees. He couldn't detect anyone nearby, but the magic was screwing with his senses. A dampening spell. It would make it almost impossible to notice an approaching threat until it was too late.

"She's definitely a mage, but it's possible she's been using witch magic." Maya never slowed her pace despite the danger. Obviously she was more worried about the altar than any traps that might be lurking in the darkness.

"Why?" Ravyr was genuinely baffled. "Witch spells can't compete with the wild magic of mages. Your power comes directly from the source."

"Which means it can't be mutated. Its power can be used for good or bad, but it's raw energy. Like the wind. Or the waves of an ocean. They might be harnessed to do great things, but they can also destroy. The power doesn't make the choice. The user does."

"And a witch's spell?"

"It can be twisted and transformed into something evil at its basic level. Like infecting good cells with a disease. Unfortunately, it also corrupts the user."

Ravyr didn't fully understand, but if Maya was worried, then he was worried. "If you suspect that's what she's doing, shouldn't we be tracking down Alison before she can use the spell?"

Maya at last slowed, her hand reaching out as if searching for an invisible signal. "First I need to destroy the altar. If it remains in the woods it could fester and pollute the land. Or it could be used by a human witch who would have no concept of the dangers." She cocked her head to the side then abruptly turned to the south. "This way."

They walked in silence, their pace slow and cautious until they reached a circular opening. Standing in the deep darkness of the thick underbrush, Ravyr studied a wide stump that had been carved with strange symbols. They meant nothing to him, but he could detect that they'd been done in the past few weeks. The altar hadn't been in this location for very long. On top of the stump was a shallow copper bowl filled with water and painted with four faces that pointed in opposite directions. North, south, east, and west. There were also at least a dozen candles of various sizes. And just behind the stump was a cheval mirror in a sturdy oak stand. It didn't look special. It was oval and stood at least six foot, but beyond that it could have come from any human furniture store.

Surrounding the stump and mirror was a narrow circle that had been dug into the ground and filled with layers of salt.

"What is this for?" He at last broke the thick silence.

"I don't know. Maybe she was trying to summon something?" Maya furrowed her brow, clearly not satisfied with her conjecture. "Be careful. We don't want to trigger—"

Her words were cut short as a branch snapped, the sound echoing eerily through the opening. Ravyr released a low growl as he belatedly realized the demon had been skulking in the dark, his presence muted by the dampening spell. It was only dumb luck that he hadn't tripped over the creature. He silently chastised his failure to detect the danger.

As if realizing that he'd given away his location, the demon tossed aside any attempt at stealth and loudly crashed through the trees, heading deeper into the woods.

Ravyr stiffened, torn between the need to capture the bastard who'd tried to blow them to smithereens—twice—and the primitive instinct to remain with Maya and keep her safe.

It was Maya who made the decision for him. "You go after Bastian." Her expression was set in stubborn lines. "I'll deal with this altar and hunt down the mage."

"I don't want to leave you." He turned, wrapping his arms around her and tugging her until she fit against him with spectacular perfection. She tilted back her head, and his unbeating heart squeezed as his gaze traced the delicate beauty of her pale face and the deep pools of mystery in her eyes before moving to linger on the scars that ran the length of her jaw. The scars did nothing to mar her beauty, but they were a painful reminder of how close he'd come to losing her. "Not again."

Her expression softened, a tiny shiver racing through her. "I'll be fine." She laid her hands against his chest. "We have to stop Batu." She grimaced as his lips parted to insist they didn't know if it was her former master behind the deadly plot. "Or whoever is pretending to be him," she conceded.

Ravyr clenched his jaw, his fangs throbbing with a combination of fear, frustration, and razor-sharp desire. A potent mixture. But he hadn't survived over the long centuries by allowing his emotions to overshadow his common sense. Maya was right. It made sense for him to track down the demon while she dealt with the mage.

"Be careful." He lowered his head, pressing a hungry kiss against her lips. There were some emotions that logic couldn't control. Lust, passion, and the intoxicating suspicion this woman was destined to be his eternal mate. He lifted his head to gaze down at her with a brooding intensity. "If I lose you..."

He ended his sentence with another kiss, relishing the feel of her fingers digging into his chest as she shuddered in pleasure. At least he wasn't alone in his aching desire, he acknowledged, his body tensing with a gnawing need to fulfill the hunger pounding through him.

With a raw groan, he forced himself to lower his arms and spin away.

He would cling to the memory of her flushed face and passion-darkened eyes until he'd captured the damned demon and he could return to the woman who was destined to be his.

Chapter 12

Maya watched as Ravyr vanished into the darkness, her fingers lifting to touch her lips that were throbbing from his kiss. It took every ounce of willpower not to toss out a spell that would hold him in place so they could continue where he'd so abruptly left off.

In her mind she could vividly imagine leaving him bound in her magic as she stripped him naked and explored every hard inch of him, first with her lips, and then with her tongue. He would taste of raw power and masculine desire and she would glory in her ability to control him.

Was it wrong? Maybe. But she knew beyond a doubt that Ravyr would be a masterful lover. His passion would be all-consuming as he devoured her—not only her body, but her blood—before allowing her to soar into a glorious release. And while the anticipation of a good, hard banging made her heart thump and her palms sweaty, she wanted to have plenty of playtime before he took command.

Releasing a shaky breath, Maya forced away the delicious images clouding her mind and forced herself to concentrate on her surroundings. If the demon had been hiding nearby, there was a good chance the mage was lurking in the area. Either because she was using the dampening spell to hide her presence in the hopes that she could try another attack when Maya and Ravyr dug their way out of the tunnels, or, more likely, she was waiting for new orders from her boss.

Cautiously moving forward, Maya studied the altar, searching for some clue to reveal why it had been created. In the olden days, gullible humans assumed they could summon demons and control them inside the circle of protection. But no mage would ever believe such nonsense. Still, it was possible that Alison was trying to summon something else. The hope of acquiring mystical power wasn't just a human failing. And Alison would know she was no match for Maya in a head-to-head battle.

Busy tracing the glyphs carved into the stump, she was distracted by the soft tread of approaching footsteps.

Ah. Alison. Right on cue.

Covertly reaching into the satchel that had managed to survive the magical flames along with the fall to the bottom of the pit, Maya grabbed a vial. The younger mage wouldn't dare to approach unless she had a spell prepared to cast. The potion would extinguish the magic long enough for Maya to launch a counterspell.

"Why won't you die?" Alison ground out, and Maya felt the sizzles of heat arrowing in her direction.

"Better mages than you have tried." With a flick of her wrist she sent the vial sailing through the air, a hard smile curving her lips as it hit the invisible spell and shattered to create a green cloud of smoke. The magic fizzled to nothing more ominous than a brush of warm air as it swept past Maya. Her smile widened. "And failed."

Alison's jaw clenched as her spell missed its mark, but her expression was mocking as she strolled toward the altar.

"You mean Courtney?" She snapped her fingers, sparks dancing in the air as she released a burst of power. "Amateur."

Maya didn't bother to flaunt the magic pulsing through her blood. She'd survived horrors that the younger mage couldn't even imagine. She didn't have any need to prove her strength.

Besides, she wanted the other woman to wallow in her smug conceit. Overconfidence was the first step to defeat.

Maya held her ground next to the stump, silently weaving a protective web of magic around herself. For the moment she needed answers more than she needed to punish the arrogant bitch.

"Did you hire Courtney?"

"Unfortunately." Alison tossed her golden curls that were silky smooth in the moonlight. As if she'd recently taken the time to wash and condition her hair. She'd also pulled on a long black fur cape. Was she just vain? Or was she planning on meeting someone? Hopefully her employer. Maya was anxious to have a word with him. "All she had to do was lure you to the Slaughterhouse Club and make sure you couldn't escape. She couldn't even do that right."

Maya felt the magic settle over her, shimmering with a faint silver glow. "So you killed her?"

Alison strolled another few inches closer. "It was necessary. Plus I wanted to try out my new spell. Did you like it?"

Maya grimaced, recalling Courtney and her companion's bizarre decomposition. Once the mage was properly locked away, she intended to discover exactly what sort of spell she'd used.

"And the explosion that destroyed the house?"

"That was Bastian's work." Alison shrugged. "He's a useful tool."

"Why?"

"Why is he useful?" Alison widened her eyes, deliberately being as annoying as possible. Not that she needed to go above and beyond. Maya already wanted to throat punch her. "Oh, he has all sorts of useful talents. He's stronger than an ox. He's completely without morals. He's stupid enough to be easily convinced to do anything I ask. And he's a beast in the bedroom, which, honestly, is just a bonus."

Maya refused to take the bait. "Why did you have Courtney lure me to the Slaughterhouse?"

"Because I was offered a reward I couldn't resist."

"By who?"

"The Master, who else?"

Maya clenched her hands. She really was going to throat punch the bitch. "Batu?"

Alison's brows snapped together, clearly outraged at Maya's lack of respect. "The *Master*."

With a shrug, Maya dropped the issue. She wouldn't know who the mystery leader was until they were face-to-face. Until then it would be dangerous to leap to conclusions.

"If the Master wants me dead, then why send you? Why doesn't he personally get rid of me?"

Alison sniffed. "You aren't important enough for him to be bothered."

Him. So at least her assumption that it was a male was right.

"And what happens when he discovers you aren't up for the job?"

Alison's face flushed at the deliberate taunt. "I'd heard you were arrogant, but I hadn't realized you were stupid. I deliberately led you to this spot. Now you're going to die."

Maya's smile never faltered. "Really? Does that mean I finally get to meet this elusive master? Or is this just a chance to kick your ass?"

With a dramatic flourish, Alison tossed back her cape so she could lift her arm and point over Maya's shoulder.

"You want to meet him? He's waiting. Look."

"Right." Maya rolled her eyes. "Like I'm going to fall for that old trick."

"Maya."

Ice-cold horror blasted through Maya as a rough male voice whispered her name. She recognized that voice. It'd haunted her dreams for the past forty-five years.

Unable to halt the instinctive movement, she whirled around, fully expecting to discover Batu standing just behind her. All she could see, however, was the mirror shimmering with a weird silver mist. As if it was glowing from within.

Caught in the trauma of her past, Maya failed to sense the danger of the present as Alison abruptly charged forward and slammed her hands against Maya's back.

"Die, you bitch."

Although she was protected against magic, Maya had no defense against a direct physical attack. Stumbling forward, she swiveled her body in a desperate attempt to grab the nearby mage to prevent a painful fall. Her hand closed around the neckline of the cape, but the fur was too slick to hang on to and her fingers slipped away.

She did manage to snag a gold chain that the younger woman had hanging around her neck, but it snapped beneath the pressure. Instinctively she clutched the chain in her hand, tumbling in an awkward motion toward the nearby mirror.

Expecting a painful connection with the heavy wooden frame, or even the pain of shattered glass slicing into her skin, Maya was completely unprepared when she simply kept falling. Like Alice through the looking glass.

Only when she finally stopped falling, she wasn't in Wonderland. At least she didn't think it was Wonderland, as the misty silver fog she'd glimpsed in the mirror shrouded her.

Was she *inside* the mirror?

Genuine fear pierced Maya's heart as she turned in a slow circle. She'd imagined many hideous ways to die. Usually at the hands of a vampire.

But she'd never considered the possibility of being trapped in an endless mist. It suddenly seemed like a horrible way to spend eternity.

Standing as still as possible, Maya closed her eyes and calmed her nerves. As much as she wanted to run screaming through the mist, panicking wasn't going to solve anything.

If she entered this strange place, then she could get out. Right?

Clinging to that thought, she reached out with her senses, searching for any hint that she wasn't alone. There was nothing. No, wait. That wasn't true. There was no one nearby, but there was a distant echo of someone familiar.

"Hello?" She strained to reach out. "Can you hear me?"

"Now what?" a female voice snapped.

"Tia?"

"Who else?"

"I need you."

Maya opened her eyes, watching as the mist swirled and Tia stepped into view.

She looked remarkably solid, as if Maya could reach out and touch her. And there was no missing the irritation smoldering in her dark eyes.

"Well? Now what?"

Maya waved a hand toward the mist. "Where am I?"

Tia blinked, as if she hadn't noticed the strange location. Then, deliberately, she glanced around. "I'm not sure." She pursed her lips, returning her attention to Maya. "Tell me what happened."

Maya ignored the older woman's air of command. Tia assumed she was the boss. No matter what the situation. "A mage shoved me into a mirror."

Tia stared at her in confusion. "Excuse me?"

"I was battling a mage who is somehow connected to Batu and she shoved me into a magic mirror," Maya explained in clipped tones. "Now I don't know how to get out."

The confusion remained, but an unmistakable interest replaced the irritation in the older woman's eyes. "You're sure it was the mirror that was magic and not just a spell surrounding it?"

Maya considered the question, replaying the moment she'd tumbled forward and landed against the mirror. There'd been a weird sensation, as if she was sliding through water, but it hadn't been magic. At least no magic she'd ever encountered before.

"No. I passed through the actual glass." Her tone was more confident than she felt. Honestly she didn't know what the hell had happened. "It was part of an altar the mage built in the middle of the woods."

"Tell me what you know about her."

"Nothing beyond the fact that she calls herself Alison and she's connected to whoever is trying to kill me." A warm pulse of heat against her palm distracted her, and with a frown, she glanced down at her hand to discover the golden necklace still clutched in her fingers. The metal was glowing in the mist. Maya opened her fingers to stare down at a small golden disk attached to the chain. There was something etched on it. She lifted the necklace, studying the elaborate design in the silvery light. A gasp was wrenched from her lips as she was smacked with the realization that she'd seen an exact replica of that unique design.

"What is it?"

"The mage was wearing this."

She held out her hand and Tia stepped forward to study the small disk. "Shit." The older woman jerked her head up to meet Maya's shocked gaze. "It matches the one that Batu wore."

"That can't be a coincidence," Maya breathed, feeling queasy as the gold pressed against her skin.

Was it tainted? It felt like it. Or maybe it was just the thought of her former captor that made her nauseous.

"No, it's not a coincidence," Tia agreed, her expression hardening as she stiffened her spine. "And he wasn't the only one."

"What do you mean?"

"I know where we are. Follow me."

With movements that lacked her usual grace, Tia turned and headed away from Maya, the mist parting before her like a silvery curtain. Maya followed. The older woman was visibly bothered by the medallion, never a good thing. Not when Maya had witnessed Tia battle a rabid horde of demons with a smile on her face. But if the older woman knew a way out of the weird fog, then Maya would follow her to the gates of hell.

But not without questions. "Tell me what's happening."

The words came out as an order, not a request. Tia wasn't the only one who could be bossy. Thankfully the mage was too distracted to take offense.

"The night Batu tried to kill me, I had finally managed to break through the layers of magic that hid his inner sanctum," she said, angling through the mist as if she knew exactly where she was going.

"And you didn't tell me?" Maya's breath hissed between her clenched teeth.

She didn't know why she was shocked. It didn't matter that Tia had sworn a solemn promise that they'd work together to uncover the secret they both knew Batu was hiding. And that they would stand side by side as they exposed whatever evil he was so anxious to keep locked behind the impenetrable barriers. Tia was going to do what Tia thought was best for Tia. End of story.

"I wanted a quick glance before coming to get you."

Maya snorted. "More likely you wanted to see if there was a treasure you could steal without having to share."

Tia's pace never slowed. "When did you become so cynical, old friend? Once upon a time you had faith in me."

"Don't call me that."

"Old?" Tia tossed a mocking smile over her shoulder. "Or friend?"

"Someday," Maya muttered.

"But not today."

"No, not today," Maya agreed as the mist started to thin, revealing a large cavern chiseled into the bedrock.

They stopped, standing side by side as the silvery fog continued to fade, exposing a narrow fissure that ran from the floor of the cavern to the ceiling.

"Tia?"

The mage pointed toward an arched doorway across the cavern. "I was here. I came through that entrance."

Maya took a hesitant step forward only to jerk to a halt when a ripple of magic swept over her, as if she'd stepped through an unseen barrier. Suddenly a line of dark shapes was visible near the back wall.

She dipped her hand into her satchel, studying the bulky forms that were covered from head to foot in thick robes. Their faces were obscured and there was no hint of auras, but they had to be demons. A half dozen of them.

"Guards," she hissed when Tia did nothing to prepare for an attack.

"They're not real." Tia's voice was distant, the scent of scalded cloves swirling around the mage. "They're memories."

Maya's tension didn't ease. This place had the feel of a dream, but that didn't lessen the danger. "Were they real when you came here?"

"Yes. Exactly where they're standing now." Tia licked her lips, nodding toward the nearest figure. "Look at their robes."

Maya sucked in a calming breath, forcing herself to study the dark, flowing material draped over the guards. In the dim light it was nearly impossible to see anything beyond a faint hint of crimson marks on the silky material directly over their hearts. Just then, Tia whispered a soft spell and a flame bloomed into a perfect sphere near the ceiling of the cavern, spilling a reddish glow over the figures. It was enough illumination to allow Maya to make out the stitched pattern.

"That's the same symbol." She clenched the medallion in her hand, feeling it throb as if it recognized this place. "There has to be a connection."

Tia nodded, but before she could respond a tremor rippled beneath their feet, like an earthquake. In the same moment, the nasty stench of sulfur blasted through the air. Maya gagged. She'd told herself she'd follow Tia to the gates of hell to get out of here, but she hadn't expected them to open and spew out such a noxious odor.

Not that the smell was the most worrisome turn of events, she belatedly realized, as the swish of satin against stone warned her the guards were on the move. She took a hasty step backward, but they remained impervious to her presence as they strolled toward the middle of the cavern and formed a straight line, facing the far wall. With an eerie silence, they slowly knelt and bent their hooded heads.

"What's happening?"

She didn't really expect Tia to have an answer. This went beyond weird to downright scary.

"I don't have a clue." Tia confirmed Maya's fear. "I barely managed to step into this chamber before Batu sensed my presence and dragged me out. That's when he decided I'd outlived my usefulness and started to drain me of my magic."

Maya was grimly battling back the memory of Tia on her knees with Batu draining the magic out of her when she was distracted as the fissure that snaked through the stone began to widen as if it was being pulled apart by invisible fingers.

"Something's happening," she whispered.

There was no tingle of magic or shaking of an earthquake, just the wall splitting in half.

Maya's heart skidded in fear as she peered into the spreading gap. It didn't open into another chamber. Or even to the jungle outside of Batu's lair. Actually, she didn't have a clue what it opened into. The landscape was something out of another dimension. Or another world. A flat, never-ending desert that was barren of any plants. And the sky was a putrid green with two moons that circled what looked like a black hole.

Oh, and the gut-churning stench of sulfur that flooded the air.

Tia sucked in a shocked breath. "Do you smell that?"

Maya shuddered. "How could I miss it?"

"I recognize that odor." Tia's gaze remained locked on the open fissure. "That's the place where Valen and I were trapped. The afterlife."

Maya had heard about Valen and Tia's unplanned journey into the world between the living and the dead. It was where the soul of the vampire supposedly waited to be resurrected in a brand-spanking-new body.

"Why would the demons be opening a portal to the afterlife?"

The question had barely left Maya's lips when the demons lifted their arms over their heads in a synchronized motion. It looked like they were saluting the opening until Maya caught a glint of steel and realized they were clutching daggers that held a sheen of magic rippling over the blades. Blades forged and hexed to kill with one blow.

Maya dipped her hand back into her satchel. The creatures appeared indifferent to their presence in the cavern, but if they decided to attack, things were going to get ugly. And painful. She wanted to take out a few before they could reach her.

But even as her fingers closed around a vial, the daggers slashed through the air, plunging downward until the blades pierced directly through the design stitched on their robes and into their hearts.

Maya froze, watching in stunned disbelief as the demons fell forward, dead the moment the steel blades slid through their flesh. But the horror wasn't over. The wounds in their chests pumped out large rivulets of blood that trickled into groves that had been dug into the stone floor. The dark liquid flowed toward the shallow trough that led directly toward the wall. At last it pooled at the base of the fissure, sizzling as it touched the strange image flickering in the gap.

There was a loud crack that echoed through the cavern, as if the stone was protesting the touch of the blood. Then as slowly as it parted, the stone wall started to knit back together. Maya shook her head. If this was magic, she'd never seen anything like it. Perhaps back in the days when mages could fully touch the wild magic it would be possible to move mountains, but...

"Maya."

Her tangled thoughts were distracted by Tia's sharp tone, and turning her head, she discovered the older woman staring at the center of her chest.

Maya glanced down, her brows snapping together at the shimmering strand of magic that appeared to flow from her heart toward the distant gap in the wall.

"What the hell?"

She couldn't sense the strange cord. Not even when she tentatively touched it with the tip of her fingers. Desperately she told herself it was an illusion, some sort of weird effect created by the cavern. And she might have believed her anxious hypothesis if a loud screeching hadn't forced her attention back to the gaping wall to discover it was no longer moving. A small crack was still visible, held open by the shimmering thread that was directly attached to her chest. As if she was somehow keeping the gap from completely closing.

"Maya." Tia grabbed her upper arm, giving her a rough shake. "We have to get out of here."

Thankfully jerked out of her shocked paralysis, Maya allowed Tia to tug her across the cavern to dart through the arched opening and into the chamber where Maya had battled against Batu. Maya refused to glance toward the spot where the vampire had died—or at least where she'd assumed he died—just as she refused to glance down and see if the weird magic was still shining out of her chest.

It was enough to concentrate on escaping the nightmare without adding to her blistering anxiety.

They were entering the vast throne room when the mist abruptly returned, boiling through the air as if it was alive. They quickened their pace as they continued toward the main doors that would lead to the terrace overlooking the jungle. They didn't need to be able to see through the mist to find their way. Not after endless years of being trapped in the lair.

Halfway across the chamber Maya felt the first tremor beneath her feet. Not an earthquake, but raw male power.

Her heart slammed against her ribs. "There's someone ahead of us," she warned in a low hiss.

Tia tightened her grip until her nails dug into Maya's flesh. "We can't stop."

"Actually, you can."

Maya and Tia grunted in pain as they ran face-first into an unseen barrier that was as hard as a brick wall. Reeling backward, Maya broke free of Tia's grasp, her arms windmilling as she struggled to keep her balance. Only when she was sure that she wasn't going to fall on her ass did she glare toward the tall form stepping out of the mist.

"You," she growled, not at all surprised at the sight of the obscenely handsome male with long copper hair and eyes that glowed an iridescent green in the silvery light.

The male—the one she suspected was Joe—studied them with an irritated expression.

"This is no place for you." His gaze shifted to Tia. "Either of you."

Astonishingly, Tia slammed her fists on her hips, her expression equally irritated. "What are you doing here? Did you follow me?"

Maya blinked in confusion. "You know him?"

Tia clicked her tongue. "He was in your shop."

"Seriously?" She glared at the male. "Why were you...wait." Maya turned her glare toward Tia. "What were *you* doing at my shop? You're supposed to be in Colorado."

Tia shrugged. "Looking for you."

"That's one explanation," the maybe/maybe not Joe retorted in dry tones.

Maya hissed in annoyance. Right now she had a truckload of problems. It wasn't the time or place to add more.

"This is all getting too weird." She focused on the male in front of her. "How do we escape this place?"

The male lifted his hand, his power thundering through the air. "Allow me."

Maya stumbled backward. She didn't know what was about to happen, but she was confident she wasn't going to like it.

"No. Wait."

"What's happening?" Tia stiffened, but Maya didn't have time to warn her. Even if she wanted to. Which she probably didn't. One moment she was backing away from the finger pointed in her direction and the next she was knocked unconscious, the pain and fear forgotten as she drifted in an endless darkness.

Chapter 13

Following behind the fleeing demon, Ravyr made the strategic decision to allow Bastian to escape. The male had to know his only hope of surviving was by reaching the protection of his mysterious master before Ravyr could catch him. He also made two calls. One to the chauffeur waiting at the Yalick estate, ordering the demon to return Maya to the Witch's Brew. And the other to Valen, warning him that there was a dragon scale manufactory in his territory.

Then, he zigzagged his way through the dense trees, heading ever deeper into the nearby mountains as he followed his prey. He had no idea where they were headed, but he wasn't surprised when he felt a small pulse of magic beneath his feet. Any demon, or even a vampire, who was going to build an evil lair away from the main Gyre would seek out one of the small pools of magic that seeped through the crevices. It didn't provide the same amount of power, and they could disappear without warning, like a bubble being popped by an unseen force, but they gave a temporary boost of magic to those creatures who preferred to lurk in the shadows.

Slowing his pace, Ravyr paused at the edge of a large clearing, cautiously surveying the white stone structure with a slate roof that was built next to a stream gushing with water from the recently melted snow. Ravyr guessed that it'd once been a sawmill that had been abandoned by humans years ago. And at a glance it *still* looked abandoned. It wasn't until he noticed that the rocky ground had been carefully cleared of obstructions and coated with a shimmering layer of magic that he was certain that there was not only something inside, but that it was also worth enough to spend the money for a magical barrier to keep out trespassers.

Was this Bastian's destination? Only one way to find out.

Giving up any pretense of stealth, Ravyr walked forward, wincing as he hit the barrier, and forced his way through. The powerful spell was designed to repel any intruder not given the secret password. And while his immunity to the magic meant he could pass through without any physical harm, it didn't keep him from feeling as if he was walking through a woodchipper.

Once through the barrier, Ravyr raced forward, his movements a blur to most watchful gazes. He never slowed as he reached the heavily boarded door, busting through the thick wood with enough force to send splinters flying through the large, open space.

Skidding to a halt, Ravyr ignored the chaos of screaming goblins and fairies who rushed toward the exits at the far end of the taproom, turning over tables and sending mugs of grog tumbling to the flagstone floor as they fled. He assumed this was an illegal safe house and the customers were afraid that Valen was sending in a raid party to search for criminals. Thankfully, he didn't give a shit about them. The only demon he was interested in was Bastian.

Oh, and the large goblin currently walking toward him with a shotgun pointed at his head. It wouldn't kill him, but healing would take time and energy he didn't have to waste.

"How did you get in here?" The goblin was well over six foot with bulging muscles beneath his T-shirt and jeans. His hair was greasy and long enough to brush his wide shoulders.

He had the cocky assurance of a male who was used to giving orders and having them obeyed.

It was going to be a bad night for him.

Ravyr folded his arms over his chest. "I'm looking for a demon named Bastian. Hand him over and there won't be any trouble."

"There's already trouble." The demon waved the shotgun as if Ravyr had failed to notice it. "I asked you how you got in here. You aren't on the list."

Ravyr peeled back his lips to expose his fully exposed fangs. "We can do this the easy way, or the way where I tear this place apart stone by stone."

"The Cabal doesn't have authority here."

"No?" Ravyr glanced around the open space, taking in the barren walls and the open beams overhead. "Granted, it's a pile of shit, but Valen will be interested to know he's lost control of his territory." He returned his attention to the goblin. "Are you the new master?"

"This is a neutral location where demons pay to be safe. Regardless of who is hunting them."

Ravyr's smile widened. "Listen carefully. I'm not in the mood for a pissing match with a demon with more balls than brains. Fetch Bastian before I rip your heart out and eat it."

The male's brash confidence faltered, his gaze flicking toward the razor-sharp fangs. Was he beginning to wonder if he could pull the trigger before Ravyr could rip out his throat? Ravyr could answer that question.

No way in hell.

There was an awkward pause as if the male was considering his limited options. Then, with a timing that made Ravyr's fangs clench, the temperature in the taproom dropped and a frost crawled over the glasses stacked on the bar. Abruptly, the male squared his shoulders and tilted his chin.

"You won't be so tough when the owner gets here," he warned.

"I can't wait."

Ravyr turned to face the door at the back of the room, prepared for the vampire who was rapidly approaching. He frowned. He couldn't catch his smell, as if there was some sort of spell muting his scent, but there was something familiar about his power signature.

A second later the door was shoved open and a large vampire with long brown hair and a square face that looked like it'd been chiseled out of granite appeared. His dark eyes smoldered with anticipation and his fangs were exposed as he visibly savored the violence that trembled in the air. Wearing camo pants tucked into heavy boots with a green T-shirt that was two sizes too small to emphasize his thick muscles, the male swaggered toward the center of the floor.

Ravyr rolled his eyes. "Primus. I should have known."

Intent on impressing the crowd that was no longer there, the vampire belatedly glanced in Ravyr's direction.

"You." The older male jerked to a halt, his eyes widening with genuine horror. "Shit. I thought you were dead."

Ravyr blew him a kiss. "Surprise."

"Why are you here? Did Sinjon send you?"

"Why would he send me?" Ravyr deliberately glanced around the empty space. "You're not doing something bad, are you? Perhaps running an illegal safe house?"

Abruptly reversing direction, Primus scurried toward the door he'd just used for his grand entrance.

"Get everyone out," he called toward his servant.

"What's happening?" the demon demanded, obviously disappointed that his boss wasn't providing the ass kicking he'd been anticipating.

Primus didn't bother answering, but Ravyr pointed a finger in the demon's face as he strolled past.

"Don't move."

Easily following the trail of the fleeing vampire, Ravyr cautiously stepped through the door and headed down a narrow flight of stairs. He wasn't going to risk rushing headfirst into a trap.

Step by step he headed downward, his nostrils flaring at the moldy stench thick in the air. They were close enough to the creek for the damp humidity to seep through the dirt, and Primus was clearly indifferent to the mildew and fungus that was layering the walls with a slick green goo.

Ravyr was careful not to touch anything as he reached the bottom of the steps and followed a narrow hallway lined with heavy steel doors. He assumed the doors led to the individual safe rooms that demons could pay extra to rent. Which meant there were probably additional layers of magic to protect them.

He wasn't going to risk an injury when he could simply force Primus to hand over the demon.

Slowing his pace, Ravyr headed toward the end of the hallway. The vampire was nowhere in sight, but his power pulsed through the cramped space. Was he hidden behind a web of illusions? Ravyr scanned the walls, at last catching the fuzzy distortion in a shadowed corner. It was like the ripple of a mirage, offering the eye a vision that wasn't there.

With a grim determination, Ravyr reached through the illusion, feeling the hot rush of magic before his fingers were closing around Primus's throat and he yanked him forward.

Primus hissed in frustration, but he wasn't stupid enough to try to escape as he dangled from Ravyr's crushing grip. "Damn, you're a pain in the ass," he rasped.

"So I've been told."

"How did you find me?"

"Obviously I need to have my karma cleansed. Or my chi balanced. Or whatever the hell is supposed to get rid of bad luck." Ravyr shoved the vampire against the wall. "The last thing I want to do is waste my time dealing with you."

Realization that Ravyr hadn't come to the remote sawmill specifically to hunt him down spread across Primus's broad face. Along with a faint shred of hope that he might survive the night.

"Why would you have to deal with me?" His lips formed into a sickly smile. "You told me to stop dealing in the slave trade. So that's what I did."

After Sinjon had taken command of the vampires, he'd requested Ravyr to infiltrate the slave market where hundreds of demons were held captive and sold to the highest bidder. It'd been illegal to deal in slaves for centuries, but few members of the Cabal cared enough to bother shutting them down. It'd come as a shock when Ravyr had collected the identities of every leech involved in the revolting organization and had them arrested. They were even more shocked when Sinjon had ordered them to be hexed to keep them from entering any Gyre.

Over a dozen leeches were cursed to roam the world without any hope of regaining their place in vampire society.

"And instead you opened an illegal safe house." Ravyr squeezed a fraction tighter. "You never learn, do you?"

"Yes, I swear I'm learning." The dark eyes widened with genuine fear. "I'm repenting for my days of abusing demons. Now I'm helping them. You should be pleased."

Ravyr pretended to consider his explanation. "I suppose you could plead your case to Valen. This is his territory, after all. But if I were you, I wouldn't count on any sympathy. In fact, there's a good chance he's going to throw you in his deepest dungeon for a very long time."

Primus licked his lips. "Surely we can make some sort of arrangement between the two of us? No need to drag Valen into this. He's a busy male with his new mate and all the trouble he's had over the past few months."

The idiot's not wrong, Ravyr silently conceded. The last thing Valen needed was another problem added to his to-do list. And this wasn't like the Yalicks' drug trade. A few demons hiding in the middle of nowhere weren't going to be his top priority even if he didn't have a million other things on his mind.

"Perhaps we can make a deal," he said, layering his voice with a faux reluctance.

"Just tell me what you want and consider it done."

"I'm looking for a goblin. His name is Bastian, or at least that's the name he used when he was in service to the Yalick clan. He would have come in just a few minutes before me."

"Hmm." Primus wrinkled his brow. "The name doesn't ring a bell."

"Fine."

Ravyr abruptly released his grip on the male's throat and reached into his front pocket.

Primus watched him with a wary gaze. "What are you doing?"

"Calling Valen."

"Wait. I just remembered." Primus reached out, although he was wise enough not to touch Ravyr. "Actually, we do have a demon who recently arrived and demanded one of our hourly rooms. He seemed to be in a rush."

"Take me to him."

With a jerky nod, Primus inched his way past Ravyr and retraced his steps up the hallway before halting in front of one of the steel doors. He reached into his pocket and pulled out a heavy iron ring that held old-fashioned keys.

"Careful, Primus," Ravyr warned as the male pushed one of the keys into the lock.

"I've learned my lesson, Ravyr. I'm not going through another disembowelment. It took me weeks to heal," Primus growled, not bothering to glance in Ravyr's direction. "I'm just opening the door."

Ravyr grimaced. He'd forgotten the male had attempted to escape after he'd been captured and sent to Sinjon's dungeons. The price was a very slow, very painful disembowelment that was usually performed in front of the other prisoners. It helped to reinforce the idea that it wasn't worth trying to leave before Sinjon was ready to let you go.

An effective tool.

Turning the key, Primus backed away, giving Ravyr ample space to step forward, grab the knob, and give the door a small push. Silently the door slid open a crack, just enough for Ravyr to see the flicker of candlelight on a small nightstand. Someone was inside.

Bastian?

The door slid another inch, but before Ravyr could lean forward to peer through the opening, the stench of death smacked him directly in the face.

"Damn."

Pushing the door fully open, Ravyr stepped into the room, already prepared to discover the goblin's corpse. What he wasn't expecting was to

Alexandra Ivy

find the male sprawled on the narrow bed, his body already in an advanced stage of decomposition and his eyes sunk deep in his skull. As if he'd been dead for days, not mere minutes.

Just like Courtney.

"Dead end," he muttered in frustration. "Quite literally."

Behind him, Primus sucked in a shocked breath. "What the hell? I don't know what happened in here, but it isn't my fault."

Ravyr muttered an ancient profanity, but before he could vent his irritation on the vampire who was trying to pretend he was invisible, he felt the vibration of his phone.

Pulling it out, he read the text from the chauffeur he'd left to take Maya home.

Still waiting on the mage.

Ravyr shoved the phone back into his pocket and, without glancing toward the cowering Primus, ran down the hall and up the stairs. He'd accomplished precisely nothing and now Maya was missing.

What else could go wrong?

A question that should never, ever be asked.

Chapter 14

If Maya had been a heavy drinker, she would have assumed she had a hangover from hell. Unfortunately, she preferred tea to alcohol, which meant the throbbing headache and piercing stab of pain behind her right eye was no doubt caused by a blow to her skull.

She groaned as she struggled to clear the fog from her brain. Over the past year she'd managed to knock her head on the ground more than once. It was a habit she'd prefer to avoid in the future.

Debating whether she could slip back into unconsciousness to avoid the worst of the relentless discomfort, Maya froze when cool fingers stroked a light caress over her cheek.

"Maya."

The deep, rich voice eased her burst of fear, and she cautiously lifted her lashes to study the male kneeling beside her. He was close enough for her to see the silver that rimmed his turquoise eyes shimmering in the fading moonlight, and she reached up to press her hand against the fingers that lingered against her cheek.

"Ravyr." She studied each fiercely carved feature, not sure if he was truly there or if he was a figment of her battered brain. "Are you real?"

"I'm real," he assured her, his expression worried. "What happened?"

Good question. She hesitated, searching through the fuzz to dredge up the memory of how she'd ended up flat on her back in the middle of the woods. Eventually she formed the image of robed forms and a shimmering cord latched to her chest before she was being knocked out of the vision by a super rude mystery being.

Joe the jerk.

She groaned again, touching the knot on the back of her head as she struggled to a seated position.

"You're hurt." There was an edge of anger in Ravyr's voice as he wrapped a protective arm around her shoulders.

Maya was shocked by a sharp, overwhelming urge to lean forward and rest against his broad chest. She was tired and scared and she had a boo-boo on her head that made her brain hurt.

Grinding her teeth together, she pulled away from his arm and forced herself to her feet. It wasn't a rejection. It was an instinctive need to prove she could be strong without his assistance. "It's just a bump."

An indefinable emotion rippled over his face before he smoothly straightened and glanced toward the opening.

"What happened?"

"I'll tell you later," Maya promised, moving forward with an unexpected limp.

She'd obviously injured her hip when she'd been thrown out of the vision. She hadn't even noticed until she tried to walk. Grimly she continued toward the stump at the center of the clearing.

Ravyr remained where he was, no doubt watching her in confusion. "What are you doing?" he at last asked.

"Making sure the altar is destroyed."

Disgust raced through Maya. How could she have been so stupid? She'd been so distracted by the shiny bowl and candles she'd completely ignored the true danger. The mirror. At least until Alison had shoved her face-first into the stupid thing. Once she was close enough to her target, Maya bent down and picked up a heavy stone. Lifting it over her head, she swung her arm forward, launching the stone to smash against the reflective glass. A second later the mirror shattered into a thousand satisfying shards that scattered over the ground. She didn't know what sort of evil magic had been used to create the mirror, but she did know it was gone.

At least for now.

Turning, she called on the last scraps of her magic and weaved them into a ball of raw power. Once it was solid, she aimed it directly at the stump and sent it flying. The spell hit the weathered wood with a loud sizzle before it exploded. It wasn't an impressive blast—she was too drained for a big boom—but it was enough to split the stump in two and send the bowl and candles soaring toward the trees.

Ravyr abruptly stepped forward to join her, his gaze sweeping over the bits and pieces of the altar that were now scattered like confetti.

"Better?" he asked.

"Not really, but it's the best I can do." She frowned, making a mental note to return and cleanse the area of any residual magic. The mirror was broken, but she needed to make sure that nothing could crawl out of the oak frame that remained standing at a drunken angle. "At least for now."

Ravyr nodded before glancing toward the sky. "It will be dawn soon. We need to get back to the city."

"I'm ready." Maya limped toward the narrow pathway that led out of the woods. "More than ready."

Ravyr kept a slow pace next to her, close enough to catch her if she collapsed, but evidently—and wisely—resisting the urge to sweep her off her feet and carry her to safety. Her life felt as if it was spiraling out of control. She needed to maintain some sort of independence. Even if each step was sending jolts of pain through her back.

Skirting the edge of the mansion that was shrouded in a sullen darkness, they found the SUV patiently waiting for them in the circular drive. Swallowing a groan of relief, Maya managed to hold on to her grim courage until the driver opened the back door and she was able to collapse onto the soft leather seat.

Even then it took several minutes for the discomfort to ease and her heart to slow its rapid pace.

As if sensing her struggle, Ravyr was silent as the SUV drove away from the estate, going at a speed that rattled the expensive suspension as they sped down the mountain and back to civilization. The demon chauffeur was clearly aware of the encroaching dawn and determined to get them back to the city in record time.

It wasn't until they'd reached the paved highway that Maya turned her head to study Ravyr's chiseled profile. "Where's the demon?"

There was a flash of fang as Ravyr clenched his teeth. "He's dead."

Maya stared at him in surprise. Ravyr wasn't like most leeches. He kept his arrogance, along with his temper, firmly leashed. It was what made him such a dangerous opponent.

"Hopefully you got the information we needed before you killed him."

He grimaced. "I didn't get any information." He held up his hand as her lips parted to add to her scolding. "I didn't even have the satisfaction of killing him."

"Oh. What happened?"

"I followed Bastian through the woods to a safe house that just happened to be owned by an old friend of mine." He turned to send her a wry glance. "By the time I got the bastard to open the door to the room that Bastian had rented, he was lying on the bed. Dead."

Maya frowned. "Did your friend kill him?"

Ravyr shook his head. "He'd been dead a few minutes, but when I found him he was already a decaying corpse."

Maya sucked in a sharp breath. "Just like Courtney."

"Exactly like her."

Had Alison been responsible? It seemed doubtful since she was busy shoving Maya into a magical mirror. Did that mean there was another mage out there killing off the witnesses?

Frustration churned deep inside Maya, like a cauldron left on the fire too long. If they didn't discover what the hell was going on, she was going to end up with an ulcer.

"There's something I'm missing," she muttered.

"A good night's sleep?"

"There's that," she agreed dryly. "I might be able to put the puzzle pieces together after I've had a few hours in the comfort of my bed."

Ignoring the sway of the SUV and the blur of streetlights that were clustering closer together as they reached the outskirts of the suburbs, Maya allowed her gaze to trace the blunt lines of his features before sweeping down to the muscular hardness of his body.

When she'd struggled back to consciousness, there'd been a part of her that had been terrified by the thought that she was lying flat on her back in the middle of the woods with her magic dangerously depleted. Then she'd felt the soft brush of Ravyr's fingers, and she'd known with absolute certainty that she was safe. It hadn't been because they were temporary partners. Or that he was strong enough to fight off any predator.

It was an instinctive knowledge that as long as this male was near, she would never have to worry.

The SUV slowed as they swerved off the main highway and the streets narrowed. As if suddenly realizing they would soon be back in Linden, Ravyr shifted in the seat so he was directly facing her.

"Are you going to tell me what happened after I left?"

"The mage attacked just minutes later."

"Did she hurt you?"

Maya blushed as she recalled how easily she'd been distracted. It'd been embarrassingly easy for the younger woman to use brute strength to overpower her. She'd spent hours teaching Peri and Skye hand-to-hand defense for that precise situation.

"She shoved me into the mirror."

Ravyr studied her in confusion. "And?"

"Not *against* the mirror," Maya clarified. "She pushed me *inside* the mirror."

Her words did nothing to clear up Ravyr's confusion. "You went inside the mirror?"

"Yes. It was obviously some sort of portal, although I didn't recognize the magic. I've never encountered anything like it."

"If it was a portal, I assume you traveled to a different location?"

"I'm not sure if I traveled anywhere or if I was caught in a vision." Her hands curled into tight fists. The last thing she wanted was to dwell on what she'd seen, but she sensed that she needed all the help she could get if she was going to survive. "At first there was nothing but a thick mist; then it parted and I was back in Batu's lair on the night..." She forced herself to pause and gather her shaky composure. "It was the night I thought I killed him."

"Were you actually back in time?" He reached out to brush his fingers over her cheek, this time touching the scars that marred her skin. Did he assume she was upset by the memory of her violent battle with the male?

"I don't think so." She should have knocked his hand away, but she didn't. The cool touch reassured her that Ravyr was nearby. And that she was no longer lost in the past. "It felt like I was looking through the mists of time."

"Looking at what?"

She shivered despite the heat pumping through the expensive vehicle. "Were you ever invited to Batu's inner sanctum?" she asked.

"No. I tried on several occasions to sneak in, but the magic was too thick for me to penetrate." His fingers gently tucked her hair behind her ear. "Actually, that's why I was in the area the night that Batu was destroyed. I'd sensed a change in the barrier and I went there to try to sneak in."

"It was Tia. She managed to force her way inside," Maya explained. "That's why Batu was so furious that night. And why he was determined to kill her."

"Did the vision show you what he was hiding?"

"Demons. Or at least I think they were demons. They were covered in heavy robes."

"What were they doing?"

"When I first entered they were just standing against the wall. But then a fissure suddenly split open."

She felt him stiffen, as if surprised by her explanation. "There was a fissure in the inner sanctum?"

"Yes. It split open the back wall."

"Was there something inside it?"

A nasty sensation curled through the pit of Maya's stomach. She'd only glimpsed a sliver of the strange dimension, but it'd been enough to convince her that it wasn't a place she wanted to visit anytime soon.

"Tia said that the fissure was an opening to the vampires' afterlife."

"The afterlife? Are you..." His baffled words trailed away as his brows snapped together. "Wait. Tia was in the woods with you?"

"No, she was in the vision," she clarified, wrinkling her nose. "Or whatever it was."

"Even if she was in your vision, how would she know anything about the vampire afterlife? Not even our greatest scholars have been able to penetrate the mysteries of where our demon goes or how it's returned to a new host."

Maya shrugged. "She was taken there last year."

His frown deepened as he studied her with a fierce intensity. Was he wondering if she was delusional? She wouldn't blame him. A part of her desperately wanted to believe it'd all been a nightmare caused by a blow to her head. Unfortunately, it didn't feel like a delusion.

"She was taken to the afterlife?"

"She was there with Valen when Peri was battling the..." Maya allowed her rambling explanation to trail away. "It's a long story."

He slowly shook his head. "One I'd be very interested in hearing."

"You'll have to ask Valen for the details."

At the time Maya had been too concerned with Peri and her newfound magic to pay attention to how Valen and Tia had managed to battle their way through the barriers to reach her friend. Including a side trip into the afterlife.

"Describe the fissure. Was it real or an illusion?"

She considered what she'd seen. "It had to be magic. If the stones had actually been splitting apart, they would have caused a collapse of the cavern. Or at least, the lair would have been shaking from the force of the movement. There wasn't even a speck of dust in the air."

He nodded, as if that was the response he'd been expecting. "What happened after it opened?"

"It kept growing wider and wider, like it intended to swallow the entire lair, but the robed demons suddenly moved forward. I honestly think they'd been standing there just waiting for that moment."

Easily recognizing her distress, Ravyr brushed his fingertips down the length of her neck, lingering on the pulse that raced at the base of her throat. "What happened then?"

"They knelt in front of the opening and stabbed daggers into their chest."

Ravyr made a sound of shock. "All of them?"

"All of them. It was awful." Maya shuddered at the gruesome memory. "And worse, it had to be something they'd been trained to do because the blood from their wounds ran down the floor and into channels that had been chiseled into the stone. When the blood hit the opening, the fissure started to close."

He took a moment, as if trying to comprehend what power could have forced the demons to commit suicide.

"The blood was closing the fissure?" he finally asked.

"That's what it looked like."

"Did the demons die?"

"They were hidden beneath their robes, but they collapsed on the floor. I'm pretty sure they were dead."

"And the fissure closed?"

She hesitated. She didn't want to discuss what happened next. Hell, she didn't even want to think about it.

"Not entirely," she tried to hedge.

Cupping her face in his palm, Ravyr turned her head to meet his worried gaze. "Maya?"

She swallowed a sigh. He wasn't going to let it go. Not when he could sense the worry that pounded through her. Best to spit it out as fast as possible. Like ripping a bandage off a wound.

"There was a cord that kept a tiny sliver open. A cord that was attached directly to me." She pressed her hand against the center of her chest, half expecting to feel the weird thread. "Right here."

A sudden chill in the air battled with the warmth spilling from the heating vents. She'd expected Ravyr's confusion. Maybe even disbelief. But his reaction was pure fury.

"Is it a spell?" Ravyr's expression was hard as granite. "Can it be removed?"

"Not one I've ever heard of." Maya rubbed her chest. "And honestly, I don't even know if it's still there. Although my luck hasn't been good enough for it to just disappear."

The muscles of his jaw bulged as he clenched his fangs. "You suspect that it has something to do with Batu?"

She did, of course. As soon as she caught a glimpse of the cord, she'd been convinced that Batu had somehow tethered them together. That would explain why she couldn't get rid of the nightmares. And it might even be the reason someone was going to a lot of effort to kill her. What the cord was or why Batu would have connected them was a mystery.

But her gut instinct wasn't based on facts. And it would be foolish to let herself be blinded by her hatred for her former master.

"I don't know what it is," she forced herself to admit, "but I'm pretty sure I need to find out. And soon."

"We will."

He leaned down to brush a light kiss over her cheek at the same time the SUV pulled to a smooth stop. Maya hadn't realized they'd reached Linden. Proof that she was too weary to make any decisions about what to do next.

She glanced out the window. It was still dark, but there was no mistaking the rosy hint that was beginning to lighten the sky.

"It's nearly dawn," she warned, knowing Ravyr wouldn't have much time to seek the safety of a sunlight-proof lair.

"Yes."

"Are you staying at Valen's penthouse?"

He shrugged. "There are plenty of places in the city to avoid the sun."

She frowned at the vague response. Why wasn't he using Valen's lair? It would be the most convenient location. Not only was it sunproof, but it was heavily protected. Especially since the shocking attack by a member of his own Cabal a few months ago.

Nothing could get past his security.

It took a second for her to realize why he avoided the public penthouse. He'd wanted to keep his presence in the city a secret.

"You can stay here if you want." The words were out of her mouth before she could halt them.

His brows arched. "Seriously?"

A part of her wanted to say no. That there was no way she was sharing her private home—the place she'd built for the precise purpose of keeping out vampires—with a leech. A larger part, however, understood that she needed Ravyr if she was going to stay alive long enough to discover who was hunting her. And why the hell she had a shimmering cord attached to her chest.

Besides, Ravyr wasn't just another leech. He'd proved over and over that he was a male of worth. One she could trust even if he did have fangs.

"The basement doesn't have any windows and the door is protected with a warning alarm if it's opened," she assured him, pushing open the door.

The alarm had been a recent addition after Courtney had managed to sneak past her wards.

His features softened, a wicked anticipation flaring in his stunning eyes. "It's not a bad idea to stay close together," he murmured.

"Not *too* close."

She slid out of the vehicle, crossing the sidewalk as Ravyr moved to have a word with the chauffeur. Pausing, she searched for any hidden spells. She had a fuzzy memory of Tia admitting that she'd been in the Witch's Brew—along with the mysterious Watcher/Benefactor/pretend everyday Joe—just before she'd been knocked unconscious. She couldn't sense them, but that didn't mean they hadn't left behind some residual magic.

Nothing.

Behind her, Maya heard the SUV pull away and Ravyr crossed the sidewalk to join her, bathed in the soft light of the neon sign. Her heart skipped a dangerous beat as tingles of pleasure swirled through her. Dammit. Did he have to be so gorgeous? Or ooze the sort of sexual temptation that made her hands tremble as she unraveled the layers of protection she'd placed on the door?

Her acute awareness didn't lessen as they entered the shadowed coffee shop and she led him across the tiled floor. His presence easily spread through the space, adding a delicious layer of anticipation to the cozy atmosphere. Worse, Maya wasn't annoyed by the raw scent of power that mixed with sugar and spice. Or the pulse of vampire energy that spread through her home. It felt...right. As if he filled a space she hadn't realized was empty.

Trying to shake off the sensation, she reached to open the steel door to the basement. Once Ravyr was downstairs, she would reset the locks and layer the entire building in a warding spell.

"There's no bed down there," she warned. "But I keep my extra bedding stored in the closet next to the vault. You should be able to find plenty of blankets and pillows—"

He interrupted her rambling. Thank God. "You don't need to worry. I've spent most of my existence sleeping in caves or, more recently, in abandoned subway tunnels."

She nodded, shifting her feet as an awkward silence settled between them. *Turn around and walk away,* the voice of wisdom urged. *No, no. Shove him against the wall and lick him from head to toe,* the voice of insanity urged.

Caught between the two competing desires, Maya felt her breath being squeezed from her lungs as Ravyr stepped forward to brush his fingers down the curve of her throat.

"Maya."

"Yes?" Her lips felt oddly stiff, making it hard to form the word. Good grief. She was a mess.

He smiled, his eyes smoldering with a turquoise fire threaded with silver. Stunning.

"If you need anything." The fingertips skimmed the delicate line of her collarbone. "Anything at all, my door is always open for you."

Her pulse thundered as shivers of pleasure raced through her.

"I'll keep that in mind," she rasped.

"I hope I am on your mind." The fingers dipped beneath her neckline, stroking the soft curve of her breast. "And in your dreams." Slowly he lowered his head, nibbling caresses over her cheek before claiming her lips in a deep, drugging kiss. Oh yes. Her mouth parted in silent encouragement, savoring the taste of raw male. Not even the sharp press of his fangs could penetrate the erotic haze clouding her mind. Maya swayed forward, but with an unexpected motion, Ravyr was stepping back, studying her with a sensual satisfaction. He knew damned well he'd stirred her passions until they flamed through her with a fierce hunger. "Sleep well, Maya Rosen."

With a click of her tongue, Maya spun on her heel and marched away. She refused to give him the satisfaction of glancing back. No matter how badly she wanted to send him a glare of frustration.

Lifting her hand, she spoke the familiar words that would activate the nightly wards. The magic would alert her the second that anyone she hadn't personally approved entered the building. Whether it was through a door, a window, or a portal.

Once she was satisfied that she'd done everything possible to keep out the bad guys, she headed toward the stairs that led to the upper floors. The second floor was used for brewing potions and creating the spells that she kept stored in various artifacts, including her emerald necklace.

The third floor was her private apartment. Or at least it was private now that both Peri and Skye had moved out. For once, however, she didn't wince as she passed by their empty rooms. Probably because her thoughts were consumed with the sexy vampire currently hidden in her basement.

Stripping off her clothes, she managed to pull on an oversized T-shirt before she tumbled face-first into her bed. The hot shower she desperately wanted would have to wait until tomorrow. For now, nothing mattered but the exhaustion that crashed over her with the force of a tidal wave.

Thankfully, she was too tired to dream. In fact, she was fairly sure she didn't so much as twitch until a familiar perfume scented the air.

With a grudging reluctance, she lifted her lashes, which felt as if they'd been glued together. The room was shadowed. Had she managed to sleep from sunup past sundown?

Rolling onto her back, she watched as Joyce tiptoed into the room, her red hair frizzier than usual as it haloed her broad face. She was also wearing a flannel shirt and matching pants that looked like pajamas. Odd.

With a blink, Maya struggled to sit up, shoving her tangled hair from her face. She wasn't surprised to see the older woman. Joyce was allowed through the magical barriers she'd cast the evening before to work in the coffee shop and she knew where to find Maya when she was in her private rooms. There'd been occasions when the pipes had frozen or the computer system had gone down and she needed Maya to avert disaster.

"What time is it?" The words came out as a hoarse croak.

Joyce didn't seem to notice as she crossed the room to stand directly next to the bed.

"Almost nine."

Maya blinked again. The shop should have closed hours ago. So why wasn't Joyce tucked in her house a few blocks away? The older woman was a creature of habit who wouldn't be out and about at that hour unless it was an emergency.

Leaning to the side, Maya flipped on the lamp next to the bed. "What happened?"

Joyce narrowed her eyes against the sudden glow, as if she'd been standing in the dark for a long time.

"Everything's fine."

"Then what are you doing up here?"

Joyce stared at her in silence, her familiar features abruptly twisting in pain. Was the older woman having a medical issue? Without hesitation, Maya tossed aside the covers, preparing to grab the emergency potions she kept in the desk beneath the window. She could use one of her healing spells to stabilize Joyce until an ambulance could get to the shop.

"Just hold on," she urged, still on the edge of the mattress when the older woman abruptly lunged toward her with a large dagger clutched in her hand.

Where the hell had that come from? And more importantly, why was Joyce trying to stab her?

Rolling off the bed, Maya avoided the blade that sliced through the air less than an inch from her head. She landed on her hands and knees, scrambling toward the desk. There were more than healing potions hidden in the drawers.

Heavy footsteps thumped toward her, and Maya once again caught the glint of steel as the dagger carved a path toward her head. With a muttered oath, Maya dropped to her belly, waiting for the blade to fly past before she rolled onto her back and released a pulse of power.

"Stop it, Joyce," she commanded.

Joyce flinched as the magic slammed into her, but with a jerky motion she continued forward.

"I can't."

Maya's brows snapped together. Something was wrong. With an effort, she concentrated on her friend's face. Her expression was still twisted, but Maya suspected it wasn't a physical pain. It was more like she was fighting against an inner compulsion. And her eyes were cloudy, as if she were caught in a spell.

A very powerful spell.

Joyce sprang toward Maya, moving with shocking speed. Jerking her head back, Maya felt the blade cut a shallow gash on her brow. It wasn't deep enough to cause a real injury, but the blood flowing from the wound threatened to blind her.

She had to end this sooner rather than later.

"Joyce, listen to my voice." It was an effort, but she managed to keep her tone soothing. "I need you to stop."

Joyce hissed, tears in her eyes as she lifted her arm and took another swing with the dagger. Maya rolled to her stomach, planting her hands on the wood plank floor and shoving herself upward. She managed to get to her feet just in time to avoid the blade that nearly sliced through her throat.

Okay. Enough was enough. She didn't want to hurt Joyce, but there was no way the woman could battle through the compulsion spell. Not without help.

Darting toward the desk, Maya yanked open the top drawer and fumbled for a thin vial that was filled with a gray mist. She turned and tossed it directly toward the older woman's face.

Joyce ducked downward, but the vial smashed into the top of her head and shattered. The potion released, blooming into a small cloud that settled over Joyce's face, clinging to her even as she desperately used her free hand to try to wipe away the magic. The blinding potion was temporary, but for the few minutes it lasted it caused a searing pain.

Maya ignored the stab of guilt, pointing a finger in Joyce's direction as she tapped into the power that hummed through her blood. Gathering the magic, she released it in a slow trickle, twining it until a silvery strand floated in the air. Then, using it like a lasso, she wrapped the magic around Joyce's feet, effectively gluing her to the floor.

Seemingly unaware that she'd been caught in Maya's power, Joyce shook off the last of the clinging mist and tried to leap forward. This time, however, she merely swayed in place, nearly falling on her face.

Shoving herself upright, Joyce tried again to move forward. Once again she swayed and nearly fell.

"What have you done?" She twisted from side to side in frustration.

"You're not well, Joyce." Maya cautiously stepped forward. If she could get close enough, she might be able to break through the web of compulsion that was controlling the older woman. "Let me—"

"No!" A raw scream that came from the very depths of Joyce's soul ripped through the air. Then, lifting the dagger over her head, she stared at Maya with tear-filled eyes. "I'm sorry."

Maya stopped, prepared for the weapon to be tossed in her direction. Instead, Joyce stared her directly in the eye as she swung the dagger downward, plunging it into the center of her chest.

Blindsided by the sight of her friend collapsing to the floor with a blade stuck in her heart, Maya rushed forward. With a muttered word, she released the magic holding Joyce's feet and dropped to her knees. Reaching out, she gently turned the limp body over, a gasp wrenched from her lips at the sight of the blood that soaked through Joyce's clothing and seeped into the floorboards.

So much blood...

With an effort she resisted the urge to yank the dagger out and focused her mind on a spell that would slow the bleeding. Not that she had much hope. Even as Maya tried to form the words, Joyce released a ragged breath before she was lying unnaturally still, her eyes staring blindly at the ceiling.

No, no, no.

On the point of casting the spell, no matter how futile, Maya was distracted when a familiar symbol appeared on Joyce's forehead. It looked like a brand that had been burned into her flesh, but as swiftly as it'd appeared, it faded. A second later her skin was changing to a nasty shade of ash, the top layer starting to flake away as if she'd been dead for days.

Maya jerked back, horrified as she watched her friend decay before her eyes.

This couldn't be happening. It had to be a nightmare....

Alison.

The name whispered through the back of her mind, igniting her sorrow to a blazing fury.

The mage had to be responsible for Joyce's attack. No doubt the evil bitch discovered she couldn't get through Maya's wards so she used the vulnerable human as if she was a disposable weapon. One that could be destroyed if she failed. Or maybe even if she succeeded. The mage was smart enough not to leave behind witnesses.

An icy blast of air blew through the room, swirling the covers off the bed and rattling the bedside lamps. Then Ravyr was kneeling beside her, his arm protectively wrapping around her shoulders.

"Maya?"

She turned her head to meet his worried gaze. "I'm going to rip that bitch apart and paste her back together. Then I'm going to do it again. And again."

"Okay." He shot a quick glance toward the dead woman. "Did she attack you?"

"Not Joyce. This wasn't her fault. Someone placed a compulsion spell on her to kill me. When she failed..."

Her words died on her lips as she forced herself to her feet. She couldn't bear to remember the sight of Joyce's face as she'd plunged the dagger into her own heart.

Ravyr straightened, grasping her shoulders to gently turn her away from the decaying corpse.

"Did you know her?"

"She's worked for me for years. She was my friend."

He glanced over his shoulder, his power pulsing against her as he studied the dead woman.

"She looks like the others."

Maya gave a jerky nod, touching the center of her forehead. "There was a brand on her skin. Here."

"Did you recognize it?"

"Yes. It matched the symbol on Batu's medallion."

Ravyr grimaced. "I saw the same brand on Bastian. Do you know what it means?"

"I asked Batu one time what it represented." Maya shuddered at the memory. "He gave me a creepy smile and said it was his insurance policy."

"Insurance?" He paused, as if trying to attach some meaning to the word. "That doesn't make any sense," he at last conceded. "But then, most of the crap that Batu spewed didn't make any sense."

Maya ground her teeth, wrenching her thoughts out of the past. The answers wouldn't be found there.

"We need to track down Alison," she abruptly announced. "The compulsion spell controlling Joyce was created by a mage."

Ravyr nodded. "How close would she need to be to control your friend?"

Maya considered the question. She'd spent years practicing magic, and while her specialty had always been potions, she'd watched Peri preparing curses that were designed to be activated hours or even days later.

"It's possible that the compulsion was contained in the brand that was placed on her forehead."

"Would she physically have to touch her to place the spell?"

"Yes."

"How recently?"

"Within the past week."

"And to activate it?"

"She could have released her hold on the spell, like pulling a trigger. Or more likely, she had the spell designed to activate on a specific date and time."

Ravyr glanced toward Joyce, his expression hard with unease. "So she could have placed the spell days ago, and then set it into motion without being anywhere in the area?"

"Yes."

His brow furrowed as he returned his attention to her. "But how would she know you were here?"

Maya shrugged. That was the one part of the spell that didn't confuse her. "It wouldn't have mattered where I was. Once the spell was activated Joyce would have sought me out and tried to kill me, although it's rare that I'm not alone in my apartment at this time of night." A shudder wracked her body as the image of Joyce standing over her bed seared through her mind. It was going to be a long time before she could sleep in her bed without worrying someone was going to plunge a dagger into her heart. "But I suspect that Alison intended to kill me before Joyce was needed. She had to know that unless Joyce got lucky and stabbed a vital organ before I could wake up there was no way she could overpower me." Maya was forced to stop and swallow the lump in her throat. "Tonight was probably her last-ditch effort to get rid of me."

Power pulsed through the air as Ravyr's expression registered her words, the chill in the air suddenly more pronounced.

"She's on a schedule."

Maya sucked in a sharp breath. Dammit. He was right. If the compulsion spell had been set on a timer, that meant Alison considered tonight her last-ditch effort to kill Maya.

"Which will only make her more desperate." Maya wrapped her arms around her waist. "She had to have sensed her spell being triggered."

"She knows you're still alive?"

Maya nodded. "At least alive before Joyce came looking for me. She can't be certain what happened after the attack."

A grim smile curved his lips. "Then it's possible that she'll come to see if her plan worked."

Maya doubted the mage would be that stupid. She would have to know that if Maya survived she'd be waiting for her. Still, there was the chance that she was anxious enough to be provoked into doing something reckless.

"I'll cast a snare that will trap her if she gets anywhere close," she promised. It wouldn't be the first time she'd been forced to protect her home from intruders.

"You do that while I return Joyce to her home. We don't want to answer unpleasant questions from the human authorities."

Maya's heart twisted at the thought of dumping poor Joyce's body in her house and walking away. It felt...disrespectful. Then again, there was no way to explain to the human authorities why there was a decaying corpse in her bedroom.

"She lives—"

He pressed his finger to her lips. "I can find it."

A surge of gratitude eased the icy knot in her stomach. It might be cowardly to hand over the unpleasant duty to Ravyr, but she was simply too raw to deal with her grief tonight. Tomorrow she would be her usual kickass self.

"I'm going to set the snare and shut down the shop for a few days," she said. "I can't put anyone else in danger."

He brushed a kiss over her lips. "I'll be back. Pack a bag and try to stay out of trouble."

Maya heaved a sigh. "No guarantee."

Chapter 15

The town house that Tia had chosen for her visit to New York City possessed the old-world beauty of a Parisian hotel with lofted ceilings and white walls accented with brushes of gold. It also had the benefit of being tucked away in a quiet neighborhood surrounded by trees and a handful of humans. The perfect lair to keep her presence in the city a secret.

She didn't know where the demon family who owned the building had gone, and frankly she didn't care. They owed her a favor and she'd cashed it in.

Draped in a satin caftan that reached her ankles, Tia paced the salon, which was bathed in a rosy glow from the overhead chandelier. Long ago, she'd learned the art of patience. Chasing glory might feel good, but the only way to truly succeed was to meticulously plan a goal and execute it with flawless perfection. That was how she'd risen from being sold as a slave to Batu to becoming one of the most powerful, prosperous women in the world.

She imagined herself as a spider, carefully spinning webs that she spread far and wide.

Tonight, however, her patience was slipping away with every tick of the grandfather clock.

Spinning on her heel to retrace her path across the Parisian carpet, Tia heard the back door opening and closing before the heavy tread of footsteps echoed through the silence. At last. She watched as Lynch entered the salon, appearing obscenely out of place in his worn jeans and gray hoodie stretched tight over his bulging muscles. He'd pulled on a Yankees baseball hat to cover his bald head and his feet were encased in a pair of black biker boots.

"Well." Halting in the center of the room, Tia glared at her servant. "It took you long enough."

The goblin shrugged. "The city's on edge. Not many demons are willing to share information with a stranger." His lips twisted into a sneer. "Especially one they consider a mongrel."

Tia ignored the male's griping. He'd been in a pissy mood since they'd arrived in the city. A combination of worry that she might be in danger and the grinding reminder that even in the Gyre he lacked the power of most demons. His blood had been thinned by too many human ancestors. "Did you learn anything?"

"There are whispers of a new cult in the area."

Tia clicked her tongue. "Why do you think I would be interested in a cult?"

Lynch hunched his broad shoulders. "You said to ask about anything weird."

"There's nothing weird about cults. They've been around manipulating the weak and desperate since the beginning of time. Boringly predictable."

"This one's a death cult."

Tia's impatience was abruptly forgotten. "Death cult?"

"Yup."

"Tell me exactly what you heard."

Lynch took a minute to reply. The male had many fine qualities. He was loyal, submissive, and willing to sacrifice his life to protect her. But he wasn't the brightest creature.

"Most of the demons didn't know more than wild rumors," he at last said. "They blathered about robed forms and rituals and blood sacrifices. The usual."

"And?"

Lynch held up a beefy hand, his struggle to stay focused on his story evident in his scowl. "It wasn't until I found a bar in the Bronx that I eventually located a fairy who was several grogs into the evening. Deep enough to loosen his tongue. He told me a wild story about a rave he attended in an abandoned warehouse last week."

Tia's impatience returned with a vengeance. "Again, that's hardly vital information."

"He said while he was at the rave a goblin named Bastian was going through the crowd and picking out a few to invite to a private party."

"And he went?" Tia arched her brows. As far as she was concerned, anyone foolish enough to follow a random demon to a mysterious party deserved whatever happened to them.

Lynch shrugged. "He was promised there was going to be dragon scale there, along with human females. And after spending time with the fairy, I'd guess that he was already drunk when he was approached. His decision-making was probably a bit sketchy."

Tia frowned. It sounded more like common trafficking than a death cult. Even in these supposedly civilized days demons were notorious for capturing lesser creatures and selling them as slaves.

"Did he remember what happened?"

"He has a few fuzzy memories. The first was getting on a bus with a dozen other demons and heading to Long Island."

A dozen? It was a risk to kidnap that many demons at once. "What's in Long Island?" she demanded.

"Nothing. They went straight from the bus to a ferry that carried them to a private island."

A memory stirred in the back of Tia's mind. "Interesting," she murmured. "What happened after he got to the island?"

"He said they were led into a wooded area and told to strip naked."

Tia tried to imagine what would happen if she'd been led to the woods by a strange demon and told to strip. She would burn the place to the ground, including the demon.

"Why did they want him naked?"

"He thought they were going to an orgy." Lynch snorted, obviously as unimpressed as Tia by the fairy's lack of intelligence. "Until he saw the altar. And the robed forms with very large daggers."

Ah. Now they were getting back to the interesting part of the story. "They were going to be sacrificed?"

"The fairy didn't hang around long enough to find out," Lynch admitted. "He had an emergency crystal that he wore as an earring. It held a spell that allowed him to fade into the shadows. Once he was away from the group he ran to the shoreline and swam home."

"Does he know what happened to the others?"

"He claimed that he hadn't seen any of them since that night." Lynch shook his head. "But I'm guessing the bastard hasn't been sober since he escaped. It obviously scared the shit out of him. I doubt he'd recognize his own mother in his current condition."

Tia turned away, churning over what Lynch had discovered.

The information was vague and unreliable. Who took the word of a drunk fairy who might have imagined the entire evening? Then again, it wasn't like she had a dozen other leads to follow.

Lynch wasn't the only one who was struggling to find someone to share information. Her contacts either claimed they hadn't heard anything or had already fled the city to avoid any potential conflicts. Skirmishes between demon clans were not only dangerous, but they were also costly. Better to go into hiding than be asked to donate to one side or another.

Which meant she could continue to pace the floor or she could check out the strange cult. And she knew exactly where to start her search. There was only one local island that was fully saturated in the magic of the Gyre. The rest were too muted to offer more than a small pulse of power.

"Get the car," she abruptly commanded.

Lynch frowned. "The fairy wasn't in very good shape when I last saw him. If you want to question him you should probably wait until tomorrow."

"I'm not going to speak to the fairy."

"Then who—" Lynch bit off his question as he caught sight of Tia's expression. "I'll get the car."

"Wise choice."

Tia returned to her bedroom to change into the little black dress that Chanel had personally designed for her, and matched it with sky-high pumps that cost more than most cars. Then, smoothing her silver hair into a knot, she wrapped a lacy shawl around her shoulders and grabbed a clutch bag stuffed with potion-filled spheres before heading down to the waiting Mercedes.

The clothing wasn't just to look her best, it was necessary to blend in with the crowd.

An hour later the Mercedes was illegally double-parked and Lynch was escorting her through the large crowd gathered outside an elegant nightclub. Even living on a remote estate in Colorado, she'd heard of Valen's newest club, Neverland. It was the most exclusive nightspot in Manhattan. Which of course meant it was where everyone wanted to be.

Ignoring the muttered complaints as she squeezed through the line, Tia confidently approached the bouncer guarding the front door. He was an oversized goblin with bulging muscles beneath a black-and-gold uniform with long black hair pulled into a braid. His aura pulsed a bright red, which might have explained his arrogant expression. This was a male who stood high in the demon hierarchy. And he knew it.

Flicking a bored glance over Tia's expensive attire, he held a hand toward Lynch. "Invitation."

"It's in the mail," Lynch retorted.

The guard snapped his fingers. "Invitation."

Lynch growled deep in his throat. "I'll give you an invitation—"

"I'll handle this, Lynch," Tia interrupted, stepping between the two males to capture the goblin's narrowed gaze. Then, reaching out, she stroked her fingertips over his cheek, releasing her spell. "I'm Tia, and you're delighted to have me as your guest."

The guard frowned, momentarily resisting the magic. A second later, however, his features softened and he peered down at her with utter devotion. He was strong, but no match for her powers.

"Delighted," he breathed, the word pulled from the depths of his soul. "Such an honor, Tia."

"Yes, it is," she agreed, lowering her hand.

He offered his arm. "Allow me to show you to a table."

"No need." Nodding toward Lynch, she moved past the guard to step through the open door. "I'll find my own way."

"Are you sure?" The male doggedly followed her into the main area of the club, which was framed with smoked glass walls that reflected the laser lights bouncing off the dance floor. "I can get you a seat in the VIP section. Or a private balcony."

With a sigh, Tia turned to once again touch the male's cheek. This time the burst of magic shattered the devotion at the same time it wiped away any memory of her arrival.

"Return to your duties and forget I'm here," she whispered.

With a blank expression the guard obediently returned to his post next to the door. Tia focused her attention on the crowd that moved through the vast space with elegant grace. Demons and unsuspecting humans mixed together, filling the dance floor or posing next to the mirrored walls. Laughter and shouted conversations battled against the loud, thumping music, the scent of enchantment thick in the air.

Valen had created the perfect combination of elegance with undertones of sensual pleasure. No wonder it was such a success.

Ignoring the long bar where half-naked bartenders served the line of waiting customers, Tia threaded her way to the floating spiral staircases that led to the upper floor. Stomping next to her, Lynch eyed the crowd with a sour expression.

"You're growling," she chided softly.

"I hate these creatures."

"Which ones?"

"All of them." Lynch bared his teeth at a fairy who strolled past him with a dismissive glance. Lynch was twice as wide and a hundred pounds heavier, but the fairy's aura shimmered a deep emerald green. The slender creature could easily overpower Lynch in a battle. "They're arrogant shitheads who think they're better than me because their ancestors happened to be a bunch of inbreeders."

Tia clicked her tongue. She'd found Lynch in a fight club where he'd been used as a hapless opponent to rile up the bloodlust in the other competitors. Like a bait dog. She'd bought his contract and taken him back to her estate, knowing he would be forever grateful.

And she hadn't been wrong.

"Don't be grumpy." She climbed the stairs, heading to the most exclusive seats in the club. "Demons might be obsessed with bloodlines, but I'm not."

"I don't understand why we're here," Lynch complained. "If you want more information I can take you to a few local joints where you can get what you want for five bucks and a tankard of grog."

Reaching the upper floor, Tia paused to scan the tables. She'd never met the goblin she was searching for, but she'd seen his picture pasted in the financial magazines. Omar Burrell. Sometimes referred to as Lord Omar Burrell despite the fact that he couldn't claim royal blood. He was one of the richest demons in the world and capable of buying anything. Including a title.

His astonishing wealth meant he was the most sought-after bachelor in New York, and he was wise enough to enhance his playboy reputation by being seen at the latest social scene with the most beautiful women. Publicity was always good for business.

"I spent a fortune on these shoes," she murmured in distracted tones. "Do you really think I'm going to risk them in a sleazy bar with a horde of drunk demons?"

"Better than this place," Lynch groused.

Tia's gaze swept over the balconies that overlooked the dance floor. "Where do you suppose we would find someone capable of hiring two mages and who knows how many demons?" she demanded. She understood

Lynch's distaste for his fellow demons, but he was going to have to overcome his prejudices if they were going to get the information they needed. "Oh, and just happens to own a private island?"

Lynch widened his eyes. Had he assumed she was there because she liked the ambiance? He should know after so many years together that she lived in an isolated castle for a reason.

She hated people. And demons. And most especially vampires.

"You know who owns the place where they took the fairy?" Lynch demanded.

"I have a good guess," she murmured, her gaze landing on a male seated in the middle of the largest balcony.

He was tall and surprisingly slender for a goblin, with satin black hair that was smoothed from his perfectly chiseled face. His skin was deeply tanned and his eyes were the rich shade of cognac. His aura wasn't as dark as others, but it was enough of a flare to reveal the purity of his blood. Currently, he was sitting with a pretty fairy with golden hair and wide green eyes. A problem that was easily solved.

Tia tapped into the magic flowing through her veins, creating a thin strand of power that she sent toward the cozy couple. Then, wrapping it around a champagne bottle, she gave it a small jerk, knocking the bottle over and sending the expensive wine spewing over the fairy. On cue the female shrieked, jumping to her feet as she gazed down in horror at her sequined dress.

"This is ruined," she wailed loud enough to turn heads. She waved her hands in a flamboyant gesture, as if enjoying the attention. "Just look at this mess."

The male frowned in annoyance, clearly unimpressed by the female's dramatic reaction.

"Go dry yourself off," he commanded in low tones.

The female snapped her lips shut, clearly sensing she'd made a mistake, before she turned to scurry away from the table toward the back of the room. Tia brushed past the fleeing female, entering the private balcony and sliding into a seat next to the goblin.

"Hello, Lord Burrell." She reached out to stroke her fingers over his hand resting on the table. "May I join you?"

"This is a private balcony and I'm not looking for friends...." His words drifted away as the silvery swirl of magic seeped into his skin and spread through his body. It was a powerful enchantment, but it wouldn't last for long. She had to get the information she needed as quickly as possible. "Well, hello there. My table is your table." He leaned toward her, as if trying to breathe in her scent. "And call me Omar."

"Thank you, Omar. I'm Tia," she purred, glancing toward Lynch, who moved to block the entrance to the balcony.

Omar arched a dark brow, mistakenly assuming that Lynch was close by to protect her, not to keep the fairy from returning to her seat.

"There's no need to worry," he assured her, before he abruptly grimaced. "At least not in here. Valen takes his security very seriously."

Tia smiled as he offered her the perfect opening. "Perhaps, but a woman can't be too careful these days, can she? Not with..." She allowed her words to trail away, glancing over the edge of the balcony with a visible shudder.

He turned his hand over to grasp her fingers, his expression one of concern. "With what?"

"Not with the strange cult that's been kidnapping demons from the city." She turned back, catching the sick expression that rippled over his face. As if her mention of the cult had caused him physical distress.

Good. That meant he had some personal connection.

"You know about them?" he rasped.

"I assume that means you've met them?"

"No!" Omar coughed, as if belatedly realizing he'd already revealed that he had some knowledge of the cult. "I mean, I've heard the gossip, of course. Everyone in the city has."

Tia allowed him to cling to his pretense of ignorance, even as she easily sensed he was lying. "There are some saying that it's a death cult. Is that what you heard?"

The male visibly shuddered. "Yeah."

"And that they are currently secluded somewhere outside the city. Maybe on one of the larger estates." She widened her eyes. "Oh wait. You have a private island, don't you? That would be the perfect place to hide."

"I...they aren't there," he burst out, his voice harsh. "I don't know where you heard that, but it's...ridiculous."

His stumbled protest merely reinforced her suspicion that they were using his island. She leaned forward until their lips were nearly touching, intensifying the web of magic she'd wrapped around the male.

"Is it true they sacrifice demons?"

There was a short pause as if Omar was unconsciously struggling to break free of her enchantment. Thankfully he was no match against her spell.

"There might be some sacrificing," he finally admitted, his gaze darting from side to side, indicating that a member of the cult might be lurking nearby. "Or at least, that's what I've heard."

"Horrible. It's one thing to take advantage of the gullible, but to actually kill them? Why?" She studied his handsome features. "For power?"

His jaw clenched. "I'm trying not to think about it."

There was a harsh sincerity in his voice. He might have witnessed the sacrifice, but it hadn't been at his request. So why were the cult members practicing their evil rituals on his island? He held a position of authority among the demons. It seemed unlikely that they could force him to concede to their demands. Not without some sort of coercion.

"Where did they come from?"

His musky scent swirled through the balcony. Her question had offended him. "How would I know? I've told you I don't have anything to do with them."

"Surely the gossips have speculated on how they arrived and what brought them to this area?" she countered in soothing tones.

"There might be speculation, but no one has any answers." His gaze narrowed. "At least no one I have discovered."

Ah. He'd been doing his own research. Another indication that his connection to the cult was an unwilling one. Unfortunate, since he was her one lead to discovering the truth. Tia released her last burst of magic as she caught sight of the fairy out of the corner of her eye. She was going to toss a fit when Lynch refused to allow her back onto the balcony.

"What *can* you tell me about them?"

Omar flinched as the spell squeezed around him, bending him to her will. "They arrived at my—" He barely cut off his revealing words. "Arrived in the city a couple weeks ago," he hastily amended.

"Who arrived?"

"There are no specifics. The main group keeps their identities hidden behind robes that cover them from head to foot."

Tia swore under her breath. This wasn't how she did business. She asked questions and got the answers she needed. That's how she'd built her empire. Knowledge was power and she used it without mercy.

The sensation of banging her head against one wall after another wasn't doing a damned thing to improve her foul mood.

With an effort, she leashed her surge of impatience. One way or another she was going to get what she needed.

"Were there symbols on the robes the demons were wearing?"

He paused before slowly nodding, as if he was searching through his memory. "Yes."

"Did they look like this?" Using the tip of her finger, Tia drew a glowing line of magic on top of the table, outlining the symbol from Batu's medallion.

Omar released his breath with a loud hiss, his eyes darkening with accusation. "You've seen them."

"Unfortunately." She brushed away the glowing line. His words had confirmed that the supposed cult had something to do with her former master. And the reason she was in New York City. "Tell me about the mage."

He blinked. "What mage?"

"Don't screw with me, Omar." The smile that curved Tia's lips was an unspoken threat. She was at the end of her patience. "Tell me."

"I...I don't know her name, but she shows up every couple of days and meets with the others."

"Does she come alone?"

"Sometimes there's a demon with her. I think he belongs to the Yalicks." There was an edge of bitterness in his voice as he spoke the name of his rival clan. Did he suspect they were behind the invasion of his island? "And there are a couple local fairies who do the grunt work," he added.

"No vampire?"

He flinched at the abrupt question, sweat dotting his forehead as he struggled to break free of her enchantment. This was obviously a question he didn't want to answer.

"There's only one vampire in the city," he managed to rasp. "My master, Valen."

"What about on your private island?" she pressed.

The sweat dripped down his face, his muscles tightly clenched. "What are you asking?"

"Is there a vampire hidden there?"

"Don't be ridiculous. Valen would kill any demon stupid enough to invite a rival leech into his territory."

Tia wrinkled her nose at the sour stench that drenched the air. This wasn't a fear that his reputation would be damaged. Or that Valen might punish him. This was terror that went to his very soul, as if he had seen something so evil he couldn't bear to think of it.

"But that doesn't mean one couldn't sneak in and force his way onto someone's private property," Tia insisted. "It wouldn't be the innocent demon's fault if that happened."

"There's no vampire," he ground out, his face flushing and the veins of his neck visibly throbbing with emotion. "Stop saying that."

Tia's lips parted, but before she could demand to know what he'd witnessed, the sound of a shrill voice cut through her intense focus. The fairy had realized that not only was her way to the balcony blocked, but also, there was a new woman sitting in her place. She was clearly unhappy with the situation.

"Shit. I don't have time for this," Tia muttered. "Lynch," she called out, waiting for her servant to glance in her direction before nodding her head at the outraged female.

Lynch's expression tightened with a reluctance to leave her unprotected, but grudgingly he turned back to the fairy and wrapped his hands around her slender waist. Then, with one smooth motion he tossed her over his shoulder and headed toward the stairs.

As Tia had hoped, the infuriated female screamed at the top of her lungs, beating Lynch's back with her fists and kicking her feet hard enough to offer glimpses of her lacy black undies. No surprise, the entire club turned to watch the noisy spectacle, allowing Tia to rise to her feet and boldly grab Omar's sweaty face in her hands.

"Stop!"

The goblin tried to jerk away, but Tia was leaning down to capture his gaze as she released the last of her magic. Her talent as a dream teller made it easier to enter the minds of others, but she was reaching the limit of her endurance. She would have one chance to discover what Omar was so anxious to keep hidden.

Thankfully the male hadn't developed any shields to protect his mind. Typical for a powerful demon. They assumed that as long as they were bigger and stronger than most other creatures, they didn't have to worry about a direct attack. Their arrogance left them vulnerable.

Slipping into his memories, Tia skimmed over the past few days that had been spent at his apartment in the city, easily following the trail back to a dark night a week ago. She could see Omar striding through the woods, a semiautomatic weapon clutched in his hands. He'd caught the sound of demons, along with the acrid stench of smoke, just when he'd been about to sweep his date up the stairs to his bed. The interruption had infuriated him. It was bad enough that anyone would be stupid enough to intrude into his privacy, but to ruin a romantic evening was unforgivable.

He fully intended to teach the idiots a lesson they would never forget.

Charging into the clearing, he stumbled to a halt as he realized it wasn't a horde of drunken intruders who could be easily intimidated. Instead there were a dozen robed figures who were standing around a blazing fire.

"What the fuck?"

Omar lifted the gun, prepared to shoot first and ask questions later, but before he could squeeze the trigger a young woman appeared from the woods, wrapping him in strands of magic.

A mage.

Glaring in frustration, he was more annoyed than frightened, assuming that a rival clan had decided to make a move against his stronghold. It wasn't the first time, and Omar was confident his own soldiers would soon swarm the place to effectively end the threat.

It wasn't until the robed forms silently parted to reveal the altar that had been placed over the fire that he accepted this was something he'd never seen before. There was a naked body stretched on the flat stone, and at least two more bodies that were lying on the ground, obviously drained of blood and staring sightlessly in Omar's direction.

With a shocked gasp, he swept his gaze back to the altar where a robed form was bent toward the screaming demon, its face buried in the gaping wound that had been carved into the creature's stomach. Was that thing eating the demon while they were still alive?

Omar instinctively stumbled back. He wasn't opposed to causing his enemies pain. Or even torture. But this? It was sick.

He was near the edge of the trees when the robed form finally lifted its head. Omar wasn't sure what he expected. A demented goblin. Or a fairy high on some exotic drug.

Instead he caught a glimpse of a broad face with eyes sunk so deep they looked like black holes and chunks of flesh that were peeling off like a snake shedding its skin.

Was it a zombie? He'd never believed they were real, but…

His dazed thoughts were shattered as the beast parted his mouth and the long fangs of a vampire glinted in the garish glow of the firelight.

Screaming in horror, Omar turned and ran.

He didn't know where he was going, but he was certain he was never coming back.

Chapter 16

After spending several hours moving from one demon bar to another in hopes of locating Alison, Ravyr at last insisted they call it a night. Not only was dawn less than an hour away, but Maya was exhausted.

Of course, the stubborn woman wasn't willing to admit that the battle with Joyce, not to mention her acute sense of guilt at being forced to kill her friend, had sapped her strength. She would willingly continue the search until she collapsed if he hadn't insisted he needed shelter.

Her weariness did have one benefit. She'd been too tired to argue when the SUV had pulled to a halt in front of the towering glass-and-steel building in Manhattan. She'd even limited her annoyance to a narrow-eyed glare when they'd entered Valen and Peri's penthouse and a servant had led them to the guest suite.

Choosing the bedroom on the far side of the small living room, Ravyr had taken a long shower to remove the smell from the demon clubs and pulled on a pair of jogging pants and a sweatshirt he found hanging in the closet. Then, returning to the shared space, he discovered that the shutters had firmly closed to shut out the morning light and that several lamps had been switched on, bathing the elegant silver and charcoal furnishings in a soft glow.

Maya was already pacing the thick carpet, nibbling on a croissant that had been left on a silver tray along with fruit and freshly brewed coffee. Her hair was damp from the shower and she was wearing a satin robe that clung to her lush curves. Ravyr's fangs lengthened as a sudden hunger slammed into him.

Not for croissants or coffee. It was Maya he was desperate to taste. Her blood. Her lips. The sweet flesh between her legs.

Coming to an abrupt halt, Maya slowly turned to face him. As if she could sense the desire that pulsed through the air. For a searing moment her eyes darkened with a need that matched his; a profound, ruthless passion that demanded satisfaction.

Then, narrowing her gaze in frustration, she tossed the croissant on the low coffee table, brushing the crumbs from her fingers.

"I can't believe you convinced me to stay here," she groused in accusing tones, clearly in a mood to blame him for everything wrong in her life.

Ravyr arched a brow, strolling forward to stand directly in front of her. "I have many fine talents." He boldly stroked a finger over her cheek. She trembled beneath his light touch, but thankfully she didn't pull away. "A few that I hope to demonstrate very, very soon. But convincing Maya Rosen to do something she doesn't want to do isn't one of them." His fingers traced the curve of her lower lip. "You're here because you know Valen is out of town. And it's currently safer than your home."

"Are you saying I'm stubborn?"

"Are you looking for a fight?"

She furrowed her brow before heaving a harsh sigh. "Maybe." Another sigh. "Yes. I hate this."

"It's not so bad. A little posh for my taste, but I've stayed in worse places."

Ravyr swept a glance over the sleek furniture and expensive paintings hung on the walls. He'd never had a permanent lair, and until now, he'd never considered putting down roots. Suddenly, he tried to imagine himself surrounded by his own belongings. It wouldn't be like this place. Like he said, it was too posh and he wasn't really a penthouse sort of vampire. Perhaps a cabin in the mountains. Or a coffee shop in Linden, New Jersey.

All that really mattered was that Maya was at his side.

Maya shivered. "I hate that the business I struggled so hard to create has been tainted. And I hate that Joyce is dead because of me."

"No." Ravyr's tone was sharp. He wasn't going to allow her to blame herself. "None of this is your fault."

"It has to be," she insisted.

"Why?" He frowned down at her troubled expression. "What's going through that cunning mind of yours?"

"Whatever is happening now is connected to the past." Magic prickled in the air, as if Maya was struggling to leash her emotions. "To Batu."

"I agree." Ravyr knew better than to try to soothe this woman with lies. She was too smart not to realize everything happening was linked together. "But that doesn't make you responsible."

"If Batu's here to punish me, then I have at least some blame," she insisted.

"We don't even know if Batu is alive."

Ravyr cupped her cheeks in his hands, the feel of her rough scars sending a burst of fury through him. He almost hoped his old nemesis *had* survived. Nothing would give him greater pleasure than destroying Batu. As slowly and with as much agonizing pain as possible.

Her expression tightened. "What else explains what's happening?"

"I don't know, but if the bastard had escaped all those years ago, then why wait so long to hunt you down?" He deliberately paused, allowing her time to consider his words. "And most importantly, why not confront you in person? He was never a leader who made meticulous plans and set out long-term goals."

"No." She grimaced. "He was a petulant child who indulged in constant temper tantrums and impulsively hopped from one decision to another."

"Exactly." He brushed his thumb over her cheek. "If he had survived, he would have ripped apart the world searching for you. And there wouldn't be incompetent servants trying to kill you. He would have insisted that he destroy you with his own hands."

"There's a connection," she obstinately maintained.

"I agree." He gazed deep into the clear green of her eyes, for the first time noticing the emerald flecks at the center. Beautiful. "I don't know if Batu is alive or not, but I followed the pulse of magic to this location. It's a part of the same mystery."

"I hate mysteries."

His gaze lowered to her full lips, his fangs lengthening. They were a lush invitation, promising eternal pleasure.

"That's odd," he murmured.

"Why?"

"Because you are the most intriguing, mysterious creature I've ever encountered."

She tensed, as if sensing his thoughts were no longer focused on Batu, or the danger that waited just outside the door.

"There's no intrigue," she protested, licking the lips he was so desperate to kiss. "I say exactly what's on my mind and do what I believe is best for my friends and the Witch's Brew. It's all tediously straightforward and uncomplicated."

"Uncomplicated?" Ravyr released a sharp laugh. This female had captured his unbeating heart from the moment he'd seen her seated on that damned balcony. Since then she'd haunted his dreams, enticed him to forget his duty to his brothers. And now she beguiled him with glimpses of a future he'd never considered a possibility.

"Why is that funny?"

"I'm laughing at myself," he assured her.

"Because?"

He stepped close enough to feel her delicious heat seep through his clothing. The warmth spread over his chilled body, along with a tingle of magic that danced over his skin like electricity. Ravyr hissed. The sensation was excruciatingly erotic.

"All those years ago, I told myself that I had to keep a distance between us because I was at Batu's lair to discover what he was hiding," he confessed in low tones. "I couldn't allow myself to be distracted by a beautiful mage, no matter how fascinating she might be."

Pain darkened her eyes. "You accomplished your goal."

Guilt sliced through him as sharp as a dagger. He'd known she was miserable. And that he had the power to sweep her off her feet and rescue her from the male's brutal companionship. And honestly, if he could go back in time he would make a different choice. But there'd been more than one reason that any chance of a relationship had been doomed.

"It wasn't just duty that kept me at a distance. I sensed the barriers you had built around yourself from the moment I walked into Batu's lair," he gently reminded her. "You glared at me like I was a bug you wanted to scrape off your shoe."

She jutted her chin. "Do you blame me? Vampires destroyed my life."

His fingers smoothed over her scars and along the obstinate contour of her jaw. She'd used her well-earned prejudice against leeches as a weapon to deny their fierce attraction. It was time to confront their complicated history and hopefully build a new future. One that included more than a reluctant partnership.

"These barriers went deeper than your hatred for leeches," he insisted. "You'd been betrayed by someone else. At the time I didn't know it was your own mother."

Maya flinched, but for once she didn't scuttle behind her defensive shield. She even allowed him to glimpse the lingering sorrow in the depths of her eyes. A small miracle.

"My mother did what she thought was best," she forced herself to say.

"That doesn't make it easier to be the one sacrificed."

A wistful smile twisted her lips. "No, but eventually I accepted that life is filled with hard choices."

His jaw tightened. "Some harder than others."

She slowly nodded. "And there was a part of me that wasn't ready to open myself to any more disappointment when you arrived at the lair. I could deal with pain and fury. Those were emotions that I understood. Anything else terrified me."

He yearned to wrap her in his arms and pull her tight, but he wasn't going to risk destroying the moment. This was the first time she'd allowed him to see the woman who lurked beneath the powerful mage. Vulnerable. Scarred. And yet, determined to survive.

"You were afraid of being hurt again."

"It took a long time to trust that I could be happy without having it ripped away," she admitted. "And that opening my heart and my home was worth the risk."

Jealousy blasted through Ravyr. Or at least, he assumed the unhinged emotion was jealousy. He'd never felt it before. Why would he? He didn't have possessions or power or a social position. He didn't have a long-term lover or family.

None of the things that caused creatures to behave like a lunatic.

Not until Maya.

Gritting his teeth, he struggled to squash the sensation. Something easier said than done.

"Sharing your life with who?" he demanded. "The Benefactor?"

She made a gratifying sound of disgust. "Certainly not. I might trust my mysterious Benefactor more than vampires." She stopped as if considering her words. "*Marginally* more than vampires," she corrected herself. "But he's a necessary inconvenience, not a friend."

"Ah." A ridiculous surge of relief rushed through him, along with his ability to use his brain. Thank the gods. "You're talking about your partners at the Witch's Brew."

Her features abruptly softened. "Peri and Skye are more than partners. They're my family."

There was a fierce sincerity in her voice and once again Ravyr felt a prick of an unpleasant emotion. This time it was envy rather than jealousy. He'd give anything to have her expression melt when she thought about him.

"You're lucky you found each other."

A sudden sparkle chased the shadows from her eyes. "Actually, I'm not sure if it was luck or destiny."

"Why do you say that?"

"I was driving through a random town late at night and I took a wrong turn," she explained. "I was trying to circle back to the main road when I saw a woman being attacked by human thugs. Even from a distance I could sense she was a mage...a very powerful mage...but it was obvious she had no training. I stopped to help her and later invited her to join me in Jersey." She paused, as if lost in her memories. "Still, it wasn't until she walked through my front door that I realized how much I needed a friend. A few years later Skye appeared and I knew immediately she belonged with us." She shrugged. "Luck or destiny, it doesn't matter. I'm just so thankful they are a part of my life."

Despite his stab of envy, Ravyr was pleased that Maya had found her friends. They'd given her the love that she'd been denied for too long. And obviously helped her to build the Witch's Brew into a business that made Maya proud.

But those same friends had found new lives with their mates. Leaving Maya alone again.

"And now?" he asked in gentle tones.

She hunched her shoulders. "They're still my family."

"But you miss them." It was a statement, not a question. He could feel the emptiness that had settled in the center of her heart.

"Yes, I miss them." She grimaced. "Every day."

He lowered his head, brushing a light kiss over her lips. "You don't have to be alone."

Lifting her hands, Maya laid them flat against his chest. "What about you?"

He nibbled her lower lip, allowing the tips of his fangs to scrape against her tender skin.

"Are you asking if I have friends?"

"Do you have to be alone?"

It was a question that Ravyr hadn't considered. He'd never felt the urge to join with a clan or stay in one place long enough to become acquainted with the locals. Perhaps that was why it was so easy to accept Sinjon's offer to become his spy.

Being a loner wasn't a sacrifice, it'd been his nature.

"It's comfortable," he admitted. "I can come and go as I please without anyone depending on me." He kissed her again, savoring the sweet softness of her lips. Then, lifting his head, he gazed down at her with blatant need. "But I hope that in the very near future I can share my life with a partner." He paused. "And lover."

The scent of warm feminine desire perfumed the air, stirring his hunger to a fever pitch. But even as his arms wrapped around her waist, she pressed her hands against his chest.

"Won't your master make that decision for you?"

Ravyr frowned. Was that why she tried to deny the desire between them? Because she assumed he would abandon her? Not that he blamed her. He'd always believed his loyalty to Sinjon and his brothers was more important than anything. Including his own happiness.

It wasn't until this moment that he realized that he had no intention of continuing his role as royal spy. He respected Sinjon and what he was attempting to accomplish for the vampires, but his future was bound to the woman who'd stolen his unbeating heart.

Always assuming they managed to survive whatever was hunting Maya, he wryly conceded.

"I might not be a member of the Cabal, but I'm not a slave," he assured her, his hands smoothing up the curve of her back. "I can walk away whenever I want."

A blush of awareness stained her cheeks, her eyes darkening with desire. "And what do you want?"

"You, Maya Rosen." Swooping his head down, he claimed her mouth in a kiss of sheer possession. He shuddered as her lips parted, allowing him the taste of her sweet desire. And magic. So much magic. "I want you," he rasped.

Her fingers curled into the thick fabric of his sweatshirt, her back arching as she pressed against his hard body.

"You left," she accused.

He scraped his fangs down the line of her jaw. "Never again."

"No." Her voice was sharp. "No promises until we've destroyed whoever or whatever is threatening me."

He nipped at her chin, careful not to puncture her delicate skin. Not until she gave her permission.

"This isn't a promise," he argued.

"It isn't?"

"It's destiny."

Her fingers continued to grip his sweatshirt, her hips pushing against his thickening erection.

"For now."

He chuckled as he watched her accept that their desire was irresistible even as she maintained an illusion that they could control the fiery inferno. "Stubborn."

"Relentless."

Trailing kisses down the curve of her throat, he lowered his hands to cup her ass. "Ingredients for an interesting relationship."

She rubbed her hips back and forth, the friction creating jolts of intense pleasure.

"More likely a recipe for disaster," she warned.

"This doesn't feel like a disaster." His fingers dug into her soft flesh, his tongue stroking the rapid pulse at the base of her throat. A growl rumbled in his own throat. He was going to devour her. Every silken, delicious inch of her. His lips moved to trace the V of her robe. "Or this."

Magic swirled through the air, the silvery ribbons wrapping around them like chains. Ravyr was enchanted. He'd never been turned on by restraints during sex, but nothing was more erotic than the promise of being forever bound to this luscious mage.

"I can't believe this is happening," Maya breathed.

"Can't believe what is happening?"

"That I'm kissing a vampire."

Reluctantly, Ravyr lifted his head to stare down at her flushed face. "Do you want me to stop?"

With a gratifying determination, Maya grabbed the bottom of his sweatshirt and jerked it over his head before tossing it aside. "Don't you dare."

Relief cascaded through him, along with a strange sensation of gratitude. There was no mistaking the passion that burned in her emerald eyes. Right now she was seeing him as a desirable male, not a leech who'd walked away when she needed him.

He glided his hands up the curve of her back, his touch a tender apology. "I'm sorry I can't change the past."

She held his gaze, a wistful smile touching her lips. "The past created the woman I am today. It's never been easy, but I'm proud of who I've become."

"I'm proud of her too," Ravyr growled, threading his fingers through her hair as he tugged back her head to study each sweep and curve of her beautiful face. "Strong. Independent. A survivor."

Her lips parted in invitation. "Let's hope so."

"I'm not going to hope." His gaze lingered on the soft temptation of her mouth, imagining the feel of her lips stroking over his bare skin before wrapping around his cock. His muscles clenched in glorious anticipation. "I'm going to make damned sure that we have a future. Together. But for tonight I want to forget everything but you, Maya."

"Forgetting is good." She ran her hands down his chest, boldly exploring his clenched muscles. "What else do you want?"

He feathered tiny kisses along the side of her throat. "To taste you," he admitted without hesitation.

"My blood?" Maya shivered, but there wasn't fear in her scent. It was pure desire.

"Everything," he growled, pressing the tips of his fangs against her skin. "Everything from head to toe."

"Everything is a lot," she murmured.

"Yes," he conceded without apology.

"What if I'm not ready to give everything?"

He didn't bother to argue. Eventually she would accept that they were destined to be together. Until then, he fully intended to enjoy what she was willing to share.

Thoroughly enjoy, he assured himself, impatiently tugging at the belt wrapped around her waist. He needed this woman naked. Now. With an eagerness he did nothing to hide, Ravyr peeled away the silky robe to reveal the treasure beneath.

Good gods above. Ravyr grunted, feeling as if he'd been punched in the gut.

He'd suspected she was beautiful. But this...

She was beyond exquisite. Not just the soft breasts, crested with pink nipples. Or the narrow curve of her waist that flared toward her hips. Or even the flawless beauty of her satin-smooth skin. It was the proud angle of her shoulders and the confident smile that touched her lips.

This was a woman who understood that she was desirable and his approval wasn't necessary. That realization was fiercely erotic. What could be sexier than a woman who knew who she was and what she wanted?

Running his hands down the curve of her spine, he savored the warm silk of her flesh before pulling her tight against his hard length.

"Tell me what you want from me," he commanded as he gazed down at her flushed face.

"I want your touch," she whispered, her eyes smoldering with a sensual heat as she lowered her hand to wrap her fingers around his cock. She smiled when he released a muttered oath. The pleasure was so intense it bordered on pain. In the best possible way. "Your kisses," she continued, leaning forward to brush her lips over the middle of his chest. Directly over his unbeating heart. "Your body."

"You can have it all," he growled, lowering his head to trace his lips over the pillowy curve of her breast. "I'm yours. Now and forever."

Savoring the sensation of her fingers exploring the throbbing length of his arousal, Ravyr kissed a path between her breasts. At the same time, his hands stroked down the curve of her ass and between her legs. The pungent scent of her desire filled the air, and, using her low groans to guide his touch, he dipped a finger between her soft folds.

"Ravyr."

His name came out as a gasp and with a soft chuckle, he slid his finger into the warmth of her body. She arched in pleasure, her eyes squeezed shut even as she continued to stroke his cock.

"I'm here, Maya," he said, his voice harsh. "I'm not going anywhere."

Sliding in a second finger, he thrust them in rhythm with her strokes, and then, turning his head, he sucked her clenched nipple between his fangs, teasing it with the sharp tips.

Raw lust sizzled between them, threatening to burn out of control, but first, he had another hunger he desperately yearned to sate.

"Maya. I need..." His desire was so vast he couldn't even speak the words.

"Yes," she breathed.

Not giving her time to reconsider, Ravyr plunged his aching fangs deep into her flesh, the taste of her blood exploding on his tongue with shocking force. It was rich with power, the magic bubbling through him with a heady intoxication. He felt drunk, his mind spinning as the blood seared through him, burning away who he'd been to create a new Ravyr. A male bonded for all eternity to this woman.

Mine. The knowledge whispered through him with absolute certainty. This woman was a part of his very soul. As if they'd been made to fit together. And without her, he knew beyond a doubt he would never be whole again.

Ravyr growled in pleasure as he continued to drink deeply from her vein. He would have laughed if he'd heard any of his brothers speak about their mates in such melodramatic terms, but it was the truth. And he would proudly proclaim his devotion to Maya Rosen far and wide.

Lost in her own pleasure, Maya tilted her head to the side to allow him greater access as he withdrew his fangs and gently licked away the puncture wounds.

"I need more," he teased, nuzzling kisses up the curve of her neck.

"Greedy," she chided, her voice unsteady, as if she was struggling to breathe.

"For you?" He lifted his head, gazing down at her with a smoldering intensity. "Always and forever."

She held his gaze, an emotion so vast he couldn't name it easing the ancient pain in her eyes.

"Then take me."

That was all the invitation he needed. Grasping the back of her thighs, he lifted her off her feet in one smooth motion. Instinctively she wrapped her legs around his waist, her fingers digging into the width of his shoulders as she tilted back her head with an expression of surprise.

"I intend to take you, my love," he assured her, his voice a rough rumble. "Over and over."

Her soft laugh brushed his cheek as he carried her forward. "Like I said...greedy."

Ignoring the nearby couch, he instead crossed the room to press her back against the wall. Then, with an effort, he forced himself to pause and savor the sheer beauty of the woman in his arms. The elegant sweep of her features that were framed by the satin curtain of black hair, the emerald eyes that shimmered with the oldest magic of all, pure feminine temptation, and the plush curve of her lips.

A siren singing her song, luring him into the depths of her passion. And he was a willing victim.

Raw lust hammered against him with savage force as he parted his legs to brace himself and, with a slow, steady thrust, penetrated her body.

They groaned in unison as his cock sank deep into her slick heat, her nails digging into his flesh hard enough to draw blood.

It didn't seem possible, but the pricks of pain intensified his pleasure, and with a groan, Ravyr buried his face in the curve of her neck, his muscles corded as he thrust his hips in a delicious cadence that matched her soft pants of pleasure.

It was a pagan tempo. One that was as old as time...

Chapter 17

Maya had suffered from claustrophobia since Batu had locked her in a cramped closet for an entire week. At the time she'd been convinced she was going to suffocate alone in the dark. Ever since then, she'd hated the sensation of being confined. A heavy blanket would stir her anxiety. Or a hug that went on too long.

Lying tangled in Ravyr's arms, she waited for the sense of panic to hit. Not only was she pressed tightly against his naked form, but also, he was holding her in a grip that warned he didn't intend to let go.

It should have made her crazy.

Instead, an unexpected peace had settled deep in her heart. As if she'd finally found the place where she truly belonged.

She heaved a small sigh, her hands smoothing up the curve of his back. Destiny obviously had a sense of humor....

Lifting his head as if sensing her strange thoughts, Ravyr gazed down at her with a worried expression.

"Are you okay?"

Her lips twitched. Her entire body ached from their latest bout of lovemaking that had nearly shattered the bed frame. It was glorious.

"I'm tougher than I look," she assured him.

He blinked, as if caught off guard by her response. "I wasn't talking about physical injury, although I'd be horrified if I thought I hurt you." The turquoise gaze swept down her body, clearly looking for bruises. Only when he looked convinced that her delicate skin was unblemished did he return his gaze to her face. "I meant are you okay with what happened between us?"

Her lips twisted into a wry smile. "I would think my screams of pleasure would assure you I was enjoying every moment."

"A vampire can always hope."

He brushed his lips over her brow, the touch exquisitely tender. At the same time, she felt his muscles clench, as if expecting a blow.

"What's troubling you?" she demanded.

"You."

Her startled laugh echoed through the guest bedroom. She wasn't sure the exact time that Ravyr had carried her from the main sitting room to this spot, but it had been between bouts of sweaty, mind-numbing sex.

"That's not exactly what a woman wants to hear when she's lying naked in your arms."

"I've never had a mate before," he murmured.

"Ravyr."

He lifted his head to gaze down at her with a brooding intensity. "I swear, I'm not asking anything of you. It's just terrifying."

She reached up to trace his bluntly carved features. He wasn't handsome like most vampires. He had a savage, untamed beauty that had once upon a time reminded her of a lethal predator. But beneath that dangerous façade she'd discovered a male who possessed an unwavering loyalty that a woman could always trust.

Whether it was with her life or her heart.

"I'm terrifying?" she teased.

"It's terrifying to care so deeply," he clarified, his eyes darkening with an intense emotion. "If anything happened to you..."

Her fingers pressed against his lips, silencing his fear. "I defeated Batu once. I'll do it again if I have to."

He smoothed his hand down the curve of her spine, his cool touch sending goose bumps dancing over her skin. She shivered, silently admitting she was becoming addicted to the icy sensation.

"Your courage has always astonished me. Even when you were imprisoned in Batu's lair you walked through the tunnels with your head held high. Like you were a queen surveying her castle."

"I wasn't going to give Batu the satisfaction of seeing me beaten." She didn't add that she was even more queen-like whenever he happened to be visiting the lair. Her pride demanded that she disguise her vulnerability. "And I never doubted that one day I would escape. It was the only thing that kept me going."

"So what keeps you going now?"

"My friends." Her fingers skimmed down the line of his jaw. "The Witch's Brew."

"And?"

"Eventually I'll discover another mage in need of training," she said, acutely aware of how hollow the words sounded.

As if she was trying to convince herself that was the future she desired. Ravyr's expression remained brooding. "Will that bring you happiness?"

"I *am* happy."

"What about fulfilled?"

She hesitated. She hadn't lied when she said she was happy. Or at least, she was content. After years of abuse, she'd created a home, a business, and a sense of security that no one could take from her.

But fulfilled?

"Is anyone?" she challenged.

"I am," he said without hesitation, his hands pressing her tight against his thickening cock. "Now. Having you in my arms completes me. It's that simple. And that earth shattering." His brow arched as her lips curved at his words. "Why are you smiling?"

"Earth shattering," she explained. "That's a perfect way to describe you."

He appeared genuinely confused. "I appreciate the comparison, but it's not very accurate." He grimaced, obviously remembering his past. "I've spent my life in the shadows. Silent and invisible."

"Never to me." She traced the curve of his lips, feeling the sharp tips of his fangs. Another shiver raced through her. Those fangs had speared deep into her throat, drinking her blood and creating havoc in her body. The pleasure had been nothing less than sheer bliss and she honestly couldn't wait to feed him again. And again. And again... "As much as I wanted to pretend I didn't notice you... I couldn't get you out of my mind," she forced herself to continue.

"Good." His eyes smoldered with a turquoise-and-silver fire as he easily caught the scent of her desire. "I intend to stay there. Just as I intend to stay in your bed."

"A bold claim."

"You make me bold." He parted his lips to reveal his lengthening fangs. "And hungry. Very, very hungry."

Maya released her breath with a soft hiss as he lowered his head to scrape his fangs down the curve of her throat. Oh yes.

Maya.

The unwelcome voice whispered through the back of her mind. Maya screwed her eyes shut, trying to pretend she couldn't hear it. Like she was a child hoping to avoid an unpleasant task.

Maya.

The voice was sharper, more insistent. A warning that she wasn't going to be able to ignore the looming intrusion.

"Ravyr." She pressed her hands against his chest. "Wait."

He tilted back his head to study her with blatant concern. "Is something wrong?"

Very wrong, she silently groused.

Not only was her body on fire with the need to finish what Ravyr had started, but she wasn't in the mood to shatter the illusion that they were safely hidden in a bubble that couldn't be touched by the outside world.

Unfortunately, she knew the aggravating mage too well to hope she would take the hint and go away. And more importantly, there was a simmering impatience in the mental connection that suggested this was more than a social call.

"It's Tia," she told Ravyr. "She's here."

"In the penthouse?"

"In the lobby."

His muscles clenched as he prepared to leap off the bed. "I'll get rid of her."

"No." Maya grasped his shoulders, keeping him in place. "I think she's here because she has information. I need to speak with her."

Ravyr's features tightened, but he didn't argue. Instead he brushed a light kiss over her mouth.

"*We* need to speak with her," he gently corrected.

"We need to speak with her," she agreed, her lips instinctively parting in invitation.

Ravyr groaned, his hand moving to cup her breast as he buried his face in her tangled hair. "Can it be later? Next year?" His thumb stroked her nipple to a hard peak of need. "Next decade?"

Maya shivered, battling against the urge to give into temptation. As much as she wanted to pretend that they were safe from the world, she knew deep in her heart it would be a mistake to waste time. The sooner they located the danger hunting her, the sooner they could eliminate it.

After that...

Well, she had high hopes for the future.

"It feels urgent," she warned as Tia's voice once again echoed through her brain.

"Right." Ravyr's expression was hard with frustration, but his touch was gentle as he placed a last lingering kiss on her lips. Then, with one smooth motion, he shoved himself off the bed to head toward the door. "I'll have her sent up."

Heaving a sigh, Maya climbed off the mattress and headed to the attached bathroom. She wasn't going to face her old friend looking like she'd spent the night in the gutter.

After a quick shower, she pulled on a pair of cream slacks and a navy-blue sweater that she'd packed in a suitcase before leaving the Witch's Brew and brushed her damp hair until it was silky smooth. Studying herself in the steamy mirror, she arranged her features into an expression of aloof composure. This was the Maya Rosen she shared with the world.

Exiting the guest suite, Maya entered the public salon just as the heavy shutters slid up. She glanced in surprise at the large windows that offered a stunning view of the New York skyline. It was night? She hadn't realized it was so late.

Clearly the old saying was true. Time really did fly when she was having fun.

With a shake of her head, Maya turned toward the silver-haired mage standing in the center of the room.

"Tia," she murmured.

The older woman pressed her lips together, peering down her slender nose in blatant disapproval. She was wearing a black pair of slacks and matching turtleneck with comfortable shoes. Maya had never seen her onetime friend in such sensible clothing.

"A vampire, Maya. Really?" Tia clicked her tongue. "I thought you of all women had better taste."

Maya smiled. There was nothing Tia could say to make her regret her night with Ravyr.

"Ravyr is different."

"He's a cold-blooded leech. Same as the others."

Maya strolled forward, her smile fading. This female didn't have the right to criticize anyone. Especially not Ravyr.

"He's the male who was there when I needed him the most," she reminded the woman. "He saved my life."

Tia stilled, her expression suddenly wry. "Ah. He told you, did he?"

"No. I had a vision of being carried from Batu's lair." She deliberately paused. "By Ravyr."

Tia tilted her chin as if daring Maya to demand an apology. "Only after the bastard was dead. Why didn't your hero do something when Batu was tormenting us?"

Maya waved aside the accusation. She'd made her peace with Ravyr's loyalty to his people. Back then, he was focused on his duty to Sinjon, not on rescuing a mage he barely knew.

"The question I'm more interested in is why you lied to me."

"I didn't lie," Tia countered with a shrug. "You assumed I pulled you out of the lair and I didn't bother to correct you."

"Oh no. You're not blaming me for this. A lie is a lie."

"You should have asked more questions."

Maya ground her teeth. Tia was stubborn, but so was she. She deserved an answer.

"Why didn't you just tell me what happened?"

Tia made a sound of impatience. "You know why, Maya. It suited my purpose to let you think you were in my debt."

There it was.

Tia needed something from her, and she had been willing to do whatever necessary to get what she wanted.

"You didn't need to manipulate me for that." A surprising sadness tugged at Maya's heart. She'd lost her best friend when she'd walked out of that mountain hut. It'd left a hole inside her that had never been filled. "I never forgot you were the one to protect me when I first came to Batu's lair. And that it was your training that gave me the power to stand on my own."

"And to walk away from me," Tia snapped.

"We wanted different things for our future."

Tia's expression hardened with disdain. "Together we could have ruled the world. Instead you wasted your life pandering to the leeches and serving humans like you were a peasant."

"No, I devoted my life to creating a home and then filling it with a family," Maya argued. "And I wouldn't change a thing."

Tia's expression could have cut glass, but before she could continue her tirade on Maya's lack of ambition, a cool breeze swept through the room as Ravyr appeared in the open doorway.

Maya's breath locked in her lungs at the sight of the worn jeans and black T-shirt that clung to his hard body, and the glint of silver-blond hair that had been shaved close to his head. In the muted light, his eyes glowed like polished turquoise. *It's ridiculous,* she silently acknowledged. They'd spent enough time together that she shouldn't need to brace herself for the impact of his glorious beauty, but it smashed into her like a freight train each time he entered a room.

"Did I miss something?" he murmured, his gaze locked on Tia as he moved to stand next to Maya.

"Our conversation is private and none of your business," the older mage snapped.

"How did you know we were here?" Ravyr demanded, his tone suspicious.

"Seriously? Everyone in the city knows the two of you are staying here," Tia said with a sneer. "It's the chatter of the demon world."

Ravyr folded his arms over his chest. "I doubt that."

"Check out the social media."

Maya grimaced. She didn't doubt Tia's claim. Demons were weirdly obsessed with vampires, treating them with the same awe and obsessive fascination that humans reserved for celebrities. No doubt because their social hierarchy could be drastically improved by an intimate relationship with a member of the Cabal. If she'd been spotted coming into Valen's lair with a mysterious vampire, the gossip would be spreading like wildfire through the city.

Unfortunate, but at the bottom of her current list of worries.

"Why are you here, Tia?" she demanded.

Tia arched a brow at her blunt tone. "Unlike some, I haven't been wasting my time," the older woman drawled.

Ravyr reached to brush his fingers over Maya's cheek. "I assure you our time wasn't wasted."

"Oh please—"

Maya interrupted the brewing argument. "Just tell me why you're here, Tia."

Tia sent Ravyr a jaundiced glare before turning her attention to Maya. "I found your mage."

It took a second for Maya to grasp who she meant. "Alison?"

Tia shrugged. "If she's the one you claimed shoved you into the mirror."

"Where is she?"

Tia held up a slender hand. "Let me clarify. I know the location where she was meeting with her friends."

Maya refused to be disappointed. All she needed was a place to start, and she would be able to track down the bitch.

"Where?"

"A private island owned by Lord Omar Burrell."

Maya blinked. That was the last place she would have looked for the missing mage. "Are you sure?"

"Who is Omar Burrell?" Ravyr asked.

"One of the most powerful demons in the city," Maya said, her tone distracted. "But he's never been involved in politics or the squabble between clans. In fact, he goes out of his way to avoid being drawn into any disputes."

"I don't think he's involved now," Tia retorted. "At least not willingly. The cult simply chose his island as a convenient location."

Maya absently nodded. That made more sense. She'd never been invited to the private island, but she'd heard that it was isolated with heavily wooded areas that would be a perfect location to avoid unwanted attention from the local Cabal.

"What makes you think Alison is there?"

"Last night my servant located a male fairy who claimed that he'd been lured from a local rave with the promise of dragon scale and taken to the island."

"How did they get there?" Maya demanded. "It's strictly off limits."

"He claims he was taken by bus to Long Island and then ferried over to the island."

"That takes organization," Maya murmured, more than a little troubled by the realization this was more than a mage and couple of demons floundering around trying to kill her. "What else did he tell you?"

"Once he got there, the fairy caught sight of several robed forms standing around a fire," she shared in impatient tones. "He was smart enough to recognize that he wasn't there for fun and games, and managed to slip away unnoticed. The others who went with them weren't so lucky. He hasn't seen them since that night."

"Robed forms?" A chill inched down Maya's spine. "What were they doing?"

"My sources claim that it's a death cult," Tia said. "And that they've been sacrificing demons."

The words did nothing to ease Maya's sudden sense of dread. An organized group of robe-wearing creatures who were sacrificing demons. That couldn't be a good thing.

But she was suddenly distracted as she tried to imagine the smug, petulant Alison rubbing elbows with the strange cult.

"Wait. Why would a mage be interested in a cult that uses demon sacrifice? Only witches can use blood to create dark magic. Unless..."

The words died on Maya's lips as she abruptly recalled her early years living in a remote village. There had been a few magic users who had traveled through the area. Most claimed to be healers, or fortune tellers, or mystics. And a few had the talent to perform minor spells. But it was the witches who promised they could channel a long-departed spirit, or even raise the recently dead, who'd attracted the most attention.

"Unless what?" Ravyr finally prompted.

"Unless she's a necromancer."

There was a short silence before Tia clicked her tongue in disgust. "Seriously, Maya. Necromancers are a myth. Like elves and leprechauns."

"Some believe," Maya stubbornly insisted. "And they're willing to try anything, including slaughtering innocents to prove they can return the dead from the grave. A group of them gathered like vultures after the floods swept through our village. It was horrifying what some of my neighbors were willing to offer in exchange of returning a child or parent." Maya tilted her chin. "We need to get to that island."

"There's no point," Tia warned.

Maya ground her teeth. Tia was always arrogant and bossy and annoying. Tonight she was taking all three to a whole new level.

"Why not?" Maya forced herself to ask.

"This morning I went out there to search the place."

"Let me guess. They were gone."

"Every trace of them. The ground had even been salted so I couldn't follow them."

Maya grimaced. There was only one reason for a mage to salt the ground. It was to make sure her presence couldn't be detected by another mage.

"Alison must have warned them that we'd discovered her identity."

"Yes." Tia's gaze was accusing. As if she blamed Maya for allowing the cult to escape. "A shame you didn't capture her when you had the chance."

Maya turned toward Ravyr. Tia couldn't make her feel worse than she already did. She was acutely aware that she'd allowed herself to be outmaneuvered by an inferior mage.

Twice.

The only way to settle the score was to find Alison and force her to confess why she was in New York and who was behind her attempts to kill Maya. As painfully as possible. But first she had to find her.

"What if they've fled the city?" she asked Ravyr, revealing her greatest fear. If Alison disappeared now, they'd have no way of following her.

Ravyr grasped her hands, giving her fingers a comforting squeeze. "They haven't."

"How do you know?" Tia intruded into their conversation, her tone sharp.

Ravyr sent her an impatient frown. "Because I was sent to Batu's lair to investigate a strange pulse of magic. That same magic has reappeared on several occasions over the past four decades, moving from Gyre to Gyre. Currently it's here."

Tia snorted. "There was a lot of magic in his lair. Most of it taken by force."

Ravyr shook his head. "This was different. I've never felt anything like it."

Tia didn't look satisfied with the answer. Shocker. "If it's magic, I would be able to sense it," she stubbornly insisted.

For once, Maya didn't blame Tia for her suspicion. Magic flowed through the veins of a mage. How was it possible that both of them had been impervious to the strange pulse that Ravyr had sensed?

Unless...

"Not if it was necromancer magic," Maya abruptly pointed out. "A vampire would be more likely to sense anything connected with death."

"I'm resurrected, not dead," Ravyr teased, his brows arching as he lifted her hand to press her fingers against his lips. "Obviously I'm going to have to up my game."

A blush crept beneath her skin, but she refused to be distracted.

"You've been to the afterlife," she explained. "A place between life and death."

He shrugged. "More than once, presumably."

"Maybe that's why you can feel it and we can't."

"Necromancer magic." The words were soft, as if he was testing them to decide if she was on the right track or if she'd gone off the rails.

Tia had already made up her mind. "Stop it," she snapped. "There's no such thing."

Maya made a sound of impatience. "I'm not saying there is. But it doesn't have to be real for people to believe in it. If they're creating a spell out of the blood of their sacrifices to try to raise the dead, it could release more than one sort of evil."

Tia pinched her lips together, abruptly marching toward the nearby door. "Believe what you want."

Maya frowned. "Where are you going?"

"The fairy was too drunk to give much information about the cult before they disappeared from the island," Tia revealed. "I'm going to see if he's managed to clear enough of the grog-fog from his brain to answer my questions." She paused, raking Maya with a dismissive glance. "Such a disappointment."

With a toss of her head, the older woman completed her dramatic exit, disappearing from view.

"Ditto," Maya muttered, aggravated that her ex-friend always managed to have the last word.

"Grog-fog?" Ravyr interrupted her dark thoughts, repeating Tia's words. "Poetic."

Maya shook off her annoyance. Tia was the least of her worries. "She always was a drama queen."

"While you are calm, cool, and collected," Ravyr murmured.

"Not always," she admitted wryly.

"True." Tugging her forward, Ravyr lowered his head to brush a kiss over her lips. "I like you when you're ruffled. And disheveled." Another lingering kiss. "And—"

"Is the chauffeur on duty?" Maya forced herself to interrupt. One more kiss and she'd be shoving him onto the nearby sofa and stripping off his clothes.

Not that she was opposed to the idea of a naked Ravyr sprawled beneath her. In fact, her mouth went dry and her heart raced at the mere thought. But she couldn't let herself be sidetracked.

Alison was still in the city. For now. She couldn't risk allowing her to escape.

"Unfortunately," he murmured against her lips. "Where are we going?"

"The Dead Badger."

Ravyr lifted his head, his expression resigned. "Of course we are."

Chapter 18

Locating the fairy and convincing him to reveal the location of the local rave turned out to be easier than Tia expected. Probably because she'd hit him with a love spell that had him on his knees the second Lynch managed to track him to the dingy demon bar. In between loudly proclaiming his devotion, he'd offered an address, along with the assurance that the rave was indeed being held tonight, although he'd sworn off attending the dodgy event.

She taken time to scrub his mind of any memory of her before they were driving the short distance to an industrial neighborhood that was empty at the late hour.

They parked the expensive vehicle in one of the empty lots before angling toward a long, narrow structure that was built out of concrete bricks with bars on the narrow windows and a flat roof. Tia grimaced. Not because the area smelled of diesel and old tires, but because there was a low, obnoxious bass pounding through the air that was threatening to give her a headache.

The fairy hadn't been lying. The rave was going in full force, if the music was anything to go by.

"I assume we must be close?" she muttered dryly.

Lynch strolled next to her, his head swiveling from side to side as he kept watch for any danger. "There's an entrance at the end of the building." He at last pointed toward a small steel door that was set into the concrete blocks. The outline of a male casually leaning against the building was visible in the flickering light from the Exit sign. "I'll deal with the bouncer," Lynch promised with obvious anticipation.

She reached to touch his arm, bringing him to a halt. "No need."

"Why not? I can handle a fairy," he protested.

"Sometimes, Lynch, a scalpel is more efficient than a hammer," she reminded him.

Disappointment rippled over his square face. "We're going to sneak in?"

Tia grimaced at the mere thought of entering the filthy warehouse where a hundred or more demons were smashed together as they sweated and danced to ear-piercing music. It was truly her version of hell.

"We're going to wait for the transportation," she clarified, her gaze searching their surroundings.

Lynch looked predictably confused. "What transportation?"

"The fairy told you that he was taken from the rave by a bus, remember?"

"Yeah, but they aren't going to the island anymore, are they?"

"Probably not, but unless they've relocated to a place that's walking distance from here, they're still going to have to drive the demons to where they're going to be sacrificed."

"Oh. Right."

"They won't come to the front door. That would be too obvious," she abruptly decided. "We need to get to the other side of the building."

Not giving her servant the opportunity to protest, Tia turned around and briskly followed the parking lot to the back of the building, her heels clicking on the asphalt. She nodded her head in satisfaction as she caught sight of the line of metal overhead doors that were cut into the cement blocks. This was clearly the loading area for the warehouse. A perfect place to slip the demons out of the building.

"What if they don't come here to collect any sacrifices tonight?" Lynch asked, halting at the corner of the building to pull out a cigarette and light it.

Tia shrugged, refusing to contemplate failure. It simply wasn't in her vocabulary.

"Then we keep searching," she warned.

"Gotcha." Lynch blew out a cloud of smoke, careful to keep it away from her. There was a short silence, or at least as silent as it could be with the music vibrating through the night air. "Do you think it's him?" Lynch abruptly asked.

Tia absently reached into the pocket of her tailored jacket to touch the small beads that were loaded with potions. It was more a stress reliever than a reminder that she was carrying powerful weapons. Like Lynch's cigarettes, only without the nicotine. Or gagging smoke.

"I don't know," she forced herself to say, despite the dread that had been gnawing at her since the vision of Batu had brought her to New York. "I really don't."

"If it is?"

"I'm going to destroy the bastard."

"And if it isn't?"

Tia shrugged. She had been around long enough to know there was a possibility that someone was trying to screw with her by conjuring the image of Batu. Her past wasn't a secret, and she had numerous enemies with the time and money to lure her into an elaborate trap.

"I'm still going to destroy them," she said with a blunt confidence.

"Why bother?" Lynch released another puff of smoke. "Because of the mage?"

Tia's brows snapped together. "What?"

Lynch turned his head to send her a curious glance. "Aren't you doing this for your friend?"

"I don't have any friends."

With a rare lack of subservience, Lynch continued, refusing to heed the edge of warning in her voice. "There wasn't any reason for you to leave the protection of your estate," he pointed out. "Your enemy would eventually have been forced to travel to Colorado if they really wanted to hurt you. Far better to face them directly on your home ground."

He spoke the truth. Tactically it made zero sense to leave the layers of security she'd woven around Emerald Glade and travel to New York. Even if Batu *had* returned from the dead, there was no need to hunt him down. Eventually he would have tried to seek his revenge. Far better to be surrounded by her treasure trove of magical artifacts and potions.

As much as she hated to admit it, a part of her had rushed to New York because she knew that Maya would be in danger.

"I might be a selfish bitch, but I always pay my debts," she at last conceded. "If it hadn't been for Maya, I would have died in Batu's lair...." Her words trailed away as the sound of an approaching vehicle rumbled through the air. "Lynch," she murmured, pressing her back against the building to blend into the shadows.

Lynch tossed his cigarette on the ground and crushed the glowing ember beneath his heel.

"I see it." He nodded toward the rusty blue vehicle that looked more like an extended van than a bus.

Tia arched a brow. Whoever supervised the cult was obviously working with a budget. Odd. Batu had been many things...cruel, vindictive, and greedy...but he'd never been cheap.

"Stay here," she murmured as the van parked next to one of the loading docks.

Pulling a bead out of her pocket, Tia squeezed the glass, releasing a mist that circled around her, wrapping her in a web of magic. It didn't make her invisible, but it reflected the light enough to shroud her in a thick darkness. Cautiously moving forward, she halted a few feet from the van as a narrow steel door opened and a tall, slender fairy stepped out of the building. She could see the female's red-gold hair, which was shaved on the sides and teased high in the middle. Her silver lamé dress barely covered her ass as she jogged down the cement stairs. She looked like a bougie brat until Tia caught sight of the automatic weapon casually gripped in one hand and the dagger peeking beneath the hem of her dress.

A dangerous bougie brat.

As she reached the bottom step, a male goblin stepped out of the van, predictably wearing a leather jacket and matching pants. His head was shaved and his expression was hard.

"How many?" he demanded, pushing open a sliding door on the side of the vehicle.

"Five," the fairy answered.

"Five?" The goblin shook his head. "She's not going to be happy."

The fairy shrugged. "Fuck her."

The goblin snorted. "Easy to say when she can't hear you."

She. Tia tucked away the surprising realization that the leader was a female. At least, whoever was dealing with the sacrifices was a female.

"Look, it is what it is," the fairy drawled, as if bored by the conversation. "Do you want them or not?"

"Bring 'em out," the goblin growled, reaching beneath his open jacket to pull out a long envelope.

The fairy leaned forward to snatch it from his fingers before turning and sashaying back up the steps. Payment for her services, Tia assumed, impatiently waiting for the female to disappear into the building so the driver would stop ogling her ass and return to his place in the van.

After what felt like an eternity, the goblin at last headed back to settle in the driver's seat and Tia darted forward to place her fingers on the dented bumper. She usually didn't have to touch an object to cast a tracking spell, but if Maya was right and there was a mage involved, there might be a spell attached to the vehicle to prevent it from being followed.

Tia wanted to make damned sure they didn't lose the van as soon as it left the parking lot. This was their best opportunity to discover the master or mistress of the mysterious cult.

There was a tingle of power as she released her magic, followed by a firm tug as the spell snapped into place. A second later, she scurried back into the shadows as the steel door was shoved open and a high-pitched giggle echoed through the parking lot. She managed to disappear into the shadows when the first of the sacrifices skipped down the steps and into the van. She was a young fairy dressed in expensive clothes with the vacant expression of someone high on drugs. Next were two male goblins who leaned against each other as they stumbled down the stairs, barely able to stand upright. There was another female fairy, this one older, with a hardened expression that suggested she no longer cared what the future held. Good or bad.

The last victim trailed behind the others, covered from head to foot in a sparkly silver cape with a large fur-trimmed hood over his head to hide his features. Tia frowned, wondering if it was some sort of fashion statement; then the head abruptly swiveled to the side and she could see a face covered by a massive beard. The male paused, one brilliant green eye closing as if he was winking in her direction before he scooted down the stairs and pushed his way into the van.

Tia's breath was squeezed from her lungs.

Joe.

"What the hell?"

Trying to wrap her brain around the fact that the strange creature had just waltzed past her and jumped into the van, Tia was left staring at the taillights as the vehicle pulled away and headed out of the lot with squealing tires.

It wasn't until Lynch suddenly appeared beside her that she was shaken out of her sense of stunned disbelief.

"Is something wrong?"

"So many things," Tia muttered, squaring her shoulders as she turned toward her servant. Right now the only thing that mattered was finding out where the van was going, and who was waiting when they reached their destination. "Get the car."

* * * *

The Dead Badger was exactly what you would expect from a demon bar. The long, narrow building was squeezed between a bodega and a transmission garage with wooden booths along the walls and a bar shaped like a U in the middle.

Stepping through the door, Ravyr cast a jaundiced glance around the rough crowd. Most of the goblins and fairies mingled at the back, shooting pool or playing darts, although there were several who sat at the bar, downing tankards of grog with a speed that would make a dragon proud.

Two-for-one night was obviously a big hit with the heavy drinkers.

"Is there a reason we're at this particular establishment?" he demanded as Maya moved to stand at his side. "I'm hoping it's not for the ambiance."

She wrinkled her nose. "It does have a sticky-floor, rat-infested charm."

Ravyr didn't think she was joking about the rats. There was the distinct smell of vermin fused with sour sweat and stale grog.

"Not the sort of charm that would attract a woman like Alison," he pointed out.

"No," she readily agreed. "But I'm not sure where to start searching for her."

"Then what are we doing here?"

"When I was talking to Tia about necromancers I suddenly remembered something I'd smelled a few months ago."

Ravyr arched a brow. His acutely fine-tuned senses were usually a gift. There was no creature who could equal him when it came to hunting his prey. But the heavy stench that permeated the room felt like a physical assault.

"You smelled it here?"

She shook her head. "No, but the demon who owned the shop where I did smell it should be here."

"Who?"

"Hexx."

Ravyr dredged through his memories to put a face to the name. "The demon who planted the bomb?"

"That's the one."

"Why not go to his apartment?" he asked in confusion. "I doubt he's going to give us any information without..." He searched for a word that didn't make it sound like he was going to have to beat it out of the idiot. "Encouragement. Wouldn't it be better to question him in private?"

Her lips twisted into a cynical smile. "Just being here is all the encouragement we need. Hexx would rather be flayed and rolled in salt than to be seen talking to me in public."

"Seriously?"

With a shrug she headed toward the center of the room, her head swiveling from side to side as she searched for her prey. "I've spent the past decade selling curses, truth serums, and love potions that were used against thousands of demons in this city," she reminded him, her chin tilted at a defiant angle as the closest demons glanced in her direction and abruptly froze in fear. "It doesn't make me the most popular person."

Her chin remained high as she continued forward, ignoring the large goblin who glanced up from the bar in the center of the room. He had a mohawk and a dozen piercings and looked like the sort of male who regularly thrashed any customer stupid enough to cause trouble in his establishment, but the moment he caught sight of Maya his face turned white and the tankard he was holding crashed to the wooden floor.

"Ah. Your reputation precedes you," he murmured, enjoying the fear that pulsed through the bar as the customers recognized the powerful mage.

This woman had carved out her place in this dangerous city, and the demons understood the cost of challenging her.

"Exactly," she said, her tone distracted.

Ravyr walked close behind her, protecting her back. Most of the demons might be afraid, but there was always one in the crowd who wanted to prove he was a tough guy.

"What makes you think Hexx will be here tonight?" he asked.

"I had to come to this place a few months ago and I noticed that sign promoting two-for-one grog night on Wednesdays." She pointed toward the large sign that was hung above the bar. It was faded enough to reveal that it wasn't a special promotion but an ongoing marketing strategy. "Hexx lives a couple of blocks away. I doubt he'd miss the chance for free drinks."

"Clever."

She glanced over her shoulder. "I'm not just another pretty face."

He wiggled his brows like a villain in a cheesy human movie as he allowed his gaze to sweep down her body. "True. You have gorgeous curves and an—"

"Careful."

He chuckled as a portion of her tension thankfully eased. "Always," he assured her softly.

Turning her attention back to the crowd, she made a sound of satisfaction. "There he is."

She nodded toward the goblin with long, stringy hair who was hunched in the corner of a booth, as if he was trying to hide in the shadows. Odd for a demon who'd gone to the trouble of tattooing crimson flames along the line of his jaw and chosen to wear a black leather jacket and heavy chains around his neck as if he was some sort of badass.

Then again, Hexx hadn't impressed him as a particularly intelligent goblin.

With a smooth elegance, Maya slid onto the bench across the table from the pathetic creature. Ravyr remained standing. They'd been caught off guard too many times for him to take any risks. Nothing and no one was getting close to Maya without coming through him first.

As if realizing he was no longer alone, Hexx lifted his head to regard Maya with a blurry gaze.

"Shit." His skinny body tensed as he stared at his companion in horror. "This can't be real." Without warning, he banged his head on the table in frustration. "Someone cursed me, right? How do I get rid of it? How do I get rid of *you*?"

Maya rolled her eyes. "Stop being such a baby."

"Baby?" Hexx leaned forward. "From the moment you entered my pawnshop my life has gone to hell," he hissed. "I've lost everything."

Maya folded her arms on the table, her expression icy enough to rival a vampire. "Answer my questions and I'll disappear."

"You keep promising me that even though I've told you everything I know." The goblin sounded like a petulant child. "Why don't you go bother some other demon?"

Ravyr released a low growl, an icy breeze cutting through the stuffy air as he leaned toward the goblin.

"Adjust your attitude," he warned. "Or I will."

"Okay, okay." Hexx hunched his shoulders, glaring at Maya. "What information do you want?"

"Who supplied you with the black-market inventory you were selling out of the back of your pawnshop?"

There was a startled silence, and Hexx looked as caught off guard by the question as Ravyr was.

"You mean the stuff that was all confiscated by Valen?" Hexx asked in confusion.

"Yes."

Hexx held up his hand. "Hey, if you're here to accuse me of something, I swear I don't deal in magical artifacts anymore. I swear."

"All I want is information about a specific customer."

"Oh." Something that might have been relief rippled over the narrow face. "Why?"

"During my brief visit to your pawnshop I recall a sweet, musty scent coming from one of the boxes hidden in your storage room."

"I had a bunch of magical junk. I don't know what any of it was used for." He grimaced. "Mage stuff."

Ravyr believed the male would buy and sell illegal items without any clue if they might be dangerous. Demons possessed a few magical items, but they were completely different from mages or witches. And far too rare to fall into the hands of a low-level goblin.

"The smell was belladonna and no mage would have any use for it," Maya clarified.

Hexx stiffened, and Ravyr abruptly understood why they were at the Dead Badger. And why Maya had sought out this demon.

"Maybe not, but humans will buy anything if you tell them it has magic in it." The goblin was trying to bluff. Ravyr knew it.

"Not belladonna," Maya insisted. "It's specifically used by necromancers."

Hexx rolled his eyes, clinging to a pretense of confusion. "There's no such thing."

Maya leaned forward, her expression grim. "We both know that there are witches who believe it's possible to raise the dead."

"Like I said, humans will buy anything."

"Give me a name."

"Name?" Hexx released a forced laugh. "Do you know how many customers I've had over the years? Thousands. I can't remember all of them."

"You wouldn't have specifically ordered belladonna unless someone requested it."

"Of course I would. I have all kinds of shit."

"Fine." Maya held Hexx's wary gaze as she casually lifted her hand and gestured toward the bartender, motioning him in the direction of the booth. "We'll have a round of grog while you try to remember."

Hexx licked his lips. "You can't expect me to put a name to all my customers. That's insane."

Ravyr reluctantly stepped aside as he felt the bartender approach the table, his fangs fully exposed in warning. Maya simply smiled as she glanced toward the demon.

"Three grogs and keep them coming. We're going to be here for a while."

The bartender visibly ground his teeth, glaring at Hexx before turning away and stomping back to the bar.

Hexx gulped. "You know what, I actually just remembered that I have something I need to—"

"Stay where you are," Ravyr growled, blocking his exit.

"Yeesh." Hexx held up his hands, as if to prove he wasn't a threat. "This is bullshit." He returned his attention to Maya. "What did I ever do to you?"

"Are you kidding me? You nearly destroyed the world when you helped kidnap my best friend and the Cabal leader of New Orleans a few months ago."

Hexx hunched his shoulders. "I didn't know what was going to happen, did I?"

"Because you didn't care."

"Here." The bartender slammed down three tankards of grog, pointing a finger in Hexx's face. "Drink 'em and go."

"Crap," Hexx muttered, grabbing one of the tankards to take a deep drink. "You're going to get me banned from my favorite bar."

"Then talk," Maya commanded.

"And you'll leave?" Hexx polished off the last of his grog and reached for another tankard. "You promise?"

"I'll leave." Maya slid her hand to the center of the table, the wood beneath her palms suddenly smoldering as if it was being charred by her mere touch. "But if I find out you lied to me, I'll return to place a curse on you that will shrivel your bits and pieces into dried-up raisins. Got it?"

Hexx jerked back, his face paling. "Do you have to be so mean?"

"You have no idea," she murmured.

Muttering under his breath, Hexx lifted the second tankard and chugged the grog before he loudly burped. As if hoping it would give him courage.

"Okay, but if word gets out that I'm a snitch I'm going to be punished," he whined. "*Severely* punished."

"Being a snitch is the least of your concerns," Ravyr snarled.

Hexx scowled, but his gaze remained locked on Maya. Smart male. Ravyr could rip out his throat, but Maya could make him regret ever being born.

"Alright. Fine." He conceded defeat. "There's a coven of witches who regularly order the stuff. I don't know what they do with it and I don't care."

"A name," Maya demanded.

"The Divinity of the Darkness."

Ravyr studied Maya's delicate profile. "Have you heard of it?"

"No." Her attention was locked on Hexx. "Is it local?"

"I have no idea."

Maya's jaw tightened, emphasizing her deep scars. "Who picks up the boxes?"

"And older woman. Lettie?" Hexx furrowed his brow. It looked like it was a struggle to search through his memory. "No, Lottie. Lottie... something or other."

"Lottie Howard," Maya breathed. "Silver-haired woman who looks like a sweet old grandma who bakes cookies?"

Hexx snapped his fingers. "That's it."

Ravyr watched as Maya pursed her lips. "Obviously you recognize her," he said.

Maya nodded. "When I first settled in New Jersey, she had a large coven that was in total control of the East Coast. She seemed to think that sheer numbers gave her the right to tell me what I could and couldn't do in *her* territory."

Ravyr arched a brow. "I bet that went over well."

A humorless smile curved Maya's lips. "She lost most of her coven when I cursed her with dysentery. I heard that she was in misery for several weeks."

"Damn, woman," Hexx muttered. "That's cold."

Maya shrugged. "It was temporary, and I knew that Lottie wouldn't leave me in peace until she'd learned her lesson. She desperately wanted to prove that a witch was as powerful as any mage."

Ravyr understood Maya's dramatic response. Unless you nipped trouble in the bud, it would always come back to bite you in the ass. Mixed metaphors, but true.

"Did she practice necromancy?" he asked.

Maya slowly shook her head. "I've never heard any rumors about it, but I haven't had any contact with her or her coven for years." She considered for a long moment. "Maybe she hoped to amp up her powers by raising the dead."

It wasn't a bad theory. An ambitious witch would realize that she could never match a mage in head-to-head power. She would need an extra boost of magic to challenge Maya.

"Where can we find her?"

"She used to gather her coven in an abandoned grain elevator in Brooklyn." Maya tapped the tip of her finger on the table. "More than likely she's still using the same place."

Ravyr nodded. It took years for a coven to purify the land before they could build their altars and call on the spirits of nature. They wouldn't leave it unless it was tainted or they were forced off the property.

"You won't get in," Hexx abruptly intruded into the conversation, setting aside his empty tankard before grabbing number three. "The coven didn't just order belladonna. They recently bought several high-powered rifles and automatic weapons. Obviously they were serious about trespassers."

Ravyr peeled back his lips to reveal his fangs. "I'm not afraid of human weapons."

Hexx pressed himself tight into the corner, the tankard held in front of him like a shield. "Fine, whatever. I was just giving you a heads-up. Now...go away."

Maya reached into her satchel to pull out a wad of folded bills, tossing them onto the table before she slid out of the booth. Then, without another glance toward the anxious demons monitoring her every movement, she headed out of the bar and crossed toward the waiting SUV. She paused long enough for the chauffeur to roll down his window so she could give him the address before climbing into the back. Ravyr quickly joined her, and with a low hum, the vehicle pulled into the traffic and headed toward Brooklyn.

Chapter 19

Settling into the plush leather seat of the SUV, Ravyr remained silent as Maya reached up to grasp the emerald hanging on a golden chain, her lips moving as if she was repeating a spell. He assumed she was using the gem to store her magic. Probably a good idea. They had no idea what might be waiting for them. Even if the Divinity of the Darkness coven wasn't practicing necromancy and had no connection to Alison, it was obvious Maya had a history with the leader. Lottie Howard wouldn't be happy to have Maya intruding into her territory, and she'd be even less happy that she was bringing along a stranger.

Eventually the SUV reached the edge of the long canal and came to a halt in the shadows of the abandoned railroad tracks. Assuming this was as close as the vehicle could get without attracting notice, Ravyr climbed out and allowed his senses to absorb their surroundings.

In the distance was a cluster of buildings framed by towering silos that were silhouetted against the night sky. Like a shell of some massive creature that had died and left behind its fossilized bones. The creepy impression was only emphasized by the barren landscape that surrounded the line of structures built out of a combination of cement and red bricks.

The heavy atmosphere of decay shrouded everything in the area.

"This is the place?" he demanded as Maya moved to join him.

"Assuming that Hexx didn't lie," she said in dry tones. "Which is a very big assumption."

"Hmm." Ravyr's gaze skimmed over the open field directly in front of them before moving to the pile of rocks along the edge of the canal. "Let's look around."

She'd taken a step forward before Ravyr could reach out and grab her arm in a firm grip. "Wait, Maya."

"Why? Is something wrong?"

"Hexx was right when he pointed out that you aren't immortal," he reminded her, nodding toward the largest building. There was nothing to indicate that there was a waiting sniper hidden behind the broken windows. Everything was dark, and only the distant sound of traffic disrupted the thick silence. Still, he wasn't going to take any chances. "I'll go in and look around."

"No."

His jaw tightened. "I knew you'd be stubborn about this."

"Me?" Her eyes widened. "Stubborn?"

He ignored her teasing. "I'm not going to take any unnecessary risks."

"Agreed. I'm going with you to make sure you're careful."

Ravyr muttered an oath at her refusal to be sensible, barely resisting the urge to wrap her in his arms and toss her back into the SUV. As much as he hated the thought of having her anywhere near the mysterious stalker, he knew that she would hate being treated like she was too fragile to face the danger.

He would have to use a delicate persuasion if he was going to convince her that he had a better idea. Not his finest trait. In fact, it wasn't one of his traits at all. He had the subtlety of a sledgehammer.

"I'll do a quick sweep to get rid of any weapons. Once I've secured the place, you can join me."

"It's not just weapons that are the danger," Maya said. "If Alison is inside, then she has no doubt surrounded the place with powerful layers of protection."

"The magic isn't going to hurt me," he reminded her.

"Perhaps not, but the moment you walk through a hidden trigger it's going to alert everyone inside. I'll need to wrap us in a spell to disguise our presence. Which means we have to stick close together."

"Absolutely not. I don't want you going anywhere near that place if they have guns," he insisted.

"Ravyr." The name came out as sharp as the blade of a dagger. "Do you want us to have a future together?"

His brows snapped together. Was this a trap? It felt like a trap.

"There's nothing I want more in this world," he assured her. "But now doesn't seem like the best time to discuss it."

"It's the perfect time. If we're going to be together, then I have to know we'll be equal partners."

Yep. Definitely a trap. "Of course we'll be equal partners."

"Not if you insist on doing everything on your own." She stepped forward, her features softening. "I appreciate the fact that you want to protect me, but you aren't the lone wolf anymore."

"It just makes sense for me to clear out the weapons before you get shot." He made a last-ditch attempt to keep her out of danger.

A wasted effort.

"And alert everyone in the area that there's an intruder? There's no way you could get through the layers of alarms." She took another step forward, until they were nearly touching. "If they escape, then we'll be back to where we started. I want this over, Ravyr. And that means working together."

Ravyr turned his head to judge the distance to the nearest building. He was inhumanely fast, but if he did set off an alarm, then the coven and whoever else was inside would scatter. There was no way to keep them all inside long enough to determine which one was the leader.

Dammit, she was right.

He turned back to meet Maya's steady gaze. "Having a partner is still a work in progress," he admitted.

"Agreed."

They shared a rueful moment of acceptance. They both had adjustments to make. Some would be more challenging than others.

"How does your spell work?" he asked.

She grabbed his hands, the emerald around her throat suddenly glowing in the moonlight.

"Once I've activated the spell, it should make us invisible to whatever magical barriers they've created."

Ravyr arched a brow. "It will make us invisible?"

"Not physically. We'll still have to be careful to stay out of sight of any guards."

"I can take care of that," he promised. He might not have magic, but he could sense the presence of any human, demon, or vampire lurking in the dark.

She nodded. "The only thing we'll have to worry about is staying close to each other. The spell doesn't have a very large radius."

"Oh, that's not a worry." He gripped her fingers tight enough to assure her that he wasn't going to stray an inch from her side. "I'm going to be very close."

She rolled her eyes, but she didn't argue as she squared her shoulders and prepared to release her spell.

"Are you ready?"

"Yeah." The word had barely left his lips when the scent of sweet orchids swirled around him. Magic tingled in the air, humming with electric power as it brushed over his skin and sank into his body. Ravyr shivered. The magic was shockingly forceful, like it was gaining power as it raced through his body.

Maya's eyes snapped open, her expression confused, as if she was as startled as he was by the intensity of the magic. Then, she sucked in a slow breath as she loosened her grip on his fingers to lightly trace the shimmering symbol that was branded onto his skin.

"What's that?" she demanded.

With a frown, Ravyr studied the strange marking. The interlocking circles created a unique pattern that he'd never seen before.

"It's a reaction to your spell," he murmured, more fascinated than disturbed by the shimmering tattoo.

"It was harmless. It shouldn't have left a scar," she protested. "Could it be caused by your special talent?"

Ravyr shook his head. "My ability is to absorb magic. It should make it more difficult to keep the spell in place."

She bit her lip, as if wanting to insist that the mark was somehow related to him. It obviously bothered her to think that she'd lost control of her magic.

"Does it hurt?" she abruptly asked.

"No. It feels..." Ravyr paused to concentrate on the sensations that continued to tingle through him. There was the sizzle of magic, along with a warmth that he'd never experienced before. As if he was human. And then there was the scent. Rich orchids and lush female power. "It feels like you."

"Like me?" She blinked. "What does that mean?"

"I can sense your magic flowing through me." He cupped her scarred cheek in his palm, a sense of awe blooming in the center of his chest. "As if we've been mated."

Heat flushed her cheek, her eyes widening. "How is that possible?"

"Long ago there were mages who could create unbreakable bonds with their partners," he said. He'd read about the ancient ritual that would bond a mage with a powerful warrior or a lover, but it'd been countless centuries since the last known mating. Of course, since Peri had released the wild magic, there were lots of things that had been lost into the mists of time that were returning. It had yet to be determined if it was a good or bad thing. "The mating gave them the ability to share their emotions and pinpoint their location. Some could even heal their partner from a distance if they sensed they'd been injured."

Her brow furrowed. "That wasn't my intention."

"Maybe not here." He tapped the tip of his fingers against her temple, indicating her brain, before lowering them to rest over the rapid beat of her heart. "But maybe here."

Her flush deepened, but she didn't argue. Perhaps she could sense that she hadn't lost control of her magic but instead had accomplished precisely what she wanted, even if she hadn't fully understood what that meant.

"A problem for later," she murmured.

"Exactly." With an effort, Ravyr forced himself to lower his hand. As much as he wanted to wrap her in his arms and explore the bond shimmering between them, it was more important to survive the night. "Does it work?"

She looked confused. "What?"

"Are we invisible?"

"Oh...yes." She cleared her throat. "The spell has been activated."

"Then let's do this."

Brushing a quick kiss over her parted lips, Ravyr turned to position himself so he was walking slightly ahead. If there was a sniper, he assumed they would be on the roof of the main building. That would give them the best view of the surrounding grounds.

In silence they moved along a broken sidewalk, avoiding the large open space between the towering silos and the nearby canal. That would be the most logical place for trespassers to approach the abandoned structures. Still, he didn't allow his assumptions to keep his gaze from searching the thick shadows that surrounded them, or testing the air for the scent of a nearby enemy.

It wasn't until they were near the first outbuilding spread across the large property that he could sense the presence of demons. At least six of them.

Touching Maya's arm, he nodded toward a back parking lot. Together they angled toward the main building that loomed over them with a forbidding silence before inching around the corner. Maya released a soft hiss at the sight of a rusty van that was pulled next to an open door. It had obviously just arrived and they were in time to see several demons stumble out of the vehicle before disappearing into the building. As if they were drunk or drugged out of their minds.

"Those must be the sacrifices," Ravyr said, his voice barely above a whisper.

"We should follow them."

Ravyr nodded, but before he could position himself to keep his companion shielded from any potential bullets, he felt a dull thud pulse beneath his feet. He froze, feeling another thud that echoed through him like the beat of a massive drum.

"Maya," he growled.

Easily sensing his tension, Maya reached up to touch the emerald that glowed with power. "What is it?"

"I feel the magic."

It took her a second to realize what he meant. "The magic you felt in Batu's lair?"

"Yes." A heavy sense of evil was threaded through the pulses, battling against the sensual beauty of Maya's presence. "It's here."

"Can you pinpoint the source?"

He slowly nodded. It was beneath his feet. Which meant there had to be a nearby tunnel or basement.

Glancing back at the van that was pulling away with a squeal of its tires, Maya squared her shoulders, her expression hardening into lines he knew too well.

"You go find it. I'll take care of the mage."

Ravyr released a low growl, grasping her shoulders to turn her to face him. "What about our partnership?"

She grimaced. "Right now it seems wise to divide and conquer." She reached up to brush her fingers over the mark on the back of his hand. "Plus, we are bonded now, right? We'll know how to find each other if one of us gets lost."

He couldn't argue with that. The sense of Maya had settled deep inside him, as if she'd become a part of his very soul. It wouldn't matter where she traveled, or how long they were apart, he would be able to locate her with his eyes closed.

Not that the sense of her nestled inside him eased the fear of letting her out of his sight. She might have off-the-charts power, but that didn't make her immortal.

Unfortunately, the evil pulsing through him had never been this strong. He would never have a better opportunity to track it down and destroy the source.

Leashing the feral fury at the mere thought of Maya injured, he pressed his fingers into her shoulders, glaring down at her upturned face.

"Don't you dare do anything stupid. If that bitch hurts you—"

"I can deal with Alison." She balanced on her tiptoes to press a lingering kiss against his lips. "Once I'm done I'll be waiting for you."

He pulled her close, absorbing her heat. "You promise?"

"Forever," she whispered.

Chapter 20

Maya watched as Ravyr turned to disappear into the thick shadows, relief racing through her at the sense of him that continued to pulse through her. He might not be close enough to touch, but the feel of his presence bolstered her courage as she marched forward, entering through the same door as the sacrifices.

Whatever happened, she wasn't alone.

A knowledge that filled an empty place inside her heart. Yet another emptiness she hadn't even realized needed filling.

Not until Ravyr.

Maya clenched her teeth, forcing herself to concentrate on her surroundings. It'd been sheer luck that she hadn't been seriously injured during the previous attacks. She couldn't count on continuing luck to keep her alive.

Ignoring the squeak of the hinges, Maya stepped into the vast space with a towering ceiling. There was a musty chill in the air and a heavy sense of abandonment that assured her that the coven wasn't using this area as their meeting spot. Still, she could smell salt nearby. The witches had to be close.

Walking along the nearest wall, Maya pulled a vial from her satchel. It was a simple stun spell that would hopefully give her time to escape if she walked into an ambush. She reached the end of the wall and cautiously pushed open the steel door that led to the connected building. She grimaced as the smell of salt burned her nose.

This was it. The place where the coven had been meeting.

Sweeping her hand over the wall next to the doorway, she found the light switch and flicked it up. It took a moment for her eyes to adjust from complete darkness to the harsh glow of the fluorescent bulbs hanging from the steel rafters, but she was already prepared to see the short, heavy-set woman who was standing in the center of the cement floor.

Maya remained near the open doorway, her gaze searching for hidden dangers. The building looked like it'd been a mechanic's shop at one time with wooden counters along the far wall and the lingering smell of grease, but now it was cleared of any clutter and a deep circle had been carved into the cement floor.

Assured there was nothing hiding in the corners, Maya returned her attention to Lottie Howard. She hadn't been exaggerating when she said that the older witch looked like a kindly grandmother.

Her round face was even more deeply wrinkled than the last time she'd seen her and her cheeks a little less rosy, but her thick silver hair was still pulled into a tidy bun at the back of her head and she was wearing the same style of pantsuit that went out of fashion in the eighties.

"Hello, Lottie." Maya continued to hold the vial of potion in her hand, mentally preparing herself for the attack. There was no way that this wasn't a trap. Unfortunately, she'd reached the point of no return. This ended tonight. "It's been a while."

Lottie's lips pinched, not seeming to appreciate Maya's friendly tone. "Not long enough."

"Still bitter after all this time?"

Lottie spit on the cement, just inches from her own toes. "I curse the ground you walk on."

"Nice." Maya pretended to stifle a yawn. When she'd first opened the Witch's Brew, the older woman had appeared on her doorstep, threatening her with the evil eye and a dozen different hexes if she didn't pledge loyalty to her coven. Maya had tried to ignore her for weeks, but eventually she'd had to put an end to the woman's silly threats. Since then she hadn't given her a second thought. "Where's your coven?"

Her lips pinched tighter. "They're busy."

"Busy doing what? Trying to raise the dead?"

Lottie flushed, as if embarrassed by Maya's blunt question. And perhaps she was. Practicing necromancy wasn't something you'd want getting out. Not even in the witch world.

"Our magic is none of your business," she snapped.

"It is when you delve into such darkness." Maya narrowed her eyes. "Why?"

Lottie thankfully didn't try to deny the accusation. "I needed the power."

"For what?"

"I ruled New York." She pointed a finger toward Maya. "This was my city until you arrived and stole everything from me."

Maya shook her head in resignation. "There was no need for us to battle one another. We could have easily coexisted if you hadn't challenged me."

The accusing finger continued to point in her direction. "This is all your fault."

Maya studied the older woman's plump face. "What's my fault?"

Lottie bit her lip, as if realizing she was treading dangerous ground. "All I wanted was more magic."

"From the dead?"

"How else could I compete with a mage?"

"This was never a competition."

"Not for you."

Maya squashed the urge to continue the argument. What was the point? The witch was determined to blame Maya for her weaknesses. Instead, she sent the older woman a glare of disapproval.

"Blood magic is evil. No matter how ambitious you might be, there's no excuse for sacrificing the innocent."

Lottie blinked at the accusation. "I've never sacrificed anyone."

"Don't lie." Maya narrowed her gaze. "There are witnesses."

"She's not lying," a voice drawled as a door across the space was shoved open and a young woman stepped inside. "It was me."

Maya hid a smile of satisfaction as the slender mage strolled forward, her pale eyes burning with a smug satisfaction that Maya had been lured into her trap.

"Alison," she murmured.

"It's about time you showed up." Alison tossed her blond curls. "I've been waiting for you."

"I had better things to do."

"Just admit it. You didn't have the skill to track me."

Maya shrugged, not about to waste her time with petty arguments. Deliberately she glanced toward Lottie, who was standing in stiff silence.

"Do you two know each other?"

Lottie licked her lips. Was she scared? "She's a member of my coven," the older woman said, careful not to glance toward the younger mage.

"What *used* to be your coven," Alison corrected. "It's under new management."

Maya glanced back at Alison. "You?"

"Who better?"

"Ungrateful bitch," Lottie muttered in tones low enough she no doubt hoped that Alison wouldn't hear her.

The mage's jaw tightened, but she resisted the urge to punish the older woman.

"Not ungrateful. I fully appreciate the opportunity to learn my craft, but I was never meant to be a follower. Not after my powers emerged."

It made sense to Maya that Alison would decide she was better than the witches once she was revealed to be a mage. What she didn't understand was why she was still there.

"Why would a mage be interested in taking over a coven?" she demanded.

"Every general needs soldiers, especially when you're going to war."

"War? Who are you going to war against?"

Alison's expression tightened, as if she regretted her overly dramatic proclamation. "Whoever is foolish enough to stand in my way," she muttered.

Maya glanced toward Lottie in time to witness her grimace of disgust. "And you agreed?" she asked the older woman.

"It wasn't like I had a choice." Lottie glared toward Alison. "Not once she brought those demons into my territory."

Maya's brows arched. Witches were humans. They weren't supposed to know about goblins or fairies or vampires.

"What demons?" Maya pressed.

"The ones who crawled through the gates of hell." Lottie sniffed, still glaring at the younger woman. "I warned you that murdering people was going to summon evil creatures, but you wouldn't listen to me."

Alison smiled. "Because I wanted them summoned."

"Why?" Maya demanded.

"At first I was simply searching for anything that could give me access to the wild magic. From the moment I was transformed into a mage I could sense it just out of reach. I assumed it had to be found among the forbidden magics, since the power had been cut off for so many centuries." Her expression twisted with a hint of bitterness. "At least until your precious Peri tapped into the raw power."

Maya didn't allow the younger woman to become distracted with the jealousy that obviously seethed inside her.

"That's when you started trying to raise the dead?"

"Lottie had already trained us in necromancy, but I was the one who created an altar that allowed me to tap into the dark magic."

"Did the altar include the mirror?"

Alison nodded. "It was a means of communicating with other necromancers. It wasn't until a few weeks ago that it became something more."

"What happened?"

"A vision formed in the mirror offering me power. More power than I ever dreamed possible." A visible shiver of anticipation shook her body. "A promise it would run through me like a river."

Maya clenched her teeth. "What did you see?"

"Robed forms standing around a flat stone that was drenched in blood. In the darkness I could sense someone watching me." She paused, nervously licking her lips. "He whispered promises of power, and asked me to prepare for his coming."

"You didn't see his face?"

"No, but his voice..." She sucked in a slow breath, as if still trying to come to terms with what she'd heard. "It shattered something inside me. Nothing mattered but doing what he wanted me to do."

Ah. So the vision was a compulsion, not a premonition, Maya silently concluded. And a warning. Whoever was in charge of the robed figures wasn't just another demon. Or mage.

It had to be a creature with enormous strength to manipulate the minds of others. A vampire was the obvious answer, although even leeches struggled to influence a mage. It was something about their innate powers that protected them. Only a leech with a unique ability to compel others.

A leech like Batu.

"I'm assuming you were expected to do something to gain your new power?"

"Nothing is free." She waved a hand toward the older woman. "Lottie taught me that."

Maya ignored the implication that the older woman had been abusive. "What was the cost?"

"Killing you."

Years of training allowed Maya to keep her expression smooth. "Why?"

"He didn't say. Just that you needed to die." A cold smile twisted Alison's lips. "Honestly I couldn't believe my luck. Not only was I going to get enough magic to take control of this city, but I had the added bonus of getting rid of you."

Maya frowned, perplexed by the rampant dislike toward her by such a wide variety of strangers.

"What have I ever done to you?"

"Personally? Nothing, but Lottie told us how you tricked and cheated the local witches to destroy their covens." Her eyes narrowed with hatred. "And how you've threatened anyone who might refuse your authority."

"Tricked and cheated?" Maya glanced toward Lottie. "Care to explain?"

The older woman at least had the decency to blush at being caught in her blatant lies. "That's in the past."

"Obviously not," Maya said dryly, suddenly understanding why Alison might resent her. Of course, she didn't believe that was the entire reason. She was tainted by her lust for power.

"It doesn't matter. This day was inevitable," Alison insisted. "I would have eventually challenged you. There can only be one mage at the top."

"Idiot," Maya muttered, shaking her head at Alison's sheer arrogance. "If you were so ready for a challenge, then why send Courtney to kill me? Why not face me yourself?"

Alison snorted. "I planned the explosion. All I needed her to do was lead you into the trap. And she couldn't even get that right."

"Why her?"

"She was a member of the coven."

Maya blinked in genuine surprise, glancing back at Lottie. That explained why Courtney had harbored the same resentment toward her as Alison did, but it didn't explain how they'd been drawn to Lottie in the first place.

"Two mages in one coven?"

Lottie shrugged. "I have an eye for talent."

Maya suspected it was more than an eye. There were a rare few women who could sense the hidden powers of a mage long before they manifested. Sometimes when they were still children. She would be a unique asset in helping Maya identify potential mages. If they could get over their difficult past.

Something Maya suspected was easier said than done for Lottie.

Alison intruded into Maya's distracted thoughts. "Courtney left when her powers manifested. I tried to convince her to come back to the coven, but all she cared about was living a life of luxury. Preferably without having to work for it."

Maya shook her head, forcing herself to concentrate on her current danger. She would return later to test the level of Lottie's abilities.

Assuming she survived the night.

"Did Courtney know you were the one to hire her?"

"Of course not. She would never have taken the job."

"Why not? If you two were old friends..." Maya belatedly realized exactly why Courtney would have fled the second she knew who was behind the contract on Maya's life. "Ah, she would have realized that you intended to kill her from the start."

"Of course. I was warned not to leave any loose ends that could link me to your death."

Maya grimaced. Courtney had been a shallow, ruthless traitor who would have happily watched her die, but she couldn't help but feel sympathy for her brutal end.

"How did you kill her?"

Alison's smile widened, as if she was savoring the memory. "It was a curse I placed on her a couple weeks ago when I tracked her down at her favorite nightclub." Alison chuckled. "She was completely clueless when I joined her at her table and offered to pay for her drinks. She was even thoughtful enough to tell me that she was using a website to find jobs as an assassin. It made it simple to send her a message and hire her without her ever knowing it was me. Stupid girl."

Maya ignored Alison's smug satisfaction in outwitting her former coven-mate.

"What about the demon we found dead with Courtney? How did you curse him?"

Alison shrugged. "The curse would have extended to anyone she'd revealed her plans to when it was activated. I specifically warned her when she was hired not to share the details of the job."

"You placed the same curse on Bastian." Anger blasted through Maya at the woman's reckless lack of concern for who she hurt. Even the innocent. "And poor Joyce."

"They were all disposable tools in my quest for power."

Maya's hands curled into tight fists as she remembered the terror in her friend's eyes before she plunged the dagger into her own heart. It took every ounce of willpower not to leap forward and beat the shit out of the smug little bitch.

Right now she needed answers more than she needed the satisfaction of punishing the mage. But soon...

"How did you curse them?" she forced herself to ask. "The magic wasn't yours."

Alison frowned, as if offended by Maya's words. "It was."

"No. You don't have that sort of power."

Clearly realizing that Maya wasn't going to believe she'd done it on her own, Alison shrugged before reaching into her jacket to pull out a small medallion. Laying it in the palm of her hand, she held it toward Maya.

"I do it with this."

Maya hissed, easily recognizing the symbol etched into the metal disc. "Where did you get that?"

"A gift from my master." Alison smiled. "Lord Batu."

Chapter 21

Tia waited for the van to disappear into the back lot before she motioned for Lynch to lift her through one of the empty windows on the opposite side of the massive structure. She assumed that there would be guards waiting for the latest batch of sacrifices that were being delivered. She wasn't going to risk an unnecessary skirmish when she was so close to discovering the truth.

Once inside, she grimaced at the musty scent of stale air and the layers of filth that covered every inch of the floors and walls and the weird drips of condensation that leaked from the steel beams far above her head. It was hard to believe that anyone would choose this location as a lair. Especially a male like Batu who'd demanded the finest comforts, including floors tiled with rare mosaics and hand-stitched tapestries on the walls.

Did that prove he'd died forty-five years ago?

No, but it did mean that if he was alive, he was clearly desperate.

Which only made him more dangerous.

Not sure whether she was hoping the bastard had survived so she could be the one to kill him or desperately praying that he was gone and this was nothing more than a sick joke, Tia moved toward a distant door that had long ago rusted away. She could hear the muffled sound of voices heading in her direction, and she wanted to be in a place to watch where they were going without being seen.

It turned out to be easier than she expected.

By the time she'd reached the opening, the handful of demons were being herded into a small storage room, most of them stumbling forward as if they were still drunk or high. A second later a steel door was slammed shut by a heavy-set demon wearing leather pants and a hoodie who turned to lean against the wall, clearly designated as the guard. The poor creatures were locked inside, like cattle waiting for the slaughter.

With a frown, Tia retraced her steps, not halting until she was out of earshot of the demon.

"Where's Joe?" she muttered. She'd seen him get in the van, but he hadn't been with the victims currently trapped in the storage room. So where was he? And how had he escaped?

"Who?" Lynch demanded.

"Stay here." Tia headed back toward the doorway. "I'll be back."

"Where are you going?"

"I want to find out who else is in the building."

"What should I do?"

Tia glanced over her shoulder, annoyance stabbing through her as she met her servant's worried gaze. She hated being fussed over. She wasn't helpless. Not even close to helpless. But, for the first time in a very, very long time, she forced herself to take a deep, calming breath. Lynch had been a loyal servant for decades, she sternly reminded herself. And the fact that he was concerned didn't have anything to do with his lack of confidence in her abilities. He genuinely cared what happened to her.

"Keep an eye on the hostages. If they get moved to a new location, I want you to follow," she commanded, pointing a finger in his direction. "But don't get caught. I'll be seriously pissed if you get yourself sacrificed."

"No one's sacrificing me," Lynch growled, but he couldn't disguise his pleasure that she'd bothered to warn him.

With a shake of her head, Tia dismissed her servant from her mind. She was obviously getting soft in her old age, she decided, pausing long enough to reach into her pocket and pull out a small orb. Pressing it between her fingers, she watched as a silver mist spiraled upward, growing larger as it twirled around her. Within seconds it had shrouded her in a layer of magic that allowed her to disappear into the shadows.

Cautiously tiptoeing over debris that littered the ground, Tia pressed her back against the wall as she exited the room. The guard was busy scrolling through his phone as she inched her way in the opposite direction, but any noise was going to alert him that he wasn't alone.

Or at least it should alert him. From his bored expression it was clear he didn't think much of his current job. It might take more than a rustle in the darkness to attract his attention.

Stepping into yet another connected building, Tia halted to scan the shadows. The vast space echoed with emptiness, but she could sense the presence of several demons. Unfortunately she had no way of knowing where they might be gathered.

Only one way to find out.

Crossing the long room, Tia's steps slowed as she neared an open doorway. It wasn't the soft glow of light that alerted her that there was someone nearby. It was the tingle of magic. A magic that was intimately familiar.

Maya.

Keeping the mist wrapped around her, Tia scurried forward, avoiding the light that spilled into the room as she pressed her back against the doorframe.

"You're sure his name is Batu?" Maya's voice floated through the stale air, her voice sharp with suspicion.

Tia curled her fingers into fists, leashing the fury at the mere mention of her former master. Her greatest danger would be to allow her emotions to cloud her mind.

"Not Batu, he's *Lord* Batu," a female voice corrected sharply.

Leaning to the side, Tia caught a glimpse of an older woman standing in the center of a circle and next to her was a younger female. There was a low hum of magic, which indicated she was a mage, but not nearly on the same level as Maya. Or herself. Was it the mage who had shoved Maya into the strange mirror?

Maya's back was to her, the rigid angle of her head a sure sign that she wasn't as calm as she was trying to pretend.

"Where is this Lord Batu?" Maya asked.

The younger mage shrugged. "With his disciples and the latest sacrifices."

"In this building?"

"Unfortunately." The mage's tone was sour. "Because of you, we were forced to relocate. This is hardly the setting for a creature of his power, but it's not for much longer."

"But *you* haven't physically seen his face?"

"Why are you nagging about whether I've seen his face or not?" the woman snapped. "He's whispered through the mirror and I've been in his presence, even if he has been heavily robed. He's magnificent. That's all that matters."

Tia rolled her eyes. If it truly was Batu, there was nothing magnificent about the bastard. He was a cruel, selfish prick who would use the mage and destroy her as soon as he was done with her.

Maya made a sound of disgust, but she didn't bother to warn the younger mage that she was playing with fire. Why bother? She'd discover her mistake soon enough.

"So now what?" Maya instead asked.

"Simple. Now you die."

"It's going to take a better mage than you to kill me."

"No, just a smarter one."

"You?" Maya's voice dripped with scorn.

As expected, the impulsive mage stepped forward, putting her within easy distance of one of Maya's potions that were no doubt stashed in her satchel. Idiot girl. Even if the mage didn't know that Maya always carried an arsenal of potions that could level a small town, she should have sensed she was being deliberately provoked.

The mage tossed her blond curls, too arrogant to sense her danger. "Do you think I wasn't prepared for you?"

"You're saying this is a trap?" Maya drawled.

"Of course it's a trap, you stupid bitch."

"Let's see it."

"I don't think so." Tia abruptly stepped into the room, drawing on the magic that surged through her blood as she silently prepared a spell. "We don't have time for this nonsense," she said as Maya sent her a startled glance.

"Who are you?" the younger mage shrilly demanded.

"Shut up." Tia released her magic with a wave of her hand, not bothering to watch as the magic hit the young woman to send her flying backward, although she did hear her hitting the wall with a dull thud. "Are you done playing with her?" she asked Maya with a lift of her brows.

"I think so." Maya wrinkled her nose. "She didn't have any useful information."

"Then let's go."

"No!" The mage scrambled forward, her face flushed with a combination of pain and fury. "Stop."

"I told you to shut up." Tia casually sent the woman flying backward again before turning to head out of the room.

Walking next to her, Maya's back was rigid, as if she wasn't as delighted as she should be to have her old friend make an unexpected appearance.

"I didn't need you to rescue me," Maya muttered.

Tia made a sound of impatience. "Can't you just say thank you without trying to start a fight?"

Prepared for a full-out squabble, Tia was caught off guard when Maya's tension abruptly eased and she sent her a rueful smile.

"Thank you."

"A miracle." Tia kept her tone light, careful not to goad her companion. She told herself it was because she didn't want to start a fight when they were both on the same team. At least *temporarily* on the same team. Or maybe she was just getting old enough to concede that her pride wasn't always the most important thing in her life.

Turning back in the direction she'd come, Tia retraced her steps. Now that Maya was with her, she didn't have to sneak around. Together they could create a trap and wait for the demons—and whoever else might be lurking in the dark—to stumble into it.

"It's just a habit, you know," Maya abruptly announced.

"What's a habit?"

"Sniping at each other."

Tia nodded, although she didn't think it was entirely habit that caused Maya to resent her.

"You blame me for not doing more to save you from Batu." The words tumbled from Tia's lips. As if they'd been waiting a long time to be shared. Probably forty-five years.

"And you blame me for abandoning you once we were free," Maya countered.

Tia grimaced. Okay, that might be true. "The classic friends to enemies."

"Only we're not enemies, are we, Tia?" Maya murmured. "Not really."

Tia sucked in a startled breath, jerking her head to the side to meet Maya's steady gaze. "What are you saying?"

"For forty-five years I told myself that I walked away from you because of your obsession with gaining power." She shrugged. "I didn't want to spend my life battling for something that would never bring me happiness."

Tia didn't bother to insist that she wasn't obsessed with power. All she wanted was the ability to destroy anyone stupid enough to try to enslave her again.

Right now she was more interested in what thoughts were running through Maya's head. "That wasn't the reason?"

"In part, I genuinely had no interest in conquering the world."

"Why conquer the world when you could peddle coffee, right?" Tia couldn't resist.

Maya thankfully ignored her. "But I'm starting to think there was more than one reason I fled my homeland," she confessed. "And why I've kept you at a distance."

"Tell me."

"I didn't want to be reminded of my time spent as Batu's slave. I needed to start over and I couldn't do that if I was constantly haunted by my past."

"Including me."

"Not you," Maya protested, as if sensing that her words had managed to touch a raw nerve. "It was also the guilt I felt that I betrayed you. I knew you would never forgive me."

Tia grimaced. When she'd realized that Maya had not only left their home, but had also disappeared from the country, she'd been furious. It had felt like a dagger in the heart after she'd done everything in her power to shield Maya from Batu's cruelty, not to mention training her to control her magic.

"I didn't forgive you," she said, then with a sigh, forced herself to admit that she wasn't as bitter as she'd assumed over the past four decades. "But that didn't stop me from traveling to New York when I realized you were in danger."

Maya sent her a startled glance. "I thought you were here because you suspected that Batu survived."

"As it was so recently pointed out to me, I didn't need to contact you if that was my only reason for being in the area," Tia pointed out in dry tones. "You hurt me when you left, Maya, but if I'm being honest, I didn't have to think about you again if I didn't want to. You weren't a threat to me or my ambitions."

"That's true. My dreams are much simpler than ruling the world. But I'm not sure I understand what you're saying."

"If I held on to my grudge, then I had a reason to keep you in my life." The words came out stiff. It wasn't easy for Tia to lower her barriers, and even more difficult for her to admit that she might regret losing her oldest friend.

She took great pride in her independence. Only a weakling needed others.

Maya came to a halt, her brow furrowed as if she was carefully choosing her words. "You know, we can't heal all the wounds from the past," she finally said. "But perhaps we can heal a few of them."

Tia scowled at the dangerous longing that tugged at her heart. For the past forty years she'd been telling herself that she didn't need other people. Family and friends softened a woman. They made her vulnerable. Then again, maybe her independence didn't have to be all or nothing. There might be room to collaborate with another mage, assuming she had the proper skills and talent to be worthy of her time.

"Perhaps," she conceded.

As if realizing this wasn't the time or place for repairing their fragile relationship, Maya glanced around.

"Why are you headed in this direction?"

Tia nodded toward the doorway. "The sacrifices are locked in a storage room down the hallway."

"Is that how you found this place?"

"Yes. I followed them after they were taken from the rave." She shrugged. "Now that there are two of us, it makes sense to hide in this area. Eventually someone's going to come and get the demons. We can follow them to the mysterious leader."

"Clever," Maya agreed, pursing her lips and appearing to consider the hasty plan. "We should also weave a tracking web on the floor. That will give us the opportunity to keep some space between us and the captors without losing their trail."

It made sense, and, moving a few feet from her companion, Tia judged the angle of the door and breathed the words to the familiar spell. The magic tingled through her blood, not a full-out bubble since the threads to create the web were simple to conjure, but enough to send a shiver of bliss racing through her. There was nothing more addictive than magic.

Not sex, not money, not even power.

Just the wild beauty that hummed through her.

Then she felt the soft brush of Maya's power combining with hers, threading the strands of the web together, and another shiver raced through her body. She'd forgotten the pleasure of sharing a weave with another mage. Especially Maya, who formed the web in perfect harmony as Tia spread it across the cement floor.

Squashing the strange ache that felt perilously close to loneliness, Tia tied off the spell with a flick of her fingers.

"Where's your leech?" she demanded, well aware the male would be in the area.

He'd obviously bonded with Maya. He wasn't going to allow her to be in danger without being close enough to rush to the rescue.

"He sensed the magic again. He's hoping to trace it to its source."

Tia frowned. She still didn't understand how the vampire could sense magic that eluded a mage.

"Does he think it's Batu?"

Maya looked grim as she shrugged. "Is it possible that he survived?"

"I would say no, but—"

"But what?"

Tia's jaw tightened as she recalled the strange shimmering strand that she'd seen flow from the crevice in the hidden chamber directly to the center of Maya's chest.

"Something's still attached to you."

Maya flinched, but even as her hand lifted as if to touch the invisible strand, her eyes widened.

"Did you see that?" she rasped, stepping past Tia to stare at the distant wall.

"Did I see what?"

"There was a figure running across the back of the room."

Tia moved to stand next to her companion, unable to see anything in the thick shadows.

"Was it robed?"

"No." Maya sent her a confused glance. "Honestly, it looked like Joe."

"Shit." Tia had forgot all about the aggravating male. "Come on."

Tia sprinted forward, determined to capture Joe before he could disappear again. Maya was swiftly at her side, her expression puzzled.

"You think it was him?"

"I saw him getting into the van with the other sacrifices they lured from the rave," Tia said. "But between the city and here he vanished. I was searching for him when I stumbled across you."

"What's he doing here?"

Tia's magic swirled and hissed through her as she prepared a spell that would wrap the mysterious Joe in an indestructible net. This wasn't a pedestrian tracking spell. She was going to need all the power she could scrape together.

"I intend to find out," she snapped.

"Careful, Tia," Maya warned. "He isn't what he seems."

"I already figured that out." Reaching the back wall, Tia was forced to slow her pace as she searched for a doorway. "Where the hell did he go?"

"I'm here."

With a magic that was impossible to detect, Joe parted the shadows. Suddenly Tia could see that he'd ditched the cloak he'd been wearing to reveal his velour-running-suit-fishing-hat-bearded glory.

"What the hell?"

"Shh." He pointed toward a large drain that was cut into the cement. "We need to hear this."

Curiosity overcame her annoyance, and Tia leaned forward, peering through the opening. It was hard to make out what was beneath them. It looked like a cement-lined tunnel. A sewage drain? Some sort of vent?

She was still trying to figure it out when the low sound of male voices echoed through the air and Maya sucked in a sharp gasp, her hand instinctively reaching out to grasp Tia's arm.

"Ravyr," Maya rasped.

Chapter 22

Ravyr grimaced as he entered the large tunnel that was dug through the rocky ground and lined with cement. It didn't take a genius to suspect that he was being lured into a trap, but he refused to slow his pace as he plunged through the darkness. It wasn't until he sensed the tunnel widening, as if he was nearing a juncture, that he forced himself to halt. There was a difference between aggressive and reckless. He wasn't going to help Maya if he was dead.

Pressing his back against the curved wall, he allowed his senses to spread outward, absorbing every detail of his surroundings. The heavy weight of the silos above his head. The layer of mold that coated the cement. The faint breeze that carried the scent of moisture, revealing that the tunnel emptied into the nearby canal. But most of all, the biting chill that warned he was near a vampire.

"Ravyr, my old friend." A deep voice rustled through the darkness, like the hiss of a snake. "I've been waiting for you. Come and make yourself comfortable."

Squaring his shoulders, Ravyr pushed away from the wall and stepped into the open space that served as a juncture between the drainage system. He was distantly aware of the musty air leaking from a hole in the ceiling of the tunnel and the scent of demons and mages above him, but his focus was locked on the shadowed form standing in the center of the opening.

The creature was wrapped in a heavy cloak, but that didn't disguise the skeleton gauntness of the hunched body or the narrow face with sunken eyes and lips that had rotted away to reveal massive fangs. Ravyr hissed in shock. The male had a zombie vibe that was giving him the creeps. He was used to death—he was a vampire, after all—but this...

Batu had decayed into a walking, talking corpse.

With an effort, he squashed the instinctive desire to put space between him and the nasty cadaver, even managing to force a mocking smile to his stiff lips.

"So you did survive, Batu." He flicked a disgusted glance over the male's emaciated body, refusing to be distracted by the voice in the back of his head that whispered that this had to be a trick. He'd lived long enough to know that nothing was impossible. "At least I assume you survived. No offense, but you look like you climbed out of hell."

The stench of tainted anger wafted toward Ravyr. "Not for much longer," Batu growled.

"Why? What's going to happen?"

Batu's disturbing chuckle echoed through the tunnel. "Nothing that you need to worry about. You'll be dead by then."

"A shame." Ravyr halted several feet away. He was still convinced this was a trap, but he was hoping he could get the information they needed. "But if I'm going to be dead, then perhaps you wouldn't mind answering a few questions that have been nagging at me?"

"Ask and I'll decide if I want to answer them or not."

Ravyr folded his arms over his chest. "What is that damned magic that is giving me a headache?"

"Ah." If Batu still had lips he would have smiled. Instead his face twisted into a weird grimace. "An ancient artifact that was chiseled out of a sacred stone. I assume it was used by dragons to store their powers, but I've never found anything like it before or since."

"Where did you get it?"

"I bought the medallion in a black-market shop over a millennium ago." Sweeping aside the cloak, Batu revealed the heavy amulet that hung around his neck. It glowed in the darkness with a greenish light, as if it was releasing some sort of magic. Ravyr had always assumed it was molded out of metal, but a closer look revealed the chiseled edges. Why hadn't he paid more attention? "It was what led me to Cambodia where the original stone was buried. And why I built my lair in that location."

Ravyr slowly nodded. He'd never heard of a stone that could hold the power of a dragon, but Batu had always been an avid collector of rare and forbidden objects. And of course, Gyres were perfect examples of how dragon magic pooled and lingered in the earth. Why not a sacred rock?

"What does it do?" he demanded.

"The medallion?"

"We can start there."

"It has several purposes." Batu stroked his fingers over the medallion, his touch slow and gentle as if it was a lover, not a lump of rock. "It can absorb the magic from demons and even mages to give me more power."

"That's why you held Tia and Maya captive," Ravyr murmured. He'd already known that the male was siphoning magic from the mages, but he hadn't been able to discover what he was doing with it.

Now the question was how much of that magic remained and if the bastard could still tap into it with his weird-ass necklace.

"They were my honored guests, not my captives," Batu growled, sounding genuinely annoyed by the accusation.

"Not according to them."

The annoyance was abruptly replaced with a cunning expression. "Let's ask." Batu tilted back his head to sniff the air, the few strands of his hair that tenaciously clung to his head floating on the soft breeze. "I feel their presence. Call them to join us."

Ah. That was why he'd allowed Ravyr to get so close to him. He assumed that Maya would follow him into the tunnel. But Tia? How had she found this place? More importantly, could they trust her?

He shrugged. A worry for later.

"I'm not done with my questions," he insisted.

The annoyance returned as Batu snapped his bony finger at Ravyr. "What else?"

"You said the medallion has more than one purpose."

"It does."

Ravyr ground his fangs. "What are the others?"

The silence stretched, as if Batu was weighing the benefit of appeasing Ravyr long enough to lure Maya into the tunnel against the pleasure of simply killing him.

Apparently, Batu's desire for Maya edged out his thirst for blood. "It connects this body to my demon in the afterlife," he grudgingly confessed.

"Wait." Ravyr took a second to process what the male was saying. "Your demon is in the afterlife?"

"Yes."

"So Maya did kill you."

"Only temporarily."

Ravyr shook his head. Vampires might be considered immortal, but they weren't eternal. Their physical form was capable of being destroyed, sending the demon spirit into the afterlife to await a new body. That broke any connection to the previous existence. That was how it'd always been.

But Batu's physical body was still functioning—in a creepy, zombie sort of way. So either the demon should be inside him, or...or hell, he didn't know. None of it made sense.

"What does that mean?"

"When I discovered I had the ability to open a doorway to the afterlife, I knew I had a unique opportunity."

"To what? Cheat death?"

Batu released a low growl, as if he was frustrated by Ravyr's inability to appreciate his amazing skill.

"Not cheat death. To *control* death," he chastised. "It's the ultimate challenge."

"We're vampires. We already possess the ultimate dominion over death."

"No. We're not eternal. We're resurrected."

Ravyr shrugged. "Same thing."

"It's not," Batu snapped. "Our memories and powers and everything that makes us unique are destroyed. Our very essence is..." He spread his arms, the motion slow and methodical, as if he struggled against the weight of his shroud. "Poof. That's not eternal life."

Ravyr stored away the evidence of Batu's weakness as he concentrated on what the male was saying. Once he had the information he needed, he would decide how to destroy the evil bastard.

"It's a clean slate," he said, deliberately provoking Batu. "Being alive forever would be as boring as hell. This way we get a new start. Like a reset button."

On cue, Batu stepped forward, his sunken eyes glowing with the same greenish light as the medallion. The male had turned himself into a decaying corpse, convincing himself that he'd become nothing less than a god with the ability to control life and death. He wanted to be glorified, not told that his sacrifices were a wasted effort.

"The end of who we are with no guarantee we will be given the same gifts and advantages," Batu snarled.

"Meaning you're too lazy to start over."

The bony fingers clenched and unclenched, as if Batu was battling against the urge to attack Ravyr.

"Not too lazy, too smart," he snapped. "Why give up what I have acquired over the centuries when I can keep it?"

Ravyr didn't argue. Any vampire who'd gained enough power to become a member of the Cabal and given control of a Gyre would leap at the opportunity to maintain their current existence. There were no guarantees when they came back that they would have the same powers. It was far more likely they would be a servant. Besides, his only interest was discovering Batu's powers and how they connected to Maya.

Connected quite literally.

"How?" Ravyr demanded.

"I used the mages' magic to store up my power."

"In the mystery stone?"

"Exactly."

Ravyr recalled the endless hours he'd wasted trying to break through the magic surrounding Batu's private lair.

"That's why you had so many layers of protection."

"I wasn't going to risk having Sinjon interfering in my plans." Batu did that weird grimacing smile again. "Thankfully you were clueless."

It was true. *Painfully true,* Ravyr grimly acknowledged. He'd not only been clueless when he was spying on Batu forty-odd years ago, but he'd remained clueless as he'd traveled from one place to another trying to locate the pulsing magic.

It was annoying as hell.

Refusing to be distracted, he glared at the aggravating leech. "What happened when Maya killed you?"

"My disciples surrendered their lives as they were trained to do when they felt my death."

Batu's tone was dismissive, as if the sacrifice of his loyal servants was a meaningless cost to keep his sorry ass alive.

"Why did they have to kill themselves?" he asked, his voice harsh.

Batu shrugged. "Only death can open the gateway to the afterlife."

That made an evil sort of sense, but the anger that had been simmering inside Ravyr since he'd first been sent to Batu's lair seared through him with a white-hot force. This egotistical, self-absorbed brute had destroyed countless demons and humans—for what? To become a shambling zombie who desperately clung to the hope of being reunited with his demon?

It was sickening.

His hands curled into fists as he glared at the evil creature. "And it takes sacrifices to keep it open?"

"No, the magic that is still stored in the stone keeps it open." He reached up to touch his glowing necklace. "I'm able to tap into the magic with the medallion. At least enough for my demon to remain connected to my body."

"Then why are you still killing? Haven't you abused enough demons?"

The male paused, as if irritated by Ravyr's seething disgust. "Call for Maya and I'll tell you," he at last commanded.

"I'm not calling for Maya until you explain why you're here and what you want from her."

The stench of decay thickened as Batu hissed in frustration, but he was smart enough to know that Ravyr wasn't going to budge. Not until he knew exactly what Batu wanted.

"I'm not sure how it happened, but the magic that bonds my physical body to my demon was somehow disrupted." Batu's fingers wrapped around the medallion, as if struggling to control his anger at the memory. "I should have been restored to my original form as soon as my body healed. Instead, the connection fractured as if it was being split in two. One part remained attached to me, but the other half disappeared."

Ravyr furrowed his brow as he forced himself to imagine Batu in his death throes, releasing his magic to maintain a leash on his demon as it entered the afterlife. Why would it split? The demons had done their duty and stuck daggers in their hearts to keep open the barrier between life and death. At least that's what Maya had seen in her vision…

"Maya," he breathed, certain she was the only creature powerful enough to disrupt the magic. Even if it had been unintentional.

And it would explain the shimmering strand she'd seen attached to the center of her chest.

"Very good," Batu drawled. "It's taken me years to figure that out."

Ravyr arched a brow. "Seriously?"

Batu hissed in fury, then continued. "At first I assumed that it must have been one of my disciples who disrupted the magic. Unfortunately, the ones who hadn't sacrificed themselves fled after my supposed death. The cowards." His eyes glowed an eerie green. "For over forty years I've tracked them down one by one to destroy them."

"That's why the magic moved," Ravyr muttered, still confused. "But why didn't I sense it all the time?"

"There was no need to activate the magic until I located the demon and was prepared to sacrifice them."

"Along with dozens of others? Was that really necessary?"

Batu looked baffled by the question. He'd obviously never wasted one second regretting the blood that he'd shed.

"The more death, the more powerful the magic."

Ravyr shook his head. "Evil."

"How am I evil? I don't make the rules," he protested.

"You just bend them to give you what you want no matter the cost."

"Why not? There are winners and there are losers." Batu tilted his chin, looking ghoulish with his protruding cheekbones and rotting lips. "I will always be a winner."

Ravyr pointedly glanced down at the emaciated body that was barely capable of staying upright.

"Not always."

A low growl rumbled through the tunnel as Batu struggled to maintain his composure.

"Maya was an unfortunate obstacle in my plans, but like all obstacles she'll soon be removed."

It was Ravyr's turn to battle against his surge of fury. This male had brutalized Maya for decades, not only draining her magic but also holding her captive in his lair, caged like an animal. Ravyr would do anything—sacrifice everything—to destroy this male before he could lay another finger on her.

Silently assuring himself that he was close to having all the answers he needed before he shredded the male into ribbons so tiny they could never be stitched back together, Ravyr asked the question that was still bothering him.

"How did you realize she was the one you were searching for?"

"When my demon sensed her friend Tia in the afterlife. I suddenly realized that I had been a fool to assume that it was one of my disciples who'd splintered the bond. It had to have been magic that caused the fracture. Maya's magic." Batu glanced over Ravyr's shoulder, as if hoping the mage was lurking in the shadows. "Until she's dead, I'm doomed to be caught between life and death."

Ravyr didn't have the full story of Valen and Tia's journey into the afterlife, or how they'd escaped, but he suddenly wished they'd found some other way to save Valen's mate. Batu might have never connected Maya to his death-cheating snafu.

Then again, Ravyr would have been stuck chasing the decaying fool from one end of the world to the other. And worse, he wouldn't be planning a future with Maya.

He had to hope that this was what destiny intended, he conceded.

"So you came to find her?" he asked, no longer interested in Batu's explanations.

All he wanted now was to keep the male distracted so he could edge close enough to attack.

"Once I had things in place," Batu admitted.

"What things?" Ravyr took a deliberate step to the side, watching Batu turn so he continued to directly face him.

The male could still move, but he certainly didn't have his previous grace. But Ravyr was more interested in how the thin fingers flexed around the medallion. As if he was afraid that Ravyr was going to try to take it away from him.

Which led to the question...what would happen if he did wrestle the medallion from Batu? Would removing it from the vampire be enough to interrupt the magic? Or did it have to be destroyed?

Not that he had a clue how to destroy the thing. Dragon magic was above his pay grade.

"My disciples had to locate a proper lair," Batu explained. "I couldn't risk entering the city and alerting Valen to my presence. Not until I'd accomplished what I came here to do."

"The island."

Batu nodded. "A perfect spot. Isolated and yet close enough to maintain the power of the Gyre. Until you ruined it."

"It's what I do." A humorless smile twisted Ravyr's lips as he took another step to the side, and a few inches forward. He wanted to be close enough to grab Batu before the male realized he was in danger. Or before anyone could leap out of one of the tunnels to protect him. He assumed the disciples were somewhere close by. If they realized their master was being threatened, they would no doubt rush to his rescue. "What else did you need?"

Batu waved a bony hand. "A few local demons to start collecting the sacrifices. The more death, the more powerful my connection to the afterlife."

Ravyr refused to be provoked by the male's careless tone. The only way to make Batu pay for his sins was to make sure he died in these tunnels. He took another step forward.

"Why come yourself?" he asked, genuinely curious. "Why not send your demons to kill Maya?"

"I have to be next to her when she dies," Batu recklessly revealed. "That's the only way to be sure that the magic connected to the both of us will re-form into one bond."

Ah. That was why he'd placed himself in danger, Ravyr silently acknowledged. He had to lure Maya into his presence if he was going to reclaim his demon. Then his brows snapped together as he was struck by a sudden realization.

"If you have to be together, then why the hell did you send Alison to kill her?" he asked. "Or didn't you know what your servants were doing while you moldered in the shadows?"

"Of course I knew. Just like I knew if I tried to capture Maya, she would have some nasty spell prepared to escape." The greenish glow in Batu's eyes flared, as if recalling the last time he'd been in Maya's presence. "I might hate the bitch for what she did to me, but I'll never underestimate her. Not again."

Obviously his brain hadn't rotted along with his face, Ravyr conceded. Or at least he still had enough brains to realize Maya was a threat.

"So why did Alison try to blow us up?" he pressed.

"I didn't want to risk forcing Maya into my trap, but I could offer her a temptation she couldn't resist."

Ravyr scowled. What the hell was Batu babbling about? Dodging demented mages and bone-rattling explosions wasn't exactly tempting. Then, the realization of where he was and the sense of Maya somewhere above his head forced an ancient swear word past his lips.

"You created a mystery that she felt compelled to solve."

Batu chuckled, the sound echoing through the empty tunnels. "Exactly."

"Alison never intended to kill her?"

"Oh, she thought she was supposed to destroy Maya," Batu corrected him. "It was the only way to make the game believable."

"Game?" Ravyr snapped. The past few nights were going to give him nightmares for the next several centuries.

"Life and death are the best games of all," Batu drawled.

Ravyr shook his head in disgust. "And what if she'd succeeded? What would have happened to you if she'd died when you weren't around?"

Batu appeared legitimately shocked by Ravyr's question. "Alison? That pathetic mage against Maya Rosen?" He clicked what was left of his tongue. Another creepy sound. "She never stood a chance. Besides, I knew you'd be there to protect her."

Ravyr arched a brow. "You knew I was in the city?"

"I've sensed you following me for the past four decades," Batu revealed in mocking tones. "Always one step behind me. And as clueless as ever."

Ravyr ignored the jab. What could he say? He *had* been clueless. Instead he focused on Batu's assumption that he would be nearby to rescue Maya from danger.

"What made you think I would try to protect Maya?"

"Only an idiot would have missed your besotted expression when she was in the same room." A taunting smile twisted his spine-chilling features. "And the way your fangs flashed when you thought she was being abused. Only your duty to Sinjon kept you from stealing her from me."

"Fair enough," Ravyr retorted, unfazed by his taunt. He had been besotted with Maya. Still was. He took another step forward, his muscles clenching as he prepared to attack. "But you seem to forget that my need to keep Maya safe extends to destroying you."

"I'll admit that I'd hoped your attempt to rescue her would get rid of you. I liked the thought of you splattered across New York City." Batu waved a skeletal hand. "But in the end this is probably better."

"Why?"

"Because you weren't alone in being besotted. Maya was equally obsessed. Like Romeo and Juliet." There was an edge in Batu's voice that revealed he hadn't been pleased with her interest in another male. Not surprising. Vampires were notoriously possessive. "Unfortunately for you, your story will have the same tragic ending. Both of you destined to die. Romantic, don't you think? But first..." Without warning, the green glow surrounding the amulet pulsed bright enough to momentarily blind Ravyr. At the same time a blast of heat from the glowing medallion crashed into him, flinging him against the side of the tunnel as pain ravaged through him. Obviously the medallion had more tricks than Batu had disclosed. Falling to his knees as the agonizing heat seared through him, Ravyr crawled forward, refusing to concede defeat as he heard Batu call out in a loud voice. "Maya, come say goodbye to your lover!"

Chapter 23

Despite her limited view through the water drain, Maya could clearly hear the conversation between Ravyr and Batu. Or at least, what was left of Batu. The bastard confessed everything, from the reason he'd been in Cambodia to why he'd sucked the magic from her and Tia, and how he'd sacrificed endless demons in an attempt to cheat death. His words answered her question of why she'd been plagued with nightmares for the past forty years, and why he'd traveled to New York City.

No doubt it would take months—if not years—to process everything she'd discovered, but at the moment she didn't give a shit why Batu had held her prisoner or how he'd survived. Or even why he'd tracked her to New York City. Her entire being was focused on a stark fear that clenched her muscles and twisted her stomach into a painful knot. There'd been a risk that they were walking into a trap from the moment they'd entered the abandoned building, but she'd assumed she would be the one in danger. Now she was forced to watch from a distance as the green glow slammed into Ravyr, clearly causing him an intense agony as he fell to his knees, his head bowed as if he was fighting to remain conscious.

"Ravyr!" His name was wrenched from her lips as she straightened and prepared to rush toward the nearest exit.

She didn't know where the opening to the sewage tunnel might be, but she assumed it was outside the main building. The sooner she found it, the sooner she could destroy Batu once and for all.

Of course, it couldn't be that easy. Nothing had been easy for the past year. It had honestly been like a terrifying roller-coaster ride that she couldn't get off. Before she could take a step, a firm hand was clamped onto her upper arm, spinning her back to face Joe.

"Let go of me," she snapped, her magic churning through her veins. "I need to get to Ravyr."

"That's not the way." He lifted his free hand to weave it in a complicated gesture.

Maya tried to jerk her arm free. She didn't have time for this male's mysterious stunts. It was a wasted effort, of course. His fingers were wrapped around her arm like a steel manacle. Soon after, her attempts to escape were forgotten as she caught sight of the shimmering strands of magic that floated in the air.

They weren't the same as hers. The strands looked like pure gold as they twirled faster and faster, stretching and thinning until they at last settled into a large oval. Maya frowned, not sure what the magic was going to do. Then, there was an unexpected pulse that shook the entire building, rattling the windows that still held glass, and sending flakes of dirt from the ceiling. At the same time, a crimson fog began to fill the inside of the oval.

"What is that?" she rasped, widening her stance as the floor continued to vibrate.

"An opening to the afterlife. That's where we need to go."

Maya sucked in a shocked breath. No wonder the building was still shaking. She couldn't imagine the amount of power it would take to rip a hole between dimensions.

She sent Joe an angry glare. "Are you insane?"

He shrugged. "It depends on who you're asking."

Maya snorted. Was there anyone who'd encountered this male who didn't assume he was...eccentric, to put it nicely?

"Why would we go to the afterlife?"

He released his iron grip on her arm to tap his fingers against the center of her chest. "To snip the connection between you and Batu's demon."

Maya grimaced. "Can't you just snip it here?"

Joe sent her a chastising scowl. "Don't ask foolish questions."

Maya met his scowl with one of her own. "I'm not leaving Ravyr."

"No? Then he'll die." The blunt word echoed through the vast space. "The only way to destroy the medallion is by closing the opening."

Maya continued to scowl. "Convenient."

"Actually, nothing could be less convenient," Joe informed her.

"I can't leave Ravyr," Maya stubbornly insisted, even as a part of her knew she was fighting a losing battle. Joe might annoy the hell out of her, but if he said the only way to cut Batu's connection to the world was to go into the afterlife, then what choice did she have? She was going to have to go.

"I'll keep your leech safe on this side," Tia interjected, the older mage still standing next to the drainage hole. "You go with..." She waved a hand toward Joe, who puckered his lips and blew a kiss in her direction. "Whatever he is."

Maya regarded her friend with a suspicion she couldn't disguise. Tia hated vampires. Why would she protect Ravyr? "You?"

A smile that would cause the most rabid goblin to flee in fear curled Tia's lips. "Batu and I have unfinished business."

Maya hesitated. She wasn't surprised that Tia wanted to confront her former master, but she hadn't expected the stab of fear that pierced her heart. The two of them might not be besties, but she wasn't prepared for her to die. They had baggage to sort through and old wounds to heal.

"He's dangerous," she warned.

The smile widened. "Not as dangerous as me."

"She's not wrong," Joe muttered, something that might have been admiration in his voice.

Maya whirled back toward the opening. As much as she wanted to be the one rushing to rescue Ravyr, the only way she could help him and Tia was to put an end to Batu. Once and for all.

"Are we going or not?" she demanded.

Joe arched a shaggy brow. "Now you're in a hurry?"

"Yes."

"Fine. Stay close."

She didn't need Joe's warning as he pressed a hand against her back and gave her a slight shove toward the crimson fog, which churned and boiled inside the magical oval. She intended to stick to him like glue.

Stumbling forward, Maya felt a heaviness press against her, as if there was a barrier attempting to keep her from passing through the gateway. A second later she was through the mist and standing in the middle of a desolate desert. The land around her was flat and barren, as if it'd been sucked of any life. And overhead the sky was a weird greenish shade with two moons that circled a black hole. Worst of all was the stench of sulfur. It was so thick it made her gag.

This wasn't a place for the living.

It was hushed and predatory and smoldering with greedy anticipation.

There was a shudder of power, and Joe was stepping through the mist to join her. Just for a second his image as a scruffy human with a messy beard and worn fishing hat flickered, and she could see the gloriously handsome creature who lurked beneath the grungy façade.

"What are you?"

He headed across the barren ground, as if he had a destination in mind. "I'm a Watcher."

Maya kept her gaze trained on his profile as she scurried to keep pace. She didn't want to think about the spooky landscape or the fact that they were in a place she couldn't escape without this male's assistance. It was better to concentrate on her companion and why he was helping her.

"What does Watcher mean?"

"We are..." His words trailed away as if he was searching for the words. "The beginning and the end."

"End of what?"

"Existence."

Maya's brows snapped together. He was babbling without making any sense. "Can't you give me a straight answer?"

Joe slowed his pace, heaving a deep sigh. As if she was unbearably stupid. "I'll try to explain in a way your mind can understand."

"So kind," she muttered.

"Yes, I am." He held up his hand as her lips parted in protest. This male was many things, including aggravating and occasionally scary, but he'd never been kind. "The only way I can describe my species is to say we truly are eternal," he said. "We were here long before the first demon crawled from their primordial sludge and even before the first dragon hatched from its egg."

"Are you claiming to be a god?"

His deep laugh rolled through the emptiness, momentarily battling back the ominous atmosphere that threatened to choke her.

"No, I can say with absolute confidence that I have no godly ambitions." He turned his head to wink at her. "Although I can sympathize with your urge to worship me; I am, after all, amazing."

Maya rolled her eyes. "Ugh."

"But I'm merely a referee to try to keep the demon world as peaceful as possible," he continued as if he hadn't heard her. "A task that I might add is one headache after another with few rewards."

Ignoring his arrogance, Maya considered what her companion had revealed. The explanation was deliberately vague, but it stirred a memory.

"You're like Lynx," she breathed, referring to the strange male in Skye's vision a few months ago. "The creature who negotiated the treaty between the vampires and the dragons."

Sorrow darkened Joe's face. "He was a brother."

"And he's dead now?"

Joe shook his head, his expression easing. "He sacrificed himself to keep the peace, but none of us are ever truly gone."

"Was he related to the fairy who called himself Lynx?" she pressed, an edge of anger in her voice. She would never forgive the bastard who'd kidnapped Skye and done his best to start a demon war.

Joe shrugged. "A distant grandfather."

Maya arched a brow. So it was true that the strange creatures formed intimate relationships with demons. At least intimate enough to create children.

"And Peri?"

Joe paused, ostensibly to scan their empty surroundings. An obvious delay tactic since nothing had changed despite the fact that it felt like they'd been walking for miles. Well, unless you counted the dry, sulfur-tainted breeze that stirred her hair and rippled over the sand.

"She has our blood in her veins," he eventually admitted.

Maya felt something close to smug satisfaction. His words just confirmed her own certainty that there was something special about her young friend. She'd sensed it from the moment their paths had crossed.

"Is that why she can tap into her wild magic?" she asked.

"It doesn't hurt, but her talent is utterly unique."

"Just like Peri." Maya smiled; then another question that had been nagging at her for months bubbled to the surface. "Wait. That picture of you that Peri discovered in her mother's cabin."

"What about it?"

"Brenda Sanguis was obviously in a relationship with one of your kind," she pointed out, referring to Peri's mother.

Joe held up a hand, as if offended by her words. "Not really one of my kind. He had a very distant connection to the original Lynx, but the blood had been diluted through years of mixing with demons and even humans."

Maya refused to react to his implication that the mixed blood made Peri inferior.

"Did Brenda recognize you?"

Joe shook his head. "Why would she? She might have been a witch, but she never realized that Peri's father was anything but another human."

Maya wasn't convinced. "Then why would she have your pictures hidden in her private papers?"

"I assume Brenda hired someone to keep a watch on Peri since she'd told her coven that she'd killed her daughter. It might have been a little uncomfortable if Peri had made an unexpected appearance."

"The images were focused on you," Maya stubbornly insisted.

Joe slowed his pace, his nostrils flaring as if he'd caught a new scent. Maya hadn't. The sulfur had scalded her nose until she couldn't smell anything else.

"It always happens if I'm in the vicinity," Joe said in distracted tones.

"Why?"

"What can I say?" He lifted a shoulder. "I'm very photogenic."

Maya made a sound of impatience. "Why?"

"It has something to do with my powers," he retorted, clearly uninterested in the conversation. "I can encourage people not to consciously notice me, but technology is always drawn in my direction."

That made a weird sort of sense. Magic and technology were always battling against each other.

"What are your powers?"

"A discussion for another time."

The words were clipped, warning her that she'd crossed a line. Maya shrugged. That was fair enough. Every species—including mages—closely guarded their secrets.

She readily shifted the direction of the conversation. "How many Watchers are there in the world?"

Surprisingly, Joe answered her question. And it wasn't even drenched in his usual sarcasm. "It depends on the need. When things are quiet, there are only a couple of us. During times of war or upheaval, there are dozens roaming around."

Maya wasn't sure whether to be reassured or frightened by his revelation. She didn't completely trust the mysterious creatures.

"Where do you go when you aren't roaming around?"

"We have our own afterlife." He sniffed, waving a hand toward their bleak surroundings. "Only it's a lot nicer. And it doesn't stink."

She studied his profile, wondering how he'd decided on his scruffy disguise. Was it to blend into the background of the streets? Or because he'd realized she had a soft spot for those in need? No matter how aggravating he might be, he had known that she was never going to run him off. In fact, she fed him on a daily basis....

Suddenly her brows arched. "And it just happens to be your turn to be the Watcher?"

"Something like that."

"So why be a Watcher in front of the Witch's Brew?"

She sensed his jerk of surprise, as if he hadn't been expecting the question. "I have to be somewhere. Your coffee sucks, but you make a decent blueberry muffin."

The casually sarcastic tone didn't fool her. Not this time. "No."

"Your muffins aren't decent?" His expression was too innocent to be real. "Harsh."

"You're there because of me," she said, absolutely convinced she was right.

He tsked her words. "That's a little vain, isn't it? Not everything is about you, Maya Rosen."

She narrowed her gaze, using the tip of her finger to jab his upper arm. "You're my Benefactor." She jabbed again and then once again for good measure. Perhaps she should be afraid of this male, but he'd been a part of her life for years. It was hard to conjure the proper respect. "You're the one who's been protecting me, right?"

"Perhaps," he grudgingly admitted.

"Why?"

"I could sense a disruption in the world, but I couldn't pinpoint the source." He glanced at her with a wry expression. "Not until I at last tracked you down."

Maya blinked. "I'm a disruption?"

"Not you personally. Although you do have a temper." His gaze lowered to the center of her chest, but not in a creeper sort of way. It was purely professional. "I was referring to the link from Batu's demon to you."

Maya's breath hissed between her clenched teeth. He'd known about the connection and didn't warn her? The jerk.

"Why didn't you just get rid of it?" she snapped.

"Because I didn't know the source or what would happen if I did...." He wiggled his fingers in a gesture she assumed was supposed to be air quotes. "'Get rid of it.'" He sniffed, clearly offended. "It's possible I could have opened a rift that would have spilled death into your world. Is that what you want?"

She huffed in annoyance. "In your words..." She did her own air quotes. "'Don't ask foolish questions.'"

"Touché." He nodded his head, acknowledging her direct hit. "I decided to offer you my protection while I waited to see what happened." His attention returned to their surroundings, his pace slow and cautious. Did he think there was something nearby? The thought sent a shiver through Maya. Leeches were scary enough when they were hidden in a human body. She wasn't sure she was ready to see one in its primordial form. "I assumed that eventually whoever had created the link would try to do something with it."

"And that's all you wanted? Just to protect me?"

"What else?"

"I recall you demanding my help on more than one occasion in return for your protection," she reminded him.

He shrugged. "Would you have trusted me if I'd offered my assistance without asking something in return?"

Okay. He had a point. "No. I suppose not."

"Besides, I'm not just here to take care of you. I have other duties. It only made sense to utilize your talents to take care of the more mundane problems that cropped up."

"Mundane?" Maya growled in disbelief. "Just in the past few months I was thrown through a mezzanine window, shoved into a magical mirror, and nearly exploded to smithereens." She paused for dramatic effect. "Twice."

Joe pursed his lips, appearing sublimely indifferent to her various brushes with death. "What is smithereens? I've never understood that term."

"You—" She bit off her angry words. This male had his own priorities, and her pain or discomfort wasn't going to change them. "Never mind. Does this mean that once we've found Batu's demon and killed it, then our partnership will be over?"

"Eager to get rid of me?"

She wrinkled her nose. Honestly, she hadn't really thought about the future. Right now it was enough to survive from one minute to the next.

"I just want this over."

Joe came to a sudden stop, his expression grim. "You're about to get your wish."

Chapter 24

Tia followed the scent of death out of the building and toward the access door to the underground tunnel. She paused at the entrance, muttering the words to an ancient spell. For decades she'd been training for the day when she would confront one of the leeches. It never entered her mind that it would be Batu, but now that she had the chance to confront him, it made all those years of hard work worth every second of sacrifice.

The words tapped into the magic that flowed through her veins, altering the power until it was no longer simmering in anticipation. It'd hardened into a solid weapon, ready to strike with lethal precision.

Holding the spell in a tight grip, Tia entered the tunnel and made her way through the darkness. There was no use trying to creep through the shadows. Nothing could sneak up on a vampire. Even if they were supposed to be dead.

Nearing a large junction, Tia wrinkled her nose at the scent of sulfur. The last time she'd caught a whiff of that nasty odor she'd been in the afterlife. Which meant Batu had to be close.

On cue, a raspy voice echoed through the tunnel. "Yes. Come to me," the voice hissed.

Refusing to acknowledge the stab of fear, Tia squared her shoulders and stepped into the juncture. She spared a quick glance toward the vampire, on his hands and knees, and surrounded by a sickly green glow, before focusing her attention on the gaunt form shrouded in a heavy robe. Batu? Shock jolted through her. She'd expected him to be changed, but this...it was horrifying. "It's you," Batu spit out in disappointment. "Where's Maya?"

Tia forced herself to step forward, her skin crawling as she studied the skeletal features of his face and the sunken eyes that glowed with the same eerie magic that pulsed from the medallion around his neck.

"Gone," she informed him.

Batu jerked in shock. "You lie."

"Quite often, but not on this occasion," Tia drawled, taking pride in the fact that her voice didn't quiver.

"Where did she go?"

"Somewhere you'll never get your hands on her."

"There's nowhere she can hide." Batu's fangs extended, appearing weirdly long without his lips. The sight sent a shiver through Tia. "She belongs to me."

"Not according to Maya."

"Then her lover dies."

"Why?" Tia took another quick step forward, angling toward the silent Ravyr. "I'm here. I'm a mage. I can do anything Maya can do. And do it better."

"Ah." Batu's wariness visibly eased. "Still jealous, are you, Tia?"

Tia shrugged. There might have been times in the past when she'd envied Maya her raw power. Everything had come so easy for the younger woman. But she'd long ago recognized that she possessed other, more important talents. And that she was quite honestly superior to any mage out there.

"Not jealous, simply tired of her being treated like she's something special when my magic is stronger, trained to perfection, and available," she retorted. "For the right price, of course."

"There's the Tia that I knew and loved." Batu released a creepy chuckle. "I've missed you."

Tia leaned forward, stretching out her arm as she allowed the magic to pulse through her. She assumed that Batu hadn't attacked because he was hoping she could lure Maya out of hiding. "Let me help you."

"The only help you can offer is to bring Maya to me." Batu confirmed her suspicion.

"I've told you, she's not here. She left the area, I swear." Tia continued to hold out her hand. "But I can replace her."

"Never," Batu snapped, as if abruptly accepting that Tia wasn't going to be able to give him what he so desperately needed. "Besides, this is your fault in the first place. If you hadn't forced your way into my private temple, I would never have been in this position."

She had only seconds before he struck out. "What did you expect? If you hadn't made the hidden chamber off limits, I would never have been curious about what you were hiding." She inched sideways, trying to put herself as close to Ravyr as possible. She wasn't arrogant enough to think she could kill the male, even if he was damaged. But with Ravyr's help they might be able to overwhelm the bastard. First, however, she had to disrupt the medallion's magic. Something that she feared was easier said than done. "Really when you think about it, you have no one to blame but yourself. Let's kiss and make up."

Batu frowned as she leaned forward close enough to feel the heat from the glowing medallion.

"Stay back."

"Don't worry, I just want to help."

"You? How could you possibly help?"

"Like this." Releasing the spell that was thundering through her, Tia watched in satisfaction as Batu stumbled back, his face twisting with pain as shimmering shards of magic stabbed deep into his frail body. At the same time, she leaped to stand directly in front of Ravyr, her momentary delight shattering as she absorbed the punishing power. The piercing agony was crippling, threatening to crush her bones to dust. If it didn't stop her heart first. No wonder it'd sent Ravyr to his knees. "Shit."

"As reckless as ever, Tia," Batu growled in a harsh voice, unable to disguise his own pain as her spell continued to batter him. "This time there's no Maya to rescue you. This time you die."

* * * *

Maya sensed Joe fade into the background, as if he was deliberately avoiding the confrontation. And maybe he was. He said he was a Watcher, not a Doer, so she assumed he wasn't supposed to directly interfere in what was happening.

Or maybe he was using her as some sort of bait to lure Batu into a trap. It wouldn't be the first time he'd deliberately put her in danger.

Either way, Maya wasn't going to wait and hope he decided to step up. Not when Ravyr was being tortured. Walking forward, Maya clenched her hands and tilted her head to a proud angle. Inside she was a seething mass of terror, but by damned she wasn't going to give Batu the satisfaction of seeing her fear.

Approaching the dark shadow that she assumed was Batu's spirit, she watched as it abruptly jerked in her direction. Had she managed to startle the creature?

Maya. The voice echoed in her mind, sending chills of unease down her spine. *What a nice surprise. I've been looking for you.*

She halted a few feet from the shadow, trying not to notice how it flickered in and out of focus, as if he was an illusion, not a real form. The only thing solid was the crimson strand of power that was running from the middle of the darkness to connect directly over her heart.

Maya shivered, battling back a surge of panic. She wasn't going to let herself think about the fact that the creepy strand had been connected to her for over forty years. That was a nightmare for later.

"So I heard," she forced herself to respond.

How did you enter this dimension?

Maya shrugged, barely resisting the urge to glance over her shoulder and see if Joe was lurking nearby. "Does it matter?"

Not really. The scent of sulfur thickened. *Once you're dead I can return to the existence you so rudely interrupted.*

"Or...hear me out." She lifted her hand, her stomach churning as the form continued to flicker in and out of focus. The thing was making her nauseous. "I can finish what I started all those years ago and kill you. Once and for all."

A hollow chuckle echoed through her brain. *You can't do it.*

Couldn't she? Honestly, Maya had no idea. The only thing she knew for certain was that it wasn't going to be for lack of trying. Pretending to sniff the air, she forced a smile to her stiff lips. "Then why do I smell your fear?"

It's not fear. It's regret. His voice abruptly lowered to a creepy purr, as if he hoped he could distract her with his dubious charm. *I never wanted to hurt you, Maya. We should have been partners, not enemies.*

Maya snorted, her fear momentarily overshadowed by her surge of fury. "You can't be serious. You bought me like I was a piece of property and then proceeded to hold me hostage for years. Oh, and don't get me started on the pleasure you took in tormenting me."

Don't be so dramatic, he chastised. *You were my guest.*

"Guest? I wasn't allowed to leave your lair."

That was for your own protection. The world is a dangerous place for mages.

Maya made a sound of disgust. "The only danger was you. Not only did you drain my magic against my will to fuel your perverted death spell, you punished me whenever you felt the urge to cause me pain." She flicked her hand in a gesture of blatant disdain. "Not to mention your tedious habit of threatening to murder my family if I tried to escape."

The darkness shuddered, as if reacting to her anger, but the cajoling voice continued to whisper through her mind. *Admit it, Maya, you would never have become the mage you are today without me.*

She narrowed her eyes. "For once, you're right," she admitted. "It was because of your ruthless torture that I forced myself to hone my magic into a weapon I could use to destroy you."

And yet you failed, he taunted.

"Once." Maya was acutely aware of the passing time. And that each second she wasted was another second that Ravyr was in agony. Or worse. She had to do something, but she honestly had no idea how a spell would work in this place. She could feel the magic flowing through her veins, but it was sluggish. Like molasses rather than bubbling champagne. On the other hand, it seemed equally doubtful that her potions would work here. Not only was the atmosphere different, but Batu wasn't solid enough to hurt.

Solid...

Her gaze lowered to the strand shimmering between them.

Batu might be a spirit, but she was very real.

Reaching into her satchel, she searched for the vial that was warm to the touch. Once she located it, she clenched it in her fingers, leaving her hand hidden in the satchel as she breathed the words of a familiar spell. She would have one desperate shot at this. She needed to make sure that Batu was distracted.

With an unnecessary flourish, Maya tilted back her head as she shouted the last words of the spell and released a bolt of magic. As she'd hoped, it hung in the thick air with a visible lack of enthusiasm, simply floating between her and the glob of Batu's spirit. Like a petulant cloud.

Ha, Batu crowed in delight. *You failed again.*

"Well, you know what they say."

What do they say? he mocked.

"If at first you don't succeed..."

You will never... The words trailed away as Maya pulled the vial from her satchel and shook it to ignite the combustible potion inside. The liquid bubbled inside the glass container, the smell of acrid smoke competing with the stench of sulfur. *What are you doing?* A hint of worry threaded through the voice in her head. Good. Even as a spirit, the creature was worried about fire. *That can't hurt me. Not now.*

"No?" Her smile widened. "Let's see."

The darkness pulsed, growing larger as if it was preparing to attack. Maya clenched her teeth. This was it. Now or never. She didn't bother tossing the potion in Batu's direction. She accepted that she couldn't hurt his spirit. Instead, she shattered the vial in her hand, allowing the potion to spill over the center of her chest.

Searing heat spread over her, eating through her clothing and into her flesh. Like acid. But with grim determination she ignored the excruciating pain, concentrating on the potion that had reached the strand that bound her to Batu. With a desperate urgency, she used the magic she'd released earlier to squeeze the potion forward, forcing it to crawl along the crimson threads. The pain pounding into her intensified to an excruciating level, but the sudden burst of fear she could sense from the spirit kept her tenacious courage from shattering.

No, it hissed in her mind.

"Yes."

The potion neared the darkness, suddenly flaring with a blinding glow of heat. *Stop!*

"Never." Maya lifted her hand to protect her face as the heat burst into flames, consuming the spirit. "Not until you're dead."

Bitch!

The word echoed through her mind in a shrill screech, the darkness collapsing beneath the weight of the fire. Maya watched as the spirit withered and at last faded into the sand. She didn't know if it was dead forever, or if it could be resurrected, but she was certain that the connection between them had been well and truly broken.

Lifting a hand to cover the raw wound that seeped an alarming amount of blood, Maya fell to her knees. She'd managed to destroy Batu, but she didn't have the strength left to try to escape the afterlife. Closing her eyes, she concentrated on the bond that remained locked inside her heart.

The one that held her to Ravyr.

Someday they would be reunited. She clung to that belief as consciousness drifted away.

* * * *

Ravyr felt the grinding pain ease as Tia leaped in front of him. Using the brief respite, Ravyr forced himself to his feet. He'd be damned if he died on his knees. Unfortunately, once he was standing, he realized that the mage was already on the point of collapse. Within minutes the magic would destroy her and he would be back on his knees.

"Tia, get out," he commanded.

"No." She bleakly held her ground. "I promised Maya I would save your frosty ass."

Maya. Ravyr touched the mark on his hand, frowning when he realized that the sense of her was muted. As if she was a long distance away.

"Where is she?"

Tia swayed, her face hard as she battled against the magic. "You don't want to know."

"Dammit." Ravyr ground his fangs. "She promised not to do anything stupid."

"And you believed her?" Tia released a sharp laugh. "You don't know anything about Maya Rosen, leech."

He stepped forward, prepared to shove her out of the path of the magic. "I know we're both going to die if you don't get out of here and get help."

She turned her head, as if she intended to chastise him. But even as her gaze narrowed, she visibly stiffened.

"Do you feel that?" she rasped.

Ravyr's brows snapped together. Had the pain tipped the mage over the edge? He didn't feel...

Wait. He did feel something. The green glow continued to surround Tia, but it was fraying along the edge of Batu's medallion, as if it was running out of power.

"Yes," he hissed.

"Get ready."

"For what?"

"That." There was a final pulse before the magic was shattered and the glow disappeared. "Now, leech!"

Ravyr didn't need Tia's command to rush forward, grasping the still-warm medallion in his hand and twisting it until the chain tightened around Batu's scrawny neck. The vampire screamed in fury, but there was an unmistakable resignation in the sunken eyes as Ravyr continued to twist the chain, not halting until the links had cut through the fragile neck and Batu's head bounced across the cement.

"Is he dead?" Tia demanded, her voice shaky.

Ravyr watched as the medallion he held in his palm darkened, a curl of smoke crawling over the carved symbols before the thing crumbled to dust. At the same time, Batu's decimated body exploded in a puff of ash.

Distant wails of loss echoed through the opening overhead, revealing that Batu's disciples had felt his passing.

"He's dead," Ravyr assured her, caught off guard when she abruptly turned around and headed back down the tunnel. "Where are you going?"

"Alison is going to try to make a run for it. I intend to make sure she doesn't succeed."

"Maya." Her name came out as a croak.

Tia turned, her expression wry despite the lingering pain etched on her pale face. "She'll come for you. She's nothing if not loyal. Even to those of us who don't deserve her."

The sheer certainty in her words eased Ravyr's flare of panic. "True."

Lifting her arm, Tia pointed a finger in his direction. "Listen, leech, if you hurt her—"

Ravyr interrupted the ridiculous warning. "It's not possible. I would die before I allowed anything or anyone to cause her pain. Including myself."

"Yes, you would die. That's a promise."

With a toss of her head, Tia disappeared into the tunnel, and Ravyr leaned heavily against the cement wall. He had to gather his strength before he started his search for Maya.

As if the mere thought of her had stirred the tracking spell she'd placed on him, Ravyr felt a tingle race up his arm. It was as if Maya's magic was tugging at the mark. Was she trying to lead him toward her? Did she need his help?

Shoving away from the wall, Ravyr was attempting to locate a direction when a sharp odor of sulfur tainted the air and a sudden hole split open. A second later, Maya spilled out.

"Maya."

Leaping forward, Ravyr managed to catch her before she hit the ground. Cradling her against his chest, Ravyr ran a desperate gaze over her limp body, his heart clenching as he caught sight of the wounds on her chest even as relief blasted through him at the steady beat of her heart. She was injured, but she would live.

With careful movements, Ravyr lifted his hand to press his thumb against the tip of his fang, breaking through the skin. Then, holding his thumb directly above her chest, he allowed his blood to drip into the wound. Instantly the flesh began to mend, the skin healing over with remarkable speed. There would probably be a scar, but nothing mattered beyond the fact that she was alive and in his arms.

Perhaps sensing his tidal wave of relief, Maya's eyes fluttered open, a smile curving her lips.

"It's done."

Chapter 25

Maya strolled down the street, her lips curving into a smile at the sight of the neon sign that glowed brightly against the night sky. The Witch's Brew would soon reopen after weeks of renovations that had transformed the basement into an elegant lair that now consumed the entire block. Ravyr had insisted that it was necessary to buy the surrounding buildings, not only to make sure that their privacy was fully protected, but to give her room to expand the business in the future.

She hadn't argued.

With Peri's assistance she'd hired a full staff to run the coffee shop and bookstore, leaving her ample opportunity to concentrate on her magic-for-hire business, which had now been expanded to include temporary bodyguard services, with Ravyr providing the muscle and her magic offering an additional layer of protection.

After tonight, she was considering another expansion for her business, but that would have to wait until she discovered if the seeds she'd just planted actually produced results.

Coming to a halt in front of her shop, Maya removed the protective spells as she glanced around the empty sidewalk. It felt strange not to see Joe slumped against the lamppost. He'd become a familiar landmark. Like the fire hydrant. And potholes. But while she occasionally—very occasionally—missed his snarky presence, she'd been adamant that he find someone else to pester.

She had a new Benefactor, and he came with all sorts of perks.

Need stirred through her at the thought of the glorious male. Ravyr had been gone less than a week, but she already ached to have him back. It felt like she was missing a part of herself.

Shoving open the door, Maya stepped into the shadowed coffee shop and immediately released a bolt of magic as a dark form rose from a nearby chair. Wrapping strands of power around the intruder, she shoved him against the wall even as she slammed the door shut behind her.

She heard a grunt, but a second later her magic was being absorbed by the male, who was wrapping his arms around her waist.

"Hello, Maya."

She chuckled. She'd already known who was waiting for her. Not only from the chill in the air, but also because no other creature could have gotten through the layers of magic she'd placed on the door.

Leaning against his rock-hard chest, Maya wrapped her arms around his neck. "You're home earlier than I expected."

The glow from the streetlights angled through the window, silhouetting the stark lines of his profile.

"Home," he murmured softly. "I like the sound of that."

"Me too." She paused. They'd spent the past weeks recovering from their battles with Batu and his demented disciples, and creating a lair that would be comfortable for both of them. But in the back of her mind had been a gnawing fear that Ravyr would be forced to return to his previous duties. Finally, Ravyr had judged her recovered enough to leave for a few days and made the journey to speak with his master, face-to-face. "Does that mean Sinjon agreed to your resignation?"

Ravyr nodded. "He did."

"No late-night calls that will send you dashing around the world?"

"Nope, no dashing." He bent his head to brush his lips over her forehead. "I am officially retired. Just like you retired from your duties to the Benefactor."

She shivered, pleasure racing through her. When both Peri and Skye had assured her that sex with a vampire was the best thing EVER, she'd refused to believe them. How could sex be good with a frigid creature who was stabbing his fangs into your neck? Now she couldn't believe that she'd ever been content sleeping alone in her big bed. All she wanted was Ravyr lying next to her, his hands roaming her body as he drank greedily from her vein.

"Good." Her voice was suddenly husky with desire. "I need you here."

His hands drifted down her back to cup her backside. "I'm not sure I can bake any muffins or brew coffee, but I'm incredibly talented with a mop. And you should see me with a sink full of dishes."

"Mopping floors and washing dishes aren't why I need you here," she assured him, rubbing against his thickening erection.

"Ah. Luckily for you, I am a vampire with numerous skills." He kissed a path down the length of her nose before teasing her with soft kisses. "But first."

Maya blinked as he lifted his head to gaze down at her with a searching gaze. "Yes?"

"Did you take care of your witch problem?"

Maya nodded. It'd taken days to finally hunt down Lottie Howard, but tonight she'd finally cornered her hiding in a dingy motel in Queens. The older woman had been too defeated by Alison's conquest of her coven and the necromancers who'd invaded her territory to put up any fight. Any plans to punish the older woman for festering such hatred toward her had died the second she'd seen the witch's slumped shoulders and dull eyes.

Instead, she'd offered the woman a reason to continue living.

"Lottie has decided to disband what was left of her coven," she assured Ravyr, knowing he wasn't going to be entirely pleased that she hadn't locked the woman in a cell and thrown away the key. "But I requested she remain in the area."

"Because it's easier to keep an eye on her?"

"In part."

Ravyr studied her with a sharp intensity. "And the other part?"

"She has a remarkable talent for detecting mages before they come into their powers. If her senses can find them early enough for me to take in and train, I could help ease their way into their powers." She pressed her fingers against his lips before he could protest. "We have an empty building next door. It would be the perfect place to bring in mages from around the world to study together."

His jaw was clenched, suggesting that he wasn't entirely pleased with her explanation, but he was wise enough not to argue. Vampire business was his to deal with and mage business was hers. End of story.

"And Alison?" he instead asked.

Maya grimaced. "She's currently staying in Colorado with Tia."

Ravyr arched a brow. "Staying with?"

"What else?"

"Hmm." He grimaced. "I don't envy her."

"Neither do I." Maya didn't doubt the young mage was howling in regret for having used her powers to tamper with the dead. "Tia makes a bad enemy."

His tension eased as he stroked his hands up the curve of her back. "Not for you."

"No, that feud has been buried in the past."

"Along with Batu."

She nodded. The nightmares weren't entirely gone, but they no longer bothered her. Not when she had this male lying next to her. "Exactly where he belongs."

"The one thing left is to concentrate on our future."

Holding his gaze, she reached out to grasp the hem of his black T-shirt, yanking it over his head and tossing it aside.

"I prefer to savor the moment," she confessed, leaning forward to explore the rigid muscles of his chest with open-mouthed kisses.

"Ah." He shuddered as she licked his nipple. "I like how you savor."

She scored her fingernails down his bare back, hard enough to leave marks. "I could savor better in our bed."

With an elegant ease, Ravyr was sweeping her off her feet and heading toward the back of the shop.

"Your wish is my command."

Excitement scalded through Maya. She'd missed this male more than she'd dreamed possible. And now she had the promise that he would always be at her side.

It was all she needed to be happy.

"Not only gorgeous and sexy, but wise as well," she murmured.

"And hungry," he growled, pulling open the steel door and heading down the flight of stairs to the remodeled basement, now filled with luxurious furnishings and top-of-the-line tech gadgets that Ravyr was collecting after years of ignoring anything modern. He headed directly to the bedroom and lowered her onto the center of the massive bed covered in a soft ivory comforter. "You forgot hungry. My beautiful mage. I was away too long."

"I've been waiting for you," she assured him, lifting her arms in welcome.

With quick movements, Ravyr stripped off his clothes before joining her on the bed. "Just like you promised."

"Forever," she whispered, her hand moving down to grasp his erection.

* * * *

Pacing the elegant gold-and-crimson carpet she'd personally chosen for her private study, Tia ignored the leatherbound first editions that lined the bookshelves and the expensive wine that her servant had decanted and placed on the sidebar.

She felt...restless. Yes, that was the word. As if she had an itch she couldn't scratch.

The trouble was, she didn't know what the itch was, or how to scratch it.

Hoping to squash the sense that she was standing at the edge of a brewing thunderstorm, she'd abruptly decided to release the cantankerous Alison from her cell in the dungeon a few hours ago and requested that Lynch drive her to town. She'd made sure the mage understood the dangers of toying with powers that were beyond her pay grade, as painfully as possible. She'd also taken the precaution of placing a curse on the younger woman that would make her very sorry if she ever decided to go rogue.

It wouldn't be pretty.

Turning to retrace her steps, Tia's musings were interrupted as Lynch stepped into the room and offered a deep bow.

"It's done," he announced.

Tia halted, studying the large male with a narrowed gaze. "Did you stay and make sure that she got on the bus?"

He shrugged. "She was the first one on. I don't think you have to worry about her coming back anytime soon."

"Good." Tia pursed her lips. "If she learned her lesson, she might make a decent mage one day."

"And if she didn't?"

A hard smile curved her lips. "Then I'll give her another lesson. One she won't forget."

Lynch nodded. "Is there anything else?"

Tia glanced toward the heavy, old-fashioned clock set on her desk. Midnight. It was later than she realized.

"Not tonight."

With another bow, Lynch turned to disappear from the office, closing the door behind him.

Once alone, Tia glanced toward the wine waiting for her, along with one of her favorite books. Everything was settled. Batu was dead. The surviving disciples rounded up by Valen to be properly punished. Alison had been released from her cell, and Maya was happily settled with her leech. There was nothing to do but enjoy the peace.

So why wasn't she enjoying it?

With a click of her tongue, Tia headed across the room to lay her hand on top of the heavy globe. Maybe a relaxing dip in the pool would settle her nerves. Or, if nothing else, it might give her some insight into why she couldn't shake the edginess humming through her.

Magic tingled in the air, along with the scent of dirt and moss as the hole in the floor slid open and Tia climbed down the steep stairs, her silk caftan brushing the stone floor as she crossed toward the natural spring in the center of the cavern.

Only it wasn't just moss that perfumed the air, she abruptly realized, her steps slowing as she neared the edge of the pool. There was a distinct scent of copper that teased at her nose. Along with a power that suddenly thundered beneath her feet like an earthquake.

Dammit. Magic hummed through her veins as the water bubbled and churned before a tall, broad-shouldered male with long, burnished hair abruptly appeared in the center of the pool. Narrowing her gaze, she glared at the sculpted features that were impossibly perfect before lowering to take in the wide, naked chest that tapered to a narrow waist.

Thankfully, his lower half was hidden beneath the waters, she silently acknowledged, as desire blasted through her. It'd been a very long time since she'd been with...anyone. And the raw intensity of her awareness was as shocking as it was unwelcome.

"Joe." His name came out as a hiss. "How did you get in here?"

He smiled, his gaze taking a slow survey of her rigid posture and tightly clenched hands.

"You think there's any place I can't enter?"

"That's not the point," she snapped. "It's rude to intrude into someone's home without permission."

His brows arched, as if he was offended by her accusation. "But it wasn't without permission. You called me."

"Bullshit. I don't know who you are or even *what* you are," she protested, pretending she hadn't grilled Maya on everything she knew about this creature before she'd left New York. At the time, she'd told herself it was necessary to be prepared in case Joe proved to be a threat. Now that he was standing in her home...well, there might have been a bit more to her interest, she reluctantly conceded. "How could I call you?"

"You called me in your dreams."

Heat crawled beneath her skin as Tia flushed for the first time in centuries. "You mean my nightmares," she muttered.

The emerald eyes glowed with a sudden fire as he took a step forward. "It didn't feel like a nightmare. In fact—"

"Stop." The command came out as a squeak. "Don't you dare take another step."

He chuckled. "Afraid what you'll do if you see me in my full glory?"

Yes, absolutely. He was right when he claimed he'd been in her dreams. She'd fantasized about him over and over, but she'd be damned if she admitted her fascination. Not even to herself. When it came to lovers, she was careful to choose partners who could never be a threat. Not in or out of bed.

This male...he was completely and totally off limits.

"You should be afraid of what I'll do." She lifted her hand, magic dancing over her fingers with fiery sparks. "What do you want?"

The emerald eyes darkened. "So many things."

"Tell me," she snapped.

He paused, as if realizing she'd reached the end of her patience. "I need your assistance."

She frowned before she abruptly realized what assistance he meant. "Ah. Of course, Maya kicked you to the curb, didn't she?"

Joe shrugged. "It was a mutual decision."

Tia shook her head, her chin tilted to a stubborn angle. "I've already been a pet mage to an arrogant male. Never again."

"What about a temporary partnership?"

About to insist that he leave her in peace, Tia abruptly hesitated. She hadn't reached her level of success by being hasty. In truth, her greatest asset was her cold logic and willingness to make hard decisions.

She didn't know much about Joe, or what the role of a Watcher entailed, but she did know he was the most powerful creature she'd ever known. It would be beyond stupid not to discover what he could offer her.

"What do I get out of it?" she demanded.

He blew her a kiss. "Besides me?"

Tia rolled her eyes. "Yeah, besides you."

"I'm open to negotiation." He folded his arms over his bare chest. "Name your price."

A slow smile curved Tia's lips. "Oh, this is going to be fun."

www.ingramcontent.com/pod-product-compliance
Lightning Source LLC
Chambersburg PA
CBHW021002250225
22521CB00011B/22